THE STRINGS THAT HOLD US TOGETHER

KENDRA MASE

The Strings That Hold Us Together

To the stories and writers who inspired me to build a world of my own.

Trust the overthinker who tells you they love you. They have, most assuredly, thought of every reason not to.

— LK PILGRIM

CHAPTER ONE

*H*e was the most beautiful man in the universe.

For some reason, the statement felt the truest out of any Katherine had ever thought to herself.

Through heavily lined eyes, the raven-haired man smirked as he turned with simple grace on stage. Katherine noticed him for the first time during her deliveries to the converted theater now housing DuCain, an S&M club that prided itself on passion as much as pain. His body, though not tall, still managed to take up as much space as anyone else who commanded the stage.

He stood, shoulders back, proud and utterly, most definitely, in control. He took another step toward the woman across from him. She smoothly moved like melted candle wax down to her knees.

Each movement was a deliberate, smooth performance. The viewers in DuCain lapped it up like sweet cream.

Katherine couldn't look away. That grin pulled her in like a siren, luring her out to sea, and she couldn't swim. As he stalked over to the woman, it was all Katherine could do to imagine the calluses of his hands as they ran down the back of her arms, just like he did to his pliant victim. She felt the light sting of knots being tied tight against her skin as she was pushed up against the wide cross.

Jack leaned closer, breath sending fire over her bare shoulder. A sigh of delight crossed her skin, amusement as he noticed the nervous thrill of shivers down Katherine's spine.

"Stunning," he whispered.

A hand cupped her thigh, skimming where the garters she'd taken to wearing since she started working for her aunt's shop peeked out just underneath her skirt.

"Don't worry. You're safe. I got you."

She believed him.

Her body believed him. She loosened her weight into the hold of his single palm. She melted into the taut comfort of the binds that held her up on the stage for everyone to see.

Everyone would see her.

"Little Em!"

Tearing her gaze away from the stage as the crowd cheered, Katherine swung toward the bar. On the other side, she met the amused expression of the club's owner, Nik. A few others must've also noticed her pause, or rather, her longing.

It wasn't the first time either.

Clearing her throat, she prepared the same phrase she practiced every time she entered the club a little too late on her delivery rounds, a little too leisurely.

Nik didn't make her stutter it out. They shook their blond ruffled head with a grin as they poured another tall glass of moody liquid behind the bar. "If you are here to drop off, you know where to go."

Katherine clutched her bags to her ribs as she scuttled away from the pressure of eyes following her every move. It wasn't long until she became lost in the crowd. Her heart calmed the farther she dove into people who didn't give her a second look.

Not the couple in latex.

Not the woman with dark roots and platinum blond hair swinging side to side with her clip-on ponytail.

Not the raven-haired man on stage, Jack, she stared at through wire cat-eye glasses.

She was invisible.

For most of her life, Katherine had been this way, whether she wanted to be or not. It only became more prevalent since she started working for her aunt as a sort of apprentice. She did as she was told and complained only later when her aunt handed her a cup of tea and asked how her blisters were doing. A dozen sores were hidden beneath thin canvas shoes she traded her ballet flats in for after her second day traversing up and down city blocks. She got lost more than the number of packages stuffed with leather and lace that she had to deliver.

The first few weeks she'd started working alongside Emilie was painful in every sense of the word, yet Katherine was glad she remembered her eccentric aunt in the city who only came to visit the suburbs once every year or two after Katherine's mother left.

It was also a very good thing Katherine knew how to use a needle and thread.

A family trait, apparently, Emilie remarked with pleasure when Katherine arrived on her doorstep.

So was people leaving them.

If it wasn't, Emilie would've never opened the small lingerie shop to begin with. Using the money left over from when her husband screwed her best friend and left almost eight years ago, where would they be otherwise?

Katherine would be on the streets, regretting not replying to any of the universities she was accepted into after her high school counselor insisted upon her applying. Emilie would never have turned the bespoke boutique into one of the most beautiful places to window shop in Ashton—at least in Katherine's opinion.

Her aunt managed it all on her own, save for the occasional design intern from the art institute a few blocks over. Emilie dreamed, designed, cut, and sewed almost every single item that was sold within the shop. And if there wasn't something there that a customer liked or a size they didn't put on display, her aunt simply told them to come back by the end of the week.

When they did, they'd find their perfectly imagined frills wrapped up in lilac-colored tissue paper.

Anything else they needed that Emilie couldn't produce with her own two hands, she sourced. Most of which Katherine now held in the bag she carried past the red Private sign and down the stairs into DuCain's infamous dungeons.

"It would be either silly or stupid for me not to cater to all my clients' needs, Kit," her aunt informed her not long after she started. Emilie smugly smiled that day as she taught Katherine about each one. "In my opinion, it would be the latter."

After the past few months running deliveries and meeting all of Emilie's patrons, including those who made the low sounds through the cracks of dungeon doors, Katherine had to agree.

Dropping her bags to the ground of the storage room, Katherine nearly groaned with relief. They started to make her shoulders sweat from the final stretch of summer heat bleeding through the city. Pulling out each item, Katherine easily got to work replenishing DuCain's supplies. The storage room was a mess the first time she arrived in the club, wide-eyed and unprepared, but now, after reorganizing the shelves, everything had its place.

Thigh-high stockings went on one shelf beside the fishnets. Gloves went on another along with the sanitary wipes Katherine must've replenished the most often out of everything at DuCain. For obvious reasons, she imagined thinking back to the hallway she came down.

Finally, the last of her deliveries were at the bottom of her bag. Enclosed in individual boxes, shiny new and the most-essential riding crops waited their turn. Katherine smiled at them as she stood up on a chair to reach one of the highest shelves in the closet. She slid each next to other daring implements. Floggers, canes, and clamps—it didn't escape Katherine how, at some point, they turned into casual terminology.

Stepping back down, the door across from her crashed open, slapping against the black concrete wall. Neither of the two who shoved their way inside seemed at all startled by the loud noise.

Katherine, on the other hand, froze. Halfway back down to solid ground from her folding chair, she tilted to the right and caught herself before she fell the rest of the way.

"Shut up and hurry." Katherine immediately recognized the voice of the command, and if she didn't, the sight of her plowing the rest of the way inside would've been all the reminder she needed.

Besides the fact that the woman was nearly nude, yanking up a pair of exceedingly tight leather pants over her hips, deep red curls fell over her shoulders, caked with glitter and hairspray.

Avril Queen.

The burlesque star first made her mark in Ashton before taking on the rest of the world. Katherine had seen her before on her deliveries to DuCain as well as at the sensational dance lounge, Rosin, where she often mended costumes and restocked plenty of glitter. Katherine always said she'd have the courage to dress up in something perfectly Moulin Rouge, and watch the solo dancers as well as the chorus numbers permeated with dirty jokes, champagne, and the very Queen of Burlesque herself. But now, she was directly in front of her.

Queen's C-cups glinted with handsewn crystal pasties Katherine knew well, seeing similar pairs in the shop as well as bespoke photos Emilie kept of pieces she was most proud of. All of them usually managed to adorn the redheaded vixen in front of her.

When a deep voice sounded, Katherine still hadn't managed to open her mouth as she stared from Avril to *him*.

The two of them were always something of a pair. Katherine, however, could never quite figure out in what way. They lay on the edge of the stage together some afternoons as crew adjusted the theater lights above them. They laughed and shoved each other, his arm looping over her shoulders whenever they moved.

They were like magnets.

An amused expression passed over Jack's face as he rolled his lined eyes.

And it was only right that the most beautiful man also had the most beautiful eyes in the entire world. Bright and flecked with shards of honey.

As those eyes landed on her, she felt herself inhale, and then they swept right past as if she wasn't there at all.

For a second, Katherine wondered if she truly became invisible.

"Grab your stuff and let's go, Queen. You're already making us late." Jack gripped the side of the door as he stood waiting. He tapped a watch he didn't wear.

Avril shuffled through a bag Katherine hadn't realized until then was stuffed deep into the corner.

For months Katherine had seen them, and like when she stared at the raven-haired professional dominant, she imagined what would happen if she ever managed to muster up any ounce of courage. She surely had a bit of it, she was certain, even if it was just to say hello.

And now—

Topless, yet completely at ease, Queen threw something at Jack.

He caught it in one hand, looking down at the corset.

"Not my fault you decided to get a little handsy on stage and they wouldn't let you off before a second encore."

"Says the woman who decided to give a surprise performance."

Avril pursed her lips in satisfaction. "Nik was practically begging."

"So you say."

Studying the corset, Jack twisted it one way and then the next until he found the laces caught together in a large knot. Katherine noticed with wide eyes. With a single finger, he gestured for Avril to turn around. "You realize I usually only have to deal with taking these kinds of things off, right?"

If he pulled on the corset, while twisted like that, he could ruin the piece.

Katherine couldn't hold it in anymore. Something deep inside erupted before she could clap a hand over her mouth at the horror she was about to witness.

"Stop!"

Both heads snapped toward her. They both were oddly calm, as if they truly didn't notice her standing there watching them until then.

Or, more likely, didn't care.

Katherine's bottom lip stuttered, trying to find the right words before she went on.

"Stop. Please." She glanced at Jack, extending her hand out to the man who continued to stare at how it quivered as if she was some strange creature he never encountered before. "You're going to ruin it."

Queen raised her delicately colored eyebrows. She took the corset back and tossed it directly into Katherine's hands.

Katherine volleyed the piece before gripping it tightly in her fingers, looking at the woman in front of her who suddenly didn't look much older than she did.

"Well?" she asked, glancing at Jack, still standing next to her. "Lace me up, darling."

Lace her up. Right. Katherine carefully began to unknot the problem sections before she approached Avril. Reaching toward her breasts, she paused.

Avril only looked more amused. "Tits up? Don't worry, this isn't my first rodeo."

No, Katherine gave a light laugh. She couldn't imagine it was. Rounding Avril's back, Katherine settled the cups into the right place. It fit her like a mold, perfectly. One gentle tug and pull at a time, Katherine restrung and tightened Avril Queen into a corset, just the way her aunt had taught her.

Lacing had been one of her first lessons, and one she practiced often on herself when she was left too long in the workroom. If there was one thing Emilie specialized in, it was magnificent, magical corsets.

She felt Jack's eyes settle on her as he watched her work, up until the very last tie in the center. Katherine smoothed her hands over either side of Avril's now prudently cinched waist.

"There you go," Katherine nearly whispered.

Avril twisted around with a grin. Her canines were sharp as they punctured her lower lip. "You're Emilie's new girl, aren't you?"

Katherine opened her mouth to answer but once more nodded in acceptance. Yes, that was exactly who she was.

"Name? Or would you prefer me to keep calling you darling?" Avril joked with a smirk back at Jack.

"I, uh…" She finally cleared her throat. "It's Katherine."

Avril's brow crinkled. "Doesn't quite fit, Kitten."

"That does."

Katherine's eyes flickered to the deep rumble of a voice again. Jack's face fluctuated, confused between enjoyment and pain as he stared off toward the floor. Dust was more entertaining to him.

With a shrug, Avril was already grabbing the bag she dropped as she got dressed and headed back to the door. "We'll work on it.

Let's go. Mr. Grump-ass over here is becoming easily insufferable."

Jack had already tilted himself back into the hallway, taking a step back toward the emergency exit.

Avril was halfway when she looked back. Her bloodred lips curved.

"Well? Are you coming or not?"

CHAPTER TWO

"I'll make it easy and tell you the right answer. It's yes." Avril Queen, the most talked-about woman in Ashton, looked at Katherine. She looked at her as if she might've been someone interesting as her hand clasped around Katherine's wrist and pulled her along. "It is Saturday, after all."

"What's Saturday?"

"What's Saturday?" Avril looked scandalized. "Did you hear this girl, Jack?"

His eyes flicked between the two of them, giving Avril a dark look. "Oh, I heard."

"Saturday is basically a holiday," Avril explained as they pushed open the emergency exit to the parking lot. No alarm went off.

"Reed is calling me again." Jack glanced down at his phone screen before pulling open the door of an army green–colored Jeep. Hopping into the driver's seat, he let it drop into the cup holder.

"The idiot." Avril gave a shake of her head. "Are you going to answer?"

"Have you been?"

Avril turned back to Katherine without answering as the two of them squeezed into the car. It was clean, surprisingly so.

Avril turned around in her seat to make sure that she was behind her. "And holidays, of course, mean…"

"Is this going to turn into a guessing game?" Jack muttered, turning the key until the engine came alive, rumbling beneath Katherine's feet.

Avril seemed only encouraged. "Celebration time. You're not dead."

"Yet."

"You made it through the week. If you don't have a party on a Saturday, what are you really doing?"

Not sure if she was looking for an answer, Katherine stretched against her seat belt. She peered out the front window as they'd already turned back onto the streets, crowded and filled with lights beginning to flicker on as the night set in. "Working, usually."

Jack's index finger tapped the wheel as if in agreement.

Avril only narrowed her strikingly green gaze at him.

"I didn't say a word."

The only one who continued to say more than a few was Avril. She talked to Katherine as if they had been friends for ages rather than a few minutes. She barely took a moment to breathe between stories. She touched up her lips in the mirror as she rambled about the burlesque lounge, Rosin, and parties, and gave slight mention to her boyfriend.

She kicked her heels up on the dash before Jack swatted them down.

Jack slowed at a light and took a wide turn onto the bridge. Katherine crossed it once before when she first entered the city. Though she couldn't see it now in the darkness, she was sure that the charcoal-hued water of the Ash roared beneath them. Across the bridge, luxurious townhomes built what had to be over a hundred years ago lined the horizon.

Each was trimmed in various tints and oddly shaped windows.

"Will he be here?" Katherine asked, glancing toward Jack to see if he reacted.

Avril popped her lips, capping the tube of scarlet. "Who?"

"Your boyfriend."

Jack snorted.

"No. Definitely not," Avril answered, her tone a noticeable octave lower than before. "This isn't really his scene."

"You mean your life?"

It was Avril's turn to give a dark look to the driver. He, however, was too busy focusing as he pulled into a spot along the curb. Avril hopped out the passenger door before he managed to put the car in park and left the door open as she trampled up the steps of a dark violet home, tall and narrow.

Standing there for a moment, the structure arched above the cracked sidewalk.

Other people greeted Avril the moment she made it to the door, everyone similarly dressed in tight jeans and heels. Faces were made-up with makeup and glitter, exactly how Katherine always imagined once upon a time that parties would look. Low light in the entryway welcomed her as she stepped inside.

Emilie wanted her to get out of the shop. She'd almost begged for weeks. Or more likely, from the moment Katherine arrived. But Katherine rarely walked farther past the block the shop was located on until her aunt assigned Katherine delivery duties to put an end to her hermit tendencies. They were no longer an option, but her opponent.

Her aunt probably cheered with every step Katherine took into the ornately decorated townhouse, even if Katherine was certainly not dressed for whatever occasion she was now a part of alongside Avril Queen—and Jack.

Katherine swallowed. She hoped saliva covered nerves.

As the door shut, a warm form pressed in behind her.

With a glance back, Jack still barely looked at her through his dark lashes, nearly closed to his cheekbones as he took a deep breath. In a single hand, without notice, he slipped the couple of canvas totes Katherine had, now limp and empty, layered over her one shoulder.

They collapsed in on each other as they fell on a bench, where about a dozen different keys were also left in a homemade pottery dish.

"Thanks," Katherine was about to say. The words almost passed her lips, but not by the time Jack already moved past her.

In the living room, a group of others greeted him with raised hands.

Jack smiled that easy grin he always appeared to have, touching at least a single corner of his lips, except for when he looked at Katherine. He flopped down on the ottoman next to a girl with loose strawberry waves.

She tugged on his shirt until he swayed into her. His grin only faltered slightly as he brushed a single peck to her plump lips.

Oh.

Right, of course.

Katherine glanced away, forcing herself to look anywhere but the living room or her shoes, dingy and worn.

Katherine had been to a party before. She'd been to more than one. She wasn't much of a fan of them, or at least never considered herself to be, but maybe she had a little bit of Emilie inside of her, daring her to go out. Find life.

They just never ended particularly well.

The feeling was back in her stomach, heart thrumming as people looked at her curiously, knowing that when she ended up going home, no one would notice that she was gone.

No one noticed she was ever there to begin with.

But then again, none of those parties were anything like this. Warm and bright and stark with stretching noise from the music, never overtaking voices of stories yelled between one another.

The townhouse was everything Katherine did and didn't expect in a home owned by a Queen. She stepped down the sleek tiled hallway where an ornate rug ran all the way to the kitchen, where three people leaned over the edge of the marbled kitchen island. Antique sconces curved off the walls and cornice adorned the ceiling wherever Katherine looked up.

No one stopped her as she wandered. She studied all the knickknacks left on shelves and the postcards that littered the front of the fridge from places all over the world. Notes were written on every single one, not just for show. Katherine only stopped herself once she made her way back around to the living space again, pausing to scan the tightly stuffed bookshelves on either side of the archway.

Her fingers traced over lightly worn spines.

"Do you read much?"

Katherine took a step back, startled at the voice next to her.

"I only ask because it's usually only one or the other around here," the man murmured lowly. Dark brown curls women would kill for pressed around his cheekbones as he assessed her. The smallest of smiles popped out from his lip, exposing a crooked canine.

Switching his drink from one hand to the other, he extended a damp palm. "Reed."

Reed. Katherine remembered that name from the car. The one that was calling Jack.

Peering from his hand back up to his face, she quickly realized she was supposed to take it. "Right, um, Katherine."

He nodded, releasing her, but not before lifting the back of her palm to his lips.

She watched as his full lips gently brushed against her skin, sending a wave of nerves all the way up to her elbow. A few curious eyes turned.

"So, you're the one that Avril brought along from DuCain. Emilie, the seamstress's new apprentice, correct? I'd say that we were due for a new face, but..." Reed let his words trail off with a single shrug. "Are you hiding?"

Lips parted and still feeling the heat from his mouth on her knuckles, Katherine's eyes flicked back to the room before the two of them.

Reed only shook his head and brought his glass of murky, clear liquid back to his lips again. "I see my deduction skills haven't wavered. I was worried since I haven't been back for a bit."

"You've been out of the city?" Katherine ventured.

"Traveling, sort of. I'm finishing up the final stretch of my Ph.D. but have been luckily able to do it wherever I choose, whether that be here in-house or the south of France."

"So you chose not to do it here."

Biting the side of his tongue, Reed weighed her words, looking around the room again.

This time it was Katherine who couldn't help herself, noting as they landed on a wavy-haired guy by the fireplace. His soft cheeks were pronounced when he laughed, though he tried to cover it by looking down into his drink.

Interrupting her stare, Avril pounded back down the stairs. She swung around the railing, changed out of her corset and pants. She easily found herself a seat in someone's lap.

Reed blinked a few times, taking a long sip of his drink until ice clanged against the side of the tumbler. "I needed a change of pace, you know?"

"But you live here?" Katherine said carefully, trying not to seem awkward when she didn't move away.

"Yes, Avril and I have been together since high school. And ever since Queen got to the city, she wanted one of these houses, and damn, if she didn't get one the moment she managed enough cash. The look on the realtor's face was priceless." Reed shook his head at the memory. "It's become something of a house for all of us since then. We've, however, done most of the decorating."

Obviously. Looking between the two of them, Reed and Avril, it was hard not to notice that they were something of a matching pair. Well dressed, tailored, and filled with an air of... well, something Katherine never had. She wondered how formidable the two of them were side by side.

"You have good taste."

That small yet wicked smile that made the corners of his eyes tight was back. "Thank you."

"Can I ask you something?"

He raised his eyebrows. "I think you already did."

Katherine clamped her lips shut.

"Go on."

"How?"

"How what?"

Katherine looked over the room, at Avril and the house, as if that would encompass it all.

Reed's eyes widened with understanding. Perhaps it wasn't the first time he was asked such a question. "Walked into the wrong place at the right time. You know she used to work for your aunt, right?"

Katherine nodded. Emilie mentioned it once when they first went over where to go and who to know.

"A short tenure, but one nonetheless when Avril needed nothing more than a job, your aunt was basically the only person who would give her one. Queen was seventeen when she stumbled onto Rosin's stage one night. Cherry, the owner at Rosin, nearly kicked her out then and there, but instead..." Reed shrugged.

"She became Queen."

Reed only followed Katherine's gaze to where it rested on Avril before pulling away, not wanting her notice. If she did, she didn't do anything but turn her chin. Smile at her friend.

"Are we going to play or not?" Avril called out across the room.

Reed set his empty cup aside. Without looking toward Katherine, he made his way into the center of the den. "If you insist."

"I do."

"I'm still going to win."

As Katherine watched the two of them banter, Avril pushed off whoever she was using as a human backrest and grinned at the challenge. All around her, the rest of the small gathering of people already smiling boozy smiles began to collect in the living space. They pushed Katherine with them until she was in the corner of a wide circle.

"We'll see about that, Reedy darling."

Immediately, people began to set up what looked to be a large game of duck, duck, goose. Only in this version, shot glasses from every state littered the floor. The coffee table was shoved out of the way, and Jack reached back onto one of the rounded built-in shelves, retrieving what looked to be a large deck of cards.

He presented them with a flourish.

"Why, thank you, love. But don't think it will get you any bonus points," Avril reminded.

"Wouldn't dream of it."

"Good, then, ground rules," Avril went on. The final person standing as the rest of the group sat down. Even Katherine found a spot, squeezing between two people who only gave her a light smile.

She attempted one of her own back.

Across, Jack extended his legs out in front of him, taking up space as the lanky woman next to him attempted to tug on the loose sleeve of his shirt again. His eyes merely shifted to her and back to Avril standing in the center, locking there, and not once moving as she spoke.

"Should you really be the one to go over them?" Reed asked tiredly.

Avril grabbed one of the few bottles of liquor off the floor and pointed it at him. "Shut up. Anyway." She flashed the label to the crowd. It was nearly golden, and the response was one of oohs and ahhs. Words were printed in a fiery red. "You stocked well, as if you knew this would happen, Reed. Lion vodka?"

A few chuckles.

"What's Lion vodka?" Katherine tried to whisper to the girl next to her.

Her eyes flashed, leaning in to explain. "It's some kind of inside joke from the first game they ever played. I wasn't there though."

Reed again only smiled good-naturedly. "I thought I would give you the opportunity for a comeback."

"If you don't cheat."

To that, Reed said nothing before Avril finally sat down among them.

Did she already go over the rules?

Did Katherine miss them?

Katherine glanced over to Reed, hoping the charismatic man would give her some kind of hint, possible cheater or no.

Having fun yet? His expression seemed to ask.

Avril cleared her throat, slapping the deck of cards down toward the center of everyone. It was only then that Katherine realized that they weren't just any normal sort of playing deck. Illustrations in gold and red smeared over the edges, hand painted, much like the tarot cards Emilie had at the apartment.

From another life, her aunt had said when she noticed them.

"Welcome to Passion and Prose, kinksters. One card slip, no trades, unless, of course, you are willing to trade something really good." Avril wagged her garnet brows. She'd already uncapped the glass bottle of golden alcohol, like that of the gods' nectar, pouring shots on the floor no one reached for even as they overflowed. "If not, take what you get and drink."

"To figure out who goes first, it's the name of the game. You take a passion; you turn into prose, dirty limerick—we are very open people here. Voters vote wins. Understand? I really don't care either way. Reed!" Avril swung her gaze to him expectantly. "Care to share first? Being the big bad P&P winner last time and all."

"If you insist." He grinned.

"But before we begin, let's raise a shot to our newbie, shall we?"

A few eyes glanced toward Katherine.

Katherine tilted her chin down to hide the heat spreading up the back of her neck.

Avril's hand grazed Katherine's as she leaned across the circle anyway and handed her a tiny glass.

"Cheers," Avril said, lifting her own.

Sitting up, Katherine touched the rim to her lips as the small crowd easily followed through with Avril's suggestion with her. The liquor was smooth with a hint of spice and slid down her throat with less than a burn. A few whistles went up of appreciation.

"And one more for good luck?" Avril said, handing Katherine another.

The girl on the other side of her playfully jostled her shoulder.

Friends, her brain easily told her before it paused, questioning what she was doing before a single word stood out.

More.

That was all Katherine ever wanted to be. For years, she tried through her smiles and easy compliments she gave to strangers when they were alone. More.

Taking the shot, Katherine weighed the narrow glass from Montana in her fingers. The pressure of eyes hung on her shoulders, and the liquid sloshed back and forth near the rim. She could be the someone else she always thought of herself as. She could be the girl she always wanted to be and dreamed of in the back of her mind while the world kept moving all around her, never coming to a halt.

Suddenly, looking into the shot of golden alcohol, it all made sense.

Across her, Avril grinned as she met Katherine's eyes, as if she heard exactly the convincing Katherine led herself through. Something similar reflected in her expression as she lifted another shot with Katherine and swallowed it down at the same time.

Cheers.

CHAPTER THREE

*T*he first time Jack realized he was in love with Avril Queen, she stood up on a rickety table in some idiot underclassman's apartment. Double-fisting, one hand cupped a bottle of bourbon, more empty than full, while her other twisted around another poor sap's collar as he shook his head at the display. He was either stupid or far too used to being on the other side of the gorgeous fury.

Jack ended up leaving that party early. Too sober and feeling too empty as he pulled his Jeep around the front of the apartment complex, he waited for the asshole in front of him to make a left-hand turn farther uptown.

But then his unlocked passenger door swung open. Quickly, it slammed shut, and the idiot and the redheaded fury of a woman stuffed themselves inside his car.

Emerald green eyes turned up at him from where their owner knelt down, a tight fit under the glove compartment.

"Drive."

He did, without a thought, he drove. He weaved around the car in front that sat stagnant despite their turn signal and tore into the street while the guy sitting next to him maneuvered backward between spurts of laughter.

"That hasn't happened in a while," he choked out.

The vixen only grinned as she extended her legs out in front of her. Seeing the sparkle of glitter coating her chest and rhinestones stuck to either of her winged eyes, Jack's gaze narrowed.

"Do I know you?"

Her grin only widened as if a vampire preparing to eat him as her next meal.

For some reason, Jack didn't mind the possibility.

Instead, she extended a hand.

Jack gripped it with slender fingers, adjusting his other hand to take the wheel.

"Avril Queen," she chimed. "At your service."

Her lips, however, then pursed, looking down to his hand at the same time as if she wasn't quite ready to let go. Curiosity began to permeate the car, along with bubbly adrenaline. "But, do I know you from somewhere?"

Unfortunately, she did.

She also made sure he got a new job before the sun rose, telling him to make his own left turn as they got to the next light, heading back to the unlit streets downtown.

Jack asked her why she did what she did—he gave up asking himself a similar question long ago, Queen reached out her hand and brushed her thumb along the very back of his jaw he'd clenched tight, as if there was a speck of dirt there.

Her hand came away clean, nothing there that he could see, even as she rubbed the pads of her fingers together, tapping one after another to that thumb.

She only smiled, though a twinge of sadness crept up the back of Jack's throat as he watched it form. She shrugged. "I don't meet just anyone for the hell of it, Jack."

He huffed out a breath at the way she said his name. A single syllable with all the meaning in the world. He shook his head and looked at the city, much like he did every single day and night after he met the formidable burlesque dancer who was not yet twenty-one at the time, yet somehow already managed to have the world twisted around her wrist like a charm bracelet of favors.

A few of them most certainly belonged to him, prepared to pay it all back one day.

Jack ground his teeth all the way up the steps of Avril and Reed's castle along the river. Pen gripped his arm like a vise, trying to hold herself up. Passion and Prose finally came to an end. No one could shuffle the deck without dropping half the cards in the process for another speed round.

As of Thursday, of all days, Queen returned from wherever she had been hiding for the past month with her high and mighty boy toy who, Jack had already tried to inform her though it fell on deaf ears, was also an asshole. Either way, she came back with a vengeance and plenty of liquor to numb the harsh emotions Jack still couldn't put his finger on all night as he stood next to her.

Penelope, on the other hand, he could tell exactly what she was feeling as her lips scraped up the one side of his neck where his shoulder met, and he felt her heat and arousal on his tongue like cinnamon.

Emotions, no matter whose they were, stuck to Jack like specks of glue and glitter left over from a night out. They made his blood run cold and his brain twist, like trying to find the correct answer to a complex math problem, and he was never very good with numbers. He never knew why, or if it was just him who had the constant joy of other people's meltdowns alongside his own, and he never cared enough to ask.

Only Emilie, a shopkeeper who supplied Avril with her costuming and DuCain with everything else, called him an empath of sorts. Sensitive.

He snorted at the word. If there was one thing he wasn't, it was that.

By the time he managed to haul the slim frame of Pen into his room, the guest room he'd been staying in since June after his roommates left, Jack grunted from the effort.

He didn't know any of the three roommates he had last well besides the fact they stole most of the cereal he bought, but still, for some reason, Jack figured that he would've been told—or maybe he should've noticed before suddenly his landlord was handing him the full bill he sure as hell wouldn't be paying alone. Living alone.

Coming back to Queen's castle, half Jack's shit he left behind the last time he needed a place to stay was still in the closet. It was as if he never left, however messy and pushed back the random pieces of his life from a few years ago were. A duffel bag of his first toys when he started at DuCain was propped up against an electric keyboard. Who knew who that belonged to?

Almost eight years he'd been living on his own in this city and he still hadn't managed to do anything with his life that made it, well, his life.

Unlike his roommates, who suddenly all up and found their own places in a newer high-rise with girlfriends, or in new opportunities leading them to new places.

Scooping his head underneath Pen's slim arm, he carefully sat her down on the edge of the gray plaid duvet. Looping her hands around his neck, she didn't let go, even as her head lulled to the side.

At least her eyes were still opened. Most of the time, when he ended up dragging her home from a party, she was more a corpse than a woman in her late twenties who constantly insisted she had her shit together.

She sure looked it.

"No," Penelope whispered. Rubbing her lips together, she blinked as she looked up at Jack with glassy eyes. They traveled over his shoulders and down his arms, never quite meeting his face. "Kiss me."

"Pen."

She tilted her chin. "Kiss. Me."

He let her pull him down an inch. Jack adjusted his hand on the bed before his lips gently found hers, already damp from her tongue. She pushed her body against his, knowing exactly what she wanted and where this would end up while her lips twisted, seeking more from him while her movements were empty.

They always were when they held each other, evoking the reaction they wanted. For the past few years since he met her at Rosin, dancing for the first few times, it had been this way. Avril didn't like her—and likely because Avril didn't like her, Jack wanted Pen all the more. So, he had her.

She certainly had him whenever she wanted, like an open invitation for one of them to wreck the other whenever they cared enough to.

A finger tugged at the belt loops of his jeans.

He forced out a small chuckle at the wanton gesture. Better than shaking his head at it. "Get some rest, Pen. You're drunk. You can fuck me whenever you want another night."

"Is that right?"

Jack said nothing. He only tasted below her ear, where he knew she would make a tiny gasp.

She didn't disappoint at the very least.

"Well." She nipped at his ear. "Not forever."

Jack stilled, letting her fingers trade-off from his pants to seek the top of his shirt. She gently pulled at it again, encouraging him to take it off. His hands remained braced over her, against the bed to hold him up.

"We both know that."

"Hm." Jack nudged her with his chin, making a sound for her to go on. He wanted to hear what she had to say as she continued to sloppily drool over any available section of skin.

"Like I've said," she sighed, warm against him. "It's not like you're the kind of guy a girl like me takes home to meet the parents, right?"

Jack froze at the words, however unsurprised he was to hear them. Something in his chest still pitched forward at the blandness as she said it.

Cupping her chin, Jack squeezed just enough that Pen had to meet his eyes.

She gave a tiny squeak of surprise, but her eyes dilated just before Jack let his lips crash hard down onto hers. He kissed her until he could barely breathe. He kissed her the way he could always kiss girls, until they groaned into his mouth.

No, not just some guy anyone takes home to their parents.

Holding her bottom lip between his teeth, Jack gave a tug before letting her go, stepping back as she panted on the bed.

She almost pitched forward, reaching for more.

Jack shook his head. "Sleep."

"You aren't going to join me?"

"Water," was Jack's only explanation as he ran a hand through his hair. His fingers fixed at the base of his neck.

Her eyes rolled, rimmed from blue mascara. Pen didn't say anymore, however. She sighed and rolled over on the bed. Unlike him, she'd lost her pants early in the Passion and Prose game when it took a turn for a strange combination of Never Have I Ever and strip poker. All that was left was her thong she must not have taken off from the show tonight, the back edge trimmed in peach-colored lace.

He didn't look at her again when he stepped out into the quiet hallway. A few murmurs from others that didn't want to risk not making it home in the state they were all in hummed through the space. It was a rough night. A rough game.

Even he had never gone so far into it as he had tonight, blinking a few times to adjust himself to the light and the fact he had no shoes. He let his hand slide against the wall to keep himself upright as he made it back to the stairs.

Before he went down, however, Jack wandered farther down the hall. Three people, in various states of dress, pulsed against each other in Reed's room, the gentle tones of music playing from a phone inside, though no one bothered to shut the door before they began their final fun of the night. Neither did Jack. He continued until he nudged the door open with his toe.

Inside the deep red and rose–colored bedroom that looked like it belonged to another dimension, the large bed against the wall was strewn with sheets and blankets piled up over each other before they fell onto the floor, never to be picked back up. Gentle voices murmured inside.

Reed laid there, still in his dress pants and collared shirt half unbuttoned. The glimmer of his rings he wore over his fingers glinted in the dark as he gripped Queen. She laid on his chest, eyes closed as she breathed, but not asleep. Not yet.

Jack could not count how many times he had seen a similar scene before. The two of them were always a package deal, even now when Reed didn't come out as often as he once did with Avril, Jack his replacement. Every time, Jack questioned. Should he go in? Should he join them? In some of his more inebriated states, he did. Avril opened her arms wide and pulled him into the mold without question.

Today, Reed's head lulled back to the door. He caught him standing there. Raising his eyebrows, there was the slight tilt of his chin, an offering.

Jack's shoulders slumped. He was tired, and he knew how comfortable Queen's bed was.

But it was also cold. Everything about her when he caught her off guard the past few days had been.

Something about Avril, as he glanced at her again, tight in Reed's gentle protective hold, it sent his stomach churning. Jack was unsure what to make of the stark contrast of unabashed happiness and trickling fear whenever she drank too much, emotions raised too high lately. All of it brimmed over until the thoughts and feelings swirling around him as he tried to make sense of them became static.

Jack let the one corner of his lip quirk at Reed in appreciation, but shook his head, lifting a hand to his mouth for a drink, turning back to the stairs.

Reed only turned back to glance at Avril, eyes rimmed with dark purple circles before he shut them with her. Two exhausted royals.

Not bothering to look for anyone else, Jack, at this point, could make his way to the kitchen with his eyes closed, and almost did. His lashes fluttered low as his eyes burned. If not from lack of sleep, from glancing in the living room where someone was passed out on the couch, and on the floor still remained the wreckage of the game Avril had made up during one of her first Saturday night parties.

The problem with Passion and Prose, however, Jack always said, was that no one ever really knew the rules. They changed with every game, either because everyone was too lazy to write them down or because once anyone was finished, there was a high likelihood that no one would remember most of the game the next morning anyway.

Shot glasses from each and every state as well as tissues, chips, and empty bottles of tipped-over liquor littered the space.

He waved a hand at it, continuing down the hall to the kitchen. He hoped Reed already alerted the maid that showed up each month what she'd find and tipped her well. Queen was back in action, that was for sure.

Closing his eyes again, he grabbed a glass out of the cabinet before turning around to the faucet. He was still having trouble figuring out Reed's new filtration system.

A sniff caught his ear as he turned toward it.

"You all right?" Jack looked down at the small frame curled up against the kitchen island beside him. He almost thought he managed to be alone for a second there, but he knew better. It was almost too quiet.

The girl, tucking her loose curls behind her ear, nodded, not looking up at him.

It was still too quiet.

With a deep sigh, Jack let the water run into the glass before grabbing another and filling it just the same. Lowering himself down, he gripped the edge of the granite for support.

Fuck for the second time.

The world tilted. And here he was thinking he didn't have that much to drink. He couldn't even remember the chick's name next to him. She was the one who beat them all at their own game tonight. Literally.

She looked a lot smaller than he remembered curled in on herself like that. A lot younger too, not that he was sure they asked how old she was.

Not like anyone was going to call the cops about corrupting minors with the Queen.

He rolled his eyes at the suggestion.

The girl next to him continued to stare anywhere but at him, eyes locking on the swirling tile lightly coated in dust as it continued under the stove as she zoned.

"It's okay, ya know—if you're not," Jack said, clearing the gruff sound in the back of his throat. "Just let me know because I'm pretty sure I'm up to my quota of drunk girls who've gotten sick on my shoes."

If he was wearing any.

The girl continued to stare at the floor in front of them, as if counting the tiles.

"The last time I was here, I think I counted about thirty-eight before I got bored. Me and Queen were having a rough night and didn't bother to sit at the table to eat a box of cereal at around midnight. Made me feel like a kid again." Jack rambled on for some reason, not really sure why he was still talking. Or sitting here. He didn't really want to go upstairs, for one thing.

He took a sip of his water and a deep breath.

On the inhale, he could taste an odd combination in the back of his throat coming from the girl. Herbal and honey.

It lulled into him, sticky and seeping. "An answer would make me believe you more. If you are still going in the all's well in the kitchen front direction."

A sound broke out of the back of her throat. It wasn't exactly a laugh but was.

Encouraged, Jack waited for more, relaxing his own back against the cabinets. The last time he was on the kitchen floor that night with Avril, he remembered it being a lot more comfortable.

"I'm..." Her voice was soft, as if she was forcing herself to whisper out of some sort of shock. "I'm at a party. A party in Avril Queen's house."

"And you beat the shit out of everyone in P&P. Who knows when that last happened?" Never, if Jack remembered correctly. Avril and Reed had the game rigged for years, not that anyone cared enough halfway through playing.

The girl glanced around herself again, and Jack wondered what she saw. Crystal chandeliers and plush furniture that cost more than most people's first home? A mess of bottles lined up by the back door when someone obviously couldn't find the right recycle bin?

She shook her head at whatever it was.

"Queen." He stretched out his arm before letting his fingers catch, pulling at the roots of his hair. "She has a habit of doing that to people."

"What?"

"Collecting them." Adopting them was more like it. He might as well welcome whoever this chick was to the family tree at this rate. Orientation passed with flying colors. Of course, he still had no fucking clue what her name was. "Her lost things. I'm—"

"Jack," the girl cut him off before he could continue.

Finally, she turned her full attention to meet him. Her eyes weren't just dark brown like he thought before when he glanced at them. They were warm and looked directly into his, even as she wrapped her arms around her knees. She effectively turned herself into a small ball.

"I know exactly who you are."

Pursing his lips, of course she does. Probably heard all the back-alley compliments and insults.

"No." She noticed his expression, trying to find the right words to make whatever it was she was thinking sound better. It was a hard sell, he was sure. Was told. "Not like that. I mean, the moment I walked into DuCain for the first time a few months ago, I asked. I asked who you were."

"You did?"

Inhaling as if it took all the courage she had, she nodded.

He really doubted that was all she had in her now.

Of course, he also had to shake his head. "I'm going to sound like an asshole then, not that I'm sure you'll remember this."

Her dark eyes flicked to him in distaste. *They'd see.*

"What is your name? I don't think—I didn't ask."

For some reason, it felt like his tongue was too big for Jack's mouth all of a sudden, words not finding the right spots like they normally did. He took another long gulp from his glass.

"Oh," she breathed. "It's Katherine. My name."

"You don't sound sure."

"I'm pretty sure I sound a little drunk."

Jack grinned.

Finally, she pushed herself up to sit next to him, no longer slouching. She swayed a little and Jack couldn't help but imagine her head fitting right there between his chin and shoulder.

He blinked a few times, rushing a hand through his hair to ground himself.

"My aunt, she calls me *Kit*." She grimaced.

"Not a fan?"

"It's not like that." Kit. It did really fit her better, and she attempted to rephrase, but too quickly she gave up, leaving it as it was in the silence. Closing her eyes, Jack watched closely. "Only she and my mom ever called me Kit."

"Is that a bad thing?"

"My mom left when I was little."

He didn't know how much time passed before her eyes opened again, going back to the same glazed-over expression he found her with, eyebrows furrowed at the ground.

"What are you thinking about?" Jack asked.

"Why are you talking to me?"

"That's what you are thinking of?"

"Partly," she stared. "I kind of thought that you didn't like me."

"Why do you say that?"

"Maybe I'm dreaming."

"You dream of me?"

She narrowed her eyes.

Interesting. "Humor me, then."

She pulled her gaze away from him, repositioning as her hands clasped one another.

"I'm thinking now..." Again, her teeth clenched shut as if debating. How painful it must've been to be inside of this girl's head. Kit's. "I'm thinking about the last time I was at a party."

"A good one?" He had side stories that he kept for just this situation. Nowhere to go. Only reputations to uphold.

Only, her shoulders slumped, back to tracing the patterns below her. "No. Not at all. I thought I'd go because everyone was going. Why not say yes for once? But then..."

"Then?"

"I got there, and I was invisible."

Jack knew the feeling. Like everyone was all around him, but no one noticed, or at least cared.

"It has always been that way though."

"You have superpowers?"

She shook her head, a hint of a smile teasing her lips. "Just me. I've never been important enough to be not invisible or forgotten about. That night one person did talk to me and I was so surprised, they turned to get me a drink and they never came back, and you know what? Then I wasn't surprised. Not in the least."

Jack's lips parted, any sort of smirk he had schooled his face into for the past so many years of his life, somehow, slipped.

"How could I be? Everyone leaves in the end, and then it is just me again having to figure it all out. Sew it all back together with frayed pieces of string."

Jack shook his head, jaw clenched, until he was looking up at the ceiling, taking a few deep breaths. A few speckled stains from misdirected ketchup and champagne splattered near the center.

"I'm sorry," she said hastily. She glanced away from him and shut her eyes for a long second. "I shouldn't... I have a problem sometimes with oversharing. When someone talks to me. Pretend I didn't say anything at all. Maybe I didn't, drunken dream and all."

Before he could think of something to say, her quiet voice cut into his third ridiculous option that began with, *I see you.*

"What are you staring at?"

At that, Jack could answer without hesitation. "The stars."

Kit leaned back to look up with him. Her head knocked against the cabinet with a thunk.

He grimaced for her.

"I don't see any."

"They're there. You know, just through a few layers of house and drywall and smog most likely when you make it out of the castle's assortment of knickknacks that have probably accumulated in the walls by now."

Too many people have lived in the house during the short time since Queen bought the place out from under some other socialite or money-grubber who would likely have painted the outside something less ostentatious. Grayer, rather than animated purple or whatever she called it that took at least three coats to get to her particular royal shade.

Anyone who needed a place to crash or live for a few months while they managed to find themselves a place in Ashton had it, including Jack. He took up the empty guest room back when he first met Avril—and now.

He forced himself not to glance toward the stairs again.

Instead, he focused on the stars. Far, far away.

Sucking air through his teeth, Jack's lips ballooned as he let it back out. "My mom, she used to say whenever you were having a bad day, just look at the stars."

Kit's forehead wrinkled, but still, she continued to stare at the ceiling. Her words slurred together. It was still easier to understand over Avril's drunken Irish brogue.

"Why is that?"

"Because." Jack wanted to shrug. He didn't really remember what she said. For some reason, he remembered at least four different sayings that all seemed to come from his mother. Or Avril, always mentioning something about how the planets were out of alignment when she pretended to try and read his fortune that usually ended with his receding hairline. "You never know when a wish will decide it's time for something to come true."

"Are you wishing for something?"

"Probably should be."

"Well, don't tell me what it is."

Jack glanced down at her, still focusing even as another curl bounced from the top of her head in front of her eyes. He resisted the reflex to brush it away. Funny little creature. "Why not?"

"Because then it won't come true." She shook her head at him like he was the sorriest thing she'd ever witnessed.

"Well, I'm a terrible secret keeper."

"Hm."

"Will you tell me what your wish is then?"

Kit narrowed her eyes at him again.

So that would be a no.

"Maybe I'm just not a party person," she said instead.

"You?" Jack glanced down at her, and if anyone had asked him a few hours ago, maybe he wouldn't disagree. "Nah. You look like you still have some potential yet."

Kit breathed a dry laugh.

"I, unfortunately, can't say the same."

"No?" Her eyes still peeked up at him through heavy lids.

"Nope. Love parties. Birthdays. Weddings. Holidays. Baby showers. Weekends—you name it and I'll be there," Jack replied with conviction.

"Baby showers?"

"Who doesn't like a good baby?"

Kit smiled the moment he let out a single sharp laugh. He could almost imagine her standing behind a cake coated with yellow frosting of her own.

"I've never held a baby before."

"You've never held a baby?" Jack raised his eyebrow. "One of life's most fearful joys and you've never held that tiny head in your hands and felt as if you are constantly one step away from messing up and making it hate you for the rest of your life? You're kidding."

She shook her head.

"Wow. I grew up in a big family. Babies abound." Jack's smile flinched as he thought about it. He looked back at her again, assessing how she continued to look at him. Her eyes never left his face. "Birthdays, I guess, too."

Kit smiled again, this time a little bigger, holding back a laugh he almost dared her to sound.

"What is it?"

"It's my birthday."

Jack balked, looking her over from the top of her head where she piled dark curls into a topknot to her sneakers. She had to have been joking.

"It's the truth," she said before he could ask. "I didn't tell anyone. Not Emilie, anyway."

"Why not?"

"I don't—I didn't want to cause a fuss."

"What do you mean, that's the whole point of birthdays. You can do whatever you want, basically anyway."

"Basically."

"How old are you?"

Kit turned to him and raised her eyebrows, not just one.

He wanted to laugh. "What? You somehow at the ripe age of forty-two?"

She shook her head.

"Twenty-three?"

Pausing, Kit shook her head again.

Now it was his turn to look confused. He was sure that right now, he would get as many guesses as he wanted, but he didn't take them. "Tell me."

Sighing, she looked up to the ceiling before coming back to him. "I don't want to."

"Why not?" Jack smiled again.

"Because I feel old. I feel like I should be, somehow, though I know that sounds ridiculous." Her tongue got caught on the final word.

Jack only shook his head, thinking of the things she'd told him.

"I don't think so."

She stared at him again, and for some reason, Jack was sure that this girl was staring straight through his eyes and attempting to rummage around his brain. He wondered how she was doing with that. He could use a few answers himself. Her eyes were a soft brown, but not just brown, like melted caramel with specks of blue just around the edges that caught the light from the back patio light.

"Twenty."

"What?" Jack blinked, trying to pay attention to what they were talking about.

"That's how old I am. You can't tell anybody."

Twenty? He almost asked her again, just to be sure she was telling the truth. Twenty years old.

Jack ran a hand through his hair, remembering where he was at twenty. Sleeping at work and praying no one would notice after he told himself he had nowhere else to go. He couldn't go home, he figured then.

Now he really couldn't.

Twenty.

"I think you already forgot, Kitten, that I'm not good at keeping those."

"Well then, don't think of it as a secret. Think of it as... an oversight," Kit corrected.

An oversight.

Jack thought back to the bottle of Lion vodka Kit managed to down earlier. "One hell of a birthday cake. Kit?"

"Hm?"

"Can I ask you something?"

"Only if it's to marry you."

"Funny."

"Only if it's a joke."

Jack's teeth punctured his bottom lip to hold back a laugh building. "Do you think that I'm—What do you think of me?"

Penelope's words ran through his head again.

He wasn't someone you'd ever take home to meet your parents. He couldn't even go home to see his own, so much so he might as well have been a little bit invisible in his own right.

At the very least, according to Pen and the rest of the downtown Ashton area, most of whom had been in his bed, Jack Carver was not someone you wanted to be *yours*.

He turned his head toward Kit again, who'd lifted her gaze from the ceiling back at him.

Her eyes turned sad, glassy, like they burned when she finally shut them. "I think you're magnificent."

Magnificent? His mouth was so dry he couldn't manage to tease her with the word like he would anyone else.

"Jack?"

His name coming out of her mouth had no edges, it sounded odd to his ears. Not a bark or shrill, like chimes. It was a soft whisper, like she was breathing.

"Are you all right?"

"Me? Perfect. Always." Jack tried a smile again, but it seemed less than it was before. It almost hurt as he brought his hand to his jaw and rubbed.

"You sure?"

"Just need to clear my head."

"Okay, then." She didn't look convinced.

"I'm serious."

Kit pressed her lips together. "I didn't say that you weren't."

God, she didn't even know him.

"How about you? How do you manage to hold so much top-shelf liquor?"

Kit's eyes slowly drifted back to his face, and this time, that small smile teased him. He wanted to see it break through the dark shadows of the house, but it only held right on the edge. "I already threw up in the bathroom at least two times."

Jack closed his eyes to hold back his amusement. *At least.*

"Attagirl."

Not long after, Jack found that the girl's head did fit rather seamlessly into his shoulder as she slouched farther and farther into him. And though she was tiny, this chick was solid as he lifted her up into his arms, depositing her back on the oversized sofa in the living room. Grabbing the blanket, he laid it over her lower half, making sure that she was still turned onto her side. That way, though, it looked like he was crushing her glasses, large from where they perched on the bridge of her nose.

Carefully extracting them, he set them aside on the table, swiping away some crumbs.

"Sleep well, Kit."

Pen was still in the same position he left her on top of the sheets, shirt riding up higher than it was before exposing the peach thong waistband.

He wondered if Kit made it.

CHAPTER FOUR

*W*rapped in Avril's sheer scarf, Katherine walked across the bridge to get home. It wasn't a long walk, though she never took it before. As she imagined just last night in Jack's car, she could hear the gentle yet deep roar of the dark water streaming below her feet.

Pausing halfway across, Katherine watched the water catch on rocks and edges. She looked back toward the string of houses with a Jeep parked in front.

She was at a party last night. She was at a party with Avril Queen.

A smile pulled at Katherine's lips. It lifted her chin up toward the still dim sky, catching a single star, or maybe it was just a plane flying by, dim and still slightly hazy.

Vaguely, Kit remembered her mother, who used to tell her stories. When she was in a good mood, she would point out the figures that stars made, though Kit never was able to form them. She'd tell her of their lives and tragedy and love, just like her own.

Then they would disappear, just as she did.

Now, the stars were fading out. Cars honked their horns and the air buzzed against Katherine's skin.

They were nothing but a flashing possibility, like Jack and her... staring at the ceiling.

She hadn't wished like him then, but now, for the first time in a long time, Katherine looked up to the stars just in case she hadn't already used up her quota for a lifetime and wished.

CHAPTER FIVE

*E*milie left the door open for her. She knew this, because the shop wasn't open on Sundays. It was closed to everyone. The only exceptions were a select few clients who frequented for custom bespoke pieces Emilie told Katherine in no uncertain terms that she would be crazy to turn away. Not with that kind of money—and the kind of fun she had making the pieces with silks that slipped through her fingers and lace she only saw on royal wedding gowns, let alone garnishing the goodies of some rich priss.

Emilie's pink lips spread into a grin as the front door caught on the old rusted bell. It hadn't been polished since it was put up whenever the shop was made a hundred years ago. The chime gently rang above with a high-pitched trill. It might as well have been a bomb.

Katherine winced.

"My, my, and here I was wondering if I would ever see the day when my sweet little niece would come back in here doing the walk of shame."

Katherine squinted, turning her gaze back toward the stairs. "There is no shame."

What there was, however, was her need for a shower and a few gallons of water. She licked her lips at the thought.

"I'd should hope not. Own it, lovely." Emilie leaned over the worktable in the back room, coated in a warm yellow light streaming through the windows. It only cast shadows where the sun had to bend around sheaths of tulle and across the uneven floorboards. "And with Avril Queen, no less."

At that, Katherine paused and looked back at her aunt, visibly shaking with delight. "Impressed?"

Her aunt only shrugged. "I told you."

"Told me what?"

"That you needed to get out and see the world. How you'd meet important people."

Katherine rolled her eyes. "I think you said fun people, not important."

"One and the same when it comes to life."

Sure it was. "You just think you're psychic."

She only shrugged, not denying it, and put a hand to her heart. "I'm just so proud. You would make me even prouder, of course, if you managed to get back here on time. We have work to do."

Katherine shut her eyes at the work she knew her aunt was referring to. Along with balancing the books and learning the ins and outs of running a small business with menial math skills, since the first week, Emilie had insisted on beginning to teach Katherine her one and only talent that made her business the renowned spot in town. Corsets.

The most divine of them had been plastered on Queen's body for the past few years, showing up in magazines and ordered from anyone from showgirls to women who knew sublime underpinnings when they saw them. Once, someone even commissioned her aunt to make a few for a historical film. They weren't cheap, but even Katherine sighed with pleasure whenever she ran her hands over the delicate boning while lacing them up on the mannequins positioned before the large bay window.

They were works of art.

Art that Katherine found rather quickly; she was not skilled in making. She insisted it would be much better, as well as profitable, to keep her on making simple sets and keeping up with Rosin's many burlesque costumes in need of minor repair.

All the pieces she had ruined in the past three months should've counted as a sin.

"Practice, practice," Emilie only said quietly from her side of the room, clearing her throat again.

Katherine wished that was all it took. Unlike Emilie, she had little grace in her fingertips when she didn't know what she was doing. She also didn't have the knowledge of studying historical underpinnings for most of her life. Her knowledge of sewing came from the same magazines her aunt was once featured in and adjusting hemlines on clothes she bought from the thrift shop she used to work at.

Trying to make up time, Katherine had been studying late at night, flipping through Emilie's books of fashion and the varied shapes and structures of the sixteenth century onward. There was always another page though, ripped covers and tracing paper stuck inside while her aunt made fun of the host on *Wheel of Fortune*.

"Don't give me that look! Change and make tea, will you?" Em tossed her head back to screech before sucking in a large breath of air to cough. She laughed louder as she watched Katherine cringe, trying to hide it within a single nod. "Thank you. There is some aspirin in the medicine cabinet."

"Uh-huh."

"Kit, baby?"

Again, Katherine paused and looked back at her aunt. Her carrot-colored wig was a little lopsided as she tapped the back of her scissors to her cheek coated in blusher. "Yes?"

"So proud."

Katherine gave another very visible eye roll as she made her way up the narrow staircase leading to the apartment beyond.

As if the storefront wasn't enough for her aunt, freshly divorced with no place to go, the little storefront complete with somewhere to live, built standing against other tiny top-heavy buildings on either side of her, was dropped straight out of nirvana.

Plus, Emilie always loved Ashton after being outside in the suburbs for most of her adult life, trying to fill an empty back-yard with children she never pictured herself having nor ever did. She told Katherine the wonders of Ashton the moment she picked her up from the bus station.

You're going to love it here, Kit, baby. This is a city built on the ashes of dreamers.

The ashes? Katherine asked.

What else do you rise from?

Katherine peeled off her clothes as she trailed through the one-bedroom apartment. Stepping inside the avocado green tub and shower combo, the water ran only lukewarm, yet Katherine hadn't complained. Its refreshing quality was now a godsend as it beat down on her. She scrubbed with homemade soap Emilie purchased from the farmer's market each week, causing the street to smell of lilacs and sandalwood.

The towels were rough, yet clean, as she dried herself off and reached into the medicine cabinet. She rubbed away the dewy bits of steam that clung to the mirror with the back of her hand. On the bottom shelf, toothpaste only had the lid half twisted on and a dozen different trial-sized moisturizers were tested and forgotten about. Squinting without her glasses, Katherine read the labels of at least a dozen orange canisters of pills left behind from when Emilie fought her battle with cancer two years back.

Little reminders blocked the way to the aspirin that Katherine knocked back, dipping her head under the faucet to wash them down.

Almost all of Emilie's home was that way, filled with things and photos, even though she spent more time down in the shop than she ever did upstairs. Depression glass littered cabinets and different kettles and teapots lined the yellow stove, which Katherine hesitantly noticed looked like it was hooked up to a gas line circa 1950s. Wallpaper painted everywhere in the small space from floral to stripes, including in the bathroom where it started to peel from years of long steam-filled showers.

Piles of pink quilts were draped over the pull-out couch in the back corner living room that most recently was reorganized into Katherine's bedroom. Shoving away the sheets to find her things lined up along the edges, she hadn't brought much when she came to stay with Emilie, everything still folded in the open-faced suitcase.

A simple cotton dress fell over her shoulders, along with a sweater. Though the air was getting cold, she didn't bother with tights. Padding over to the kitchen barefoot, Katherine filled the kettle up with water along with a glass for herself. The stove clicked twice before bursting with a familiar blue flame.

Hair drying and the second glass of water down, her head no longer felt as if it was going to fall off her shoulders. Katherine grabbed a tray, putting two mugs on top along with a few pieces of overdone toast she popped whenever she smelled burning— whether it be the toast or the appliance itself. Either way, she slathered each slice with butter. Only when she poured the water over Emilie's preferred oolong to Katherine's earl gray did she stop moving.

She braced her hands on the table and breathed a cool breath up through her bangs.

Her glasses fogged.

What she wouldn't do to install one of those little food

elevator things to send all this down to Emilie so she could collapse on the couch for another few hours. Instead, Katherine slipped on Emilie's gifted pair of slippers left by the door, and carefully maneuvered down the metal steps one at a time.

"And here I thought I was the old woman," Emilie commented when she finally saw her. "No time to lose."

Dropping the tray on one side of the table, Katherine didn't respond to that. Instead, she shoved a large bite of toast into her mouth. The crust had gone soggy from the butter and she swallowed it down with an even larger gulp of tea, refilling by the time Emilie waited for hers to cool.

She took her first sip, looking across the room good-humoredly. "Whenever you are ready, you know where to begin. I'll help."

"No, you won't."

"But it sounds nicer if I say I will," Emilie countered. "Come on, I showed you everything I know by now."

Then the real question was why Katherine couldn't make a corset by now?

Katherine gathered all the supplies she needed. The last and the time before last, she produced the world's least decorative corset, let alone suitable for any body type. So now, Katherine glared at the tracing sheets Emilie gave her for a basic frame. Fabric was cut, boning was laid out in the exact places it was supposed to be. She had followed everything she needed to do perfectly before she looked up from the table.

Emilie had gotten up at some point and disappeared from her spot in the corner, likely to take a nap or get something to eat. Katherine ate all the floppy slices of toast.

The store was stagnant as she took a deep breath, knowing what she had to do next. It was the point of the process most times where everything went wrong.

Putting it together.

Though they were closed, it wasn't often they had a packed shop any day, so most of Katherine's sad attempts at this point were never seen by anyone, thank god, but her. She tortured herself enough about each, knowing they were what brought Emilie in the most per purchase.

Katherine had been trying to convince Emilie that her time would be better spent elsewhere at this point, but still, nope. They—Emilie's shop needed a better online storefront for the past month. When she told her aunt this, she was only given "the look."

Emilie's eyes would widen slightly, in between shock and the oddest glare Katherine had ever been witness to.

She didn't test what might've come next if she went on pestering her aunt about it.

Instead, she continued to work on her own late at night when she wasn't forced to pinch her fingers in the corset that belonged in the scrap bin. She'd pull out the laptop after she heard Emilie set a radio clock alarm in her room. The static of Barry Manalo pulsed before silence cracked through the floorboards, adjusting to the cold fall temperatures.

So far, the website was coming along. The biggest issue Katherine kept having was the fact the shop had no name, and Emilie didn't appear to care to give it one anytime soon.

"You realize you have to do more than stare at the pieces of a corset to make it one, correct? I thought I taught you better." Emilie moseyed back down the final stair back onto the first level, foot hovering over the floor before settling down.

"I had no idea," Katherine said dryly.

"Now I know why you don't drink," Emilie murmured, not looking up from where she went back to work, ripping seams out of a pair of bikini-style panties. "You're mean when you're hungover."

Katherine's forehead wrinkled. "I'm not mean."

"Whiny then. Is that better?"

Somehow, it was.

Katherine, nonetheless, did not answer, instead she began to assemble her corset for the umpteenth time. It wasn't as if she'd completely given up all hope that with one of these efforts she would look at it and it would resemble a corset, it was just well. It was better to not be disappointed.

Instead of crying, she only groaned, looking at her failed attempt, again. She didn't understand what she was doing wrong. Emilie didn't understand what she was doing wrong. She classified Katherine from the start as a quick study. A lingerie prodigy of a sort that made Katherine smile for days as she made her way down the stairs before the sun was up. But this.

This.

"It's not as bad as your last one, lovely. Progress." Emilie's attempt to sound encouraging did nothing to soothe the look on Katherine's face. She might as well have murdered the corset. At least then she could hide the carcass. "It takes time, and this one looks salvageable."

Katherine shut her eyes and took a deep breath, feeling the frustration build up the back of her throat.

"I know you. You'll get the hang of it."

"You know me? You were barely around my whole life until I came knocking on your door."

Emilie's eyebrows rose.

Maybe Katherine was a mean hungover person.

"And who let you in?"

"I'm sorry."

"I know." Emilie didn't look the least bit upset about Katherine's rash words. If anything, a little shocked. "It's challenging. But you are doing well—don't give that face. You are. You have years to master this. You will most likely end up being even better of a designer and seamstress than I am and ever was."

"You're amazing, Emilie."

"Eh." She raised her hands, wiggling her fingers. "Eventually, I know the arthritis sets in. The tea helps."

"I'll make us some more."

Emilie only shrugged, thinking as she looked over Katherine's work. "You'll get it."

"Wow, that is one ugly corset."

Twisting toward the front door, it shut before hitting the bell, not that it mattered. Their visitor already made their way across the shop floor to them. Expecting to see one of their regulars popping in for pick up, instead, Katherine was met with the five-foot-tall vixen wearing heels just as high.

"Hello, Avril."

"Long time no see, Ems," Avril said, hopping up on the table and looking at Katherine's aunt. "Aren't you a hard-ass, putting your dear niece to work after she slammed a game of P&P last night."

Emilie looked at Katherine with raised eyebrows. Her disappointment turned back into impressed. "You know how I do business."

Avril only hummed in assent, kicking her legs back and forth as she turned her attention toward Katherine. "Hey, darling, glad to still see you around. I didn't scare you off last night, did I?" Avril tossed her one shoulder forward.

Taking a deep breath, Katherine gave the smallest of smiles. "Not in the least."

"Fantastic."

"Anything we can do for you, Avril?" Emilie asked again, peeking up from behind her tiny spectacles as she pulled out tiny slices of string she pulled apart to start over.

"Your new apprentice here is actually exactly who I was looking for. I have a bit of a task today to complete and I need some help."

Help. From her?

"I'm..." Katherine looked back and forth between her and Emilie, who stared at Avril for a long moment. "I am working."

Avril raised a groomed eyebrow.

"Go," Emilie said.

"But—"

"You already ruined one attempt at a corset today, and I doubt you want to make it two. Take her, Queen. Take her away right now."

"Fabulous," Avril said. Her hair, pulled back into a curly ponytail ready for a heist, tossed over her shoulder as she led the way for Katherine to follow.

Emilie, however, spoke up by the time she made it halfway across the floor. "Avril?"

Avril twisted over her shoulder.

"Be careful."

She smiled at Em. "When am I not?"

"I mean it."

"So do I," Avril replied with a shake of her head. "See you later."

Katherine snuck through the crystalized front door before it slammed behind Avril. Her strange new friend appeared to already be hauling herself up into a familiar army green Jeep, only it looked like the owner was not already inside.

Coming around to the passenger side, Katherine looked at Avril as she slid on a pair of black cat-eye sunglasses, engulfing half of her face. "Jack let you borrow his car?"

"Jeep," Avril corrected, turning the key in the ignition. "He is very sensitive about the word car, don't ask me why. And borrow? I wouldn't quite say that."

That didn't make Katherine feel at all assured of what was going to come next, but she climbed in the passenger seat much more gracefully than she did the other night. With a small laugh, Avril reached for the stereo and blared the music as they sped through traffic with alarming speed and dexterity. Katherine held on to either side of the seat as her heart raced, trying to keep her foot from pressing the imaginary pedal under the dashboard.

By the time they swung into a spot behind a tall building, all silver and windows, Avril unbuckled her seat belt.

"Where are we?"

"A quick pit stop before we head back to my place and figure out what is happening with you and all that." She waved a hand at Katherine's outfit. "An old friend is having a small get-together tonight and I'm inviting you. Consider it being my plus-one."

Another party? Katherine threw the car door shut to a beep behind her as she jogged to catch up with Avril. For a petite girl in heels, the vixen could move.

Nodding at the doorman, Avril walked across the entry like she had been here dozens of times before. She hit the button for the elevator and waited for it to ring, and suddenly the two of them were up nine floors.

Avril inserted a key into the lock and twisted open the door to reveal a spacious apartment with wide light-filled windows even as the sun already began to set on the day, earlier and earlier.

"Whose apartment is this?"

"My boyfriend's."

"Where is he?"

"Out of town. For another week at least, so he says."

"And he just lets you hang out here?" Katherine asked, looking around. It was all so clean, especially compared to Emilie's space, cluttered with color and knickknacks. Everything here was so... contemporary.

Wandering over to the living space, even the white shag rug looked like it had never been stepped on, let alone had wine accidentally spilled.

Avril paused as she assessed Katherine. Whatever she saw seemed to be okay. "Technically, I live with him," she slowly explained, punctuating the statement with a sigh.

Katherine balked. "You live here?"

"So he thinks," she sighed, moving back toward the bedroom. The bed was made, pillows perfectly arranged on both sides. "When he is in town, I live here. When he isn't, well, I live how I want to live."

Katherine remembered the night before when she said how Avril's friends and her parties were all his scene. Her eyebrow furrowed at the thought.

"He loves me, so basically wants me here all the time anyway so we can be together," she said though she looked away from Katherine as she said it, shifting through different sets of jewelry Katherine couldn't imagine her wearing left on the dresser. Dainty and delicate strings of bracelets and pearls. "Territorial type, you know?"

"That nice?"

"He has really good arms."

"How do you know if someone has good arms?" Katherine wasn't sure if she ever noticed arms before on a man.

"Oh, you know," Avril assured her.

Katherine still couldn't manage to put a face to the man Avril was with. Perhaps even loved enough to move with him to the monochrome apartment without a coffeepot.

"Ah-ha!" Avril shouted.

She'd since moved to the closet while Katherine quietly opened drawers at random, as if waiting to find something out of the ordinary besides too much cashmere. Something about being here in the quiet was almost unsettling.

She was starting to sound like Emilie.

Avril shoved shoes to either side of the floor. "Found it."

"What?"

"The final piece of what I'm wearing for my show next weekend. I already looked at the townhouse and Rosin. I was almost positive one of those bitches snatched it." Avril looked at the scarlet shimmers of the panties before glancing back around the room. "But no, it has already had its grand night since it ended up here, likely after a show."

"Isn't that the one Emilie made? On the poster?"

Avril grinned. "With my ass on a throne? The very one. Maybe I should wear something else. I have a few things that haven't had their chance to shine."

Her smile slowly faded.

"What is it?"

"Nothing. Just, I think I'll be taking an extended break."

"From your boyfriend?" This perhaps was the first thing Katherine wasn't surprised by in this place.

"Dancing."

That, on the other hand— "Why would you do that?"

"We all need breaks sometimes, Kit."

Even things that made them shine like the brightest star in the world?

"Be happy for me."

Katherine blinked.

"All right."

"That's it, all right?" Avril asked. For a second, Avril almost looked disappointed.

Katherine only nodded.

"Fine then. We better go and get you fixed up so we can celebrate. Yeah?"

AVRIL FLUNG Jack his keys from where he lounged on the living room sofa. It moved since she was at the townhouse this morning. Now, the long velvet couch turned toward the fireplace.

Jack caught the bundle in one hand. "Did you really think I wouldn't notice that you stole my Jeep?"

"You let me take it in the first place, didn't you?"

Tossing his head side to side, Jack didn't answer, only stuffed his keys into his back pocket. It looked like he must've been asleep when the incident occurred.

"Kit." He nodded toward her.

"Hi."

"We are going to get Kit here cleaned up."

"Oh, so you know—"

"Not another word!" Gripping her wrist, Avril pulled Katherine up the townhouse steps toward her room.

Katherine let herself be dragged, trudging up the red oriental runner her Keds sunk into with each step.

She turned to the left over the railing again, just to see if she could spot Jack. Instead, her eyes caught on a framed photo they were talking about before of a girl who was unmistakably Avril in the lower hall. In low light, red and shadows, she posed with her legs over the arm of a chair—no, a throne. Her head fell back as if in ecstasy, yet still managed to hold on to a coronation crown only outshone by a radiating grin.

Queen.

How could she just let it all fall behind?

"Keep up!"

Avril's room looked like Rosin on steroids. Plush carpet creased under each step and silk sheets scattered on an unmade bed. Deep rose-colored curtains fanned down from the corners of the windows and collected in a pool on the carpet where even more boxes sat, yanked out from the closet, sealed.

Avril ripped open one of them before pushing it off to the side with the rest.

"Who has this much shit?" She snaked her gaze around her shoulder to look at Katherine.

She still looked around the place in awe, cautiously entering in case she accidentally stumbled upon a different dimension.

"Seriously, sometimes I'm glad I get to forget about it when I go back to my other place in the city. I swear I am going to find a garter from the renaissance when I open the closet."

Katherine expected the closet to be big, packed with hangers. If the rest of the place told her anything, it was that Avril was no minimalist like her boyfriend.

Avril's closet must have led to another dimension.

"Well, help me. Do you want to go out looking like that, or not?"

Katherine looked down at her loose-fitting dress and sweater combination.

"Let me rephrase. When you think of yourself, is that what you are wearing?" Avril asked with a smile. A hand went up as if offering her the world.

"Um, I guess not."

Katherine knew that must've been the right answer when a half hour later, article after article of clothing was tossed in the general direction of her head.

"Those might look cool."

Katherine attempted to get the pair of very tight pleather pants higher around her legs. How Avril managed to wear them so often must've been considered a miracle. Katherine stopped before she got to her hips.

"I don't understand why I am trying these on."

"How can I see how my clothes look on you without you trying them on?" Leaning back on the edge of her bed, Avril tapped her bare foot against the plush rug. "It's only logical, Kit, and, come on, those look good on you."

Maybe if she didn't have thighs.

"Give them a chance," Avril insisted, cheering her on as she managed to finally get the button closed. "See? Style. You have even more curves than I thought under all those baggy shirts."

There were certainly not going to be any of Katherine's usual baggy T-shirts or unfitted dresses in this place. Looking back into the mirror, she ran her hands over the pants that felt like a second skin. They did look better than she expected them to. "I look like—"

"A woman? A miracle, I know."

"I look like you."

"Well." Avril lifted her chin. "I do have a great style."

Katherine's hands next found their place on her now very prevalent waistline, pleasantly constricted by the '40s bullet bustier top that also managed to shove her boobs up unnaturally toward her neck. She let her gaze linger on them as if they could be two more opinions.

"I expected you to shop at places..." Katherine couldn't quite find the right words.

"Different? Expensive? Oh, I do. But the sorts of clothes that come from vintage thrift shops feel sort of like home. Didn't always get to walk into Chanel and terrorize the sales associates after all."

Katherine blinked.

Avril continued. "Look, I was called a stripper before a burlesque star and a fetish model in Playboy once or twice when I first started out. I am from the wrong side of the tracks, Kitten. Not some fancy agency in LA."

"I didn't—"

"I know. I have made myself who I am since the moment I met Reed. Everything turned around then." She waved a careless hand back to the hall.

"He is my one and only. Best friend from high school. Onetime lover. Business and historian extraordinaire, that made my red lips and curvy hips much more '40s and less '90s Playboy. I could pull off the latter all by myself," Avril said haughtily. "His family took me in for a while after they got tired of me sneaking in through Reed's bedroom window during high school. We are the kind of soul mates that were never meant to sleep together."

"They took you in?"

Avril nodded and began to lift Katherine's hair in her hands, twisting it toward the nape of her neck. "I was in the system for a while. Not the first thing that I tell people, of course."

"Why not?"

"Queens are royalty. Royalty does not deserve to be counted in the statistics for daughters from a broken family turned stripper. Of course, I have no shame. Obviously," Avril said. "And look at you. In your prime to be a new Queen. You look hot."

"I am not hot."

"Yes, you are. Your forced B-cups are telling me so, Kitten."

"Why do you call me that?" Why did she remember Jack calling her that?

Katherine glanced back down at her Sandy from *Grease* impression so she wouldn't glance toward the opened door.

"Besides the fact that you are being a pussy right now, standing like that?" Avril rolled her eyes, bored as she wandered around the room, not particularly focused on her as she spoke. "Because we are all waiting to hear you purr, of course. But then again, you will also need lipstick. Now go back in and try on something else."

"I just... I really hate pants."

"So does the rest of the world, but to be socially acceptable, we have to wear clothes unless you want to join a nudist colony."

"No." Katherine held back a pained laugh. "I just mean—I don't wear pants a lot. They are like boa constrictors for your legs."

"Boa..." Avril glanced over her shoulder and rolled her eyes, but Katherine could tell she was amused.

She expected to be more nervous around Queen, but at some point, between being invited into her boyfriend's home, being a part of grand theft auto, and forcefully stripped down to her underwear and put into clothes that felt constricting to Katherine, the jittery feeling that had been going off in her veins like Pop Rocks dulled.

"Fine. Go and pick something out for yourself then. There have to be a few things in there."

Wandering farther back into the closet, Katherine's eyes

settled immediately on a simple black skirt. On another shelf, she found a pair of seamed stockings and a black lace garter belt like the ones she made back at the shop.

Perceptibly, Avril did not mind her indulging.

One at a time, Katherine rolled the stockings up her legs, clipping them at her thighs easier than she did with the plain garters she wore out for deliveries last night, slipping toward her knees when she started to sweat. In one fell swoop, she dropped the wide circle skirt to the floor, like something out of a movie, and stepped inside.

She shed leather for crinoline, prickling her calves under the lining and added a short-sleeved sweater that cut in toward her center. She couldn't imagine Avril wearing, let alone missing them.

Glancing around as she felt the fit, her attention was snagged on the mirror plate atop of the built-in drawers. The mirror reflected rows of glittering earrings and thick collars of jewels. In the one corner of the tray, Katherine's fingers carefully brushed against gold and silver encrusted brooches inlaid with jewels, different precious stones of every color.

She expected most of Avril's jewelry to be in her face, but these were simple. Delicate, even.

An amethyst winked at her as she picked it up.

"You found my treasure trove."

Startled, the heavy metal of the brooch clanged back against the dusty mirror it laid on with the others. "Sorry."

Paying her no attention, Avril reached to pick up another pin. The bezel was decorated with what looked like tiny rubies, glittering in the shape of a rose. "They were my mother's."

"Your mother?"

"You sound surprised." Avril glanced up from the pin with good humor, but only for a moment.

Katherine was surprised. In a way.

"Where did you think I came from? Straight out of the woods?"

From hell? The idea of Avril crawling out of such a place with her bright red hair put a small smile on Katherine's lips. The words 'and eat men like air' also came to mind.

"I was born on a bathroom floor, just like anyone else," Avril said, not looking up.

Turning the pin over her fingers still, Avril paused as she stared at it.

The next moment it clanked back down on the tray and she traded it for the other pin that had been in Katherine's hand only moments before. Dropping to her knees, she shoved up the edge of Katherine's, or rather Avril's, skirt until Katherine was holding it in her own hands.

"What are you doing?"

Avril hid beneath the fabric and tugged on the strap of her new garter. Just on the edge of the belt's fabric, she shoved the pin through and into Katherine's skin twice before snapping it closed again. "There. I saw a girl do that when I was touring in Venice. She wore a lot of shorter skirts than you, of course, but *there*."

"Avril."

"Our little secret."

"Avril." She couldn't accept this. Then another one was also attached to her. And a third that sparkled brighter than any star.

These brooches were Avril's mother's.

Katherine watched the amethyst set stone glint one more time at her. "Avril, I can't—"

"Shut the fuck up and take it," Avril snapped.

Katherine froze in sudden silence. It rang between them.

"Take it, please."

Katherine, unsure what else to say, nodded.

Continuing to move, Avril reached back from where she was

kneeling and grabbed a pair of simple black heels not far off the ground.

The block heel easily slid onto Katherine's feet, nearly as comfortable as her sneakers were.

"There. Take whatever else you want too. I barely wear what I see is your style anyway. The skirt suits you. A few inches long on me," Avril went on. "Come and look at yourself."

Following orders, Katherine wandered back into Avril's room where the air was cooler, less dense than it was in the closet. Stopping her before she could turn to see herself, Avril captured Katherine's chin in her hand and precisely applied a swipe the shade of magnolia blossoms over her lips.

In the mirror, reflecting back at her, Katherine looked—she swallowed. She looked like she always imagined she could if she managed to find just the right things at the thrift store in the morning before they were all picked out.

Avril's green eyes caught hers. It was only then that Katherine realized that they were rimmed, bloodshot.

Queen only shrugged as she took in Katherine from heel to hair.

"What can I say, it's a gift." Her eyebrows narrowed when she caught her gaze. "What? Not a fan?"

"No, I love it," Katherine said, fingering the vintage skirt's top layer.

"Good. Looks like we are both ready now."

"If only there was somewhere you were going," a voice from the hall murmured. Jack rubbed his eyes with the back of his hands. Not only was his hair ruffled, so was his black T-shirt that hung loosely over his hips.

"What are you talking about?"

"I tried to tell you downstairs, the get-together was canceled, but even I knew not to involve myself in all of..." Jack's eyes caught on Katherine for a long moment. Eyes like honey dripped down her. "This."

"Damn," Avril muttered, looking around the room as if she was forgetting something else. "How about Keys?"

Jack raised his eyebrows in pleasant surprise while Katherine watched the exchange. "I could use a coffee."

"I can see that. You look like shit."

"Thanks."

Katherine leaned between them. "What's Keys?"

CHAPTER SIX

*S*he had been in Ashton for almost four months. Four months and she had not traversed past the few blocks surrounding the shop. To think that she was fine with it all suddenly felt like a slap in the face. She barely wanted to blink as they took narrow back streets and turns, passing the art institute positioned on the edge of the river, looking more like a coliseum rather than campus.

They made their way up through the cloister of shops. Emilie's was just around the bend before they arrived against the curb with a halt.

Jack held the wooden door where over the window was plastered with various posters and notes. Glancing at them as she wandered inside of the dim shop, she caught a few signs for part-time jobs, missed connections, and band auditions.

Inside was a cozy coffee shop. The floor extended into the back wall, similarly clustered with pieces of paper left behind, as well as signatures written in what could only be a permanent marker against paneling.

A small roar applauded the tiny makeshift stage in the one corner. A girl with her guitar flushed as she hopped off stage, taking a pen from one of many, holding them up in the air from where they sat on the floor or on worn-in couches. She walked over to the wall where her name became one new among hundreds.

"Well, look what the cat dragged in!" a loud voice clattered from behind the counter.

Avril pushed through the two of them, wrapping her arms around the salt and pepper-haired gentleman. "Long time no see."

Jack only grinned, shoving his hands into his jeans pockets as he walked closer to the till. "Hey, Marley."

Letting him go, Avril took a step back, her eyes catching on something in the back of the café. She already made her way toward whoever it was in the small, yet dense crowd. "I'll be right back."

"We'll be here. Where have you been?" Marley turned his attention back to Jack. "You can't keep just popping in and out. This old man I know gets worried."

"You mean you?"

"Of course I do," Marley said without fault. "Who's this?"

"This is…" Jack turned halfway around before seeing her still standing there, awkwardly shuffling on either foot. "Marley, this is Kit. She's new to the city."

"Is that right? Are you a student at the institute?"

At the slight pause, Jack answered for her. "She's working for Emilie around the corner."

"At the shop."

"The one and only Kink and Collective," Jack answered.

Kink and Collective? Though not an awful name, Katherine narrowed her eyes. For one thing, she definitely couldn't use it for the site she still had on the back of her mind all day after her failed corset attempt.

Marley raised his bushy eyebrows. "Is that so?"

Clearing her throat, Katherine nodded. "She's my aunt of sorts."

Jack's eyes opened a little wider. She didn't realize until then that it was probably the first time she spoke more than a few words in front of him today.

The thought alone shot a shake of nervousness toward the center of her chest. *Her aunt, of sorts?*

She looked back down at her shoes, expecting to find her Keds, but instead seeing the light shining black heels. Going onto her toes before falling to her heels, she listened to the solid click.

"Well then, I hope that means I definitely will be seeing you around these parts more. What can I get ya two?"

"I have no idea what Queen wants," Jack murmured. "But I'll just have a coffee. A big one."

"You got it."

Both of them glanced toward her.

Swallowing, she looked up to the board above. "Can I have a latte?"

"Make it vanilla," Jack added, just as a loud buzzing started up from his pocket.

Marley nodded.

Katherine only narrowed her eyes at Jack as he pulled his phone out of his pocket. He hesitated before hitting a button and shoving it back where it was. Looking straight ahead, he watched the owner make his way toward the machine, past a young employee with streaks of blue under platinum that only glanced their way.

"Do you come here often?" Katherine asked. The space between her eyebrows immediately creased, realizing how that sounded.

Jack only shrugged. "Once in a while. I used to work here."

"Really?"

"I told you I was terrible at keeping secrets. Most of the time, lying comes with the territory."

He told her that last night. Right when she was. "About that—"

"One coffee and one latte with a shot of vanilla." In what had to be record time, Marley pushed their two drinks over in what may have been the largest mugs Katherine had ever seen, let alone held in her two hands.

As she lifted her cup, she brought it to her lips, sipping the hot liquid just enough so as not to spill.

Jack watched her.

"Come on," he directed. Lifting a hand, it came to rest near Katherine's lower back, guiding her over to the mostly open mid-century couch with blue faded velvet upholstery.

Sitting down, Katherine felt like she was molding into the cushion and not the other way around, still, she took a deep breath, trying to calm herself down as she sat so close to Jack. The place overall was packed, likely having something to do with what looked like open mic night and all the students with backpacks piled on top of another.

Clearing his throat over the continual noise, Jack caught her attention. He set his tall mug down on the mosaic coffee table in front of them. "Hey, what you were saying back there, just so you know—"

"Don't," Katherine tried to cut in, clutching her mug closer to her chest. It was probably better if she didn't know whatever it was.

"I'm sorry," they both said at the same time.

Jack huffed a laugh.

Katherine glanced down at her feet. She was still unused to seeing anything but her beaten-up tennis shoes once again. She didn't think she'd ever had this nice of a pair of shoes, ever. She'd probably cry when she scuffed them.

"I must've made a fool out of myself last night, I'm sure."

Jack shook his head. "No, you were actually surprisingly coherent."

"Then my rambling?"

"Was charming for a drunk birthday girl, I assure you."

If he said so. She still felt the heat of a blush rising to her cheeks. From the bits and pieces she remembered of the two of them sitting on the kitchen floor, well, it reminded her of when she was little in school and there was always someone to talk to, like a friend. Even if this was Jack.

The raven-haired man and scary professional Dom her brain couldn't stop buzzing with disbelief about when she found him sitting next to her.

She dipped her head back down to her ravine of espresso. The taste was slightly bitter, but also sweet and creamy.

"You've never been here?" He cringed, looking around Keys just as someone new got up to the open mic. It spit out a screech of feedback.

"No."

"It's so close I figured you probably would've stopped in at some point since you got to the city this past summer."

"How did you know when I got here?"

He paused. "You're not the only one who asks people questions, Kit. Seriously though, why haven't you been out? You basically missed a prime Ashton season. The winters are too cold and gross to do anything worthwhile."

"I don't exactly leave the shop much."

"Why not?"

"I don't know. I don't have to?"

"No, but you don't have to be scared in Ashton. At least not most of the time."

Emilie told her that.

"It's not that. At least not all the time," she said, phrasing her words similarly.

He noticed with a light smile.

She couldn't look at Jack when he did that. It was like when he smirked, the devil came out to play just like he did on stage at DuCain, and she couldn't concentrate or find the right words.

Already she barely felt like she could do that. Most of the time, she was sure it was like he was talking to a child who didn't know their alphabet yet. "I have a lot to do in the shop. Emilie has been training me and I don't always have the time…"

Peeking back up, Jack was still smirking at her.

They both knew that was all a bit of a stretch. Especially whenever she left the shop, she got a wave of Emilie's hand and a shout for her to have fun. A careless sense of permission.

"I don't want to let her down."

"By going out?"

He didn't understand. She barely understood, but she owed Emilie in a sense.

She shrugged.

"How did you end up here, then? Working for Emilie?"

The moment she moved in with Emilie, her aunt acted as if she had always been there, no questions asked. "My father left after I graduated," was the best answer Katherine could come up with as she worked out what to say next.

"What do you mean?"

This was usually where Katherine stopped. Her eyes flicked to Jack, trying to gauge whether or not he was actually interested.

"You don't have to tell me if you don't want to."

"If you want to know." For some reason, Katherine shrugged, willing to give it. She settled farther into the couch seat, glancing so she didn't nudge the other girl with glowing skin and perfectly straight hair next to her, tapping her pencil against the edge of a workbook. Music notes were scattered across it.

"He was a single father for a long time. More or less. He wasn't around a lot."

He did what he had to do, but not much more. He left money for groceries or takeout and enrolled her in school, however, a year later than the rest of her peers. Otherwise, he was gone most of the day and usually the nights at work.

Her father was a business director of a bank of some sort— she wasn't quite sure. Katherine never had the time or nerve to ask what he did when he was dressed up in his worn business suits. They were patched instead of traded out for new ever since Katherine's mother left. She was four when her mother abandoned them. The only reason she remembered the exact date was because it was her birthday. A pink cake with yellow flowers.

When Katherine's father left her, he picked a much more unassuming date.

One very hot day, she walked home from her job at the thrift store, squeezed into a strip mall not so far that it was painful to walk to, even in the rain. "I came into the house and saw the note on the table. He left for a last-minute job opening in Chicago. Couldn't pass it up. He also left the number for my aunt."

Though it would be a lie not to say she didn't have to go searching for it among the receipts and birthday cards he would never let her throw out. Kitchen drawers were always full of paper and mess, as if her father were building a nest instead of a home for Katherine to grow up in.

Jack's forehead was as creased as hers as he listened. Maybe she said too much.

She had a habit of doing that.

"He wasn't much for pleasantries. Goodbyes. I mean, at least he put the house up before he left," Katherine tried to rephrase. That didn't sound much better, heart pounding in her chest took up the room between the words she rushed through. "The realtor called before I left for here."

"That—that really sucks. You just packed up and left home?" His expression turned slightly stunned as he sought more words that weren't there.

Katherine couldn't blame him. "Well, there was a deal at the bus station for terrible Tuesdays, so."

Jack paused before finally giving a short laugh. "Did you just try to make a joke?"

Katherine bit her lip and said nothing.

"It was good."

She was terrible with jokes. Even her English teacher said her narrative papers came off as self-deprecating.

"I took the bus in when I left home too," Jack said, easily pulling the heavy weight of his attention away from her. She was able to breathe as she listened. "The city is a far cry from where I was."

"Where did you grow up?"

"South from here with the rest of the rural hillbillies. Grew up on a farm actually."

"A farm?"

"What?" Jack countered. "Can't see it?"

"No," Katherine said, but she smiled.

Jack snorted at the attempt to hide her emotions.

She definitely could see it.

The dark vampire coming to debase the dark city streets turned into a cowboy. She could see a wide-brimmed hat and a strip of wheat hanging from his curled lips. She leaned farther into the love seat to get a better view of him as a strip of light traveled over his nose all the way down his chest, where a dark mark trailed out of the corner of his shirt.

He cocked his head at her expression.

He didn't have to say it.

She was staring again.

Covering it with another sip of her coffee, she realized she must've been doing so all along. It was halfway gone. "So a farm, like, with sheep and horses?"

"Cows. I'm a big fan of cows. Better behaved than any of my three brothers." Jack smiled at the thought. Oddly enough, it was a different sort of smile than he had given her before, lighter, but when he looked at her, the expression faded. "Sorry to pry again, by the way."

Katherine shook her head again, still stunned he was talking to her. And how she managed to talk back. "Don't be. No one ever asks."

"So! What are we talking about?" Avril jumped between the two of them as she sat down.

"Who were you talking to?"

"An old friend who is none of your business. Unfortunately, it looks like everyone is down for the count this weekend."

"It is Sunday."

"Sundays are for quitters. Speaking of which, you both are going to be having a good time with me at Rosin on Saturday, right?"

"I have a thing before, but I'll be there."

She nodded before turning to Kit. "And you. Pregaming with me and the rest of the Rosin gals?"

"Kit is actually going to be with me beforehand."

Both of their heads swung toward Jack.

"Don't worry." He took a sip of his coffee. "We'll both make it back to Rosin with plenty of time to spare before and after."

Blinking twice, Avril leaned back as she stared at Jack. "You better."

"Where are we going?" Katherine asked after another moment. Was Jack inviting her out?

"It looks like you have a severe lack of knowing just how amazing Ashton is. We are going to fix that. And I also have some work to do before we head over to Rosin, but all in good time, Kit."

"Am I not invited?" Avril asked.

"No."

She glared at him.

"What? You have warm-ups and shit before the show, do you not?"

With a roll of her eyes, they all had the answer. "Fine. But you could at least extend the offer to be polite."

"Me?"

"I know, since when has that word been in your vocabulary?"

Katherine couldn't help herself; she barked a laugh.

The student now squished next to her on the couch turned her head with a look.

Katherine pressed her lips together as both Jack's and Avril's eyes landed on her. "Are you two done? I'm tired."

"We just got here."

"And the open mic is almost as bad as folk night."

"Folk night wasn't that bad," Jack countered.

"Only because you went home with the one singer."

Jack nodded, thinking back, his face slowly transformed into an appreciative smile. "Oh, right."

"So we're going?"

"Let me just tell Marley goodbye."

Avril turned her focus back to Kit as they sat. "What? You don't look too pleased. Don't want to go back to your ball and chain yet?"

Katherine shook her head, it wasn't that, but she knew what would be waiting for her when she did. Finishing her coffee, she set it on the table beside her.

"What? Not living up to dear Em's expectations? You wouldn't be the first."

"No, it's just." Katherine shut her eyes with a smile. It sounded so simple out loud, silly even. "I can't make a corset."

Avril cocked her head. "You mean that ugly ass thing I walked in on you trying to put together?"

"I can make nearly everything else in the shop, but corsets." She shook her head as she looked around the café. Books were even lined up under the bay window seat. If she'd gone to school, would there have been a shop just like this she'd be sitting in? "I just can't get it right."

"They can't all be that bad."

Katherine looked the Queen of the night dead in the eye. "They come out so lopsided every time that the only person who would wear them is the one French queen who liked painters to depict her with her favorite breast hanging out."

Avril made a low-humored sound. "At least you have an audience."

Katherine only shrugged. She was only born a few centuries too late.

"I want it," Avril said suddenly.

Katherine lifted her chin to look at her again. "What?"

"Your corset. The first one you make that you have the tiniest bit of pride or whatever it is your anxiety-riddled brain feels. I want your first corset."

"You're kidding."

"Do I look like I joke, darling?"

No. No, she didn't. At least not right then.

"Whether or not I'm here." She looked around her as if looking for the gods to be watching her as she said the words. At the very least, the SLAM poet may have been. "I want it. Hell or high water, or you have to bury me in the ugly son of a bitch, I want it."

Katherine didn't realize she was smiling until she was. "Deal."

Avril's eyes flashed in devilish delight at the word.

"A deal it is."

Jack rounded back around, twirling his keys around his finger. "Did I miss something?"

"The start of a beautiful friendship, my dear."

"Those are the devil's words right there," Jack responded to Katherine with amused sincerity.

She only gave a small shrug.

Then why did she just feel like she'd just spoken some of the best words of her life?

CHAPTER SEVEN

*E*ach stair creaked under her weight, but Katherine was barely paying attention as she mounted them back up to the separate door leading to the apartment.

She was going on a date with Jack.

Or not a date, but she was spending Saturday with him. How did this happen? Besides the fact that he didn't ask her first so she could say no, she was going out on the town with Jack... Jack... she wasn't sure what his last name was, but that didn't even matter. Nor did the fact that she never pressed to know what they'd be doing.

She was going to see Ashton with Jack.

Locking the door behind her, Katherine dropped her bag by the door and walked farther into the apartment, glancing around the place where the kitchen light and a lamp in the living area were switched on to a low glow. However, there was no Emilie.

Pausing on a creaky length of wood, Katherine heard something that from the past months she'd already gotten used to when neither her aunt nor her could sleep. Katherine grabbed a heavy quilt from the pile layered on the pull-out bed and wrapped it around her shoulders as she followed the deep bellow of sound.

Music, loaded with heady singers, pulsed with each step Katherine took downstairs toward the workroom. The record player ground out lyrics of '40s swing over the sound of Emilie sewing to the beat with each tap from her fluffy slipper to the machine's pedal.

The quilt puddled around Katherine like a cape as she waited in the doorway.

There was an easy movement Emilie had while sewing, as easy as breathing.

Katherine watched her now as each detailed curve of pastel yellow bloomed from Emilie's practiced fingers.

Emilie peeked up over what she called her sewing specs of narrow wire glasses, noticing her. She gave a little shimmy as she stood up to the beat, dropping everything to make her way to Katherine.

She shook her head.

Emilie only responded with another roll of her shoulders. She extended her hand out in front of her as the chorus started, and Katherine had no other place to go but to take it.

Pulling her farther into the workroom, Emilie lifted her arm and twirled Katherine around once before they were both there in the middle of the shop, dancing and knowing that no one was watching except for Betsy, the sewing machine, who had long since stopped whining.

Katherine closed her eyes and wiggled her hips down and back up again to her aunt's hoots.

Laughing, she smiled wide, just as wide as Emilie, who gulped down big streams of air from the strenuous movement. She sat back down in the bowed chair, covered in a pillow and blanket.

She sighed. "Back already?"

Katherine nodded.

"Did you have fun tonight?" her aunt asked her again.

"I think I'm going out on Saturday."

"On your own?"

Katherine glanced down and breathed a short laugh. "No."

Emilie nodded sagely. "You look lovely, lovely."

Debating her answer, Katherine let out a deep breath, thinking about Avril and Jack.

How Jack smiled at her, even if it was only for a moment.

She could tell that smile was only to be seen by her.

Katherine shook her head as something tangled tight inside her. It knotted and turned taut until it wrapped around and around each of her ribs, like a spool of string in her chest. "I think so too."

"Good. Then come here and help me with this."

CHAPTER EIGHT

*W*hen Jack realized that he was in love with Avril Queen, it felt like he was slapped around the face and left to sting. She promised him that she would be on her best behavior on stage with him at DuCain during one of his first packed night performances.

That meant very little when it was obvious she had already told the rest of the world she was always poised to be at her worst.

For some reason, he didn't think that he had to worry about that when it came to Kit.

But then again, he didn't really know that either. For the past week when Avril was home, she teased him about the fact that he invited the girl out before he worked that Saturday evening without thinking after they talked for less than an hour at Keys.

One minute, Kit was some sweet new girl to Ashton who can barely string together a sentence without stuttering. He thought Queen took pity on along with her tendency to collect the sort of shiny things Kit made.

And then the next... he couldn't put a finger on it. All he knew from what he overheard was when Queen was bumping shoulders with the brown-eyed little seamstress, teasing her, she fed off it. Kit managed to snap back with more wit than Jack ever imagined anyone could possess wearing a fifties housewife skirt.

What the hell was he thinking?

Jack ran a hand through his hair like a nervous tic. If he kept it up, he would likely end up with a forced receding hairline like his dad.

They were another thing he couldn't stop thinking about ever since he talked about them with Kit and all her questions, he couldn't help but find himself answering with a sort of ease. Now, when he closed his eyes to get some sleep before going to work the next day, his calendar in the past week oddly full and exhausting, Jack saw the farm.

He saw the willow trees where leaves caught on the rain gutters and remembered how high his brother had climbed one near the barn before he fell, grunting out noises with every branch he hit on the way down.

His thoughts and schedule had only been interrupted when Penelope would not stop fucking calling him. After not answering a dozen times, he would have thought she would've gotten the message.

He didn't want to talk to her.

At least not right now.

He knew what would happen when he finally did pick up. She'd yell at him. Then she'd complain about him ignoring her in that constant screech she did when she was pissed, then he'd screw her to shut her up, or at least make the screeches more manageable. Maybe he'd reach over to the arm of the couch in her studio apartment and knock over the god-ugly lamp her parents gifted her for a housewarming.

It didn't sound too awful right now, actually.

If anything, it would equal the odd discomfort that clenched his chest tight with anxiety until he tasted sour apples on the back of his tongue, like poison. He couldn't imagine how Kit managed to deal with whatever this feeling was all the time. She was sharp with anxiety and always on the edge of feeling like tiny strings were pulling her ribs apart, medieval torture style.

He felt it the moment he stood out on the sidewalk outside of Emilie's shop. Kit clomped down the side staircase leading up to the apartment. Her loose tennis shoes slapped each red-painted step.

She gave an uneasy smile, tucking her hands into the pleats of her yellow skirt as she stood in front of Jack. "Hi."

"You ready?"

"Where are we going?"

"We will see."

"So you don't know?"

"I didn't say that," Jack said. "I'm just saying we'll see."

She raised her eyebrows.

"It has come to my attention that you have seen very little of all this city has to offer. Today, we are going to change that." Jack started to walk, and as he planned, Kit followed a step behind.

Unlike everyone else, where he only felt extreme changes in emotion—maybe they were standing too close—Jack felt a sudden leap of interest up the back of his neck, sharp and pointed.

"That's it? You want to show me around the city? I thought you said that you had plans before inviting me when Avril asked."

"I do," Jack admitted. "But consider this a continuation, or whatever comes back to the main event."

"Warm-up?"

Not quite. Jack gave a turn to look at her when he thought of the word. "Preliminary."

"Preliminary?" she asked. "So, what happens if I fail before the main event?"

"You can't fail."

Again, the eyebrow raised.

"It's basically impossible. Fine though, if you can answer this one question, we will be set for the day."

"Okay."

"Truth or dare?"

Kit's lips snapped closed with whatever answer she thought she was going to give to his question. Shit, this girl was about to fail the simplest of fifty-fifty answers.

"Gotcha. Good thing I already know where this day is starting."

She nodded. "Where's your car?"

"Jeep," Jack corrected.

"Jeep?" Kit repeated. He was pretty sure he heard her give an eye roll. "My mistake."

All his brothers and his father were truck people, and for some reason he could never get over calling his Jeep a car. When he said car, he pictured a grandma behind the wide wheel of a Nissan.

"No offense taken. Today, we are walking. You said you liked walking, didn't you?"

"I used to walk everywhere back home. We lived in town, so nothing was too far out of the way. A good thing, considering we only had one car my dad was always in—" Cutting herself off, she realized she was rambling. "Yes, I like walking."

"And there is no way better to see Ashton. So, I'll ask again." Jack extended his one hand out in front of them as if debuting a grand show. The city was their oyster. "Ready?"

With a single nod, before he dropped his hand, she slapped hers inside. "Lead the way."

Keeping her hand tucked in his so she wouldn't realize that wasn't his intent to begin with, a few more turns down toward the river and the two of them passed the art institute complex.

Her neck strained as she looked up into the shady trees arching over the sidewalk and academic buildings.

"Will you tell me where we are going now?" Kit asked.

"We're here."

Pausing, they stood in front of one of the many museums in Ashton, this one was, however, sponsored by donors of AIA. A mix of alum and excelling student work, anyone's name inside was likely one you'd seen a good dozen other times before, head-lining shows or gallery openings across the world.

"You haven't been here, right?"

With a heavy sigh, Kit looked up at him from below as he mounted the wide marble steps to the entrance. "I haven't been anywhere, Jack."

Such disdain for him suddenly. He grinned with a tug on the hand she just seemed to note with wide eyes she was still holding. He gripped gently, but enough so that she wouldn't let go now. He had a feeling awkwardly letting go now, for Kit was likely worse than holding his hand in public altogether.

Flashing his old residency ID at the front desk, the woman barely gave a second glance at the two of them as she waved them through. Up first, art.

Finally letting go of her hand, Jack extended his to either side.

"Truth or dare?"

She stared at him.

Fine. "Dare, then."

"I didn't say—"

"You hand over your stupid decisions when you decide not to make them. Dare," Jack repeated, thinking of something just enough. "Let's make art come alive, shall we?"

Her soft brown eyes narrowed. "What do you mean?"

They needed an example.

Gaze caught on the portrait on the other side of the square box they were in, Jack walked over and turned out. His face perfectly mimicked the utter scorn of the man in the portrait, however overexaggerated.

Covering her mouth, Kit popped a laugh. It echoed once before she stopped it.

"Yeah?"

She nodded, a shot of sweet joy as she tugged his arm once and ran to the other room. Inside was a take on a couple during what appeared to be the tango. Looking both ways to see if anyone was looking, she lifted her arms upward, a single leg shooting back.

Slipping into the man's space, Jack paused before giving her a single twirl over the hardwood.

She beamed at him, looking for their next target.

Posing like the ballet dancer in the image, on her toes, Kit froze before moving on into a deep curtsy.

Jack barked a laugh, attracting the eyes of other visitors.

"Magnificent," he said, the word striking a chord with him.

Magnificent, she described him as that night on the kitchen floor.

His turn, Jack slowly folded himself into a slight sitting position, mimicking the marble statue, a la *The Thinker*. Kit smiled with a light clap of her hands.

Pulling her with those hands to the next exhibit, they pointed out which outrageous haute couture added by design students they would be most likely to wear. Each of the original sketches appeared next to the model in oil pastel.

Kit stopped at each, looking back and forth from idea to conception.

Pointing to a gaudy purple suit with pointed lapels, she raised her eyebrows as she looked Jack over. "It definitely brings out your eyes."

"My eyes?"

She smiled widely, still taking in all the small details. "They are the first thing I ever noticed about you. Or second—Do you see the way this dress is cut here? I could never be so precise with my scissors. Unless it is the type of fabric..."

"What was the first, then?"

"First what?"

Jack felt a little embarrassed he had to ask, luckily, she was still charging ahead, stopped before a peach-colored evening gown. It shimmered under the enclosed glass lights. Like a conductor, Jack watched Kit's hand almost trace the structure of the ensemble, sweeping up where it gathered at the one hip.

"What was the first thing you noticed about me?"

Pausing her trance, Kit blinked a few times before she looked at him. The expression that crossed her face appeared as if it was somehow obvious. His eyes, for one—he'd never heard that before.

Usually, the attention was focused on well, other places.

Biting his lip, he leered at his own thought.

"Your smile—or smirk. Yes! Just like that," she whispered instead of yelling. "It's so smug, always about to pop out. When I first saw you on stage at DuCain, you were stalking with that grin right across the stage to Miranda. I think that was what her name was?"

Mel. Jack remembered the last time they were on stage together a few months ago before she left. They were good partners. She moved to LA to finally pursue an acting career with the cash she managed to save up.

He tried to remember clearly how play was set up between them. What was the mass reaction? The night only came back in bits and pieces, mixing with all the rest. Only Kit was out in the back of that crowd.

"Your smile." Kit assented with a nod, though a hint of sourness snuck through. "That's the first thing I noticed about you."

"You look disappointed."

"I'm not. It's just..."

Just. He stared at her, waiting. "Just what?"

"I'm not used to smiles. So, when you smile at me and invite me out like today, it makes me feel special."

Jack still waited for her, seeing something else forming on the tip of her tongue she was debating.

"But you smile at everyone."

"I guess."

"So how does someone know it means something different when you smile at them?" Kit asked.

"Like what?" He wasn't sure what she was getting at.

"Like we're friends."

Jack's brow furrowed. "We are friends, Kit."

Even if he just realized it himself. That sharp understanding dawned on him, sudden and sure.

He nodded once. It might as well have been set in stone.

"Come on, there is one more exhibit here to see."

Walking out of the darkness setting the bright-colored fashions apart, the bright lights against black and white walls felt stark in comparison. Various types of frames throughout the eclectic corner of the museum's photography collection greeted them through another hall.

Before, when he first got to Ashton, Jack would spend hours in this space alone. All of his old favorites were still there. The picture of a couple, openmouthed, screaming as they splashed one another with the Ash waters. You could see how the droplets were uncharacteristically dark in gradient compared to the average stream. There was also a picture of a backpacker, arms open wide under the bright sun that reflected off his glasses on a mountain, likely not nearby or even in the country.

He always told himself he'd find that mountain one day.

For now, Jack shook his head at the reminders and smiled toward where Katherine was drifting across from him, easiness in her step. Only a tinge of torment still lingered between the strange string connecting them, as if waiting in the wings for its time to shine again. For how he thought the day might've gone, Jack was having...fun.

"Jack." Kit's voice dipped as she said his name, and he could see why. Pointing a finger toward one of the dark frames, Jack shut his eyes, knowing exactly which photograph Kit was looking at, lips parted in sudden awe.

A dark sky filled with stars. A face was upturned to stare at them just as the sun went in, framing them in brilliant reds.

CHAPTER NINE

"*T*hat's your name," Katherine said, as if it wasn't obvious.

Shutting his eyes, Jack shifted from one foot to the other. "Yeah."

"What do you mean, yeah?" Katherine suddenly couldn't contain herself. "This photo is amazing. You're in a museum!"

His one eye peeked open, mouth skewing to the side as if suddenly amused by her reaction rather than the hint of embarrassment she almost swore she detected—though that couldn't be true.

She never pictured Jack to be someone who got embarrassed.

"You're a photographer."

"Sort of."

"I wouldn't call this sort of!"

One of the security guards in the corner leaned forward with a finger to his lips.

Jack mimicked the movement as he took a few steps closer to Katherine. She turned back to the photo to stare at it again in admiration. It was beautiful. So beautiful that she let herself look over the name, shocked at the one she saw.

Jack Carver.

That was him. Right next to her.

"When I was back in the institute. It might've been one of my only great photos, and everyone had to put something into the pot at the end of the year to show to the board. Though I was gone, my professor submitted this with my name attached."

"But you took this?" She still couldn't believe it, pointing an inch away from the print again before dropping her hand.

Jack smiled, bashful. "I did."

"Why didn't you say anything?"

"I don't know."

"You do too. Did you want to see if I would notice?"

"It was another life."

Katherine raised her eyebrows. Both, since she could never do just one, however ridiculous it made her look. For a while there, she didn't care how she looked. She smiled, thinking about the past hour, running room to room, and standing beside Jack with a grin of her own.

She shook her finger at the photograph again, captured in its sleek black frame.

"What?"

Following him back away from the photo out into another section of the gallery, she couldn't get that image out of her mind. "Truth or dare?"

"I already know what you want me to say."

"So?" Say it. She dared him.

He rolled his eyes. "Truth."

"Tell me about it."

"About the photo?" Jack asked, answering before Katherine could agree along with adding the few other dozen questions she had. "I took it at a party. All my pictures I took for school usually came back on Monday from parties. I was warned about it a few times but…"

He just kept taking them.

"But you went to the institute?"

"For a short period of time." That hand went back up to his hair as they continued to walk back the way they came. They took a short detour through a printmaking exhibit. He huffed. "It was why I came to Ashton. I wanted to be a photographer. I walked into the institute and landed myself a last-minute spot, banking on any scholarships they would give me after saying I was basically off the streets. At that point I had a backpack and a portfolio of pictures I took with an old camera from home."

"That's amazing." To think she thought she came to Ashton with little to nothing.

Jack did come with nothing and acted like he had nothing to lose. Everything to gain.

"But what happened?"

"Why am I not a world-famous photographer?" Jack joked, though it came out a tad strained.

She glanced behind her toward where they came from.

Jack looked ahead, talking softly. "My professor, as I mentioned before, didn't appreciate the fact of how each Monday I would turn in photos from the party I crashed the night before, however well formatted. He told me I knew how to work a camera, which I did, but that I had to do the assignments or else, well. It wasn't my finest hour.

"I ended up liking Ashton and the parties a lot more than I liked college. I dropped out. They kicked me out. Either way, that photo was my legacy of this place. I always wondered if they regretted losing out on me when I left after that."

"Do you?"

"Do I what?"

"Do you regret leaving?" Katherine asked gently, realizing exactly the sort of question she was asking when Jack bit his lip in thought.

"Yes and no. Looking back, sure, I started a degree I didn't finish, doing something I knew I always wanted, but honestly, I don't know. Who would I have been if I'd stayed? Would I have met Avril and started working at DuCain? Met you?" He nudged her with his shoulder as he waved to the front desk on their way out. Sunlight greeted them as he held open the door for her.

"I ended up working at Keys, sleeping in the stacks for a while before Marley found me out, as well as all the other ways I was trying to pay back the student loans I'd already racked up and they were interested in getting back. Not long after then, I met Queen and started my other vocation."

"You didn't give it up though."

"What makes you so sure?"

She shook her head. "I just can't see it. You, giving up your dream. Photography."

His eyes lit up with another string of amusement. "Maybe you're right. Or, maybe not."

Katherine rolled her eyes.

"That's our last stop of the day. We are crashing a wedding tonight."

"You're kidding."

He laughed, noting her lack of enthusiasm. "I am. At least mostly, this is my photography gig these days. I guess you're right, I don't want to get too rusty. I take pictures of drunken grooms and women wearing different shades of white, and tonight before we head to Rosin for Queen, you're coming with me."

"They won't care if I show up?"

"They barely ever notice the photographer. You'll be fine. Now, onward." He extended his hand out when he hit the bottom step.

"There's more?"

"You think an hour and a half constitutes the whole day?" Jack looked at her. "Hell no. Truth or dare?"

"Truth."

"Boring." He scrunched his nose.

Katherine only smiled as they continued to walk, her following each careful turn along the water's edge as they got closer to the upper side bridge. The structure was bound on each side with swirling metal. It looked more like an art piece than a working bridge, cars and cabs honking at one another as they sped over top.

Underneath the bridge, vendors with large covered pop-up tents littered either side of the paved bank walkways.

"Another farmer's market?"

"Tea or coffee?" Jack suddenly asked.

That was an easy question. "Tea."

"Perfect."

It was only then that Katherine smelled why. Another farmer's market of sorts, yes, but along with traditional wears, spices and powerful flavors hung in the air. Moving toward one of the vendors, glass containers lined tables filled with dried flowers and herbs.

Tea leaves.

Katherine glanced back in pleasant surprise.

Lifting each of the lids, Katherine dipped her nose down to smell the different aromas. Herbal teas were at one end, black and breakfast at another. Each fought for her attention as she took her time, glancing at Jack, who did the same as he looked around.

Pausing, Katherine nodded, pointing to the large jar of May Day tea. Emilie would like it. Rose, chamomile flowers, corn-flowers, orange peel, wafted over her senses like a gentle caress. Handing over the cash from her tiny pouch at the bottom of her tote bag, the woman behind the counter smiled at her, filling a colorful canister.

Carefully taking it from her, Katherine moved to the side to look in her tote, trying to find a corner where it wouldn't be knocked over.

"Here." Jack extended another small container to her, this one white with colorful specks on the outside. It looked like sprinkles.

"You didn't have to buy me any."

"Well, this way, in case you conveniently forget to tell anyone next year, you'll at least have some of this."

Squinting at him, Katherine glanced down at the canister. Birthday Tea. Black tea infused with vanilla, rosehip, berries, and marigold. "Thank you."

Smiling at it, she set it next to the other, tucked between the umbrella Emilie insisted on taking before she left and emergency sewing supplies she had zipped up in an embroidered pouch.

"Do you always carry that bag?"

"Not always, but I didn't know what we were doing today," Katherine explained. Plus, it was perfect for carrying her latest purchase. "Was that the truth? Is it my turn now?"

Jack rolled his eyes.

"Only fair."

"Go on."

"Truth or dare?"

"Truth."

She dipped her chin. "What did you want to do with your photography? Or going to do?"

He gave her a look as she fixed her question, interested as his hand went back to his head. It was like a twitch. The question made Jack, of all people, uncomfortable.

About to take it back, Jack answered.

"You know those photos in magazines? A lot of them are bought off contract photographers. They basically can go and live anywhere as long as they are taking great photos to send back. For the longest time, that's what I wanted to do. I wanted to travel over the world and see everything, I would take photos of everything even if it meant climbing mountains and waiting for that single moment for the sun to peak." Peeking at Kit, his smile curved only the one side of his mouth, soft before looking forward again.

Somehow, as she listened to him, Katherine could almost forget that Jack did anything else but the thing she just found out he loved.

"You should still."

"Maybe," Jack said. "Maybe in another life."

Looking at him with disbelief, he didn't look, but she knew he could feel it burning into his cheek. There was a single freckle right there on his jawline.

"It's my turn now. Truth or dare?"

"Truth."

His lips twitched as if he knew why she kept choosing that one. "Strangest place you've ever had sex."

She knew he was asking to catch her off guard, his entire demeanor now looming over her. Katherine, however, held his gaze, unwilling for him to see the sudden flush as she thought of her answer. She'd already thought of them asking eventually, like someone at the bar demanding a driver's license where she didn't have the correct age listed.

She'd be labeled a phony in a world uniquely ideal, even if she'd started to look the part ever since the other day, rummaging through Emilie's old clothes and finding more than enough vintage skirts and dresses for any occasion—for once the pack-rat tendencies coming through for Kit.

The hem swung back and forth against her calves as if in subtle confidence. "My head."

Pouting his bottom lip, he only nodded. "Must be a real mind fuck in there."

Katherine breathed a relatively loud laugh. "You have no idea."

For one thing, she was almost certain that the last time anything interesting happened there, he had the leading role. She turned away, looking forward as they started to walk again back up onto the main road. "Truth or dare?"

"Dare."

Katherine's lips parted and closed as she tried to think.

"Didn't have one ready, huh?"

"I'll think of one."

He shrugged. "Don't worry, we'll keep it on a tab. For now, truth."

They paused before an entrance she almost thought was to the metro for a moment, a small group climbing back up the stairs.

"Ever seen a dead body?"

CHAPTER TEN

"*W*hat is this place?"

"The Ashton catacombs."

"Like the ones in Paris?"

Jack shook his head. "Much less impressive. No, Ashton's catacombs are more metaphorical due to the positive note of the city never being closely involved with any death causing wars or surviving the debilitating plague."

"So, what is this place?" Katherine asked.

"Ashton's roots." Jack paused as they came up to a name engraved into the side of the wall. *Gretchen Lou.* "Ashton was created on the river in the very beginning as a creative commune. Now, to remember them, their names are down here. It is a crypt though too. If you do something good for the city, you can still request a spot down here, so you'll always be a part of Ashton."

"That's kind of beautiful."

Jack gave a thoughtful nod as they continued to walk through the narrow tunnel. It was even colder than the breeze outside. Katherine curled her arms around herself, pausing when she caught a name that stood out to her. Some were marked with different symbols, whether it be from the original commune, art implements pressed into metal, or simple stars etched. Katherine gently touched one. Her finger trailed over another design, a thin, almost shimmering red line that twisted and turned before connecting to another section, another name.

"What is this line?"

Jack paused, stuffing his hands in his pockets. "Have you ever heard of the strings of fate? There's a legend that says that those connected by the red string are destined to meet."

"Like soul mates," Katherine whispered, looking at the two names next to each other.

Jack nodded.

Only a few others were also walking over the compacted dirt floor, either for a shortcut or to read each line of the people who made Ashton what it was.

"Why did the commune stop?"

Jack shrugged. "Progress, like all things I imagine. There are still marks where they impacted, though, and people still carry on the tradition of Ashton being a creative place for dreamers. There is a whole road, maybe we'll pass later if you'd like."

Katherine glanced up at him in the shadowy darkness only broken through by recessed lights. "I'd like that."

For a long moment, Jack looked down at her, clearing his throat. "Oh, look here. See? Leeson Modiste."

Squinting, Katherine knew the name sounded familiar.

"The street you live on. Modiste." Jack filled in, noting her trying to work it out in her head. Was that because she didn't know her own address yet? She hadn't needed to when she never left. Now though?

Katherine nodded twice. Modiste. A fitting name for a lingerie shop.

"When the commune disbanded, the city was basically up for grabs. That's why there are so many streets with people's names. Most of them you'll catch down here."

Taking deep breaths, Katherine looked up through the silence while the city streamed loud and screaming above them.

"Truth or dare?"

Jack turned, but fast enough.

"Truth," Katherine answered. "Thank you for inviting me out today."

A soft look spread over his face. "The day isn't over yet, Kitten."

KATHERINE WASN'T SURPRISED that the catacombs opened beside a bookstore where all the other stories were kept.

They milled in the aisles, Katherine picking out favorites while Jack pointed to the few he actually managed to read for school. There was a surprisingly decent assortment of them, including *Catcher in the Rye* and Jane Austen.

"Don't judge my tender heart."

Katherine wouldn't dream of it.

Next door in the park, each of them got a crepe from the vendor, much better than any hot dog stand. Katherine got a Nutella one while Jack got a crepe with savory cheese inside. They traded a few bites before digging in, setting up camp on a formation of rocks where others were also picnicking, wrapped in warm sweatshirts and baseball caps.

"You have a little chocolate there." With his thumb, Jack touched her face. Sweeping up the blob of Nutella, he neatly deposited it into his own mouth. He sucked his thumb before it came away from his lips with a pop. "You're right, the sweet ones are good."

Katherine's mouth turned dry. She vigorously nodded. She had never been so jealous of a thumb. Pointers when she was on the other end, and fourth ring figure when there was a ring there for more than just decoration—but never a thumb.

Looking elsewhere, Katherine watched children toss a

frisbee back and forth, throwing pebbles at it when it got caught in the tree. On the other side of them, a few people laughed as one of them got up from their blanket where a woman was leisurely sitting back up from what looked to be a nap.

"What's going on over there?"

Jack turned to follow her gaze. "An old joke. It's a statue people visit. They say it gives luck."

Leaning around the corner, Katherine watched as the guy walked up the bronze statue and immediately cup the figure right between stiff thighs. Her eyes widened, more so when she saw after he pulled away that the spot had been rubbed shiny after so many others doing the same.

"Isn't there something like that in France?"

"Aren't you a Francophile?" Jack teased.

"I always wanted to go. When I was little, I used to check out books from the library." Katherine explained. For some reason, France was always *France*, some magical place where all the fairy tales were set.

"And read up on the most frequently rubbed statues?" Jack shook his head. "Why am I not surprised? Unlike the statue of Victor Noir—don't be so surprised, I know what you are talking about—here you feel this guy up because it's said that he had the biggest balls in all of Ashton. Stealing wives, leading empires that turned the west side into a financial dream."

"Did he really?"

Jack shrugged. Maybe.

Pushing up from the boulder they sat on, Katherine made her way over to the statue. She could use a little luck. If she was ever going to get the website passed Emilie with a name and every-thing so the shop could continue to thrive, she was going to need a lot of it. If that came from her rubbing her hand against a dead man's statute, well, so be it.

Pausing in front of the guy, the statue was a lot larger than she thought it was from where she was sitting. Still, she slapped her hand right against the man's memorialized junk.

"Look here!" Lifting his phone, Jack grinned widely as he snapped a photo. "Oh yeah, that'll be making the album."

Katherine laughed, still holding her hand against the statue's groin.

He twisted the screen for her, even though she was too far away to see. "And that excitement."

"Be quiet."

"I was talking about the Ro Bro here," Jack said. "Who wouldn't be over the moon to have your hands on them?"

Slowly, Katherine's laughter dwindled as she walked away from the statue. She sniffed, leaning into Jack's side. "So, what's next? Skydiving? A bus tour?"

"We have reached the end of the preliminaries, unfortunately. Now it's time for the main event."

"I passed?"

Jack stared at her for a long moment before rolling his eyes. His arm wrapped around her shoulders as they moved back to the park's entrance. "With flying colors."

ON THEIR WAY back to pick up Jack's camera and equipment, they first walked through the street Jack spoke of earlier in the crypts. The moment they came close to it, the area seemed to pulse with a sort of imaginative energy that made Katherine take a deep breath. For a long street, the ground and buildings on either side were coated in paint, chalk, and anything in between.

They walked over words of encouragement and faces of important people depicted with vivid velocity.

Turning around, Katherine stared at Jack. It didn't even feel like they were in the same city anymore. It was more of a dream she walked into, filled with light and color and people adding to it wherever there were empty spaces. "This is amazing. Ashton is..."

She couldn't find the words, not because she couldn't think of the right one this time, but because there were too many.

"Ashton likes you too," Jack said, extending a hand with a light purple piece of chalk. "Want to add your own mark?"

In front of them, on the brick wall, a little girl ran away, back into her mother's arms as Katherine and Jack approached.

At the very top in puffed letters, *I Dream...*

Taking the piece of chalk from Jack, he picked up a blue from the ground and stood next to her, already slicing color onto the building.

I Dream...

Katherine wrote down the first thing that came to mind.

Jack nodded at what she wrote. "Seems reasonable."

I dream to find home.

"Come on. Let's go or else we are really going to be late." Taking her chalk from her hand, he dropped both pieces into the wicker bin as he walked them away toward the rainbow road leading them back to civilization.

Peeking over his shoulder, Katherine caught what Jack wrote.

I dream to find what I need to.

CHAPTER ELEVEN

*J*ack never saw as much of the city as he did today. He set out with a minor task when he showed up at Emilie's. Show Kit the city. Now, he couldn't stop smiling all the way back to the castle. He dropped Kit off to get changed, though he thought she looked fine and then headed back to the townhouse to do so himself. No one was home, the space oddly quiet as he pulled on his average wedding shoot uniform of a button-down and dress pants.

He smiled at her as she climbed back into the Jeep and beamed right back through a coat of reapplied lipstick that matched the color of tiny flower pins in her hair, swept back on the one side.

"I was worried you were going to forget about me," said Kit.

"Pshaw."

"Pshaw," Kit sounded back.

She was ridiculous. "Never. I did promise a grand finale, and I followed through. Are you ready to head to your first Ashton wedding?"

"First wedding."

"Really?"

She bit her bottom lip as she made herself comfortable. "Truth."

"Damn, then we really need to make it on time though I can't promise that it'll be anything special." He grinned wider and he noted the tinge of red that spread from her cheeks. "You clean up nice."

"I should say the same to you. You look good, all corporate in a suit." Katherine looked down at herself, swinging the light pink tulle side to side. "Emilie has quite the collection."

"Of suits?"

"Frilly dresses. Though you can certainly stop over and try a few on."

He shook his head. Her wit somehow continued to surprise him. "Wouldn't want you to be overcome with how good I'd look in that number you have on."

She only kept smiling, taking a deep breath.

"You good?"

"Wedding shoot and then Rosin?" she confirmed.

"Yep. With little time to spare. What, are you tired already?"

He could tell from the set of her eyes, forcing them to stay open behind her glasses that she was, still, she shook her head, and for once the silence didn't bother Jack. They made their way to the hotel, sprinting by the time they got to the elevator to take them to the top floor. They were really cutting it close.

Guests were shoved into the enclosed space with the two of them. Jack squatted down, letting himself droop with his camera equipment about his neck.

Like a piece of machinery, he knew where every piece was. Each fit into his hand with ease. Camera and lens, an extra battery was shoved in his back pocket.

Glancing up, Kit watched him.

"Do I see that you're impressed, Kit?" Jack asked, coming back up to stand again. He lifted the camera and kicked the button toward her face.

She blinked a few times along with the others in the elevator before the doors opened, looking around for the source of the flash. Then her gaze was caught on the view.

The sunset petering downward against the tall buildings. Oranges and pinks streaked through the aisle where the groom already stood, waiting.

Stepping out, Jack guided her to the side. "If you can, find a chair near the back. The ceremony, from what I was told, isn't going to be too long. I have to go and get a few snaps of the bride before she walks. All right?"

Still struck by the view, Kit nodded.

"Good. See you in a bit."

Turning around the curve into the side rooms, it wasn't hard for Jack to find where the bridal party was. Popular music played as girls slipped into dresses at the last minute. They threw curls over their shoulders. Jack quickly angled, finding light as he shot the photos of everyone, some more candid than others, as he came to expect at most weddings when people noticed that he was there, when really, he should've been invisible.

Behind him, the bride was just stepping into her own white monstrosity. She shed her silken robe as she stepped into the dress layered in sequins and tulle.

"Suck it in." What looked like her mother encouraged.

"I am."

"Well, do it some more, the zipper is—"

The bridesmaid on the other side froze in utmost horror. Lips parted, she stared at the piece of plastic-covered metal now caught between her fingertips, and no sucking in would ever fix that. "Oh my god."

The mother of the bride had similar sentiments, walking away altogether out the door.

"What? What just happened?"

From behind him, someone jostled his shoulder. Doing a double take, it was Kit that passed him, moving toward the stunned bridesmaid before anyone could utter another word. She waved a hand for the zipper holder to take a step back, visible in the mirror's hazy reflection.

"Hi," Kit breathed, taking in the broken situation. "Don't panic."

"And who the hell are you?"

Jack almost couldn't help himself as his camera dropped, coming into contact with his sternum. He took a step forward, but it didn't look like he needed to.

Kit rounded the front of the bell-shaped dress, they were eye to eye.

Hesitating only a split second, Jack noticed as her hands pause before settling themselves on the bride's wrists.

"I can help. But I need you to take a deep breath for me, okay?" Kit asked, though by the looks of it, the bride's face was more likely to implode, a pinkness taking over her entire face from her cheeks to her forehead. "We need to get you down the aisle, and we don't want to wreck your makeup. It looks gorgeous. This is just a little zipper problem."

"It broke," the bridesmaid, still beholding the damage, stammered.

The bride turned back to Kit; teeth clenched. "Are you telling me I'm too fat for my dress?"

"No, no," Kit spoke quickly, hearing the sniff of the woman. Her voice turned soft and soothing in a way Jack hadn't heard from Kit before. Strong and in control. "My name is Kit, and I'm a… seamstress. These things happen. It wasn't you or anything, the zipper just got caught on itself is all, like when you're a kid and your jacket doesn't go up after tugging on it?"

The bride nodded, understanding.

"You're going to be fine though, okay, don't move. I have a kit here in my bag I am going to get. We're going to fix it."

Kit with her kit.

"How? Are you going to fix the zipper?"

"Nope," Kit said pertly, taking this chance to stalk back behind the bride, dropping her tote bag covered in dull faded quotes and illustrated florals at her feet. She rummaged through it before pulling out a small sewing hit.

Of course, it was still bigger than any travel size. As if the implements inside were weapons, she whipped out a needle, swiftly stringing it as she compared to different spools that appeared to be the same shade of white to the dress. Narrowing her eyes, she fixed her glasses farther up her nose.

She concentrated with a huff, the spring finally going through. Three times the charm.

"We are just going to sew you into the dress," Kit said with a light smile.

Jack said nothing, lifting his camera again away from his stomach, focusing it on her and the bride as she worked.

"You definitely won't have to worry about your dress or anything else going anywhere tonight," Kit added. "It will surely make ripping it off later tonight all the more thrilling too."

A few of the ladies giggled, including the bride, who choked back a sniffle.

Jack smiled at the exchange as Kit handed the bride a tissue to catch any misplaced tears. "Better it be your dress a little ruined than the day, right? Now, stand still."

"Thank you."

"Mhm," Kit answered as she rounded her lips together. She motioned for the bridesmaids again to hold the dress in the correct position.

"What kind of seamstress did you say you were again?"

Pinching together the fabric, Kit began to weave the broken dress back together, a white shell becoming whole.

Before she could answer, Jack spoke up. A few glanced, forgetting he was there. "Kit works in lingerie design."

The bride's smoky eyes widened in delight. "Really?"

Kit bit off a piece of string, still focused as she nodded. "I scandalize people wherever I go."

Jack barked a laugh.

She glanced up at the sound, as if shocked that she made it come out of him. "Well, I can't beat 'em like you, Jack. I just joined 'em."

Yeah, he guessed she did.

"You'll have to tell us where you work then for our next bachelorette party," the bride said. "People do that with lingerie, right?"

The others in the room murmured their agreement.

"I'll leave a card for you," Kit said, but it didn't look like she was fully listening anymore. Her eyes were only on her work, hands moving as if she'd found her way around a shredded wedding dress a hundred times before.

Kit kneeled as she worked, slowly stitching broken things together.

The camera clicked with the shutter as Jack lifted his camera up and took the photo.

Glancing upward, Kit narrowed her eyes at him.

He looked left and right around the room. Where the hell did the sound come from?

Where did this woman in front of him come from? At the beginning of the week, she was quiet and demure. Now she sat on her knees and took over. The image clouded his thoughts at how she laughed just as loud alongside him all day, making fun of him, even.

Now this.

Hiding his face, trying to focus on his own work, Jack took another picture to capture whatever it was in front of him.

When Kit was finished, she combed through the tiny pieces of hair stuck to her forehead. "There."

"That's it?"

"You should be set to marry the love of your life."

"Thank you. Thank you so much, you are a lifesaver."

Kit hid her timid grin as she looked down. Carefully, as if there was a set order to her organized mess, she stuffed everything back into her embroidered pouch of emergency sewing supplies.

As if on cue, the mother of the bride stumbled back through the doorway. She glanced down at Kit. "Finally, something that works today. Let's go, everyone. Chop-chop. Time to start."

Bridesmaids gathered. They pulled their pastel bouquets tight into their chests. The others smoothed out the bride, fixing hair and holding up the train on their way down the hall.

Jack adjusted alongside Kit, dropping a pair of ornate tiny scissors she left on the floor back into her pouch. "Very smooth."

With a zip, her supplies dropped back into her bag. "It was nothing."

"No," Jack said, again taking a moment to do what he hadn't yet since he saw her wilted on the kitchen floor. He looked her up and down. He felt the pinch of sharpness before settling into something sweet, like cinnamon sugar. The sensation coated his mouth. "It wasn't."

JACK GOT TO WORK. Without pausing, he maneuvered seamlessly through different sections for the ceremony, knowing where people would look and where they wouldn't. Though this wasn't what he dreamed of when he thought he wanted to be a photographer, he still managed to be good at it.

That's what mattered.

He took photos with an expression in mind. He watched for when a face began to lift, and vows were being said. He caught it all, shoving down a cousin's phone lifted up in his way as he went with a dirty look. The bride traveled up the aisle and traveled back down to cheers as she gripped her newlywed husband's hand, which was a good thing, considering he looked a bit lopsided.

Peeking over his shoulder, Jack caught Kit near the back. She clapped with the rest before her gaze met his. Raising her hands a little higher, she gave him a small round of applause as well.

He returned a gentle bow before trailing out with the rest of the group to the rooftop. He continued on his mission, rearranging and posing the bridal party—and then reposing again when the mother of the bride insisted on something different—until he had so many pictures of the oversized group, the toasts, and reception partiers shooting shots back, he was nervous about the number of memory cards he brought for his camera. Only once did he experience an instance where there wasn't enough space to hold them all.

Grabbing a glass of water off the table, Jack slammed it back, setting it on another tray as he caught a rather puffy pink dress standing outside near the edge of the rooftop. "So, how is it so far?"

"Not too bad." Awe crossed her face as she inhaled, looking out over the city. Her arms balanced on the ledge.

It was definitely a view from here, now dark and sparkling.

"So, this is it."

"How do you like it?"

"I can't believe that I went so long without seeing any of it," Katherine admitted, wistful. "It's beautiful. To think only last year, I had no plans, no idea that I would end up here. With you."

"Yeah, every mother's dream."

"What do you mean?" Kit asked, confusion trailing like a snake around each word, constricting.

Jack glanced back down at his camera. His finger traced the shutter button as he shook his head. "Nothing. I know the feeling."

Pulling his camera off his neck, a cool chill of air caught where the strap pressed.

"Let's dance."

"What?" Kit looked down at her hand. He promptly lifted it into his. "Are you sure? We're going to get in trouble."

"Nah, what will they do? Kick the camera guy out before they cut the cake?"

"There's cake?"

"Later."

She huffed. *Fine.*

He barked a laugh at how easily she was convinced. "I've been told I'm a pretty good dancer."

Leading her onto the crowded dance floor in the center of the room inside, the temperature changed, sticking to wherever his white shirt pressed against skin. He raised his dark eyebrows, but it was as good as any smile. He gave her hand a quick tug.

She fell into him with a yelp. "You know, I'm not sure I've ever really danced before."

"Now that might be the saddest thing I ever heard."

Kit shook her head. "Not with someone."

"Still pretty sad," Jack murmured as he rocked on either foot, side to side.

Kit remained as stiff as a board. One hand drifting to either side of her waist, Jack felt her shiver under his touch, though that could've just been a layer of—what was it again, crinoline? He tried to guide her hips one way and then the other.

"Loosen up."

Her face scrunched. "It feels awkward."

"How?"

"Like..." She looked around. "I feel like everyone's eyes are on me."

"The only eyes you should be worrying about are mine, Kit."

"I'm not sure that makes me feel any better."

His eyes flared, and his right hand trailed around her to her lower back. It didn't look like she was paying attention to what he was doing anymore as she looked around. With his other hand, he turned her chin back to him.

Eyes on me, Kitten, Jack wanted to say.

Instead, he cleared his throat, eradicating the words. "Have you never seen *Dirty Dancing?*"

"I live with Emilie. What do you think?"

"Well, for someone who has seen *Dirty Dancing* at least a half dozen times at this point, I would have thought you'd be better at this. Didn't you practice the moves alongside Patrick Swayze?"

"Did you?"

He raised an eyebrow. "You act like I should deny it. We are going to have to get some fishnet tights and some fifties music in here if we are going to make a popper mambo-er out of you."

"Emilie also must have a few of those things lying around."

"She rarely disappoints," Jack agreed.

Kit began to relax at that thought. Slowly, she swayed over her toes. It was also rare that he found someone so perfectly his own height. Often enough, Jack found himself looking up at his partner, not that it ever bothered him. But this, this was nice.

His eyes narrowed as he looked for something similar in his partner's expression. "Something wrong?"

She shook her head. "I'm glad I found Emilie. Like I said, and you say, she's wonderful. My only family, even if she did feel obligated to take me in."

"Why do you keep saying stuff like that?"

"Like what?"

"Like no one wants you around. Like you're all alone in the world," Jack said.

Kit shrugged like she did before, unsure as she let him pull her body against his. They continued to sway to the music as she aired her thoughts, letting him take her wherever he wanted to go which oddly enough was closer and closer to him until her breaths truly had nowhere to hide.

A realization with the twinge of cold frostbite slid through his veins.

She really thought she was alone. She probably thought she was good at it, and now he suddenly wanted to prove her wrong.

He gave her a twirl like he did earlier in the art gallery. Though this was no tango, it was just them. He pulled her back in, flush to him as he easily slid a leg between hers. To keep them both balanced, of course.

"Emilie didn't take you in because she felt like she had to, you know?" Jack said. "She thought right away you had talent. From what I've seen at Rosin, I have to agree with her."

Kit narrowed her eyes at him and let her head fall back. "When did you talk to Emilie?"

Jack paused for a beat but didn't miss one as he led. "Before you came. I picked up a few packages so Emilie wouldn't have to take the trip out to DuCain. She was getting things ready for you to come and needed help opening the couch bed. It was so rusted at the joints. Emilie couldn't remember the last person who slept on it."

Kit gave a small smile. Finally, her hips were loose as they danced.

"Jack?"

He hadn't taken his eyes off hers.

"Why don't you go home?"

"What do you mean?"

"The day at the café, you talked about your family, and how you talk about Emilie, well, why don't you go back to visit them? What happened after you ran away that was so horrible that you couldn't go back? You made Ashton your home, but unlike me, you have somewhere else to go to, don't you?"

Breathing air through his teeth, at that, Jack glanced away for a second. "It's a long story."

"Tell me."

"Why are you so interested?"

"I dare you."

"Are we still playing?" Jack asked, rocking into her again with each steady beat as the song turned into another. "Because for some reason, I think it's my turn, not yours."

Now her eyes were only on his, if he hadn't caught her attention before. A tiny bead of sweat collected on her jaw. He wanted to lift his hand and brush it away. He wanted to dip his mouth and let his lips graze right there—and if it was anyone else, maybe he would've.

Jack watched it tremor and curl under her chin as she spoke. "I thought you liked to play. Or do you not do that on dates?"

The question was out of her mouth, and he saw her regret it immediately.

"Even if I am a fake wedding date."

"You're right," Jack said. "If this was a real date, Kitten, you'd know it by now."

Though maybe he wasn't even sure. Not all the way. As her eyes flared up at him, the thick sweetness he only knew as desire now coated his tongue again, his mouth. His eyes flicked to her lips.

"*Excuse me*, but we are not paying you to enjoy our celebration," a voice cut in.

Immediately, Kit pushed back, faltering in balance as she stepped away. Her eyes widened before she swallowed, chastised.

The mother of the bride snapped at them, her bird's nest falling toward the one side of her head from where it was earlier. Jack took a step back away from Kit as well, though his hand lingered right on the inside of her wrist where her heartbeat fluttered.

He felt the moment Kit's stomach sank. He felt it in his own, like he had been called to the dean's office at school after getting them to sign his papers to leave the institute. They looked at him with even less disdain than the mother of the bride did now, while the dean told him how disappointed they were in him after they took a chance.

A flash of anger pulsed right back through him, knowing the exact heavy feeling rolling through her.

Shame.

"Of course, ma'am. Was just giving my good camera some time to recharge before they cut the cake, unless you would like me to leave early?"

She glanced between the two of them before looking away. "I see."

Jack raised his dark eyebrows toward his camera as he clicked the screen back on. "Right, well. Looks like it is all good now. I better get back to work."

"I'm, uh," Kit stammered before collecting herself. She took one deep breath as she looked away from Jack, both of them retreating from the edge of the dance floor. "I'll be right back."

He'd be here, but he didn't get to say it before she made her way, slipping into the crowds. He glared at the back of the mother of the bride's head, already tilting her head back as she laughed like a hyena with another guest.

Lifting the camera, Jack zoomed in on her mouth and took a picture, all while hearing Avril in the back of his mind.

Karma's a bitch, Avril often said whenever she managed to keep her mouth shut and smile.

He did the same right now. Maybe karma would be, but for now, Jack rolled his eyes and focused on the other side of the venue where the open bar was. He got a pat on the back when he took a shot of tequila and slugged it back with an older gentleman. He hated tequila, but...

Fuck her.

CHAPTER TWELVE

*R*eaching for a towel, Katherine let water pool over her fingers before she tapped it against her forehead. She just danced with Jack. He danced with her and his body was against hers as her heart pounded.

It might've been the best moment of her life.

Best days. Period. And not just in Ashton.

She shut her eyes and took a deep breath. When she opened them, she met her flat brown eyes in the mirror. She was nothing special, but she felt like she was, if only for a second, when she was with Jack. Maybe this date—no, it definitely is not a date. She already went through this with herself and then again from him, however nice he was about it.

Glancing to the door, she paused as she caught two different pairs of feet under the corner stall.

Meeting her eyes again in the mirror, her mouth was parted in an oh.

Right, probably best if she got out before—

The couple pushed out through the flimsy metal door, flushed and tugging at their clothes. Only, it wasn't just any couple in the hotel. Eyes widening, she recognized these two, though it obviously was not mutual. Snapping her mouth closed that had dropped open in shock, Katherine threw the paper towel away before her hands were dry. They slipped helplessly on the door handle before she got it open.

The two chuckled behind her. He buttoned up his shirt while she adjusted the recently won garter high on her thigh.

No way.

Katherine didn't know what to do. Not saying a word as she made her way back into the penthouse ballroom. It didn't take long to relocate Jack, striking against the crowd even when he meant to blend in that simple white shirt. His top button had come undone.

She jogged up to him, not blinking as she gripped the loose hem of her dress in hand. She was surprisingly steady on her heels as she crossed the dance floor. All she needed was to be caught up in some variation of a conga line right now.

"Jack. Jack!"

Doing a double take as she came barreling toward him, he looked incredulous, snapping another photo before taking her in. "What?"

"I think…"

"What is it, Kit?" He glanced around the room again, maybe looking for that bridezilla mother or where he needed to move next, but his gaze swung right back to Katherine.

She grabbed onto his sleeve. He looked down at her hand, face softened.

"I think I just caught the groom fucking the maid of honor in the bathroom."

His head snapped back up to meet her eyes, as wide as hers were in the bathroom mirror. "What?"

Her thoughts exactly.

His mouth opened, no words escaping for a full second.

"No, you didn't."

She nodded vigorously in assent. Oh yes, she was pretty sure she just did.

A loud laugh erupted from Jack.

At the sound, she bit her lip. Cheeks bloomed with amused color that wouldn't be going away for a good while.

He wiped a tear. "You really know how to lighten the mood, don't you?"

Kit smiled as well as she looked around the place, spying the two perpetrators leaving the bathroom behind the bride's mother. Jack's cheeks might've flushed pink, but her—she might've rivaled the cherry tomatoes at the salad bar.

"Not for long," Katherine murmured, eyes wide as the screams tore past the playlist of sweet forever love.

Out from the corner restroom, it didn't look like she was the only person to notice the star-crossed lovers piecing themselves back together after their tryst.

Jack lifted his camera, and Katherine couldn't take it anymore. A gasping laugh peeled past her lips too.

"No, stop. We can't laugh at the train wreck," Jack murmured, pulling her into his chest as she shook, a fit coming over her and she couldn't stop it. It was only slightly muffled by his collar. "This is basically a crime scene."

"Is that why you're taking pictures?"

"Just a few more for posterity. They aren't going to want any of the others now. Tell me, do you know if they can get a speedy annulment if the person the groom sleeps with isn't the bride?"

"Stop it."

"No. Truth or dare?"

"I thought we weren't still playing."

"Truth or dare?"

Katherine paused. She wasn't sure what he wanted her to pick, but her lips had already formed the words before she could think about it either way. "Dare."

"Let's get out of here." Jack gripped her hand as he guided her out alongside him. It was warm, sturdy. So was his smile, clear and bright compared to all the others he'd given her. That he ever gave anyone Kit admired at the time, so dearly, up on a black lacquer stage.

Those smiles were ruined for her now.

"We're going to be late with the scandal you caused."

"I caused nothing."

"Mhm. Sure, Kitten. Either way, for once, we may actually be on time tonight." Jack extended his hand.

She didn't even consider not taking it this time.

THE SIGN WAS MOUNTED with swirling red neon lights.

Rosin.

The head knocker on the front door was encrusted in rusted gold, but it was the first time Katherine ever really noticed it after walking through the front door dozens of other times. An older couple of ladies in fur-collared coats laughed as they exited, paying her no mind.

In school, Katherine had heard of clubs. She heard about senior weeks and the kind of dark places where people danced under strobe lights. She could imagine them blinking in and out, concealing couples that snuck off into the corners where only a few could see them. DuCain was not one of those kinds of clubs. Neither was Rosin.

Red and gold shone through the entryway into what was once a foyer.

"Anything to check?" a man in tight pants and a black suit vest with nothing concealing muscular shoulders asked. He smiled with frighteningly bright teeth under the low glow of Tiffany lamps. Each a different pattern, they lit the pathway of music to match the art deco lines of wallpaper that screamed Gatsby. Katherine could practically see the tower of champagne.

"We're headed back to see Queen," Jack answered, gripping onto Katherine's neck while he laughed into her skin. "My god, what have you done to me?"

He hadn't been able to stop laughing all the way back downtown.

The crowd was thick in the room aside from them. Women giggled with well-defined cupid bows. Katherine watched as the clustered crowd around the bar cheered with pleasure as a woman dressed only in gold jingle pasties Katherine had to repair nearly every week whipped her breasts one way and then the other. It looked only slightly painful.

The two of them made their way past and up the stairs, to the dressing rooms Katherine had been in before via the back entrance. Still, her gaze always bounced over the glitter, hairpieces, and limp lingerie slung over the back of each chair. She almost didn't notice Avril occupying one near the back corner.

A halo echoed around her petite form from the lights. Her robe hung open to each side. Standing up in high stilettos, the movement nearly caused her chair to spill back onto the floor. Queen was straight out of a fairy tale; if only the princess was a Queen and the Queen was the villain. Bright red curls were perfectly coiffed around her freckled face, painted with merlot lipstick. She threw a loose strand over her shoulder.

"Finally. Here I thought I would be going on stage without my best and newest supporters."

"Reed's not here?" Jack moved past Kit to give Avril a hug.

She accepted it with a roll of her eyes.

"He needed to catch a last-minute flight out with his group. Boring, but we all know he doesn't like to fly alone." Avril answered, sounding a little out of breath by the time Jack finally let go of her. "Thus, why you are the best, my dear Jack."

"I live to please."

Her eyes flicked between them, Jack and Katherine. "You two look like you had a fun day."

Katherine licked her lips, but not before Jack answered. "Something like that."

"Well, let's get this show on the road, shall we? Before Cherry comes up to whip all our asses."

"You were waiting for us?"

"I can only shower you with so many compliments, darling."

Without further ado, Avril stood on her sky-high heels, strutting down the back-twisting stairwell. Katherine followed along with them, back down to the bottom where the other dancers, including the few they had seen on stage, stood watching the red jeweled vixen in a trance while transferring loose glitter from one pair of boobs to another.

One of the newer girls immediately did so to Avril, rubbing it into her skin while holding her hair away from her shoulders.

"Thanks, darling. My tits didn't quite look show ready till now."

"Finally! Where were you?" A very tall woman with curly blond ringlets framing her face swung through the backstage crowd, even pushing back the glitter process to look Avril in the eye. "I thought I would have to send out another Queen search party."

"Not my fault tonight, Cherry," Avril said without a glance in the burlesque club owner's direction. There was only a wink at Katherine as she turned out toward the stage. A dark red curtain separated them from the crowd, hooting at a goddess dancing on the shimmering granite bar top dressed in nothing but a bright yellow banana skirt. "Had to adorn myself in the new crown jewels as well as wait for my adoring fans."

She'd decided to wear her iconic number then, after all.

Katherine looked her up and down. Seeing one of Emilie's favorite corsets she ever made in person was so different than just the pictures. A deep embroidered red, it might have been one of the most spectacular Katherine had ever seen as well.

It caught on the lights above.

Avril let out a smooth shot of air from matte lips to the floor.

When her eyes came back up, chin tilted down, the vixen was taken to a whole new level. A whole other otherness. And the moment she stepped out of the curtain, the hoots and hollers of a pleased crowd turned into a roar.

Katherine turned her head to look up at Jack, who stood still behind her with that beaming grin. "Happy we made it?"

Crossing his arms over his broad chest, he didn't notice she said a word. His eyes, everyone's eyes, were on Avril.

About to ask again, Katherine closed her lips and instead followed the gaze, seeing exactly what Jack did from the moment they walked into the dressing room. A queen.

Katherine glanced down at her own pink dress collecting at her knees before looking back, squished between dancers, looking at the same thing.

Avril took each slow step, taking her time to get to the center of the small stage. She tossed a chair around and straddled it. One tall thigh-high black boot was on each side, red hair, red everything, dark as the bloodred lips she spoke with. The Queen was alight with fire.

"Hello, darlings." Avril's deep rasp of a voice was not loud, but certainly loud enough for the people already pressing closer to the small stage.

After another moment of stares, she grinned, slowly beginning to slap her one hand to her thigh. One thigh and then the other, she drummed slowly, lifting her boots until a clap was a stomp to the ground. Katherine put her hands together to clap to the rhythm with the rest of the crowd following the strange tempo she created. As she continued with everyone through the silence that had gathered in the club, her body ground into the seat of the chair, shoulders rolling to the beat. It was her own music she was making.

A single hoot broke through and Avril's laugh was an anthem

that clattered through the room in a vibrant echo between a witch's cackle and a child's purest joy.

She waved each of her hands at the crowd. Keep it going. More. More.

Avril grooved her body up the back of the chair until she was standing, clapping in beat with the music slowly pulsing around the club, a part of this surprise anthem that gained more than any past shout.

She had yet to take off a single article of Emilie's carefully sewn pieces. Yet they were all hers. Every single person. Every pair of eyes, transfixed.

The dancers who vied for the same presence.

Hers.

Jack's.

The woman beside Katherine hummed, Cherry. Looking up at her, it was easy to see that the woman held as much presence as she did height, plumped lips and heavily lined eyes looked out from backstage in just as much awe as the rest of them.

She gave Katherine a short nod, knowing who she was through her deliveries and last-minute alterations from the dancers.

Katherine attempted to clear her throat. "She's amazing."

"She's Queen," was all Cherry had to say. Her voice was almost sad, something in it not quite right.

Attention drawn back to the dance, Avril began one step at a time to the music, she never stopped moving her hips, smirking and teasing the crowd as she unlaced the corset Katherine had just laced up moments before, wrists flicking one way then another. Showing a peek to the crowd, she held it against her, swaying her hips side to side before letting it fly loose with a flourish.

She held them all in the palm of her hand, slowly peeling her stockings away from the garters after slowly untying each very high boot.

Avril, Queen, whatever her name was; she could be Persephone, ruling hell. One hell of a Queen indeed.

Smiling like a devil, wide and bright, she enchanted one and all with each article of clothing that fell and received a flirty kick behind her. Beautiful, strong, graceful, and unabashed, Katherine couldn't quite settle on a word to describe her as she moved.

Avril shook her breasts of sparkling pasties once more out to the crowd, giving a wide-mouthed twirl once, twice, on her tiny pointed toes. Her eyes, before going for a third, caught on something in the crowd. Feet turned to ice.

Pulled out of her stupor, Katherine leaned farther out to see around the edge of the curtain, but she could not see anything in the darkened crowd, whatever had seemed to startle Avril. Avril, who when Katherine turned her gaze back, was already back to grinning toward the crowd, licking her lips in one slow motion as she gave a bow.

And then another.

Another.

As if it was truly her last, like she said, Avril gave one more and tilted that chin up to the lamplit sky that finally found its one and only star.

Katherine knew that look, that look of understanding, that look of love so much like the one Katherine had when staring at her old sewing kit and model she left behind in the old house where she and her father lived for eighteen years. A room and a house that were still empty, filled with broken furniture from the thrift store and scratched cabinets.

Katherine, however, like the rest of them, only clapped as their Queen rushed off stage, shoving past Jack's arms and the concerned gaze that followed her all the way back up the winding staircase.

CHAPTER THIRTEEN

*J*ack stepped to go after her, but the crowd was too thick. Katherine had to yell for him to even notice she was still there, trying to get to the stairs with him. Before either of them could, however, Avril was already hurtling back down, duffel bag over her shoulder and dressed in a tight minidress.

The glitter on her chest continued to catch light all the way out the back door.

"We need to go out now," Avril quickly said, tugging Katherine to follow her toward the back door.

"You don't want to stay till the end of the night with the girls?"

"I just want to go out and celebrate!"

"What are we celebrating?" Jack asked, catching up behind the two of them. Shoving the barred door open, the chilled hair pulsed against Katherine's face.

Avril didn't answer. "I just want to go out and drink and see everyone."

"DuCain then," Jack supplied. He glanced back at Katherine as they made their way to the Jeep. "Unless you're still tired."

"Tired?" Avril twisted around, horrified by the word.

Setting her jaw, Katherine shook her head, trying to catch Jack's eyes, that seemed to land everywhere else. "No, I'm good."

Avril whooped. "Let's go then!"

All the way to DuCain around the block, Avril told them about the day she had from Pilates to dance class to rehearsal and finally the performance with the girls, and then on her own. "I haven't had so much fun in that place in ages."

"We had some fun today, ourselves, didn't we, Kit?" Jack asked as he pulled into the parking lot behind the looming theater.

"Jack showed me all around the city."

Avril's eyes twinkled. "Where'd you take her?"

He shrugged, shutting off the Jeep. "Wherever the city took us."

"I saw Jack's photo at the museum."

"I'm impressed."

"Why?" Katherine asked.

She shrugged, opening up her door. Katherine immediately followed suit. "Jack is very touchy about his art."

"Queen."

"What? It's true, isn't it?"

Katherine turned to look at him as he opened the side door. "Were you nervous?"

"No."

"He's always worried it will ruin his big bad dominant rep."

"What?" Katherine laughed at that. From what she had heard as well as seen of Jack's reputation of being the most in-demand dominant at DuCain recently, with little to no days off, she doubted his reputation could be tarnished by being an art school dropout.

In fact, it seemed to fit.

Jack shrugged again and said nothing just as Nik caught his eye from the bar. Waving him over, a few people already stopped Avril. Trying to give her room, Queen gripped Katherine's forearm, keeping her pinned under the attention until they too finally made it to the bar. Two drinks were already waiting for them. Avril drank them down rather quickly. Cringing at the burning sensation of the hard-brown liquor, Katherine pushed hers toward her friend.

That was what Avril was now, her friend.

"Why, thank you, darling." Avril took another sip to show her appreciation before waving over the bartender. He smiled at Avril, though Katherine had never noticed him before. One side of his head was shaved, while the rest flopped over to one side. "What do you want?"

"Um..." Katherine floundered for a moment before Avril stopped her, leaning over the bar.

"Any ideas what that means?"

The bartender looked Katherine up and down. From below the bar top, a crystal glass was produced. "I think I got it."

He pushed the glass toward Katherine.

Both of them watching her, Katherine slowly lifted the cup toward her lips. Expecting the sharp burn of whiskey, she was pleased when the clear liquid only made her twinge before settling. Her eyes widened.

"Gin girl after my own heart," the bartender said, cleaning off the top of the counter before moving away. "Let me know if you two need anything else."

"We will!" Avril called before settling back onto her stool, legs dangling where only her heels reached the bar beneath her feet.

Katherine took another sip of her drink. She didn't know what it meant that she liked gin, but she did. It tasted herbal and light.

"You look rather comfortable."

With a smile, Katherine only shrugged. She guessed Avril was right. She was pretty comfortable at DuCain, even more so than at Rosin, when she felt like half the girls were always asking for extra sequins to be sewn on or chatting around her for hours without including her in the conversation. Here, everything and everyone just was, including Katherine.

"Don't worry. I won't tell anyone, darling dearest. Not even Jack, though I'm sure he'd be thrilled."

Katherine narrowed her eyes at her friend, sliding her cup back and forth. "Be thrilled about what?"

Avril raised an eyebrow. "I'm hoping you're kidding because even right now I know you know. I can see it in your eyes. You may be intrigued if nothing else, but then my kink-dar is way off."

Kink-dar?

"Your one of us. I don't sense a sliver of vanilla on you. Not even vanilla bean. Nope. No matter how good you think you are at hiding it. You like it here and not just for the phantom of the opera-esque décor."

Oh. Katherine felt heat rush to her face, thinking about how openly she looked at everyone. She didn't realize it was so obvious. "Avril—"

"I love how you say my name, you know. Never Queen," Avril said. "It's like you know exactly who I am. I feel like I am getting to know you too. Seriously, don't look so ashamed. Be ashamed if you weren't a little kinky. The world is a lot more fun this way. Or at least being in bed is."

Glancing back toward the other side of the bar, Jack stood with the same tumbler of whatever it was he was drinking between his hands. His loud guffaw of laughter was easily recognized no matter where Katherine could've been in the club. The corner of her mouth twitched at the noise.

"Ah, I see now." Avril narrowed her eyes, a look of satisfaction taking them over at the sudden change of subject. "You really want to fuck him, don't you?"

"What? I—no!" Katherine didn't say that. She didn't say anything like that. Of course, she didn't just want… to… fuck him.

She absolutely did.

"He must've made quite the impression on you today. You wouldn't be the first girl, you know."

The thought made her mind spin with different images of him she had in her head before she even met him. Them, kissing, his breath on her neck, on that stage she would never actually have the courage to step one toe on. Katherine shook her head, hoping the images would fall from either ear, especially now they were all confirmed to be uncreative when it came to wanting him.

Looking around, she saw how other perusing eyes, women and men alike, caught on him, wondering if he'd look back.

He didn't.

"You can, you know," Avril murmured. She brought the rim of her glass back to her lips, almost finished with her second—or was it more? Katherine looked down to notice her own drink at some point refreshed. "Want to fuck him, that is. Or you could play. I'm not sure if you are actually ready to fuck him."

"What are you talking about?"

"Jack. I thought we already went over this?"

They did, but, since when were Katherine and Jack up for discussion? Did Avril not notice how he looked at her? Like Avril was the brightest thing in any room.

Katherine shook her head side to side, coming up with a better excuse.

"He has Pen." Even if it was complicated, whatever that meant.

"And what do you know about Penelope?" Avril cringed as if her name had a nasty flavor. Luckily, I was easily wiped away with liquor.

"I know that she and Jack are a thing."

To that, Avril tipped her glass in agreement.

"And that they have been, apparently, for a long time, which must mean something. They want each other, so they have each other..."

"Penelope can eat my ass. He does not have her, and she will never ever have him whether or not I have anything to say about that trollop."

"What do you mean?"

Avril looked at her. "Why don't you think Jack can't go home?"

Katherine only waited. She knew if she did long enough, Avril would come out and say it.

She rarely disappointed. "Little Pen, though the two never complained about exclusivity, saw Jack out with another girl, a guy, who knows, a few years back before he was supposed to make the trip home after five years. He'd been so freaked out to go home and basically tell his parents that he was a dropout. 'Course, Pen did him one better."

"She outed him to his family."

Avril's eyes widened a millimeter in confirmation.

"That..."

"Bitch." Avril raised her glass. She clinked it against Katherine's though she didn't raise hers with her. "Perfect choice of words, Kit."

"How is he still with her?"

She shrugged. "Our poor Jack has always been a little disillusioned about himself, in case you haven't noticed."

Katherine didn't, or at least, she didn't think that she noticed, not until right then. She thought about him smiling with his camera and hesitating as he talked about him and his family. Looking at him across the bar, it was suddenly clear that maybe Jack, who looked like he had it all—the looks, the friends, the talent and joy—really didn't see himself as much at all.

But that couldn't be right.

"Then again, I was surprised when he told me that he was going to go home and not tell his family about his life to begin with," Avril went on. "Because though we all know Jack is charismatic, has a great smile and an even better cock that can get him out of almost any sticky situation, it doesn't mean much in the long run."

"Because he's awful at keeping secrets." Katherine already knew that.

"You could give Jack a hundred pussies and he would let them all out of the bag." Avril nodded, slouching back into her seat.

"Of course, I don't want to say he's not good at keeping things to himself, you know? I am saying that he doesn't shut up," Avril clarified. "And that, I'm warning you, can sometimes end up being a very dangerous thing. One way or the other."

Katherine opened her mouth again to ask something, but not before Avril cut her off.

"So, are you going to celebrate the Queen vacating her throne or not?" She raised her glass again. "What a great day for everyone. Must mean something."

With a short laugh, Katherine raised her glass as well. The top edges clanged together. "Cheers, Queen. Thank you."

Avril rolled her eyes. "For what?"

"I'm not sure yet," Katherine said simply, nose already in her cup.

Maybe there really was a drink she enjoyed.

Looking around, her eyes catching Jack on the other side of the bar to make sure he hadn't heard anything, though he didn't look again, a few others glanced toward Katherine this time. Maybe Avril was also right about her being more comfortable. She was in her dress and hair dolled up, just how Avril said she should always look.

How she imagined herself to be.

Right now, Katherine imagined herself as Kit, on the edge of a bar, smiling with Avril on a Saturday out before Avril took whatever vacation she was likely already plotting for her time off.

She didn't think anyone was wondering what the hell she was doing here.

Not even her.

Though that might've been the gin talking, she drank the rest back in a single long gulp.

Running her tongue over her teeth, Katherine smiled. "I'm sure it's something."

After another drink and laughing so hard, the couple next to them joined in on the conversation. Avril rubbed her lips together before she stood up from the bar. Her red French-tipped talons gripped Katherine's forearm for balance.

"Be right back, darling," Avril sang quickly as she swayed toward the bathroom.

This time when Katherine looked, she caught Jack on the other side of the tiny crowd they'd created, incorporating himself into them with easy conversation. His eyes trailed Avril before finding Katherine.

She mouthed the words, *I'll follow her.*

Twisting past a throng of bodies, Katherine saw her bright hair slip through the backstage doors toward the bathroom.

If anything, in the past hour or so they'd been here, the club only became more excited, people laughing and black-striped whips snapping through the air over the bass of the music each of her own steps pounded to. The stage caught her attention more than anything else, more than Avril, who fully disappeared.

On stage, a man pushed a woman in a strappy leather harness down, dragging the tip of what looked to be a horse's riding crop down the length of her already welting spine. As he lifted it again, Katherine expected a gasp, a flinch from the woman, but nothing came, not even the crop as the man smothered her back with his own chest in a passionate embrace as he held her. The hiss from the woman's lips only escaped then, in a sort of wheeze. Of pain?

Pleasure.

"Like what you see?"

Flicking her chin high up to the man standing right beside her in a loose-fitting button-down already half open, Katherine couldn't help herself from staggering toward the wall.

"Sorry, didn't mean to startle you."

"You—you didn't," Katherine managed to say, taking in the blond monster of a man. "Sorry, I was just—"

He gave a small smile. "Distracted? How about I get you a drink and we can have a chat?"

"She's already well-handled in that department, thanks."

A steady hand settled on the top of Katherine's spine, just below her neck. She almost flinched at the sudden intrusion. Her body prepared, ready to leap away like a frightened house cat, but not when she caught the edge of startling eyes burrowing into the man in front of them before she did.

In the past few weeks, she had seen Jack in passing. Never had she not seen some form of smile or smirk gracing the corners of his face. Perhaps this was the reason. Without it, standing just a bit taller behind her, he looked like he could create enemies as quick as he did admirers.

CHAPTER FOURTEEN

"*I* apologize." The man, towering over Jack, took a step back. "I just saw her with Queen. Didn't think she was yours."

"You thought wrong."

Katherine blinked at the two of them, remaining still. All she could feel was the heat somehow emanating from the three fingers Jack still had holding on to the back of her neck, touching her.

"Jack. Jack."

His eyes flicked down to her face, the strange and sudden fury waning to a sudden flush. The man across from them took it as his moment to slowly slink away from the two of them, wandering around the tables back to where his friends were, including a girl who happily wrapped her arms around his shoulders.

"Jack."

Did no one respond to their names anymore?

Maybe they all just had too many of them.

Eyes, usually full of bashfulness, now were just frozen. He

stood there until his hand finally fell away. Cold air swept over where the imprint was when Avril pushed between them.

He turned toward his friend, loosening his wide-set shoulders.

"Come on, I'll take you home."

"Who said I was ready to go?"

Though Avril did seem light enough on her feet to hold each heel tight to the floor, there was no mistaking the way the top of her head slightly tilted to the side. It was as if gravity was beginning to take over on her petite form, dragging her down by her scorching curls.

"We'll go back to the townhouse then, but we are going home," Jack repeated. He began to walk away.

"Ain't no rest for the wicked," Avril muttered. "Is there, Kit?"

"What are you talking about?"

Had she seen Jack and her a minute ago? Had she planned it? How he put his hand on the back of her neck like—like...

Katherine put a hand to her head, sure to feel pounding against her skull as the wheels turned but was met with nothing.

"You met the Ripper and the Queen and now the Devil. My, you have a way of drawing them in. And, well, you certainly started to make a name for yourself already," Avril lifted her head sloppily as she made her way toward the front curtained door.

Ripper?

Katherine followed without getting to question what Avril meant. At least a dozen heads turned, noting Katherine in her vintage pink and frilly dress she hadn't changed from the wedding. They looked her up and down like she was a new prized cow.

Of course, Katherine glanced farther back to see Jack on the other side of the bar. Jack did say that one time he was a big fan of cows.

Avril draped over Katherine's arm and pulled them both

toward the Jeep in the parking lot outside. Her high-heeled boots cracked over gravel.

Rushing up behind the two of them, Jack opened the passenger door, helping each of them haul themselves up into it. He helped Avril in with a gentle push. Slamming the door shut while Jack rounded the front, Katherine leaned toward Avril's ear. "What were you talking about, inside?"

A laugh burst through Avril's lips. The sound must have been loud enough for Jack's head turned before he made it the full way around the Jeep.

"Your knight in shining armor there is the dungeon master, darling." Avril shook her head. Katherine was moving much slower than normal. "And it appears you are a very shiny new toy to dungeon masters."

That made no sense.

"Jack?"

Jack swung himself into the driver's seat just as his name escaped Katherine's lips. "Yeah?"

Say something.

Avril's eyes flicked between the two. Katherine held on to the shoulder of Avril's seat.

She said nothing.

Jack shook his head and turned the key. Soon they were back on the road, heading right across the bridge.

Katherine almost spoke up again and told Jack to drop her off at home, but instead, she stayed silent, still in the back seat. She watched the lights bounce off the water all the way to the upper side bridge she and Jack visited that morning.

"So much for a wild night to remember, huh, Queen?" Jack said.

Avril shrugged. "I'll have to remember the ones that matter."

By the time they pulled in front of the townhouse, Avril's eyes were half closed. She didn't protest as Jack gathered her in his arms and carried her past the front door and up the flight of stairs to her bedroom.

Katherine shut the door behind her as she slowly followed.

The townhouse seemed quiet, so much so she heard the click when she turned the dead bolt. Then she felt the weight slide around her shoulders, so heavy that she considered leaning up against the door and sliding down it right then and there. Instead, Katherine forced herself to take a step forward, and then another, into the house.

Katherine kept walking, listening to the steady cadence of her shoes wherever there wasn't a rug. The stone countertop was chilled under her shaky fingers when she finally paused to take her turn to close her eyes, leaving them like that to soothe the sudden burn making its way up her throat.

Jack loved Avril.

Her mind about it all was suddenly as clear as the liquor she drank. Crystal.

It made sense. Out of all the options she'd thought through, it made the most sense out of everything. Jack and Avril. Not him and Pen, not—how could she have ever thought that Jack would have liked her anyway?

They were friends. Avril's friend that turned into his friend. They were just a couple of lost things that loved people they shouldn't.

She took a deep breath.

Another.

Slowly, she let herself drift down onto the kitchen floor, skirts flaring out to either side of her hips before kicking off her heels. Though comfortable, she noticed the dark red at the back of her ankle where they bit.

"Are those..." Standing in the archway to the hall, Jack's eyes were intent as he stared down toward where her skirt had snaked far up.

Looking down, Katherine stared at her simple garter belt,

which was more than just peeking out through the tulle. Holding one stocking up while the other pooled below her right knee, the image was a stark contrast to the three brooches that dug into her hip when she didn't stand straight. Much like now.

He had to have noticed them when they were dancing earlier at the wedding. The feeling of their bodies so close, closer than Katherine may have ever let herself get to someone before sent a wave through her again, settling low in her stomach.

Or maybe he didn't notice every place they met like she did.

There was no question, however; at some point, Jack had seen Avril's crown jewels before.

"I've been keeping them safe," Katherine explained softly.

After another moment, without a word, Jack nodded. She wondered if he too had come to understand that something wasn't quite right with the Queen. At least not tonight, or the past week. Her sitting here might've been another clue.

She shivered at the air that snuck through the vent under her feet. Crossing her arms over one another.

"You're cold."

Katherine shrugged.

"Then why do you sit there on the kitchen floor?" He asked, a hand lifting to the side as if to point out all the more appropriate seating Katherine did consider before passing by. The throw blanket over the back of the couch did look all the more inviting.

"I don't know," Katherine replied. "Sometimes I think the best thinking is done on kitchen floors. Dancing too."

"I thought you said you didn't dance."

"I said I never liked to dance alone."

"I guess you're right," Jack tipped his head, a hand going up to run a hand through the darkness. "You're a little tipsy tonight too."

"She just kept ordering more."

"Yeah, I think she has a lot on her mind too," Jack said with a sigh, his eyes catching once more on the glimmering antique pins. "Do you know what is up with her?"

Katherine bit her lip, finally looking up at him through heavy lashes. He looked good even now, with his hair mussed and shirt untucked. Of course he would. "She says she is taking a break."

"From performing?"

Her head bobbed.

A perplexed look passed over his face. "You want some company?"

"I should probably get back..." Home. "To Emilie's."

"For a little then," Jack amended. He groaned as he lowered himself down next to her, but he didn't stop until he was all the way down on the floor, his back flush with the black and white celestial tile.

"Okay. For a little then."

"Then, I'll drive you back. You shouldn't be walking the bridge this late at night alone."

She stared at him for a long while, watching as he stretched his hands above his head before settling. Friends. That is what they were and for some reason, letting her heart settle back into a slow beat, Katherine could be okay with that.

She should be grateful, even, to have a friend like Jack.

All her life, she knew better than to believe it when people called themselves a friend. Almost always, they turned out to be more like acquaintances that stayed around a little while. They called everyone a friend.

Just like when Jack smiled at everyone.

But this was different.

It had to be. "Thank you."

Eyes popping open, his honey-hued kaleidoscopes stared at her a long second before asking, "For what?"

"Inviting me with you today... worrying about me walking home. It meant a lot."

"Don't worry about it."

"But I do," Katherine said hastily, not letting him say anything else or change the subject. She knew it was the gin talking now, but for now, she didn't care. "I worry all the time. I know it, and I still do it. I worry until my heart races and I let it. So, it meant a lot that you invited me along today, whether or not it was from pity—"

"It wasn't. Pity," Jack said. His voice steady as he took in the many tense creases sure to be forming over her face. "Okay, maybe at first, a little. I was hasty and didn't want to back out after I invited you, and I had no idea what today was going to be like or if it was going to be awkward."

His definition of awkward and hers were clearly different.

"But Kit, today was a great day."

There was that smile again, this time half hidden from sucking on his cheek.

The things he could make someone do with that smile.

"It was," Katherine agreed, a little choked. "A good day. It was nice to feel like I had a friend."

"We are friends, Kit." He smiled wider.

Katherine swallowed the heavy clump in her throat and nodded. "Okay."

"We are."

"I know."

"Good. You know, I worry too."

He did?

"But, don't Kit. You'll get everything you deserve whether or not you think so. A nice handsome guy or girl or whatever you want in the world. Home."

That was what she dreamed. He remembered.

With a decisive nod of his own, Jack hauled himself back up and dug his keys out of his pocket. "You need some water first, or are you ready to go home?"

"We can go."

The ride went quickly as they went back across the bridge. He talked to Katherine about needing to download all the pictures they took together today even if the client wouldn't want them, like she had something to do with it.

She didn't correct him, though.

"I want to see them."

"'Course. I'll let you know when I sort them," he agreed as he pulled up in front of Emilie's.

Before she hit the sidewalk, his hand shot out, grabbing hers. "Kit."

She looked down at it before looking back up at him. "Yeah."

"Seriously. Thank you."

"For what?"

He snorted. "For coming with me today. It was a good day."

Reaching over, Katherine gave the hand she held all day a gentle squeeze, though it didn't feel perfectly the same anymore. "See you soon, okay?"

"See you soon."

CHAPTER FIFTEEN

*N*o one called Katherine the next day, or the next week. No one called the week after either. It dawned on her that maybe she should just get up after she finished work and march her way across the river to Avril's city-side castle, but she didn't.

If they wanted her there, they would say something to her. And if not...

She'd been getting a lot of work done at the shop in the past few weeks. She had reorganized displays, created a homepage and shop page where she would eventually be able to put pictures of all the items the shop would sell online. Katherine even managed to make a corset she could lace up, even if the chest region still was constricting in the wrong direction.

But it was there. Almost.

She could now only think of a few things that could be causing the structural issue. She sorted through them one at a time in her mind as she took a break, walking up the back steps toward the apartment where Emilie had sequestered herself for the past two days as she overcame a nasty cold that knocked her on her back. Somehow, her aunt managed to see it as a positive thing.

"This way I can see how you handle the shop when I eventually leave you here for a few days or so," she said, voice as weak and as tired as her body curled under a pile of blankets.

Katherine quietly switched out her glasses of water and teacup that finally managed to be drained since the morning. Emilie rolled over.

"How's the shop coming?"

"Slow Saturday," Katherine whispered, even though she didn't have to.

Emily hummed. "I had a few people that said they were going to stop for orders."

"They came earlier. The chiffon and—"

"Baby pink nightdress." Emily nodded as they both put their finger on exactly the piece they were talking about. Katherine wouldn't be surprised though if Emilie somehow managed to remember every piece that ever went in and out of the shop by her own hands or the occasional intern she hired from the art institute.

It was a dainty, pretty thing. Katherine wrapped it up for the customer in the morning.

"It's for my friend," the customer said, eyeing the trim on the cups. "She never buys herself anything like this, but she's getting married soon."

Katherine glanced up as she twisted around the package with matching string. "If she's interested in more bridal looks, we can always find her something in white."

The customer only shook her head. "No, that's exactly the opposite of what I am trying to do. You see, the bride and the groom still haven't…."

Eyes widened; Katherine tilted her chin down an inch. "I see."

"I'm hoping this, even if it isn't the craziest of seduction nighties, will be the gentle nudge she needs just to go for it so she's not a mess on the big day. Of course, I know that sounds like I am some sort of devil on her shoulder."

"We all need a little devil on our shoulder telling us to be selfish sometimes," Katherine said easily, immediately picturing Avril.

For some reason, as she stood in the shop, it was one of the only places that she felt she didn't have to mince words. The right ones were right in front of her. They were the articles of flimsy hosiery she made and altered for any specifications. Or occasions.

"Exactly. She wouldn't expect me to get her anything less scandalous for a gift anyway."

Katherine gave a light smile. She wondered what the patron must've done to become that scandalously well-meaning friend.

Emilie stared at her for a long moment, face drawn. "The shop suits you."

"Like I said, it hasn't been that busy."

Scooping up the cups in her hands, Katherine moved back from the bed to the doorway.

"Can I get you anything else?"

"No. Thank you, lovely."

"Are you sure you're alright? Can I call your friend or someone?"

Over the past few weeks, she had noticed Emilie's constant friend that popped in and out, stopping in more. However, she never took much time to say anything more than a hello to Katherine before the two of them scurried off to dinner or random midmorning brunch plans.

Taking a deep breath, Emilie nodded. "Just tired...feeling under the weather. I already called the doctor's office and they can fit me in this afternoon. Not a big deal. Just, could you shut the shop early and run those errands for me, please?"

"Already locked up. Anything special you want while I am out at the market?" At this point in the past few days, Katherine would be happy to pick her aunt up a whole plate of sticky buns to devour, if that was what it would take to get her to eat. Or she could buy a couple of the blueberry scones she liked from the baker with the sideburns. "No? I'll be back in a little bit."

Emilie waved the back of her hand for Katherine to stop hovering all the way out the door.

THE MARKET FELT different ever since she went out with Jack. She felt like she knew Ashton more, and all those who lived in it alongside of her, especially those of Ashton's weekly market that lined the streets of downtown east she'd been exploring on her own when Emilie didn't feel up to going out.

Like the other markets, the closest one nearby was stuffed with tiny vendors and tables laden with final fresh vegetables from local farmers in the surrounding area. She slowly was beginning to understand the appeal of it all after Emilie insisted, as an artist's town, you needed to pay patronage to the people who lived there. She made sure they got most of their perishable groceries, as well as things like soap, trinkets, and perfectly swirled tower candles from local crafters.

How else would the city maintain its core?

Pausing over one of the last tables, Katherine sniffed more than a half dozen blocks of soap before deciding the one Emilie had always been buying. The bar, hinted with chamomile and peonies, was still her favorite. Lifting two, the owner smiled and wrapped them in a thin cloth.

"If you put the handkerchief in your purse or closet, everything will also keep fresh," the apothecary owner advised.

"Thanks for the tip."

Exchanging cash from her hidden envelope for the bars, the woman caught her before she moved on. "How is Emilie doing, by the way? I haven't seen her here with you."

"Oh." Katherine shrugged. "She's doing all right. A cold caught her."

"I see." The woman frowned. "Let her know I asked after her."

"I will."

Katharine let the loose change fall into the pocket of one of her latest favorite skirts, simple and practical throughout the week when she was busy. Smoothing the pocket back into a hidden pleat, however—someone else's hand was already there.

"Hey," Katherine spoke before she realized she had the voice to do it. Tearing back a step, she met the wide eyes of her perpetrator, mind still somewhere between shock and debating if she should reach for the loaf of bread in her bag as a weapon.

"Oh my god, I'm so sorry." The girl, tall and skinny with a shaggy pixie cut, looked back toward her friend and then at Katherine again, who she now seemed to notice looked as if she was about to have a heart attack. "I didn't think. I am just *in love* with your skirt."

Katherine paused. Wasn't she just thinking the same thing?

"I can't believe I just woman handled you like that, but my city brain apparently has yet to kick back in after midterms. Where did you get it? It's vintage, right? I mean, I can tell it is vintage, but it is in such good condition."

Watching the girl's face stay in complete awe, slowly Katherine began to breathe, realizing she wasn't a moment away from being pickpocketed fifty-two cents.

The girl's friend, dark skin illuminating under the bright sun and enhanced with a sweep of gold highlighter on either cheek, shook her head. "You'll have to excuse her. I tried to stop her, but her legs are longer than mine."

Katherine started to smile. "It's all right. No harm. The skirt belonged to my aunt in the sixties."

"Damn, she must've had some style," the admirer said, grinning back at Katherine.

"She still does."

"I always wish I could fit into those kinds of things."

"There are some good shops around the city," Katherine said. Over the past few weeks in the late afternoons, Katherine started to take walks and found a few herself. "If you are willing to go hunting."

"Amazing," the girl who accosted her said with another shake of her head.

"I'm very jealous. The most my extended relatives have given me is fifty cents for gum, like, do they still think that's the going rate for Hubba Bubba? I'm Carmen, by the way."

Her friend behind her in ripped jeans and thick eyeliner gave a similarly amused look. "I'm Gina. Have you come to look around the market too?"

Katherine glanced down at her full netted bags. "Groceries and things."

"Wow. You go to school in the city then?"

"Yeah, excuse us if we sat next to you in a class and never noticed before," Gina added.

"Though I obviously would've noticed that skirt."

Katherine let out a small laugh.

Carmen only shrugged.

"No." Katherine shifted her weight to the back of her feet as she came to the realization she had never had to say aloud until then. "I live here. I've worked for my aunt since I graduated from school."

"You're kidding."

Katherine shook her head.

"Where do you work?"

On her toes, Katherine almost tried to see if they could notice the little shop around the corner, but the square was too crowded. "The lingerie shop around the corner with the lavender storefront?"

"The place with the female torture contraptions in the windows?"

Well—

"And sells, like, all the sex toys in a back room somewhere?"

Most of the sex toys were pretty much out on display so people could see and buy them.

Katherine shrugged a single shoulder in answer. If they wanted, they could stop in.

"Hey, Oli, get over here and meet our new friend!" Carmen waved a hand to catch the attention of someone behind her.

Turning, Katherine noticed the guy who previously was sitting by the fountain, only now his guitar case was closed, his instrument no longer being played for other marketgoers. Dirty brown hair sticking up on either side, it did nothing to conceal his crooked smile quickly hidden again by his lips.

"Hey."

"This is…" Gina's mouth hung there for a moment. "We didn't even ask you your name, did we?"

"Katherine."

"Katherine," Gina repeated.

"Oliver." His eyes flicked over her. "You go to AIA?"

"No," Carmen cut him off before Katherine could answer. "She lives in the city working for her aunt. She's the one with the expensive underwear and sex toy shop around the corner from Keys."

"You're kidding."

Katherine shook her head, surprised when she didn't feel a blush rise to her cheeks. Nope. That was her.

They were much more excited about where she worked than Avril or Jack was. Then again, they knew Emilie. They knew the city and the depths beneath, unlike these people who were just like her, new and taking it in by glance. Or rather, was just like her.

She smiled again, leaning the weight of one of her bags against her yellow shoe.

"You know what? You should totally come to this party going

on tonight," Carmen said, looking at Oli. "Of course, you should be the one asking since it's at your place."

"Nah, totally."

"There. You should come."

Katherine paused. They were inviting her out? It was already getting late and she had to get back to Emilie, who was likely home from her appointment with little to eat, let alone company. "I don't know..."

"Why not?" Carmen moaned. "It'll be fun. You said you're newer here, right?"

"You could meet some cool people."

Oliver waved the two girls a step back as he reached into his pocket. "Give me your number and I'll message you the address. Decide then if you want to show up at some point. Sound good?"

Katherine paused as she thought about it. What was she waiting for, really? Emilie didn't mind if she went out, and no matter how long she waited, no one else was showing up at her door to sweep her away anymore. It had been weeks.

See you later, Jack said to her.

Right. The reminder stung.

"Okay." Katherine rattled off her number. Down at the bottom of one of her produce bags, she heard the chime of her phone go off.

"There," Oliver said. "That's me. Think about it. There will be lots of people, drinks and everything. It'll be great to see you."

"Come to the party!" Carmen yelled again as she was pulled away by Gina, who smiled and waved.

Lifting her hand into the air, Katherine gave a wave herself before gathering her bags back over her shoulders. Wandering down the last row of stalls, she turned back home. Inside, she noticed Emilie's jacket on the back of the chair.

So, she was already home.

She nudged the door closed with her hip as she kicked off her shoes at the same time. Walking her bags over to the old retro table in the kitchen, literally standing on its last two legs, she leaned around the corner. Emilie's light was on too.

"Hey Em, I know you said you didn't want anything, but I saw those croissants I remembered you telling me about a while back. They are the ones you said only showed up right near the end of summer or something with the rhubarb filling. They were there! It felt like too good of a sign, to pick you back up," Katherine called out.

A sign. She was really starting to sound like her aunt.

Even if Emilie wasn't sick, by the flakey coating of them, she wasn't sure if she could've walked away from the few left at the baker's stand if she tried.

Sorting through the bags, she put away anything that needed to be put in the fridge, letting the door slam as she gathered the crinkly pastry packet in her hands. "I figured they would be a good before dinner pick-me-up!"

Walking through the partly opened doorway, Katherine perched herself on the edge of the bed. The floral comforter still tucked under the box spring. She made a show of the slightly squashed yet still delicious looking pastry.

Emile glanced slowly at the brown paper and then back to her niece.

Pausing, Katherine felt her stomach drop. Did she do something wrong? "Is everything all right?"

The silence rang for a long moment as Emilie opened her mouth, and suddenly Katherine prepared for the worst. Those were serious eyes on her, but slowly they softened. "It's nothing. The doctor just said I needed to rest."

"Oh." Katherine took a deep breath, still waiting for more. "Good."

"No pick-me-up needed. I'm fine."

"That's good. Then a celebratory pastry? A little sugar never hurts."

"I'm fine, Katherine." Her aunt enunciated each word as she pushed herself to sit up against the headboard.

Looking around the space, Katherine tried to note if anything was out of place. If her aunt had gotten a phone call minutes ago with bad news or she accidentally spilled her water over the sheets, but nothing.

Raising her eyebrows, she looked back down to the pain au delicious she bought for them. She ripped it in half with her fingers. The sweet filling seeped out onto her knuckles.

"So you've said. This is your half." Katherine pointed to the piece farthest away from her as Emilie's legs shifted under the comforter. "You know, I have been meaning to talk to you about the store too. I had been waiting, but it's been a good day and I thought that maybe we could talk about my ideas again. I know my way around and things are running smoothly. We could talk about the idea of expanding to a digital shop platform."

"Kit."

"I know that you already said that you didn't want to think about it right now, but that was months ago when I first thought of it. I have more ideas now. It would be a cinch."

The shop doesn't need to *go digital.*"

"Well, it doesn't need to, but the sales do. Though we are doing fine—"

"My sales have always been fine here at the shop."

"Of course, but I just meant that you don't have to maintain the shop on the big buyers who come in and spend a lot in one sitting occasionally. There is a huge market for pretty simple underpinnings online that makes a woman feel beautiful. Just today, the girl you made the nightgown for, it was a gift for a friend I am pretty sure had always felt too ashamed to approach a shop like ours." Especially when some people liked to call it a sex shop.

Emilie looked to the left as she gnawed on her lip. "There is nothing to be ashamed of in our shop."

"I know there isn't, but some people—"

"But some people what?"

"Some people like to be bombarded with something before they believe it. Even if we start on social media channels first, grow an online following for more orders outside our regulars and Rosin's costume fixes. They haven't ordered anything new outside the occasional re-sequin fiasco or costume one of the dancers paid for out of pocket in a long while. There are other people who would and just don't know it yet." Katherine hadn't known it, at least not to the full extent, until she got to the shop in Ashton and discovered how much she loved seeing the way different types of silk and lace looked against her skin and cupped her chest even when no one else was ever going to see them, she thought.

Ripping off a piece of the croissant, Katherine laid the flaky coating on her tongue. She talked around it. She hadn't eaten all day, too focused on that dang corset she still needed to get back to. "Then we can get the online shop up and running. I already started on the design. It is basically done save for a name and pictures—"

"The store doesn't need your ideas or to be taken to the next level right now, Kit! You have no fucking clue what I've done to make this place what it is."

Sweetness never tasted so bitter as the filling slipped past her lips and froze there on her tongue. She swallowed the bite she must've put into her mouth without thinking, all that time for the past few minutes where she hadn't been thinking.

"No, I guess not."

Emilie put the heels of her hands to her eyes.

"You need to tell me what is going on."

"What? I need to have a doctor's note to take off from work if I'm feeling a tad under the weather now?" Emilie tried to joke.

"Emilie."

"I'm fine."

"Something is wrong."

"Nothing is wrong, Kit!" Suddenly, Emilie screeched. Her hand connected with her chest at the same time, making a strong slap against her ribs. "Nothing. So how about for a moment since you've gotten here, you butt out of my life and stop trying to change it?"

Katherine took a step back, snapping her lips shut as if her aunt had slapped her instead. Maybe it would've hurt less.

"Katherine."

"No." She put up a hand, forcing it to remain steady. Pushing off the bed, Katherine cleared her throat as she cleaned up the scattered pastry crumbs. "You're right. If you need time alone, you should have it. I get it."

Emilie remained silent at that; her eyes all at once pained.

"It's okay, Emilie."

"I didn't mean it like that," she tried to explain, shoulders slumped. Her hand went limp over the sheets pooled around her waist.

"Like I said, I get it." Katherine took a deep breath to steady herself. "Um, I was actually invited out, so I might do that."

"Avril and Jack called?"

Something like that. Katherine gave a single nod. Sure.

"I'll take a key with me, so I can lock the door."

Turning on her heel, Katherine turned back toward the living room so she could change, but not before she heard Emilie's voice behind her.

"Love you, Kit baby."

Peeking back around the doorframe, Kit nodded, not trusting herself to speak as she continued to move. Letting herself collapse on the pull-out couch, Katherine held her head in her hands for the world to stop spinning around her, to stop the tears that threatened to spill when she hadn't cried in so long. She'd been proud of that.

She hadn't cried since her father left her.

Since everyone left her.

Her breath shook, and she shoved it down. Now she just needed to stop thinking and do something. The shop was already closed, and her fingers hurt from working. She needed to stop being her for a minute.

Maybe she didn't have to be, at least not this bit of her.

Moving around the space, Katherine gathered supplies as if she was starting a project, only this time, the latest project was her. She was quiet as she moved so as not to disturb Emilie. She applied her makeup in the bathroom mirror, not caring that it took her four times to get her eyeliner just right. She even opened a new pack of contacts, flinching as she inserted them and set her glasses aside.

She slipped one piece on after another. Panties, garter belt and bra in lavender shades that were for show, and more, as one of the dresses that Avril gave her fell like silk over her shoulders.

Her armor.

No, she didn't have to be her right now. She could be the person she imagined herself as, and it would all be better. Someone who went out. Someone who was put together and shiny and beautiful in the way no one could see her as invisible.

Someone people looked at in awe. Like Avril.

Like Jack.

Looking down at the brooches at her pelvis, she nodded at herself.

She could be the vixen.

CHAPTER SIXTEEN

*W*hat would a vixen do? Katherine asked herself as she left the house, trailing down the road before she even realized where she was going.

She was going to find what was hers.

Or at least figure out what surely was just another big disappointment she'd rather face.

Walking through the front doors of DuCain, the woman there only smiled, knowing exactly who she was. A few other glances came her way as well as she glanced around. No one was on stage. The bar just opened, a few people getting their first round of drinks as they found their spots.

Pausing, a young man on a leash was tugged to the other side of the room. Katherine didn't blink, keeping herself on task, pausing at the counter.

"Long time no see," the bartender smiled at her. "Can I get you something?"

"Do you know where Jack is?"

"Jack?" His eyebrows bounced upward as he shook his head. "Not sure. Maybe in the back? I haven't seen him."

Flashing a smile, Katherine tapped the bar. "Thanks."

"Nik is in the office, down by the dungeons to the right."

"Thank you!" Katherine said again as she moved away from the next group, laughing as they crowded in behind her. She walked toward the stage door, feeling eyes she no longer cared about as she shoved through.

She'd been in DuCain often enough, traversing the dark dungeons with relative ease at this point, but never had she been to Nik's office. Door closed; Katherine took a deep breath as she lifted her fist.

At the first knock, she realized the door wasn't fully shut, creaking as it rolled inward.

Two sets of eyes glanced up at her.

One of them was, as expected, Nik's glassy green pair.

The other was a girl who couldn't be much older than Katherine. Her one fishnet-clad leg kicked over her knee. She gave a small smile up at her from where she sat in one of the scattered chairs.

It was odd, Nik's office felt sort of like she'd been called to the principal's. Besides the chair, the shelves, including where a riding crop hung above the desk, were undecorated.

"Little Emilie, can I help you?"

"I'm, uh." All of her excuses were beginning to sound a little off in her head as she thought them through. She leaned back on her heels as she thought of something better than, do they know where the most gossiped about individuals of Ashton were?

The girl tilted her head to the side, a light brown curl falling out of her bun. Her fingers flicked in a small wave. "I'm Evie."

"Hi."

Nik continued to wait for her to say something.

"I'm looking for Jack," Katherine said, quickly adding. "Or Avril. Are they here?"

Nik paused, looking to the ceiling.

Evie's eyes, on the other hand, lit up.

"She's the one Jack almost took down that asshole Dev for a few weeks ago," Evie cleared up in sudden understanding.

Katherine didn't remember her there that night. Then again, she hadn't met a lot of the DuCain staff save for Jack and Nik.

"Really?" Nik raised their eyebrows similarly to the bartender. He looked her up and down.

Katherine nodded, hoping to get the answer. "Is Jack working tonight?"

"Is Jack working?" Nik repeated.

Glancing at Evie, she looked for any sign that she, too, was confused by the question.

"I've been asking myself the same question for the past two weeks. Is Jack working? No."

"What do you mean?"

"Jack hasn't been coming in except for his regulars recently. If he comes into work at all," said Nik.

"He did come in on Monday."

"Yeah," Nik agreed, throwing his hand out to the papers on his desk. "To leave me to deal with all this shit ever since his friend ditched the city from the looks of it."

"So no?" Katherine asked slowly from the doorway.

"No."

"And Avril left?"

Nik didn't answer as they shook their head down at the desk again. A calendar was laid out, as well as old flyers from the past year. They were black and gold, mostly illustrated from what she could see, taking another step inside the office. New Year's Celebration swam through the background like an art nouveau dream.

Evie leaned back in her chair. "Looks like it. There is an annual party she throws for New Year's that is apparently quite the bash. She started the planning and people have been calling for things, but..."

She was no longer there to direct the plans.

"We are just going to have to cancel," Nik said.

"But you just said it was one of the biggest events for DuCain. I'm not sure about Rosin but..."

Nik shook their head. "It was always a supportive group effort the day of, though no one realized how much planning went into it. Queen took care of the rest and made it look like a breeze. It looks a lot more, complicated, to say the least."

She had a habit of doing that kind of thing.

"Does Jack know?"

Nik gave her another tired look.

"Right," Katherine whispered. He hadn't been in.

"The decorations can't be that hard," Evie cut in, an amused lilt to her voice. "A few balloons."

"I got a quote for about a gallon of glitter today," Nik informed her.

Not a flinch of shock crossed her face. "That's a lot of glitter. Gel or those specks you throw on people?"

"That's confetti," Katherine informed.

"Whatever it is, it doesn't matter. It'll take a good chunk of money from us by not doing it, but who the hell knows what we'd be getting into at this rate, anyway, two months out and barely any plans to stand on besides all of this." Again, Nik's hands fanned around the general vicinity.

"I could find Avril's notes."

Both of them turned to Katherine.

Her room was a mess, but it looked like if there was anything to find, it would be there. She had posters and clothes from years ago. Why not a few pieces of paper?

Nik stared for a second longer. "You'll do this?"

"Well, I didn't say—"

"Evie, you'll help her."

"But—"

"But what? You were the one complaining about it not happening, plus, you said you wanted more hours."

Evie chewed on her bottom lip for a long moment, she nodded.

"Great. Now that that is settled."

Katherine didn't agree to anything. She had enough work at the shop without Emilie there with her the past few days. Her bones complained about how tired she was the moment she thought of it, tips of her fingers burning from all the tiny stabs she inflicted sans thimble.

She stood there, gaping like a fish. Her mouth opened and closed, yet she never found the right words even as Nik brushed past her, back out the door. They left her and Evie there, glancing back and forth.

Evie shrugged, pushing up from the plush chair to stand. It was then Katherine noticed it wasn't only fishnets she was wearing, like the girls at Rosin, but a small schoolgirl outfit. She put her hand out in front of her. "Nice to meet you."

Katherine slipped her hand into Evie's. She squeezed it gently. "So, New Year's Eve."

"I've heard it's quite the show. Drinking. Games. Performances. I wanted to go so badly last year, but I wasn't in the city yet."

"When did you get to Ashton?"

"May."

Not long before Katherine.

"I started working here in July, I think. Took a bit of convincing from Nik, but I think they like me well enough." She smiled, though it withered as if she were remembering something.

"You're a professional here, then?"

"Yep, I'm a sub, but enough talk for now. I have to change and get back to work. You're looking for Jack?"

"Or Queen."

She didn't look very convinced. "Well, she's likely off wooing a prime minister's son somewhere. That would be quite the story, wouldn't it?"

It would, though Katherine wouldn't be very surprised if she ran off without her boyfriend and did such a thing.

"Any other plans for the night?"

Katherine had thought she did. She had come out into the night with such purpose, and now she had a new one, but she didn't feel any lighter.

"Maybe digging up those plans you promised of Queen's?"

It wasn't a bad idea.

Katherine nodded a few times as they walked back out into the hallway. "Have a nice night, Evie."

Her eyes grinned with her smile. She skipped backward down the hall. "Oh, I will."

SHE KNEW that Avril never locked the door, though she probably should. Of course, Katherine didn't need to worry about the off chance it would be locked. Passing over the bridge, all the lights of the townhouse were on, music streamed out down the front steps as the door opened and someone came outside to smoke on the small covered stoop.

The fairy lights that never were taken down from what Katherine always imagined was Christmas were even lit, trailing around the porch columns.

A party.

They were throwing a party at the townhouse. That stinging feeling in her chest was back.

Pushing it down, she barely breathed an ounce before plastering a smile on her face toward the man blowing smoke into the house next door.

She was done being messed around with.

Done letting people think that she was less than, able to be beckoned whenever they pleased. Dropping her bag at the door alongside bright red rain boots, Katherine looked into the living room. Raising beer bottles, bodies tangled on top of each other as they talked and laughed.

Another couple on the oversized love seat in the other corner looked to be doing more of the tangling, not that anyone seemed to notice, or at the very least minded as they ground against each other, lips barely had any space between.

Katherine tried to catch the eye of anyone she knew, but she didn't know anyone. None of the same people from the last party she at least remembered pieces of were anywhere in the house. One or two might've looked familiar, but otherwise, that wasn't her goal anyway.

Turning to the steps, she paused before making it to the second one as she noticed another girl coming down. Swaying to one side before catching herself, she looked more familiar than the rest, though that could've been due to her wearing nothing but one of Emilie's more casual designs that Katherine had made more than a few of herself lately, paying close attention to the embellishments on the edge of the balconette cup.

The girl's eyes lit with glee. "Aren't you cute? Are you new? I don't think we've met."

"I made that bra you're wearing," Katherine said, hoping her staring at her breasts didn't come off too forward.

Her eyes now filled with less glee and more recognition. "Oh, thank you. My boobs definitely thank you. Of course, I've seen you at Rosin before, right? And that night when Queen brought the little Emilie back for Passion and Prose. You don't look so little anymore."

No, Katherine caught herself in the thin mirror by the door. She didn't.

She wanted to be a vixen tonight, and in her tight dress, shorter than most things she'd ever worn before, with her makeup done just as Avril had taught her, that was exactly what she'd become.

"Have you seen them?"

"Who?"

"Jack?" Katherine asked, a bit louder. "Or Avril—Queen, I mean?"

Biting her bottom lip still, she looked around but only shook her head. "I don't think she's here."

Great. Then hopefully her room would be empty.

"Who is this?" A voice came down the stairs from behind the woman with the pink eye shadow and good taste in lingerie. With dark eyes and hair carefully swept to the side the way she had always imagined lawyers or doctors, Katherine recognized him immediately as the man who caught her the other night almost a month ago as she followed Avril in DuCain.

Devil.

He grinned with his perfectly straight white teeth. "Aren't you Jack's girl?"

Looking over her shoulder toward another couple grinding down on one another, Katherine couldn't help herself anymore. She gave a light snort as she laughed. What was even happening here? Go upstairs, get the notes if she could find them in Avril's pit of despair, and leave.

But she didn't back down from Devil.

"No," she said. "I'm not anyone's."

"Is that right?"

The girl with the good taste in lingerie nodded effortlessly and slipped around her back to the party.

Katherine's eyes remained fixed on the tall, dark man in front of her.

"So, what are you up to tonight?"

"Well, you know," Katherine came up with easily, glancing down at her shoes. "Saturday."

"That's right. Saturdays are like a thing for you guys. So, you're just here to have a good time?" Devil smirked.

Again, Katherine shut her eyes as she smiled at this man Jack warned to stay away from her. Looked like she could also make her own decisions. They may not have invited her to the party, but here she was. And it wasn't just them, it dawned on her, minding her company in whatever form it was Devil was looking at her for. The understanding settled low in her stomach as his dark eyes considered her.

Whatever they said about Devil began to fade. He seemed nice enough.

He certainly looked it.

And isn't that what Jack told her? She deserved a nice, handsome guy?

Again, that stabbing feeling came back, and she ignored it. Again.

She smiled instead, trying to remember the way Jack and Avril smiled.

"Looks like it."

"Then let's make this night worth it. What do you say?" Devil extended a hand.

Before Katherine could question herself—that was all she ever did, she put her hand in his softer hand, compared to how her hand sank into Jacks, she thought to herself for just a second.

Truth or dare?

Dare. "I'd say please and thank you."

"Very good answer."

With that hand gripping hers, they walked back up the stairs one at a time. She was planning to go upstairs anyway, after all. Only now, a few of the doors were already shut. They were alone, and Devil twisted her with a single light tug.

Back flush against the wallpaper, her hand was captured, lifted, and held above her head.

She followed it, only meeting Devil's eyes. They weren't just dark, she realized. They were nearly black.

Then he brought down his mouth on hers, or near hers.

Katherine froze at the sudden intensity of the kiss. It

claimed her right below her jaw. She melted against the wall instead while her heart beat rapidly. For a second, she wondered what would happen if she said something. But she didn't, eyelashes fluttering, Katherine let Devil have her. There was nothing to say, after all. There was no fear or anxiety, just understanding.

It was only kissing, after all. Holding her, he seemed to want it all rather desperately.

Maybe Katherine did too.

Pulling only his mouth away, Devil held her in place so she couldn't move an inch if she tried.

She didn't.

Devil snickered. "I can see why Jack was so intrigued. What is your name, by the way?"

Right, because they hadn't gone over that before her lips burned from the space between theirs. Katherine angled her head toward him, but with a jerk of his chin, he let his lips land back down on her jaw, her neck—just not her lips.

"Kit," she breathed.

"Kit. I don't know how Jack messed up, but I'm Dev. Devil. The one who comes out of the shadows and reins terror over the underworld. I'm sure they've told you all about me."

"I can't say they have."

He only grinned wider, leaning back in. "Then I guess you'll be in for a pleasant surprise. Wasn't it said that Persephone wasn't actually dragged down to the underworld after all?"

Katherine couldn't say she'd heard that part of the story either, but a different one began to form in her head again, like the last time she was at a party at the Queen's castle. Thinking about the parties when she'd felt so alone until suddenly, she wasn't anymore, and someone was right there beside her.

This story was different.

There were no lies here, no ill-intent or movement at all for her to make under Devil who looked at her with only keen interest. This time, she only needed to pay attention and worry about what was all right here in front of her.

And, when it came to Devil, even with his reputation, there were no questions. Only rules and an understanding that no one would share anything but a smile about what happened the next day.

She could do that, Katherine thought. Maybe Avril was exactly right about who she was.

"But you can call me Sir, if you like, yes?"

Katherine licked her lips, watching as he followed her tongue with his gaze. She'd heard the word uttered from dozens of other lips in her time at DuCain, but it felt like a shock wave on the tip of her tongue as she said it, looking from his dark eyes down to his lips right there in front of her. "Yes, Sir."

"Good."

She couldn't help but agree, a light smile brushing the corners of her lips.

His hand left the one he led her into the hallway with, smoothing it up her waist before cupping her breast. Though not much there, she always thought, it didn't appear that Devil minded in the least.

His mouth dipped as he nipped her neck and her breast swelled.

With a gasp, Katherine melted farther against him, her single hand flexing before gripping onto his shoulder as her vision swayed. Floral greens on the wallpaper vibrated like the sound she tried to keep hidden behind her lips that she pressed tightly closed.

With another hard bite right at her clavicle, Katherine couldn't help at the sharp combination of acute pain and sudden heat that swelled in her hips that rolled into his on their own accord.

"You like that, huh?" Devil murmured into her skin and continued to rub and squeeze.

Stop. That was all she had to say, if she wanted to, now would be the time.

She knew how to shove and scratch and walk away. She was good at walking.

Stop. It was just a word as his hand flared where it met the heavy crystal brooch that steadied her. It gave her courage as the hemline of her skirt inched higher at his insistence.

The only thing she could think of right now was, *let it*. "Yes, Sir."

Her voice sounded like someone else, deep and raspy.

"We are going to have fun, you and I."

Before he could complete his promise, however, a hand was on his shoulder, and Devil was flung back into the other wall before he could right himself. Katherine's hand fell from where it was held up, her chest expanding and receding much farther than she thought now that there was no one for it to connect with.

"What the fuck did I say about staying away from her?"

Turning her head, Katherine was met with kaleidoscope eyes of seas and honey.

CHAPTER SEVENTEEN

The first time Avril ever ran off the face of the earth, she took Jack with her. They went to LA and laid on the beach filled with litter and rented an old Volkswagen van only he could drive all the way up to Washington. Slowly, the van got fuller with every person they seemed to accumulate along the way.

He learned on that trip that Avril once had a brother who rode motorcycles. He'd been out to Washington once. It was postmarked Seattle, one of the last letters he sent her to wherever home had been at the time. It was before she met Reed. Jack didn't get much more.

Not until she took him to Spain. Then, she told him about her mom and how she died. She laughed through all the alcohol they inhaled throughout the day, so he wasn't sure she was kidding at first, not until he asked Reed.

There was always something left with Avril that he felt like he didn't know. For one now, where the hell was she?

On the other hand, he knew exactly where Pen was.

"Get out."

"What are you talking about? We're having fun."

"Fun?" Jack couldn't believe this. "You think this is fun, inviting all your friends over to my—Queen's house like you suddenly think you run the place now that she's out of town with her boyfriend or whatever?"

Pen rolled her eyes from where she was lying half naked on his bed. He turned around for one minute and it was suddenly like she had stripped in five seconds flat. The air filled with irritation and simple wants. "Come on, it's Saturday."

"You never were into our Saturdays."

"Our?" Pen sneered.

"Yes, our," Jack repeated, though he didn't know why. Shutting his eyes, he knew better than to look away. "What are you doing here, Pen?"

"Well, I couldn't find you at DuCain now, could I?"

"What are you talking about?"

"At least look a little excited to see me."

"I'm not. I'm not excited to see you, Penelope," Jack said. He hated how he sounded, but seriously. What the hell was going on? He booked another last-minute wedding that called him this morning and came home to *this*.

The past few weeks, nonetheless, were a mental hell for him for some reason. They started fine, normal. He got up, worked out, went to work at DuCain and came home if he didn't meet up with a friend for drinks. Then, slowly, he stopped doing that, thinking about his conversation with Kit again, always Kit and how she lit up at his photography in that stupid museum.

What did you really want to do when you came to the city? She asked him. Why don't you go home?

He was looking at a piece of the reason why on his bed. He wasn't someone he took home to mom and dad. Apparently, in his mind, it was beginning to turn out, not even his own.

Not even when someone like Kit thought he was magnificent.

What a joke. All of this. Both of his hands gripped either side of his head.

"I'm here to make up," Pen pouted.

"There is nothing to make up."

"Now we both know that's not true. Though your silent treatment was rather annoying, come here. Let's not fuck around anymore. It's really not good for either of our health." Pen sat up, coming to open her legs on either side of him.

"Stop, Pen."

"What?" she asked with a scrunch of her nose. "You want me to say I've been jealous about who else you might've been with? Is that it?"

"I haven't been with anyone, not that it is any of your business," Jack said. "I've been busy."

"With who? I know you have been cutting hours at DuCain, so don't say working."

"I have been."

"What?"

Was he seriously still talking? "Working, Pen. Working."

She raised a light eyebrow. "Where?"

"It's none of your business." Though he hadn't been at DuCain in a while, it still seemed too soon to say anything about how he had been out with his camera more often than not. He couldn't keep taking days off, but at least when he wasn't at DuCain, he didn't have to think, not about anything.

Unlike now.

"Shut this down, now."

Pen rolled her eyes. Reaching out from where she was on her knees, she gripped the bottom of his shirt. Drawing him in for a second, he let her lips graze his. "Don't be so serious. You love parties."

Finally, something she was saying made sense.

Looking down at her mouth, Jack could calm down for just a little while, just relax and let it go. He'd worry about it later. All of it.

A subtle bang in the hall behind him sounded.

Breaking whatever spell he was under, Jack took a step back. He nearly dragged Pen and her grip on him with him. His head turned to the closed door, a tingling sensation in his chest curling around each of his ribs.

He took a step toward the door, but not before Penelope tugged him back.

"They are probably just having a good time." She pulled on his shirt again until she managed to wrap her hand around his belt. "We could be having fun too."

The one end slipped through his belt loop and clanged against the metal buckle.

Another small bang sounded. Something was wrong between his ribs...

Jack pulled away, running a hand through his hair as he took a step back.

Pen looked at him with annoyance. "What now? I forgive you, is that it?"

Putting up a single finger, he took a step back and opened the door. For a second, he thought Pen was right, it was just another one of the couples she let the castle doors open to. But then his hand gripped the shoulder of some guy with a dark pressed button-down.

"Didn't I tell you?" Jack asked, a sharp tone to his voice. He gave the man, who was a good head taller than him, a shove. Fucking Devil.

He shouldn't have been surprised, but he was. Eyes flicked to the girl beneath the big asshole, still plastered against the wall. The face that looked back at him might've been the last one he expected. Then again, it might've been because he hadn't seen her in a while. What was Kit doing here?

Jack shoved Devil again. "She has enough to worry about without adding to it with your messed-up ass."

Devil only shrugged. "I mean, not that you should be talking, friend."

Friends? Jack clenched his one fist near his hip.

"Lighten up, man. She said she wasn't yours. We were just having some fun." Devil looked to Kit for some sort of confirmation. Eyes still locked on Jack, she looked more likely to let the wall swallow her whole than answer.

Jack bared his teeth at the man. "Get out."

"Stop the whole alpha crap here, Jack."

"Do you need to get your ears checked?"

Opening his mouth, Devil looked between Kit and him again with a shake of his head. Wisely, he took one step out from in front of Jack and toward the staircase.

"Sorry, sweetheart," Devil sniffed. He straightened his pressed shirt as he glanced at her. "Another time."

Another time, Jack's ass. He stomped a step toward him. "Out!"

Everyone needed to get out.

Kit, however, hadn't moved from the wall. Her lips parted as she stared at Jack. The skirt of her loose dress, the color of Easter flowers, still hitched toward her left hip as Jack looked her up and down, the picture of flushed beauty and... nerves.

"Kit?"

"Jack?"

They both stood there for another long second. But no, she wasn't going to wait any longer for him to have the first word, was she? It was probably a good thing, Jack thought as he swallowed. He didn't know what to say.

He forgot how pretty she was.

The last thought he had for the longest time was her getting out of his Jeep, grinning with the promise of friendship on her lips and then, nothing. Avril disappeared. He disappeared, he guessed too.

Friends.

That's what he called her?

Opening her damp lips, she lined them with her tongue—

"Jack?" a voice snapped them both out of whatever thought they had. Her head snapped toward the open bedroom door to Penelope before his did. "Yeah, I'm still here."

For one of the first times, Jack wished she was just about anywhere else.

Turning back to Kit, her gaze turned down to her shoes, fixing her skirt back over the light glimmer of what could only be the brooches. She was keeping them safe, she said, for Queen.

His brow furrowed again at the thought, remembering how weird she was about anyone touching them. Especially him when he found them.

"Kit, I didn't know you'd—"

"It's fine. I was just..." She trailed off, clearing her throat as she smoothed herself back down as she blinked. "I'll come back another time. I just..."

Just.

Jack narrowed his eyes, focusing on her. But he didn't feel anything anymore, just silence in the void in the space between them.

"Jack," Pen cut in once more. Her tone this time had a bit more bite that was directed straight at Kit.

Twisting around, his eyes flared. He still had questions, yet he just kept looking at her. What was Kit doing here? With Devil? How— "One second."

Again, Kit shook her head as she moved toward the steps. "It's fine. Go ahead."

Looking between her and the doorframe of his bedroom, blessedly empty this time, Jack turned back to Kit. "Wait here. I'll be right back. Wait here and we can talk, okay? Can we talk?"

Pausing with her hand on the railing, her other reached up and tucked a piece of hair behind her ear.

"Wait here."

She nodded. "Okay."

Moving back into his room, he let the door fall mostly closed behind him.

"Finally," bemoaned Pen. She pushed off from the wall and draped herself back over him. "I thought I was going to have to start begging to get you back in here. You seem tense."

Her hands went to his shoulders.

Jack shook her off.

"No. Pen, stop." He couldn't do this anymore. The realization in its entirety startled him, but not enough to stop talking. "I told you before. We are done."

"Done?"

"Yes."

Her lip curled with confusion. "Why?"

"I can't be with someone who doesn't respect me."

"Well, we're not really together, so."

Jack stared at her for a long moment.

She seemed to get the picture, peeling herself away from him. She sat on the edge of his bed. "Wow."

He nodded in case she needed another prompt.

Then again, Pen was never short on words. It was one of the things he used to say he liked about her.

"So, respect, huh?" She snorted. "Good luck with that, Jack."

"Thank you. Now, if you would just get your friends—"

"I think you misunderstand. No one in their right mind would respect you unless you were on the other end of a flogger. That's why you got into Dom-ing for a living, isn't it? So you'd feel powerful?"

Among other things, he admitted that to her once, yes. For once in his life, he felt powerful every day. He thought for a short amount of time at least he was living and standing tall where people admired him.

But no, now it was all too clear that he did not misunderstand.

He bit the side of this tongue. "Get out."

Something in his voice, rough and low, was enough to make her falter.

"Get out," Jack repeated, louder this time. Reaching down, he threw her clothes at her. "Go and take everyone with you. I mean it this time. It's not a joke. I am not some stupid game for you to play. I'm done."

Pen clutched her clothes to her chest, even as she made no move to put them on. "Fine. Go. Have fun pining after the girls that don't want you, Jack."

Gritting his teeth, hot rage clouded his brain. "Out."

Taking a deep breath, he raked his fingers through his hair again, wanting to scream and feeling it opening up a hole in his chest. But he didn't. He held the pressure in and shoved it down and swung around to open the door at the sounds of people moving throughout the house.

But maybe she was right. Kit was gone.

CHAPTER EIGHTEEN

The first time Katherine ever saw one of her own pieces of work on someone outside the shop, the wearer was half naked inside of Jack's room.

It was a simple pair of underwear she'd made multiple of in different colors. But that pair, the frill of lace on the right side was a millimeter lopsided. The stretchy peach-colored fabric crunched in with the rest, just enough that she'd notice.

She watched as he went back to her through her room, and Katherine shook her head down at herself as she waited by the staircase. She looked at the tiny birds hidden in the wall foliage and turned to stare again down to her feet. At one point through her walking, along with the small ache around the back of her heel, she scuffed the toe—just like how she promised she wouldn't when putting them on the first time.

Now there they were, damaged.

Biting her lip, Katherine didn't want to hold it in any longer. The pressure pulsed at her eyes and up her throat and burned as she shoved it right back down the other way. She was not going to cry in Avril Queen's house.

Glancing toward Queen's bedroom, she wondered if she

could find the event notes or the planner. She saw it the last time she was here, next to the rows of lipsticks on her vanity. It wasn't worth it now, though. She could come back. Katherine needed to get out of here. She needed to leave and stop making up all these ridiculous scenarios in her head that were never going to happen.

Like when Jack pushed Devil off of her and looked at her like...*that*.

She swallowed, though something thick caught in her throat. Bringing the tips of her fingers up to her neck, thinking about Devil who had just been there. Everyone told her to lighten up and live and have fun, yet she was so stupid. She waited for someone who had left her weeks ago without reason or care, like everyone did.

From the moment she stepped into Ashton, there was this feeling she had, this odd deep feeling in her stomach that everything would change.

Who would've thought it would probably be for the worse?

Oh, that's right. Her. She did. She always thought, constantly hoping to be pleasantly surprised and devastated when she wasn't. But she wasn't going to be devastated this time.

Now, she had to be done waiting.

Katherine made her way across the bridge again, maneuvering around others, looking over the edge before she thought to catch a cab. It was probably a good thing she didn't. She left her jacket and bag back at the townhouse, not that they would do her much good now. Heat pulsed inside the student apartments she remembered seeing on one of her walks the past few weeks, only a few blocks from the institute. She didn't need her phone to ask what the address was.

People crowded the corners of the space that smelled like smoke, sweat, and cheap beer that stuck to the bottom of her shoes. She slipped past the condensed group of bodies, gyrating under the colored lights as she made her way inside.

Immediately, a body, slick with moisture, hit against her front in a sort of hug.

Katherine quickly tried to return the gesture, looking up to see Cameron with her pixie cut. It was now streaked with purples and glitter.

"Hey!" She opened her eyes wide in gladness. "You made it."

"I did." Katherine tried to smile as she caught her breath.

"We weren't sure if you were going to show. Yeah, though, rough day? Let's get you a drink and hang out. It's getting late, so some people are leaving for other spots, but all the good people are still here, I can introduce you. Everyone wants to meet you—Josie! Come here," Cameron called out toward the kitchen before she could respond. "The sex shop girl is here I told you about."

That was her. Another reason they really needed to get a name on that shop sign.

"Can I get a drink?"

"Sure! Come on." Cameron pulled her along toward where the girl yelled. Reaching over on a table, she handed Katherine a red plastic cup.

Inside it was a similar shade, thin like generic fruit punch. Lifting it to her lips, however, Katherine cringed. It tasted more like acid. Still, she kept drinking it, drowning out the conversation about classes and names she didn't know.

After a while, Katherine looked down into her cup, seeing she drank most of whatever was inside as she nodded at whatever anyone said to her. Sex shop? Nod. Meeting interesting clientele? Yes. Didn't they see her at Keys a few weeks ago with those people who used to be on the Ashton gossip sites?

Probably.

She could barely hear anything anyway above the music she'd never heard before, heavy and sharp as the beat bounced against her heart.

Pounding.

What was she doing here? She should probably be home with

Emilie, helping her get better, or starting orders for the next day or back at the townhouse—Katherine paused, gripping her cup. What would've happened if she had stayed back there? Would she have been waiting long?

What would Jack have said, looking at her like he had no idea all of a sudden who she was at all?

Or maybe he would've said nothing, ditching her in the hall after realizing she wasn't worth being jealous over, wasn't worth it as a friend or—she forced herself not to imagine any other fantasies. It was just like what Emilie thought today when Katherine brought up her ideas again, never quite fitting inside whatever lines were clearly drawn.

Someone at her elbow nudged her and asked her something.

Turning, Katherine saw it was the guy from earlier at the market. Oliver. His brown hair clung to his forehead with a thin layer of sweat. There was no air conditioning in this place. "What?"

He raised his voice, cupping his hands over his mouth as he leaned in closer to her. "I asked if you were having fun!"

Oh. Katherine looked around toward the others, who only offered swift glances from the corners of their eyes. At some point, they must've moved on to another topic.

"What were you up to today before this?"

"I worked." Katherine's eyes widened as she straightened herself from the wall she leaned against as she tried to remember to sound casual. What was in that punch? "I actually ended up at another party before I got here."

"Two parties in one night. You are a downtown Ash girl, huh? I wasn't sure." He raised an eyebrow.

"What is that supposed to mean?" No, that question wasn't right. It was too tense again. Too defensive.

Turning back to Oliver, he smoothly transferred her drink, or lack thereof, to the sticky counter beside them.

"Dance?"

Her eyebrow crinkled as she looked around, a new song coming on heavy and low as it sank to her stomach, and not in a good way. Her heart was already pounding again, all her thoughts swirling in her head, including the ones she thought she pushed down far enough earlier.

"I should go soon. I don't really dance."

"That's all right," Oliver encouraged, reaching for her hand. "Who does?"

Jack.

She shook her head at the name, remembering the way they swayed at the wedding. Like an invitation, Oliver began to lead her to the other room. Furniture was pressed up against the perimeter of the walls, everyone in the center jumped and danced together.

A chill snaked up Katherine's spine while sweat collected on the back of her neck. Swallowing another breath of air, she didn't feel so well, that thick tightness in her throat was still there.

She tried to push that all down too, though it wasn't as giving. She instead tried to focus. This was good. These are supposed to be her people to be around. They were students, the kind of people she would've been around all the time if she would've gone to college. This was one of the lives she could've led, if she wanted, if she dared, if all the people she cared about didn't leave so carelessly.

It was fine.

It was all fine.

Oliver's hands transferred from her hands to her hips.

She took a step back, gasping for an ounce of air. Nothing felt like it reached her lungs. She nearly fell into another group, mouthing the lyrics to whatever song was playing. "Sorry."

"It's okay. Two parties will do that to you."

Katherine tried to narrow her eyes, but the pressure was back, filling her head like cotton balls in a glass container. How many could you fit inside before it broke?

He had no idea what he was talking about.

She needed to stop thinking.

She tried to take another step back, and this time there was no one there to stop her from taking it. Heat rising from her back up through her ribs like a wave, heart pounding. She needed to calm down. She needed to think about calming down and taking a deep breath.

She needed to stop thinking.

"You okay?"

"I can't be here."

"Why not?" he asked. "It's just a bit of fun."

Fun. Katherine could be fun. She knew she could be even as something felt as if it was lodged in her throat.

His hands gripped onto her wrists, pulling her back into the crowd of tired, intoxicated art students dancing, even though she was not one. She would never even be like one. She was the girl who worked at the sex shop. An oddity.

Hands grazed her hips, and it was all Katherine could do not to gag on the rush of panic that surged up her throat. Anxiety clamped its damp fingers around her rib cage, banging to get into her lungs.

She gasped. "Let go of me."

No one heard her. No one ever heard her when she had something to say. No one—

"Does no one have fucking ears anymore?" The body was torn away from hers. A familiar bellow replaced it, cutting between the rush of people. It cleaved the air apart with an odd sense of déjà vu.

"Jack."

His eyes were wide as he looked at her, eyes focused, like he was trying to find an answer to some kind of puzzle.

Katherine couldn't breathe.

She thought she had felt this way a million times before, but only a few times like this, overwhelming and whole as it took her over like a fist, squeezing any ounce of life she thought she had left to give, taken. This was different. She stumbled away, trying to get to the door.

That was agony and this was—this was—she could. Not. Breathe.

The rush of emotions was too much, crashing into her.

And then it swallowed her.

CHAPTER NINETEEN

The first time Jack fell in love with Avril Queen was at a party, but now in front of him, he swore he saw his life crumble along with him. Kit's lips trembled, looking so out of place in all the noise. A rush of sour bitters hit his lungs a hundred times the amount they usually did, corroding around his ribs as effectively as a knife slicing through bone and sinew.

"Kit." Before Jack could finish saying her name, Kit's legs swayed. Catching her close to the floor with inches to spare, Jack's arms strained as he kept her on her feet.

She was shaking.

"Whoa, whoa, I got you. Lean into me."

You're safe. I got you.

No one was even paying attention as Jack led her back toward the door outside. It was too loud in the house, too hot. He barely even knew what he was doing here, and Kit—her one hand reached up with a fierce grip on his shirt, a loose button coming undone.

"I got you," he repeated, feeling the rush of emotion surging through her skin. Fear and panic and misunderstanding swirled like darkness, choking her when they reached outside. It pulsed like the loudest heartbeat, hard and heavy in a world that never stopped moving before picking up again. So fast, everything was so fast, and here they were.

He could hear her gasp.

"Just sit down, there you go," Jack murmured, letting her wobbly legs ease down on the front steps. He settled his hands on her knees.

A line of ice held her down as tears began to stream from her eyes. She shut them.

"You just need to take a deep breath for me, Kit. One big breath—My god." He looked over his shoulder at a few other partygoers, who obviously didn't understand that it was fucking October and they needed a jacket or something as they let a line of smoke escape from their lips.

They each took their turn, glancing at them from the sidewalk.

Kit hated to be stared at, he remembered.

"Get the fuck away from us—goddamn."

Kit shuddered.

"Breathe. You need to take a deep breath." Jack tried to explain as he further assessed the situation. His voice calm, eyes wildly trailing over her one more time for any pain or bruises.

The alarm was slick in his veins as it poured out of her.

"You're having a panic attack, Kit. It's all right. You just need to breathe. Look at me. Right now. Look at me and follow my breaths. In." Jack took a deep breath in before letting it out.

He tried again. In. And out.

Katherine shook as she attempted to mimic him. So simple, and yet her entire body clenched in concentration—no, in fear. She couldn't do it, shaking her head as she made a sound he could only describe as a whimper.

"Goddamn it. You better breathe right now, Kitten, or else I will literally turn you over my leg and spank you until you are gulping for air."

She tried to suck in air, the sound more like a wheeze.

"Good. Breathe," Jack ordered again, a deep, authoritative tone slipping into place as she responded. "Breathe, Kit."

After another moment, she opened her mouth and took a breath, and then another longer than the last.

"There you go. Keep going. Good girl," Jack encouraged.

She shivered.

Right. Pulling his jacket from his shoulders, it looked like Kit wasn't very prepared for the cold Ashton weather tonight either. He swung it gently over each of her bare shoulders.

"How did you find me?"

"Didn't you hear that I always know where the parties are?" Jack attempted to joke, but only because it was true. It was basically in his friend job description when Reed dropped Avril's prerequisite and they ended up at Keys one too many nights out playing scrabble. "It's basically my calling card, among other things."

"Other things," she repeated.

What did that mean?

He watched as she closed her eyes and took another breath that shook her rib cage. But her heart was slowing down, somewhat. All that was left wasn't the tense anxiety, but cool sadness. Not heavy, just plain and simple sort of sorrow like a chill on fingertips.

He wanted to grab hers as she stretched her hands out before they went back to tiny fists.

Jack cleared his throat as she blinked her eyes back open. "Do you have those often?"

"Sometimes."

Jack swiped his thumb over the soft skin of her knee again, trying to slow his own heart rate that at some point seemed to sync with hers.

"I'm sorry."

"Nothing to be sorry for, sweetheart."

"So sorry."

"What did I just say?"

She said nothing. Still, her hands shook. He always thought a seamstress's hands would be steadier. But now, even if she didn't notice, he took them in his, gently pulling them away from her face.

"What happened?" Jack asked quietly after another moment. "Do you want to talk about it?"

Kit shook her head, a stringy wave falling over her cheek.

Jack resisted the urge to reach up and brush it away.

She, on the other hand, slipped her hand out of his and did it for him.

"I was j-just." She shut her eyes again through the stutter. "Thinking."

"It does the best of us in."

Kit snorted before she sniffed. "So stupid."

"No."

"It is. All of this. I was just so stupid. I went to the market and met these people from the school." She shook her head. "I'm fine alone. I like to be alone."

"Can't relate."

"It's your fault," she gritted out between her teeth.

At that, Jack raised his eyebrows. "My fault?"

He'd done a lot of things, especially in the past few months, but he couldn't think of anything specific to her.

"You and her."

Queen.

"I was fine being alone, and then all of a sudden, for a little while, I wasn't."

Jack paused, letting her go on.

"I was fine before I met you, and I just wanted…" She shook her head again, but Jack wanted to know. What was it? What did she want? "It's so ridiculous, but for a second, I felt like I was meant to be here. That I was meant to live in Ashton and be someone with you all, but then no one called, and I got it."

"Avril took off not long after we went out together that night and hasn't been making any calls either." He guessed that didn't mean he couldn't have. But he was busy and if she needed someone…

Jack's forehead creased as he focused on her.

"I get why no one actually wants to be around me. I'm just—"

"Not just."

"Yeah. Just." Kit lifted her head and finally looked at him, and when she did, he swore he saw her take another sharp intake of air, as if just realizing he was in front of her for the first time. "That's all I ever have been. Just."

He stared at her for a long moment, his hands still on her knees. He wondered if they were talking about the same person here. He basically ran out of the house after her. He was the stupid one, turning back to Pen to begin with instead of her, who looked like he did right before he did something stupid, standing on the staircase and making promises she couldn't keep.

His jaw clenched.

"Obviously you wouldn't get it."

"What do you mean?"

"You're beautiful. Everyone fawns all over you and your naughty, sexy grin. People pay for you to beat them and say thank you after. Charismatic and charming man who probably has had girls fighting to get into your bed if they weren't willing to share."

Jack fought his own snort of amusement. "That only happened two times, max."

"Of course, you wouldn't understand."

"Understand what?"

"What it is like to be no one. Out of everyone in the world, I am no one's favorite. For all I can tell, no one can stand me. And little do they know that at this point, the feeling is pretty mutual. It's not like I ever had friends before. I barely even had a family.

My own parents didn't want me and made that pretty damn clear when they left out the front door without a word. Emilie barely even wanted me until I ended up on her doorstep. She's probably looking for a way out."

"Kit." Jack looked at her hands, balled in fists.

To be honest, right now, he didn't want to get too close. Fire started to burn in the sadness and something else he couldn't decode radiating in her. That thick honey feeling.

"Don't say it's not true," Kit said. "It is. I am nothing."

"You are not."

She shook her head.

"Don't believe that for a damn second, Kitten."

"You don't know me."

No. He didn't, but that truth didn't sit well with him either, as he held on tighter. "I know that you're a liar."

She looked at him. Good. He would keep talking as long as she kept looking at him, even like that, with thick lashes and mascara dripping.

"Or maybe you just don't own a mirror, because fuck, Kit, you're beautiful."

She snorted.

"Don't make that noise at me. I'm serious. You're a badass little drinker who can somehow manage their liquor better than, well, anyone I've really met. You are funny as well as talented. To top it all off, you're smart and know what you are doing with your life setting up a website for Emilie's shop. Kitten, look at me, I may be exceedingly dashing minus the whole height thing."

"You're the perfect height."

Jack fought a smirk. "What? You want to play this game then?"

"The pity-me game, of course. We fight until we see whose life is worse. Ready? I am an almost twenty-nine-year-old man-child who ran away from home to go to college in the city. I proceeded to get kicked out of that school to work on crappy film sets as a lighting guy for a few months, since that was all I was qualified for before Avril came along. I've never lived alone because I can't stand the quiet, and currently because of this I am living in the guest room of my best friend who put me in the friend zone with a little tender touch after I confessed my drunken, yet at the time, very real love to her."

Katherine lifted her head, eyes locked on his.

"I can't even go home for my parents' anniversary, because I am a big fat coward and am afraid that after all these years, they aren't going to like what they'll see. Sometimes I don't like what I see either. You got me thinking about it all with your deep, well-meaning questions you asked."

He could've gone home a million times, but didn't. And now he barely even knew his six-year-old nephew, let alone the few other nieces that came along after his older brother. The other day, he ended up finally calling his sister-in-law back. She tried to convince him to come home, that this was the year, but he couldn't. It was too late and—

"I'd go with you."

Jack looked back from where his eyes drifted toward the lamppost. "What?"

"To your parents. I'd go with you." She took a deep breath as she recovered. Each word was slow, thoughtful. "They call themselves your family. They'd like what they finally get to see."

Jack thought for a moment, moving himself to sit beside her on the stoop. Like magnets, she leaned into him, limp and exhausted. "We'll talk about that later. Right now, we're focused on you."

"I still think I won."

Jack only hummed in response. Maybe she did.

"I just." She caught herself. "I was alone again, and I just wanted to be normal. So, I decided to go out tonight. All this time I was never good enough—never anything. How hard is it to be normal?"

Jack shook his head with a scrunch of his nose as he looked

up. The sky was dark and hazy. "Normal is boring."

Kit said nothing. Her brow creased in concentration.

He ran a finger over it, and she didn't flinch as he carefully lifted her chin up so she would meet his eyes.

God, he was an asshole.

"Be normal with me, then."

CHAPTER TWENTY

*K*atherine's jacket and tote were still by the door, she noticed. She also noticed that the townhouse was a lot quieter than it was a few hours ago.

"I should go back home. I should get back to Emilie." Katherine murmured down to herself. She'd been thinking it the whole ride back to the house. The night seemed to drone on over Ashton, a never-ending void of darkness as she looked out the window as they crossed the even darker river. In its reflection, she swore she saw a star, but when she looked up, all that was there was a haze of clouds.

Jack shook his head as he shut the door behind them. He turned the lock until it clicked. "Don't worry about Emilie. I'll call her in the morning if you want me to."

She was probably asleep. Vaguely, Katherine nodded as she stumbled farther inside to the living room. Everything was back to its rightful place, as if no one was there at all.

The only people there now were her and Jack.

Glancing up at him, she caught him slowly assessing her, probably to see if she was going to have a major freak-out. Though it wasn't the first time Katherine had ever had a panic attack before, they still managed to catch her off guard, slowly creeping up on her and then striking like a viper when she least expected.

They wrung her out like a towel, limp and exhausted.

His hands were so gentle as they found her again, leading her around to the other side of the couch. "Come here. Do you want to go to bed?"

She shook her head.

"Yeah, a little early yet for a Saturday, huh?" Jack agreed with her, though that isn't what she meant. Dropped her down to sit, then he hauled her right back up again, leading her toward the steps. "My mistake, let's get you cleaned up first. Good?"

She nodded again before she realized what he meant by that, they were back upstairs maneuvering through the hallway they were in earlier tonight. Katherine glanced at the wall she'd been pressed against by Devil's hands before being led into Jack's room. Opening his drawers, he filled her arms with soft cotton in every shade of navy and gray.

"You can use Queen's bathroom if you want, through her room."

Katherine was still staring down at the pile of clothes, forgiving in her hands as her fingers clenched around them. With a nod, she moved back into the hallway. What was she doing here? She didn't let herself answer, didn't have the energy to as she walked through Avril's room at the one end of the hall. The ostentatious space suddenly felt comfortable, knowing where she was going.

Dropping her—Jack's—clothes on the counter, Katherine immediately saw her reflection in the mirror. Lights brightened on either side. Black eyeliner and mascara dripped from where it was carefully laid, smearing down her cheeks. She let the water run, scrubbing her face before she noticed all the expensive cream cleansers and lotions in front of her. She smoothed each over her face until her skin was clear again, eyes remaining a little raw from tears and her contacts.

Blinking a few times, she reached up and carefully threw one contact and then the other in the trash. Obviously, she wasn't thinking now, the world a blur.

"Jack?" she asked once, wondering if he was waiting outside the door. Hearing no answer, she called out a little louder.

Immediately, Jack appeared from where she craned her neck around the bathroom doorway. "What's wrong?"

"Can you get my bag? It's by the door downstairs. My spare glasses are inside."

With a nod, he disappeared.

Letting the bathroom door mostly close again, Katherine kicked off her shoes and let them clang against the large clawfoot tub. It was a bathtub, truly, of dreams. She could imagine just filling it to the brim before slipping in with all the soaps lined up by the crooked witch window above.

Taking a deep breath, Katherine instead reached for the hem of her dress, tugging it upward to go over her head, but somewhere along the way, it was caught. Stuck, Katherine turned around to a deep chuckle.

She froze as hands unraveled her from wherever the fabric had caught on the loop of her bra, helping her tug the silk the rest of the way over her shoulders.

Jack stood in front of her, a small smile quirking the side of his mouth. Taking her dress, he folded it with surprising care before laying it over the edge of the tub. Then, slowly, Jack fell to his knees before her.

Katherine's eyes widened at the sight. Something inside of her chest caught, and she wondered if he could tell she wasn't breathing.

He started with the brooches. With ease, he pulled the metal away from the lace, pinned and unpinned. Then his arms reached around her, catching her eyes as he did. Deftly, his fingers unclipped her garter belt and put it next to her dress on the lip of the tub basin. One at a time, he pulled a piece of clothing off the counter, starting with sweatpants.

They were only slightly too big around her hips, cinching them inward as far as they would go. The oversized T-shirt slipped overhead. Once it passed her shoulders, Katherine tugged the hem down, oddly not shy in front of Jack. Or maybe that was just because she couldn't fully see him, not until he slipped her bulky plastic frame glasses she only wore when necessary over her nose.

He pushed them up a little farther with a single finger. "No longer blind."

Katherine gave him a small grateful smile, looking down at herself. She felt like she was coated in the world's comfiest blankets. He was dressed similarly. "Thank you."

"You're welcome. Good?"

She shook her head, not yet trusting herself to speak.

"Good," Jack answered for her. "Let's go back downstairs then and continue this party, shall we?"

Party? Following him out from Avril's room, immediately Katherine's gaze caught on the Queen's vanity. A large planner folded to the month prior was laid out. Grabbing the heavy bound pages as she walked, she watched the muscles in Jack's back move as they made their way to the living room. Blankets were spread over the cushions, the electric fireplace under the television on and pulsing with warm air.

"Sit," Jack ordered, standing in front of the couch.

Not willing to argue, Katherine did as she was told.

Another blanket was draped over her. Pulling it to her chest, Jack smiled. He flopped down next to her, but not before reaching for the glass of water on the table. Handing it to her, he waited for her to take a long sip before putting it back.

"Not going to lie, I think I like these turns of events," Jack groaned as he got comfortable. Raising the remote, the television flicked on.

His eyes narrowed toward her hands. "What do you have there?"

Oh. Katherine looked back down at her lap. Avril's two-year planner still sat there. "I may have gone looking for you first at DuCain."

"When?"

"Tonight."

"Tonight?" Jack's eyebrows raised.

"I didn't find you, obviously. I needed to get out of the house, away from Emilie, who was also mad at me and I was mad at you so, it all sort of fit."

He didn't say anything, knowing that she had more.

"When I was there though, I ran into Nik and they told me that you weren't really working anymore," explained Katherine.

"I needed a break."

She'd heard that one before from someone else in this house. But this time, tucked in on either side, she wasn't as nervous to ask questions. "What do you mean?"

Jack shrugged a single shoulder as he glanced toward the television. His eyes worked side to side as if trying to figure out an answer himself. "Like I said before, when I found you earlier. You brought up a lot of questions for me."

"I'm sorry."

"No, it's a good thing," Jack assured. "Or maybe it is. I don't know. I just dropped a few shifts, is all, trying to figure it out. I called an old friend I used to live with and asked if he still knew anyone working in photography. I just got home from another smaller wedding today and walked into all this."

"You mean the party without Avril?"

He nodded before running a hand down his face. "That's the one. Pen seemed to take it upon herself to fill her shoes."

To that, Katherine said nothing. She looked back down at

Avril's planner, opening it back up and skimming through the first few pages of her contact information and random names listed that made no sense to her. She never knew Avril had a public relations representative.

"You left before I came back out to see you in the hall," Jack said.

Katherine replied with the first thing that came to mind. "You left me in the hall."

"I did." Jack paused, looking at her. "I wanted to make sure that Pen left before I talked to you. I told her to leave and take her friends she invited with her, minding of course that one of them was with you in that hallway."

Mouth dry, Katherine nodded. Right. "You're mad at me too."

His eyes narrowed. "Why would you say that?"

"Because of how you looked at me when I was with Devil."

"I'm not mad at you."

For some reason, she couldn't believe that.

"Honestly, I would be the most hypocritical person in the world if I was mad at you, Kit. There is nothing wrong with wanting someone, even acting on it," Jack breathed a sigh as his lip curled. "Even if it was Devil."

"What is your problem with him?"

"I just don't like the guy," Jack said.

Katherine raised her eyebrows.

"He used to work at DuCain. He was the old me, in a sense. The big Dominant of DuCain who got the calls. The guy who made the money. He gave me a hard time when I started."

"Is that all?"

"He was this asshole who thought he had everyone in the palm of his hand with a snap of his pudgy fingers," Jack went on. He didn't have to think long for insults. "He's basically a trust-fund kid who wanted to turn bad when the rest of us are just this way, trying to live the best life we enjoyed or knew how. Luckily, he left only a little after I started. He unfortunately pops back in now and then whenever he gets bored and wants to ruin lives, I imagine."

"Is his name really Devil?"

Jack rolled his eyes.

She'd take that as a no. "So after, you came back out into the hall for me?"

"I did."

"And I wasn't there."

He nodded.

"I'm sorry," Katherine said before she realized. "But you found me."

"I did."

"Thank you."

He shook his head, waving the mention away. "At first, I thought maybe you didn't want me to, but I just—I have this feeling sometimes, and you showed up here."

"You were worried."

He paused before he nodded.

"Thank you."

"Stop."

"I mean it," Katherine said, and she did. She wasn't sure what she would've done, what would've happened if he hadn't shown up. Would she have let herself be pulled into Oliver at that party? Or would she have ended up outside for air, crawling home and crying on the pull-out couch, trying to be quiet so as not to wake Emilie?

Looking around, she was much happier to end up right here.

Still, he shook his head, eyes turning back down to the calendar in her lap. "You never said what happened when you went to DuCain."

"I talked to Nik, and I met this other girl who was there wearing a rather short schoolgirl uniform."

"Evie."

Katherine met his eyes and nodded. "She's nice."

"She's new."

Katherine shrugged. "Avril left."

"Off on one of her adventures," Jack confirmed with a tight smile. "At least that is what we all assume."

"What do you mean?" The space between her eyebrows creased.

"It's what Avril does. I called Reed and he didn't seem concerned so…"

"Reed and her—"

"Reed has always been her number one. A package deal, in a sense," Jack explained. "Honestly, if you wanted to know anything about Avril, Reed would know. So, when Avril runs away once in a while and Reed says that it is okay, we can all believe it."

"Even when she leaves behind her life and event planning for this New Year's thing at Rosin and DuCain?" Katherine asked.

"So that's what they pulled you in on."

Looking back down at the planner, she couldn't say anything to deny it. "They were very charismatic."

"Like Devil was."

"About, yes."

Jack barked a laugh.

"But now I am basically the planner of the entire thing it is sounding like, all because I said I could maybe come here and try to find her notes on the past year."

"So that's why you came to the castle?"

"Is that what you call it?" Katherine looked around the place. It was rather apt. "At first. I figured if you weren't at DuCain, you might've been out. I could just slip in and out for these notes. No one would ever notice."

"I would've noticed you."

But he didn't. He hadn't noticed that she was gone after that amazing day they had together when he showed her Ashton, her home, for weeks. How long would that have lasted if she hadn't shown up here tonight? How long would he have not noticed?

The thought must've dawned on him. "I'm sorry that I didn't call. I would be pissed at me too."

"I'm too tired to be angry with anyone anymore, Jack," Katherine said, "Or at least not for a long time. You say that you're a bad secret keeper, well I'm terrible at holding grudges."

Some sort of peace fell over his face.

She shrugged. At least she was the one who caused it. "I feel like I'd be madder than I'd be anxious at this point and that's... a lot."

"Why is Emilie mad at you, anyway?"

He'd caught that. She curled up farther. "I brought up some ideas for the shop again like the website and online shop."

"She's still not for the idea?"

Katherine shook her head. After today, she'd say that was a bit of an understatement. "She says it's not the right time. I feel it is. I understand the shop like she said she wanted me to. She's let me basically take over the past few weeks and it has been going well. Oddly well."

Jack smiled.

"I've had a lot of time and even my corsets have come along way, even if they aren't perfect yet," Katherine went on. "I even finished the website, besides the name of course—"

"Show me."

"What?"

Jack was already reaching underneath the coffee table, from somewhere among the chessboard and other random things, he pulled out a laptop. Waiting for the screen to light up, he shoved it toward her. "Show me."

"You don't have to."

"I want to see," Jack insisted, shaking the keyboard.

Meeting his gaze, Katherine took the computer from him. Slowly she keyed in the website builder, showing him the editing screen. She'd been too nervous to even hit preview in case she accidentally published it with a ridiculous domain name she couldn't change. Then it would really look like they were some random shop of unpronounceable scandal.

She turned the screen toward Jack.

His eyes widened as he scrolled. "This is really amazing, Kit. How long did you spend on this?"

Longer than she'd admit. "I still need to take photos."

"I can help with that."

Katherine shook her head. "I didn't mean it like I was asking."

"I was offering," Jack said, peeking up from the screen. He let her watch as he logged out and shut the screen again. Everything's safe. "What, are you nervous about modeling?"

"I would not be modeling."

"There would have to be at least one photo of the lingerie on someone, don't you think?"

Katherine stared at him for a long moment. She thought this through, and he was right, but—it certainly wasn't going to be her. "Truth or dare?"

"We are playing again?"

She waited.

"Truth."

"You just really want to see me half naked, don't you, Jack the Ripper?" Katherine asked, though she couldn't fight the small smile forming on her lips. Yes, she wanted to say. Yes.

Jack shook his head, fighting off another wide smile himself. "God, you're weird."

"You're just starting to realize?"

"You're just starting to realize that I almost saw you thoroughly fucked against the ugly hallway wallpaper earlier tonight where anyone else could see? Much worse than some boudoir on the internet if I do say so myself."

Trying to contain herself, she closed her lips and looked at Jack again, feeling the blush rising to her cheeks. He didn't say the words, and yet he was still there, looking at her like that.

"You're slowly blooming for me, Kit. Let me watch."

Blooming, was that really what she was doing? Katherine took a deep breath and shifted across the couch toward him.

Truth or dare. It was his turn.

Her eyes shifted down to his lips before moving back to his eyes again, trying to track where he was looking.

Right at her.

This could wreck everything, the one part of her brain said as she looked up at him.

The other parts whispered, somehow louder. *Dare.*

And so she kissed him. Yanking him down by the collar of his shirt so she could reach his mouth, Katherine kissed Jack Carver the way she imagined herself kissing him a hundred times before. His mouth was warm and hard with sudden shock, but Katherine kissed him, and maybe this could be enough for her, whatever happened after. Whether he wanted to be with her or—

Breaking apart, Katherine was sure that her heart might break if she finished that thought. Pounding as hard as it was, anyway, it would break right through her ribs and chest until she could no longer hide it, out in the open to gape at as well as the hole it left.

"I'm sorry," she gasped. "I've wanted to do that for…"

Forever. Since the first moment she saw Jack, even though in between, she thought there for a while that her mind was going too far to other places.

"I'm sorry."

"No," Jack stopped her, his Adam's apple bobbing in his throat. He shook his head as he blinked. This time, there was no doubt where his eyes landed when he opened them. He stared at her lips. "Don't be. I'm—I'm really sorry I didn't call you, Kit."

She shook her head, leaning back where she lounged on the couch. On the television, an old movie started to play in technicolor.

"Truth or dare?"

Jack narrowed his eyes and took a long moment in the silence between them. "For the first time I'm afraid to say dare."

"Then, truth?"

He nodded.

"Why do they call you Ripper?"

"Because," he sighed, biting his bottom lip. "I've gained the reputation of ripping out hearts."

"How dramatic."

"My middle name. You caught me."

If only she did.

CHAPTER TWENTY-ONE

$\mathcal{K}$atherine was used to waking up on couches, but this one wasn't hers. Over the past few weeks, she had ended up here, blinking her eyes open to find Jack in what looked like a very uncomfortable position on the other end. His head tilted back up toward the ceiling, legs extended so one was still on the couch while the other was propped on the coffee table.

In the mornings, Katherine started work with Emilie, who slowly but surely gained her strength back to come down to the shop, quietly working on the small pile of bespoke requests that piled up. The first time she came home after the fateful night of two parties and her new position as New Year's event coordinator, Katherine waited for the moment her aunt would question where she was or who she obviously spent the night with in that proud yet teasing way of hers.

But she didn't. Her aunt's focus remained completely on her work, offering corrections on Katherine's, when she glanced up or was brought tea, noting a loose thread or order pickup she needed to make.

Katherine didn't bring up the website again. Instead, she worked.

She put together more sets to replace the others that had been taken off the displays. She caught her finger on the sewing machine to which she did not cry. She cleaned up the shop at the end of the day and switched the sign over to closed. She tore out of the shop each day in order to make it to DuCain where Jack was often finishing up a session and conceded to helping her and Evie with the event plans.

He'd out of everyone had actually been to the previous ones and had some sort of clue what the end product was supposed to look like.

Jack told her to be there by six o'clock sharp, but he still looked surprised when she showed up on time each day.

"This is what you call normal?" Katherine asked him the first evening as she jotted a few more notes down from Avril's planner. The pages were a mess of phone numbers and minor details Katherine would've never thought of.

"Better than being alone," Jack said simply. He didn't lift his eyes from where he whipped down his equipment.

It seemed to become their motto.

From DuCain, sometimes they didn't leave right away, Evie joining them. She seemed to always be at the club. With simple ease, whether or not she knew they would be there; she'd crack the door open as she threw a sweatshirt over whatever clothes she was wearing that day. All of them hid inside Jack's preferred dungeon, sprawled out on the floor as they planned.

Among the three of them, their other motto included, *what would Queen do?*

It was met with up and down results.

"We need to set down the headliner here at midnight too," Jack said one day after Evie snuck in.

Evie poured over Avril's planner, nodding as she focused.

"Evie," Jack said again.

Katherine glanced at her too, until the girl's head popped up.

"What?" She looked between the two of them. "Threesome?"

Jack held back a laugh as he rolled his eyes. "As much as it overjoys me that you would be interested in a ménage à trois, with those welts on you and another client later on your calendar, no."

Evie rolled her eyes, mimicking him. "It's just Trevor coming to play later. It's like taking a luxurious nap in between when he tries to tickle me."

"You aren't ticklish?" Katherine couldn't help herself before suddenly asking over the top of her computer.

Evie pressed her lips together and shook her head. "I think he sees it as a challenge."

"This is not why we asked you to come today."

"No one ever asks me these days."

Jack ran a hand down his face. Before glancing at Katherine as if to say, you see what we are dealing with? "Evie."

Katherine felt her lips press together to stay closed as she smiled. She was pretty sure she loved Evie.

Handing the planner back to her, Evie curled her knees up toward her chest. "What?"

"The headliner for New Year's. I was thinking it could be you and me."

Evie's eyes widened. Her finger pointed back and forth between them. "You and me?"

With a tilt of his chin, Jack nodded. "It's up to you, of course. I know that you haven't been completely open with doing public scene work."

The girl next to her swallowed, and in that moment, Katherine didn't see the strength in Evie that she always did. Yet still, with a deep breath, Evie blew it out and started to nod slowly. "Okay."

"You know you can back out at any time."

Evie nodded again.

"No harm no foul."

She forced a small laugh as she let herself relax her back into the wall. "What better time for me to make my grand entry."

"A nice way to think of it," Jack granted. "So that's settled."

"We'll practice before, right?"

"Of course. We would never go out until you were comfortable. We can make time to figure out the semantics with no impact. That way, you'll get the pace of what the scene will be on stage. I don't go up there without a plan, not anymore," Jack agreed. "Kit, did you call—"

"Can you show me some now?" Evie cut in. "Just so I can ease my mind. This is free time."

Jack stared at her. His eyes flicked to Katherine.

Except on stage, Katherine had never seen Jack play before. Especially not in the dungeons where he spent most of his time these days between the house and the occasional photography gigs that were getting fewer now that the weather turned from chilly to cold frost sticking to the streets.

"Come on, please?" Evie shrugged, obviously noting Katherine's sudden flush. In fact, seeing it, Evie stretched her legs out in front of her, as if preparing for a nap. Her hands even curled behind her head. At the base, her hair became looser by the second. Strands tumbled down past her ears to her shoulders. "I like to know what I am getting into. As you said, I don't do a lot of scenes in public. Any, actually."

Jack chewed on the inside of his cheek. With a grunt, he pushed himself up off the dark floor. "Fine. Quickly. Get up."

"Actually, I thought maybe Kit could take my place. You said yourself the other day that she needed to learn more about the community and the roles here as she put everything together from the bottom up. Plus, I'm a visual learner."

Jack groaned, looking away, he waved a hand at Katherine. "Of course, you are. Fine. Kit. Up."

"Me?"

"You just said when you got here that you agreed to learning DuCain and Rosin so that we can market properly."

Right, she did. A sensation tingly low in her stomach, slowly, Katherine moved her laptop she was typing on to the side. Once it was safe, back in her bag, she stood up and strode across the floor toward Jack, one step at a time.

He seemed taller than normal.

"Aw, aren't you guys cute together?"

"Evie," Jack reprimanded.

Evie only continued to smile; this time unafraid at the sudden sharpness in his voice as she taunted. It was similar to the way Katherine did when she was in the shop watching Emilie put something together that was amazing. This was her happy place, filled with torture and pleasure, Katherine put together. In the dungeons of DuCain.

She wondered how many times she and Jack had played together before. She brushed the thought aside, nothing to stick on.

"Okay, so I was thinking—" Jack started.

"Uh-uh," Evie cut in from where she sat. "Don't you think to create an SSC environment you should tell Kit exactly what her role is here? Unless, of course, she already has experience. Kit?"

Katherine had to tightly press her lips together, so she didn't laugh at what was happening. She glanced at Evie, who only gave her a stranger look than she was expecting, understanding.

"SSC?"

"Safe, sane, consensual," Jack bit out.

"There is also RACK," Evie filled in. "Risk-assessed consensual kink."

Katherine gave a slow nod.

"Also, she'll need a safe word."

"We aren't doing anything." Jack again gave Evie a look that might've once sent Katherine running.

Even Evie took a second before she replied, more to Katherine than him. "You have one?"

"One what?"

"A safe word. You can use the average house word if you want, but I think it's fun to make up your own."

"What's yours?"

Evie didn't have to think twice. "Cavill."

Jack raised another eyebrow, hands on his hips.

"You know." Evie swayed as she looked up in thought. "Like Henry Cavill, the actor? I have quite the thing for him."

"How interesting," Jack replied blandly.

"Periwinkle," Katherine blurted out suddenly. It was an easy word. One that came to mind ever since she read the tag on a sheath of fabric that was delivered to the shop.

Jack turned and stared at her the moment the word passed her lips. He repeated it slowly, quietly, as if memorizing a very important vocabulary word. "Periwinkle."

Katherine nodded twice.

"Okay." He licked his lips.

"This is when you show her the basics."

"If I knew that you were going to top me, Evie, I would've brought someone else in here."

She only waited, waving her hands for them to get closer than the five-foot distance they were still standing from each other.

Yeah, Katherine liked her.

"Fine." Jack swallowed whatever was caught in his throat. "For starters, the marker of a truly good submissive is one that revels in complete obedience and perhaps even reverence toward her Dom. Isn't that right, Evie?"

Katherine heard a simple, "Mhm," from somewhere behind her.

Her eyes were focused on Jack now as he stepped closer.

"Also, the resting pose for a sub is on her knees," Jack said gently.

"Oh, um." Katherine looked around toward her heels. With a glance up to Jack and then Evie, who was watching with apt interest, Katherine slowly lowered herself down. The floor of the dungeon was not as hard as she thought it would be on her knees. Tucking her feet below her, her skirt tapered off to reveal the front of her thighs.

Running her tongue over her lips to cover any heavy breath that escaped through them, Katherine's heart pounded as she lifted her chin up and saw what she'd imagined for months.

With lips slightly parted, Jack looked right back down at her, his hazel eyes hard and narrowed.

"Eyes averted down."

"Like you're praying," Evie whispered somewhere in the distance.

As he took a small circle, walking around her, he tapped her back gently with the toe of his shoe.

Katherine sat up straight, adjusting her hands to lay carefully on either thigh where her dress's skirt slipped up at the fixed posture, no longer covering the clips of her garters.

"Good," Jack spoke, his voice rough and low.

Katherine did not move.

"BDSM." He spoke each word slowly as he continued making his round around her to make sure she didn't flinch as he got closer. "Do you know what that stands for, Kitten?"

"Yes."

"Tell me."

"Bondage, dominance, submission..." She trailed off. If her hands weren't cupping her knees, she was sure they would be shaking as she kept her voice even.

"So, you don't know," Jack said. "Let me tell you, yes?"

Katherine tilted her head.

But Jack stopped his walk. "What was that?"

She forced the word out, though not loud. She was never someone who was loud. She looked up toward him before immediately remembering and placing her eyes back in front of her on the floor.

Like she was praying. "Yes."

"I thought so, I wanted to make sure after all. Consent is key for us to be doing this, you know. What was I saying again, Evie?"

Katherine spoke up again. "BDSM."

She could feel his head whip back to her. "I don't think I was asking you, Kitten. Did I ask you to speak?"

No.

"Who was I asking?"

Katherine shut her eyes. "Evie."

"BDSM," Evie supplied.

"Oh yes, that's right. BDSM." Jack sang the letters through the space again as if he was just starting to enjoy himself, a hint of light in his voice. "Bondage, very good, Kitten. Dominance, yes, but also discipline. We may need to work on that."

Katherine cringed but opened her eyes again, sitting up straight and looking down straight ahead even as she ached to look up and give him a glare.

"And submission, as well as sadism. And M. Did I give you any hints, sweetheart?"

M. Katherine took another deep breath, settling her heart. She was here, right here, as Jack waited.

"You can answer."

"Masochism?"

"What a quick learner," Jack said, and suddenly he was right in front of her. Squatting down, he lifted her chin with two fingers. His honey gaze turned sharp like specks of gold. "Will you ever stop surprising me, Kit?"

Another deep breath. She felt oddly calm. Simple.

"Look so simple now?" Jack asked, as if he could read her thoughts. She sure didn't say anything aloud. Something more than intrigued crossed over him as he leaned in close to her ear.

"Is this what you were curious about the other night at the club when you almost slipped into the wrong hands?"

Katherine narrowed her eyes and this time when he pulled back to look at her, she only grinned, not letting him get to her. They were playing, but she was still part of the game. "Looks like I have a lot to learn."

The door across from them opened to the view of the two of them there in that position.

"It appears I am interrupting something?" A woman peeked inside. "I'm here for Evie, but you three continue doing... whatever this is you are doing." She waved her hand around the scene.

Mouth gaping, Katherine easily slipped back up onto her heels to standing. She heard a pleased clap at the swift movement from both Jack and Evie behind her. She couldn't help but spin around with an accusing glare.

"Forgive my intrusion."

"Nothing to be forgiven, Mistress." Jack stood and bowed at the waist toward the leather-clad woman.

She turned to Evie. "Coming?"

"Everyone is so giving today," Evie proclaimed as she stood up, picking up her thigh-highs she removed to wiggle her toes.

The mistress rolled her eyes.

"We were just teaching Jack's friend here the basics."

"Is that so?" the woman asked, turning back to Katherine. "Jack's friend?"

Katherine only stood there for a long moment. At some point, her throat turned very dry.

Luckily, Jack stepped in. "Kit is helping with the New Year's Eve bash since Queen isn't here."

"She isn't going to be back by then?"

Jack paused at the question. "She'll probably be back, but someone had to pick up the planning slack."

"Right." The mistress, Raquel, Katherine remembered from her past orders, glanced toward her again. "Have a nice night."

"You too," Katherine whispered as the door slammed closed.

"Did I scare you?"

Scare her?

She was still visualizing herself down on the floor with him looking down at her...

"No," Katherine spoke rapidly as she processed. "That dominatrix—Raquel. Will she think that we were... are—"

Jack was very close to her now. Taking a hesitant step back, Katherine pressed up against the wall. His eyes softened, suddenly tired, as he looked her up and down with a sigh.

"Don't worry, Kitten, your reputation is still intact. Like I've said before, if we were anything, you'd know it by now," he purred, a low rumble. The sound vibrated through her chest and settled low in her stomach.

Jack took in Katherine. She stared back. Only once she dared to meet his hazel eyes did he give an amused laugh and pull away, as if just noticing how close to one another they were. "So would your wallet. Come on. We still have work to do, but I'm exhausted."

Katherine nodded in agreement.

"Hungry?"

As their usual schedule dictated. After DuCain and event work, she and Jack almost always spent the rest of the night together in simple company. They picked up takeout or groceries and took them back to the townhouse.

They left the television on to a random channel as they ate rice noodles or worked next to each other. Katherine finally finished the final page of the website. Now truly, there were only two things standing in the way of her hitting the final publish button.

She shut the screen, pulling the blanket around herself on the couch.

"You done?" Jack asked. He was still on his computer, editing raw images until the colors popped.

"The decorations have been ordered. Cherry has been updated on the event schedule," Katherine recounted. "The headliner at DuCain has been settled."

Jack snorted.

"I like Evie."

"Of course you do. You both are shy until you get comfortable. Then, you won't shut up."

He had a point.

The corner of his mouth quirked up. "Are you staying?"

Katherine shook her head, like she always did as she curled down farther into the corner. "Just for a little, then I'll head home."

She knew that she couldn't keep staying here, leaving Emilie alone, but then again, she wasn't really talking to Katherine anyway. She'd watch the rest of whatever episode was on, then she'd go.

Unconvinced, Jack only nodded and looked back to his screen. His other hand reached out to her blanket, stretching it so it fit over her feet.

It had been nice being at the townhouse with Jack for the past few weeks. It was easy and warm. They talked and laughed, and he never questioned her taco order with extra lettuce since she proclaimed it always fell out of the top when she tried to eat it. And they never questioned the first time when she stayed over and kissed him.

A sort of memory only Katherine only reminisced on, wondering if he remembered it happening, not that it mattered.

They had a lot of more important things to worry about anyway. The event and Katherine still helping Emilie with the shop.

She could ask him right now. The realization that there was only one way to get the website up and running on her own without spending any more than she already was for hosting became abundantly clear, and he had offered.

But Katherine didn't. The television screen blurred before her eyes as she fell asleep, knowing that she would get up and head straight home to the shop again.

And then the next day, they would do it all over again.

Only today, Katherine stretched as she sat up in the dim light of an early Ashton morning. She carefully nudged Jack so he could almost think it was an accident.

With a yawn, Jack inhaled before blinking a few times. "What time is it?"

"Jack?"

"Morning."

Will you take pictures of me half naked to put online? Katherine wanted to ask. "Truth or dare?"

"It's a little early for this, Kitten. You want coffee or tea?"

It didn't matter. "Truth or dare?"

He rubbed his eyes, looking her up and down. She couldn't imagine what her hair looked like as she pulled on her glasses from the side table. He must've taken them off as she fell asleep next to him again last night.

She waited for his answer.

It came out soft, even. "Dare. Was that the right answer?"

CHAPTER TWENTY-TWO

*T*he first time he knew that there was no walking away from Avril was when he watched her have sex with someone else. He felt little as he stared at the two of them at some party uptown, in a building he wouldn't be able to pick out of a lineup. He'd convinced the two of them to go after getting an invite from an old friend who still remembered him from his time at school. Jack got his internship alongside the guy before he dropped out.

But, when he watched Avril laugh and smile, she did whatever the hell she pleased, there was only one thing he could think, and he couldn't help but think that Reed after a while, had thought the same thing.

It looked like he was along for whatever ride she had him on.

Jack didn't want to get off, though he thought about it occasionally. He thought about the possibility when she pushed him away or got so drunk, it was nearly impossible for her to mount the stairs of the castle. Or, when she rolled over in his bed late some nights after they were out and whispered the sort of dirty things in his ear he only ever thought were made up in his sickest fantasies.

But he knew that this was different.

No matter how many times he forced himself to stop whatever thought trailed through his mind late at night or even right when he woke up, it was still there, and he knew it.

Knew it from the moment he couldn't get the image of Kit kneeling down in front of him out of his mind, staring back up at him with parted lips that with anyone else, he would have smashed his against.

And she looked at him like she wouldn't mind.

Then there was also how she fell asleep almost every other night on the couch next to him. She cleaned up the plates on the coffee table, putting her laptop where they had been and told him how she was just going to rest her eyes for a minute or finish watching the end of the movie he knew she never saw the beginning of—then she'd be asleep, comfortable and safe next to him.

Most nights, he couldn't bring himself to walk upstairs to his own bed, instead, sprawling out on the oversized cushions across from her and eventually falling asleep too. He'd look at the ceiling they wished on stars through, and he tried for the life of him to remember what the hell he must've wished for that night, because it was obviously coming true.

Her constant presence swirled like the sweetness of honey that clung to his tongue. It was a craving that snuck up on him and could never be quenched like with a quart of ice cream where at least he would stop when he hit the bottom and felt the heavy sick feeling churning his insides.

And the way she looked at him—no. He shook his head, ignoring it all from the first time she kissed him. He wanted nothing more than to grasp her and kiss her back all the harder until there was no question of what he possibly thought about her. As of now, they were—well, Jack was never fond of labels anyway.

Of course, as he shoved the furniture out of the way from where rising light streamed in the front window of the house, he wasn't exactly sure what this all classified. Did friends take photos of each other? Did partners of sorts in the downtown Ashton underworld?

Letting out a deep breath, a strand of Jack's unkempt hair blew upward out from his eyes. He hadn't even made time to get a haircut recently he'd been so busy with making himself busy alongside her.

He yanked the refinished settee over the sheet he had laid over the hardwood. That should be good enough.

Jack was helping a friend with her business. That was what this was.

He'd offered to begin with and imagined her taking him up on it. But now, here they were. Running her across the bridge back to Emilie's, Jack helped sneak her in and out before Emilie looked to even be awake for the day. She gathered supplies and set one after another, knowing exactly where they were into one of those oversized tote bags she constantly carried around.

She called Emilie on the ride back to the townhouse she figured was as good as any place to do this, letting her know that she wouldn't be in until later.

The call was a short one. He took one of his own while Katherine went up to get changed, tossing his phone back onto the couch afterward so he could focus.

He looked around the living room before looking down at his jean-clad thighs.

"Calm down."

Professionalism was key. Think of it as another tab in his portfolio he'd been updating on his old website hidden in the back corners of the internet. Jack cleared his throat, rolling his neck as he made sure his tripod was at the right height.

"Can you turn around?"

He was pretty sure, seeing as she was talking to his back, he already was. Still, he froze where he was.

"You realize the day we met, you ended up half naked on the townhouse kitchen floor, right?"

"That was different."

"Was it?" Jack wasn't so sure. For one, this time, they were both completely sober. He took another deep breath. Were his hands... shaking?

"Just turn around."

"I'm going to see you in about a minute anyway."

Katherine popped her head out of the bathroom door and caught Jack's eye.

"Fine." He turned back around all the way this time.

"Thank you."

For a long moment, there was only silence ringing throughout the house.

"Are you coming out now, or am I going to have to come in there and drag you?" Jack asked before adjusting his lens again, mumbling. "Nah, you'd probably enjoy that too much."

"Probably."

His head swung up to meet Kit's nervous eyes. Her mouth pressed together in a small laugh, though.

He didn't think she would come out so quickly, but now he couldn't look away from her. She stood in front of him in a teal and gold embroidered set that looked like it was made specifically for her body from where it hit her shoulders to smoothing around her hips. She fixed one of the clips on her stocking before looking up at him. She did similar makeup to what she wore most nights when they were out. Without her glasses, her eyeliner winged out to either side sharply as the curls of her hair swept to one side.

She looked like a perfect pinup.

Swallowing, he raised an eyebrow. "Would you like to reenact the last two minutes?"

"No. I need to do this before I change my mind."

He was beginning to think the same thing. "That's the spirit."

Slowly, Katherine made her way across from him to the makeshift set.

"You are wearing them and looking like you would rather be anywhere else?"

"I'm nervous."

"Why?"

Looking around the space, she gripped her one elbow, obviously trying to think of a good reason. "I don't know."

"Well, that's a start. Kitten out of worries. Is this a first?"

"Maybe."

"I'm glad I'm here for this." He shot a picture.

"Stop. I wasn't ready."

"Okay, take your seat or stand or do whatever it is you imagine," Jack said. Stepping back around his camera, he cleared his throat again. Focus. He could do that. Looking through his camera, though, to make sure he was set up correctly, he was met with a very stiff model.

"You look like you are in pain."

"Sorry."

"It's fine," Jack said. "Just, talk to me. Relax. Safe space."

She nodded a few times, slowly drifting into less pain and more preparing for school picture day.

"Who were you on the phone with?"

"What?" Jack peeked up at her as she adjusted herself again, trying to get comfortable.

"I heard you talking on the phone. Who was it?"

"Oh, one of them was my sister-in-law calling again. She's still trying to make me go home for my parents' anniversary."

"It hasn't happened yet?"

"Nope." Jack dipped his head back down, looking at his camera and hitting the shutter button while she was relaxed. A second after, she tensed again.

"That wasn't very nice."

"Better than having photos that make your lingerie look like someone has a knife at your back."

She shrugged. Obviously, for once, Jack had a point.

"When is your parents' party?"

"November sixteenth is their anniversary," Jack said.

Kit's eyes widened. "This weekend? As in tomorrow?"

He hummed in confirmation.

"You need to go."

"I don't," Jack said, though they both could hear the sour turn of his voice. Maybe he did, but that isn't what they needed to be talking about right now. "Later."

"You always say that when you talk about your family."

"Most of the time, I mean it. Now, we are focusing on you, however uncomfortable that makes you feel. We are going to get these pictures, and everyone is going to literally buy the clothes off your body. Yeah?"

She nodded once.

"Relax, Kit." Jack smiled at her, a soft, different sort of smile than she'd seen before. Pulling down his camera, he motioned with his hands toward his chest as he breathed.

Kit followed the motion.

"Good girl. It's good to breathe."

"Who knew I was suffering all these years."

"Happy to be of service."

Eyelashes hovering over her cheeks, Katherine giggled.

The lights at the top of his camera flashed.

"I still wasn't ready," Kit pouted as her legs swayed over the side of the lounge.

He snapped another photo.

"Now that is just cruel."

"As the truth often is." Jack paused, giving her a second as he looked her up and down. She could be a lingerie model if she wanted to. A small smile graced her lips and he took another photo. Now they were getting somewhere. "Better."

"Thanks."

He pointed at her to switch the pose. Awkwardly, she turned to her other side, exposing more of where the belt attached to her sheer nude stockings. "Kick up your foot right—there. Don't move."

He focused the camera and started to take the photos again. He was used to live candid photos, but this was different. He glanced at the screen again. Good.

"The shop and now the website; it means a lot to you," Jack mused.

Kit blinked. "It didn't at first."

"When I first came to the shop, all I knew was that I liked to sew. I was decent at it and I knew what my aunt did. I guess I admired her since the first time she ever came to visit me and my father after my mom left when I was young. She was... exotic."

Jack smiled.

"But she and everything back then and even right before I came here, all felt so distant. Even when I was here, I felt like I had walked into another person's life until one day."

"What happened?" Jack asked, continuing to work as she talked. She barely noticed the fixed light flashing at different angles. Jack barely took a look down at the screen before taking another picture.

"I was working on a more complicated set Emilie entrusted me with. It took hours and I took my time trying to make sure I didn't make any mistakes. Emilie was closing up, and that is when I realized. I didn't want to go upstairs. I didn't want to sleep yet. I wanted to stay there in that workroom forever."

"So, you're going to."

"It looks like it," Katherine said softly. "Or at least I am trying to for now."

"What do you mean, for now? Do you have other plans?" Jack teased.

They both knew she didn't. Whenever they'd had a spare

second over the past few weeks working at DuCain with the never-ending list Queen put together and Kit was insistent on following, she was talking about Ashton and the shop. Somewhere in the past few months, she'd settled in.

She knew it too, as she held back a devilish smile.

"What about you?" she asked. "Have any plans? You know, besides going to see your family?"

"I can't just show up there, Kit."

"Why not?"

For a lot of reasons. Most of his good ones just weren't presenting themselves.

"You have none."

"I do."

"Sure." She grinned.

"Go, change and put on another. I think we got a few good ones."

Popping up from the settee, she skirted past Jack with a scrunch of her nose. "You have no good reasons."

Without thinking, Jack turned around and slapped her on the ass. She yelped. Turning back to him, her mouth opened in shock.

"Go."

This time she didn't tease, moving back to the other room to switch out. This time, she had a baby pink number with a matching robe. The next was a deep midnight blue silk, simple and fitted.

Taking the camera off the tripod, he looped the strap around his neck. He preferred to shoot this way, up close and personal. Maybe he could get some shots with her more off guard.

That—right there. He took two more pictures; her eyes met his through the screen.

"Don't look at me like that." He shut his eyes.

"Like what?"

"Like I hung the stars or something." He smirked, and his

honey eyes sparkled when they peeked at her. "Remember now, I'm just Queen's sidekick with a good camera. At your service—"

Kit cut him off with a roll of her eyes. Leaning forward, he knew exactly what she was thinking. The two of them were so close. Yet, she didn't move.

He took another photo, barely looking at where it was aimed. "What?"

"You must be kidding," was all she said. "Jack, to those people at DuCain, the way they looked at you—"

"The way you looked at me."

She didn't deny that. It would only cause stuttering, she was sure. "You are basically king."

"I'll take that from you, but nah. I think Reed had that title once in the very beginning of their reign and she never gave it to anyone else."

"Fine then," she conceded. "Jack. Farmer. Sidekick. Photographer—"

"And one of DuCain's own kinky therapists, at your service."

Kit laughed as she looked down at her thighs, becoming less stiff as Jack continued his movements, coming closer to her. "You know, that is how I always felt, at least maybe a little at first when you looked at me like that."

"Like what?"

"When you smirked at me."

Something in his chest stuttered.

She smiled as if daring to show him, baring her teeth.

He did the same with his own lips, spreading them wide and curling his lip in tease.

They were so close she knew that he could hear her whisper.

"Like that," Kit breathed. "Would you hurt me?"

Jack paused, smirk faltering at the question, but he didn't run or move from where he was frozen in front of her. "Would you want me to?"

He waited for her to answer, but the nerves and intrigue that coursed through him told him all the words she wished she only dared to say, she knew, clear as day.

She tore her eyes from his. Turning over to look at him over her one shoulder, she did not answer.

"Look at me."

Jack reached up, gently brushing a carefully placed piece of hair away from where it laid across her temple.

The sweetness of the gesture alone made her turn back.

"Would that make you happy?" Jack asked. His eyes studied only her face as he sat back on the sheet. His heart stopped pounding from nerves with her all of a sudden. "You want to play? Like we almost did that one day?"

"You did say..." Kit swallowed before forcing herself to say the ridiculous words. "I'm surprisingly good at playing games."

A sharp grin began to spread, ear to ear. "Only we wouldn't be playing just any kind of game then, Kitten."

With wide eyes, she seemed suddenly very aware of that.

But she didn't stop. She taunted him, mimicked him with that grin he once didn't believe could put a spell on anyone.

He had to revoke that statement.

Jack snapped another picture of her expression.

But maybe it put one right on him.

His chin jerked up. "Fine. Go put on another one. We do have more to shoot, don't we?"

She froze and stared at him.

"Do I have to repeat myself? Or did you decide you aren't up to what you started after all?"

Kit stood, eyes on him, before casting them down. "No. You don't have to repeat yourself."

Jack's eyes burned through her. What were they doing?

It felt like breathing. "Good. Go."

Pressing to her toes, she stood in front of Jack and turned on her heel.

She did as she was told.

. . .

SHE GATHERED each set together and changed into them with an ease the creator should have. The last of the pieces were simple, easy to make a dozen or more of in a sitting, but still, there was something special about them the moment they were put on. Clipping garters to stockings and adjusting straps an inch up or down, and suddenly, she was transformed in front of Jack's eyes.

Sit, stand, kneel—laugh.

He ordered the simple expressions one after another and Katherine laughed for Jack and he laughed with her right afterward.

Photo after photo he took until he saw that she didn't realize when he was taking them, when he let the camera fall to the side to adjust the lights or help her into another layer. At the end, he laced her up in a corset just like the one she'd once thought he had no idea how to fit. With a jerk at the end, he pulled the ribbons tight and smirked at the tiny gasp she made.

"Turn around."

She did, feeling the final photo taken against her back.

Then his hand slid around her waist, turning her around to him again.

"They are all beautiful, Kitten," Jack whispered.

"Thank you."

"No." Jack shook his head, grinning again. He couldn't stop himself anymore. Whether or not the world would see her in these pieces, he did first, and she had to know. "You're beautiful. When will you even begin to understand that?"

Licking her lips, Katherine stared up at him.

When did they get here?

When weren't they? Katherine's heart pounded in her chest. Warm breath touched his lips, she was so close. Staring at the dark pink painted on her plush lips, Jack wordlessly lifted his eyes from her mouth to her nose to finally her warm eyes. He took a moment to study each in case he startled her.

He was pretty sure she had begun to scare him a while ago.

Weeks—No. Months ago.

All he had to do now was lean forward and...

His thumb swept the lilac lines under her eyes. Hers widening at the touch.

"Kitten?" Jack forced himself not to move. He couldn't do this. Not unless—it was her choice. She decided. "Truth or dare?"

Her breath caught, unsure of what to say.

Dare.

Dare.

Jack cocked his head to the side, watching her struggle, panning out each situation in that stuffed-up head of hers. So many emotions bent his ribs and stung his lips, sent feeling down his stomach so low—

Katherine's lips hung there, parted.

Say dare, he nearly begged her, but instead, she said nothing.

Fine.

"Come home with me?"

CHAPTER TWENTY-THREE

*S*he thought he was going to kiss her.

Dare. It was such a simple word. Such a simple stupid word, yet for some reason, she could not work it past the back of her tongue.

Dare.

How hard was that? How hard was it for her brain to give her a little leeway and let her live life? All of a sudden, out of everything in the world, Jack Carver, the man of her summer infatuation, was about to kiss her and all she could think was, oh my god, Jack is about to kiss her and they had such a good few weeks together and what if this ruined everything?

Her kissing him clearly didn't, but him kissing her—she wasn't sure she could ever look at him again.

She was already having trouble thinking about him when she went back to pack her bag for when he was set to pick her up the next day. She was too nervous already to ask what the weather would be like or how farm-like his farm really was, so she had about twenty outfits stuffed in a duffel bag like some sort of anxiety-induced magic trick.

She couldn't kiss Jack and now she was going home with him to meet his family.

Closing her eyes, she took a deep breath the way Jack showed her how to, deep and slow as she focused on what she was doing now in the shop. One step at a time, she started her latest corset again, most of it already constructed from the other day.

She didn't need Emilie to tell her that it was time.

Emilie herself watched from afar, doing simple tasks at the register or at her desk before going back upstairs to nap after turning the sign to closed for the day. Katherine continued her work, trying not to think of anything else and almost succeeded as she hummed to whatever music she left on repeat, echoing over the cold hard surfaces. She laced up the skeleton of the corset on herself, and it fit.

She laced it back up on the mannequin and it held its shape, gently tightening just like Emilie's always did in an hourglass. Then she got to work. Pinching her fingers, she threaded darker shades of the color she already picked for the corset into the thick fabric. She braided and swirled the design and gently tucked crystals into spaces to catch the light.

Her hands ached, but after the past week, months of failed attempts, it was done. She did it. Her corset—Avril's corset already claimed—was finished.

Stepping back, Katherine felt pressure at the back of her eyes as she took in the final product set in a stunning emerald green. It might not have been Emilie-quality yet, but it was close.

"It's beautiful, Kit." A voice behind her spoke up.

Emilie stood in the darkened entryway, looking at the corset with soft eyes.

Katherine swallowed, stepping aside for her aunt to stand next to her. "It is?"

"It's perfect."

"You don't mean that."

For one thing, it might've been the most Emilie had said to

her in the past few weeks, besides critique and reminders. Katherine bit her bottom lip as she thought about how long that really was.

"No," Emilie said softly, bringing her red-painted fingernails to her lips. That hand then slowly found its way to Katherine's shoulder. "I do."

Katherine looked up at her with a hesitant smile.

"I'm sorry I've been such a—" Emilie cut herself off with a shake of her head. "There's no excuse. I know the shop has been up and down, and I know that you have ideas that are only looking out for the greatness of what this place could be. I'm just not… I'm not ready to see it all go yet, how it is now, you know?"

Katherine wasn't quite sure what her aunt meant, but she nodded all the same.

"Forgive me?"

"Of course," said Katherine. She was never the one mad at Emilie, not really.

"Look at what you've created." Her aunt gave her a gentle shake. Both of them looked at the corset another time in the fluorescent light before she hit the switch, turning them both toward the stairs. It was late, much later than Katherine had thought it was for her or Emilie to be up. "I told you you'd get it."

"Sure, you did."

"I did! You did make some ugly attempts though."

She couldn't argue with that.

"So, you've been packing to go with Jack tomorrow?"

"After I run my rounds at Rosin to make sure they are set for the weekend."

Emilie gave a single appreciative nod. "Have fun. Be nice to him. I can only imagine him going back home after so long must be difficult without everything else on his shoulders."

"I figured you would be giving me the warning against him."

She shook her head, flashing a timid smile. Her? "Where would the fun be in that?"

If Katherine could keep her eyes open, it would be a miracle. Her nerves still pulsed against her, but at the very least, were dulled at the utter exhaustion layered over her body. No wonder Emilie was feeling so tired again when they went upstairs this morning, even if she did look like she was coming back down with something again.

"Ow, watch it."

Katherine glanced up at one of the girls she just stuck with a pin. She couldn't remember her name. Calla? Lisa? Something with an A at the end, she was pretty sure. "Sorry, lovely."

She patted her hip after another moment.

"Good to go. Take it off carefully and I'll have it altered for you."

"Thanks, Kit."

She gave the dancer a small smile as she stood back up, stretching her back as she went.

"Kit, I was looking for you."

Turning over her shoulder, Katherine prepared herself when Cherry appeared, walking toward her. "What's going on?"

Cherry waved her off. "Nothing huge. Just wanted to check in on where you were with all of Queen's arrangements. Anything else I should know about?"

Katherine shook her head slowly. "As of now, no. The girls have already started to inform me of what they are wearing if they need anything altered in time. Two group numbers and three singles."

Cherry nodded without correction.

"Everything else is all set and ready for New Year's besides some minor details that will be dealt with, like setting up and getting everyone where they are supposed to be. Marketing starts next week. Oh! If someone comes by with the decorations I found in DuCain's storage while I am gone this weekend, please sign for them and then hide them away."

Cherry gave a dip of her head as she disappeared back to her office.

Knowing she wasn't one for send-offs, Katherine went back to collecting her bags. She checked the final mark on her to-do list. Since this morning, she hadn't stopped. She'd opened the shop, made deliveries and sent other orders to the post office, checked in at DuCain to make sure Evie had the details there in hand, closed the shop when Emilie looked far too pale, and still somehow made it to Rosin for last-minute dress changes and mends.

She let out a loose sigh and flung the extra duffel bag she brought to Rosin with her, knowing that she would've never made it back to the shop in time.

The Jeep idled along the curb of Rosin. Jack beeped the horn once when she yanked open the passenger side door.

"Hey."

"Hi." Katherine hauled herself in. Shutting the door took too much effort, but she managed it, luxuriating in the heat flaring the open vents.

"I got you a tea from Keys." Jack lifted the cup in the side cup holder so she knew which was hers. "I told them to leave the bag in."

"Thanks."

He peeked up at Katherine, holding her things against her chest still, buckling herself in. "Everything good?"

She nodded, though even she could feel how tight her brow creased. "Just tired. Emilie isn't feeling well again and is holed up in her room. She told me not to, but I called her friend to come in and check on her at some point today, so I hope she did. It might be the first weekend of an intentional closing for the shop."

Jack bit his lip as his fingers flexed against the steering wheel.

It was only then that Katherine realized that she was looking at his lips.

The almost-kiss, yet again, flared to mind. It was obvious now; Jack just needed a friend to go home with him. That had to be it. Jack was a very touchy-feely guy, after all.

Katherine thought of Pen and Avril and Evie... her.

"You know, we don't have to go."

"No," Katherine responded immediately, snapping herself out of her internal tirade. "We're going. It's fine. Emilie has been on and off sick for a few months. You know that. She should be fine, but between you and me, I'm pretty sure she needs to go for a check or something after all those years."

"All those years?" Jack repeated, pulling out onto the street and heading away from the river.

"I saw pictures of her when she was about fifteen, if not younger, smoking." She sighed with an exhausted sounding laugh. "Crazy to think of now, huh?"

Coming to a stop at a red light, he glanced at all her bags she began to stuff by her feet. "You bring your laptop and stuff with you?"

"Yeah, I figured we could finish the last bits of what needs to be sent out or verified with Nik later, then we are basically done until closer to the event." Katherine gave an uneasy smile. She tried to fix it again, but not before he noticed.

"You sure you are okay?"

"Yeah." She reached back down, searching for her laptop so they could get it all out of the way now. "Why would you ask?"

"You look like you are about to freak out."

"I am not." She scoffed. "Going to freak out."

"Okay, then."

"I said, I'm not."

"I said, okay then."

She flipped open her laptop and waited for the screen to turn on. "You seem worried, though. Are you nervous to go home?"

His head fell to the one side as they continued to drive. "You could say that."

"They invited you to this anniversary party, didn't they? They must want to see you."

"My sister-in-law, Leann, did the inviting, technically. She brought it up a few phone calls ago, and according to her, that is basically an engraved invitation. My family isn't..." Jack looked for the right word to pop out of the windshield. "Formal."

"What do you mean?"

"It means, along with not going home in the past eight years, only one person reached out to me after they found out where I was and what I was doing after I left the institute. Only my older brother, who wondered what the fuck I was doing with my life, came and found me once, but no one else. He and his wife call me and I video chat with them and their kids occasionally, like on holidays and stuff. My mom calls me once every few months to ask the same questions when she remembers she has another child. How am I? What have I been up to? Am I happy?"

Jack drifted off at that last question.

Katherine almost asked it herself, but she didn't.

Was he happy?

Katherine thought about her own family. She had a mother who left and a father who ran out what felt like years ago but was only months. He never called. A lot of the time, growing up, Katherine questioned whether he even thought that she was his daughter, really.

For the first time, she felt like she actually had a family when she moved in with Emilie, and it was strange, from the way Katherine overcompensated to Emilie only giving her well-meaning looks when she cleaned the shop for the third time in a single day.

"She also used to keep me updated on everything else."

"On the farm life?"

"A lot happens during farming season, thank you very much,"

Jack said. "That is why my parents' anniversary is so far into November. They got married after the last few weeks of harvest. And the end of farming season is basically like solstice, but for farmers."

"Solstice?" Katherine questioned. "Like in the summer?"

"And winter. Don't knock it until you try it. Queen always throws a huge solstice bash." Jack gave a wicked smile.

"What was that for?"

"I'm remembering the first solstice Queen threw."

"That good?"

"She rented a house out in the middle of nowhere and everyone turned up naked by the time the sun came back up in the middle of some field nearby, so I guess you could say so."

Katherine had to look away from meeting his eyes but couldn't help herself from developing a wide grin with him, trying to keep her teeth from showing. "I want to go to the next one."

"Yeah?" He raised an eyebrow.

"Don't be so surprised, Ripper."

He rolled his eyes at the name.

"How many did you say there were of you, again?" Katherine asked, turning the subject back.

"I have three brothers. So, four of us total," Jack said. "I think my mom tried for a girl after my younger brother, Jace, but she miscarried when I was about seventeen."

"Wait, what are your brother's names?"

He paused as his eyes flicked to her as he sucked his cheek.

"You all have J names."

"Jed, Jeremy, Jack, and Jace."

Katherine pressed her lips together. "Those are some messed up J names."

"I didn't pick them."

"Jed?"

"Jedidiah."

"No." Her eyes widened. That poor child—or not a child, anymore.

"My mother insists that she was sleeping when they came in with the birth certificate."

"Are their names J's too?"

"No." Jack began to laugh at Katherine's brightened interest. "Brian and Emily."

"Like my Emilie?"

"With a Y."

Katherine tipped her head. She was pretty sure she could remember all those names. Jed, Jeremy, Jace, and Jack.

"In the fall though, sometimes, neighbors would just pop over for tools they were missing as they cleaned up their places for winter, or for a beer. It was basically like Christmas. Once, when I was a kid, we set off fireworks out from the cornstalks that weren't cut down yet. Dangerous, do not recommend. We almost set the whole field on fire."

Katherine couldn't stop smiling, shaking her head. Listening to Jack's childhood sounded like a pleasant storybook. "Four boys kept things interesting."

"Oh, definitely." Jack granted, deep in thought, before he blinked. "What do we still have to go over?"

"Like I said, not much. There is just that list I gave Evie. Do you know if she got to any of it?"

"Most of it when I asked her today."

Katherine could live with that. She made a note of it next to the document.

"What about the poster designer?" asked Jack.

"I just got the file sent to me this morning. Want to see?"

At his nod, Katherine turned the screen toward him to show the poster. It mimicked the past years but kept with their art deco and gold theme she'd been going with for the decorations. Rosin already appeared in a similar aesthetic, so it wasn't too much of a stretch.

"A few minor adjustments need to be made, but he said if we had any issues, it wouldn't be an issue, so…"

"It looks really good. You didn't do that, did you?"

She was pleased he thought she could. "Oh, no."

"Who'd you get to do it?"

"I sent out a mass email to the institute's graphic design department to see if anyone would do it for internship credit."

"Smart."

"Yeah, the girl I met at the market that day, Gina, got back to me about it a few days ago. Turns out college students will do anything for internship credit."

Jack snorted.

"What?"

"Nothing."

Katherine narrowed her eyes. "You're lying."

"I am," Jack agreed. "Come on, let me have at least one bedtime story to tell you one day."

Thinking about it, Katherine shook her head. "You'll have to think of another. Tell me."

"Kit."

"It's a long car ride." She opened her eyes wide and stared at him.

"Fine," Jack conceded, though he tried not to sound happy about it. "But you owe me a deeply embarrassing story."

It couldn't be that hard for her to think of one. She waved him on.

"So, you know that I was at the institute."

"Of course."

"And thus, I too, would do anything for extra credit. Or in this case, some extra cash," Jack began. Slowly, they made their way out of the city and onto the connecting highway, crammed with other cars trying to escape for the weekend. "My internship was pretty casual. I hung lights and helped out doing random tasks on a set. Some guy, though, gave me his card and told me to call him if I ever needed some odd job work."

Shutting her laptop, Katherine continued to listen, getting more comfortable without the pressure on her lap.

"When I dropped out, I needed any job. I didn't care if it was odd or not, but I ended up for a good while setting up lighting equipment on adult film sets."

"No," Katherine feigned a gasp. She couldn't even imagine. "You worked on porn?"

His eyebrows flared, but didn't deny it. "I was there at the strangest hours helping these people, especially after Marley kicked me to the curb. He has a strict student workers policy, and he wasn't willing to break it just for me. I was also sneaking in to sleep in the back corner where he never noticed me for a good while. After that I crashed on couches and went to work on any set that needed hands. It wasn't long, of course, until—"

Immediately, Katherine could see where this was going.

"They noticed you're beautiful."

The word seemed to startle Jack out of his story. He stopped and stared at Katherine for a long moment. Long enough that she casually glanced away before looking back at him with a tilt of her head to say, *go on.*

"We both know what happened next. Or what almost happened. I debated what I was going to do, considering how good the pay was. It was the same day I met Queen," Jack said. "She got me into DuCain. I'm grateful for it. It is one rock I was glad not to have turned. Meant to be behind the camera."

Katherine gave him an amused smile when he looked at her again.

"Plus, I'm sure then nosy little seamstresses would've found my online stardom, and then I would no longer have this fun story to tell." Jack shrugged. "I found out too that photography wasn't the only thing I loved in the city."

"Performing," Katherine whispered, understanding part of DuCain's appeal to Jack now. "You do have one hell of a smile."

"One hell of a smile?" It might've been the first time Katherine noticed him blush.

So she nodded, keeping him that way. It was a good color on him. "Among other things."

He rolled his eyes at her.

"No, though. Honestly, like I said. It was one of the first things I ever noticed about you."

"Really?"

"Yeah. I always knew if you were there at DuCain when I stopped in." Katherine giggled. How different she was now. "Once, I saw you and Avril across the room, but first, I heard you laugh so loud, not caring who heard you. Whoever looked, you gave this look to right back, this smug grin."

Katherine gazed off, remembering that moment of him and Avril standing in the shadows, so perfect together. She thought about if she could've ever been someone to stand next to them and not look out of place. Could she have been someone to laugh that joyfully?

She stood there with her package still in hand and waited until Nik finally walked by and paused at the newcomer with a confused look on her face.

"Yeah, you're probably right," Katherine admitted.

"About what?"

"I would've found the videos."

Jack barked a loud laugh that filled the Jeep.

Time moved slowly as they drove.

Katherine forced her eyes to remain open. She squinted at the pothole-ridden road they made their way off the highway onto. A billboard asked her to text a blurry number to get closer to God.

She took her glasses off her face before rubbing her eyes. She set the frames in the cup holder as she leaned back against the headrest.

Jack looked forward, one hand on the steering wheel, the other casually itching the thin layer of stubble that appeared along his jaw.

Katherine reached toward the static-filled radio, music cutting in and out.

"You look tired," Jack said softly.

"A little."

"You can close your eyes if you want. I'll wake you when we get close."

"I couldn't."

"Sleep, Kit."

"Promise you'll wake me?"

"Promise."

CHAPTER TWENTY-FOUR

*T*he day Jack stepped off the bus in Ashton, he thought he had never been so in love with a place before. He hadn't been to many places, granted, but still. There was something about Ashton that was just like his mother had said, the city where she spent only a year at community college before coming home. The air thrummed through you.

Oddly, Jack felt a similar sensation inside of himself as he pulled off the highway. He remembered the windy dirt roads like they were his first true love. Glancing over, his one arm stretched over the wheel, Kit lounged in an awkward position in the seat next to him. The streaks of occasional light flew over her cheeks before disappearing behind them both.

He hadn't been home in eight years. Now he was here. With her.

Reaching over, his hand gently slid over her exposed leg. She had to be cold. Usually, she at least wore her stockings beneath even though he doubted they did anything for warmth's sake.

"Kit. Kit," he said softly with a thumb on her knee. He pulled back at her sharp intake of breath. "We are almost there."

Openmouthed, Kit yawned before she sat up. "Where are we?"

As if on cue, Jack slowed the Jeep to see the fence in front of him, and written on it in stone, *Carver Farms*.

"The middle of nowhere," Jack said anyway. Tires jumped over the dirt and rocks he could see in his headlights. The Jeep coasted into the corner of the driveway where the darkened farmhouse came into view. Turning the key to shut off the engine, Jack let out a long, practiced breath with it. "Well, we're here."

Still, suddenly he was frozen, unable to move from right here in the front seat.

Kit reached over the center console and undid his seat belt for him.

"Thanks."

It was almost midnight, and it looked like almost all the lights were off inside the house he'd once called his home and had snuck into at least a few dozen times before.

"You worried?" Jack asked as he stared at it in front of him.

"Yes."

He pried his eyes away from the structure to her. "You're supposed to say no to make me feel better. You know, for the moral support you spoke of coming with me for?"

"I've decided you probably should've brought someone else then. In case you haven't noticed, Jack, I have pretty terrible social anxiety, among the rest of my anxiety-inducing quirks, like the fact I am basically your lingerie designing sex maiden in a small town. I came from a small town—maybe not this small, but smaller and all in all, it didn't turn out the best as you also might've noticed."

He raised his eyebrows.

"Sex maiden?"

She shrugged. "I'm not feeling the most creative. I'm hungry and also terrified of what is going to happen when they look at me."

"Don't worry, they'll probably not even notice you're here once they see the prodigal son return."

"Is that supposed to make me feel better?"

He didn't know. It wasn't helping him much as he pushed open the car door and strode around the front end.

A cat appeared out of the corner of his eye. Kit had to nearly jump over it so as not to trip. She watched as it trotted off to another side of the wide driveway.

"I'm at your childhood home."

It sure looked that way.

"I'm here. At your house. With your family. With you," Kit repeated as they made it to the front door. "Do they even know I'm coming?"

"I'm not even sure they think I am coming anymore, Kit." He gave a tug on the locked door to prove his point. They never locked up.

"You're joking."

He was not. He doubted his wonderful sister-in-law, Leann, though he would come with enough conviction to bring it up.

Taking another deep breath, Jack glanced at Katherine. With only that look, her hand shot out to grab his that had been dangling at his side. Jack looked down at it, how easily her fingers fit between his.

She gently squeezed.

"Too late to turn back, huh?"

"Probably."

He knocked.

"HI, MOM."

Emily Carver was a petite woman, light hair streaked with even lighter strands of gray. Her eyes were transfixed and wide as she looked at Jack, frozen for a long moment in shock before she said anything. She lifted a hand as if pointing to something. "I heard the door and I thought—I thought it was Jace coming back."

"Sorry to disappoint," Jack murmured beside Katherine. She watched him carefully as a slightly shaken breath escaped him.

"I—we weren't sure if you were coming."

Releasing Katherine's hand that his had been slowly constricting around, Jack took the few steps past the house threshold and wrapped his arms around his mom in a hug. "Happy almost anniversary."

After another second, Jack's mom's cold disposition disappeared. Her arms wrapped tightly around Jack, hands just touching. "It's good to see you."

"It's good to see you too, Ma."

Katherine looked down at her shoes, wondering if she could blend into the stone siding. She didn't want to look at such an intimate moment. It felt like intruding. When she peeked back up, Jack was reaching toward her.

"Mom, this is my friend, Kit."

Friend.

"Hi—hello." Katherine stumbled forward with her words. She extended her hand, dropped it. "It's really nice to meet you."

"Nice to meet you." Jack's mother studied Kit's face. "You can call me Emily."

"She's Emilie's niece. She actually just came to the city to work with her in the summer."

"Oh! My old friend," Emily said, understanding. After the exclamation, though, her face turned sad. "I keep meaning to visit."

Katherine's eyes sparked for the slightest moment, confusion clouding over as her lips thinned.

"She would love if you came to the city to visit sometime," she said slowly, each word after another.

"I'll have to," Jack's mom said, nodding.

"Where are Dad and the guys?" Jack asked, noting the empty house behind his mom.

"Oh," she sighed. "For your father's birthday and anniversary gifts, all he wanted from them was to go camping out back with him."

Jack paused, looking around as he took in the darkness of the house and his mother standing in her robe. "You're kidding."

"I'm not. That is where they are. Out in the woods, somewhere." Emily nodded back toward the other side of the house. "I doubt they got far, though. Jeremy was out earlier tonight and met up with them, he was already half in his cups and Jace was throwing a fit about going out to begin with."

"Jed?"

"The only one who has ever put up with your father, as you know," said Emily, her final words dragging.

Jack huffed a sort of dejected laugh. "Yeah."

"I'm sure—you should go and join them. Like I said, I doubt they went far off the fields."

"Your friend can stay here," she added, turning her attention to Kit. "If you'd rather?"

Kit looked back to Jack wide-eyed as if unsure what to say.

Trust her to make him want to laugh right now. "She'll come with me, Ma."

After another second, his mom nodded, this time at Katherine. "We'll have to further meet each other later, then. See you in the morning, both of you."

"Night."

Slowly his mother began to close the door. She stopped halfway. "Jack."

He looked back at his mom.

"I'm happy you came home."

With that, she closed the door, and Jack followed Katherine as she padded down the front porch steps.

Once they started to move around the back of the house

where fields of flattened ground and pasture extended, Katherine lifted her head to Jack. "That didn't go too terribly, did it?"

"No," Jack said, his voice a tad lighter. "It didn't. But, of course, that was Mom."

"I didn't know that your mother was friends with my Emilie."

"Yeah, that's how I knew her in the city, remember."

Katherine paused, thinking for a long moment over when Jack came to pick her up or when Emilie mentioned him and Avril as if second nature. She nodded. "Right."

"Do you need anything out of the Jeep before we go and see how far out my dad decided to camp for the night? I don't think it should be too far, but I have a feeling I need to show my face, or else I'll have more to repent for in the morning. We don't have to stay, just for a little."

"Okay," Katherine agreed. She shrugged the loose tote over her shoulder with her more important things she always carried at her side. Her thin coat scrunched up toward her neck at the movement. "I have my bag."

He snorted. "Of course, you do."

"Are you making fun of my tote?"

He raised an eyebrow as they walked. *"If you use my fabric scissors, I will cut you."*

"But not with these scissors," Katherine finished, mostly believing it after picking up her own mini pair, also in her bag from an antique stand at the farmer's market last weekend before they shut down for the winter.

She was very fond of them.

She smirked at his sudden glee, however. Once they found the rest of his family, she wasn't sure how long it would last. "It is a very serious offense, Jack."

He shook his head, and even Katherine couldn't help but laugh. The sound was full and light through the cool air.

All the oddly printed totes were another procurement from Emilie, but Katherine liked them from the funny quotes to plain shopping ones. They all worked well enough and fit everything she needed to have throughout the day. Her arms could only hold so many immediate deliveries.

"You'll be sorry when you ever need anything out of it."

"I'm sure I will be," Jack said as they continued to walk. He stuck his hands into his pockets, slowing down so that she could keep up with him, seeming to know exactly where they were going.

It was hard for her to imagine growing up here in the middle of nothing. She could hear the wind and cracks of branches underfoot, but otherwise silent.

"Hey, Kit."

She looked up at him.

His lip curled gently at the corner of his mouth. "Look up."

Tilting her chin toward the sky, she did. Across her vision was a black sky filled with stars.

Her lips parted at the miraculous sight.

She shook her head as she looked back down at him. "What did you wish for that night?"

"What night?"

He knew exactly which one she meant.

His teeth flashed in the darkness. "I thought you said you didn't want me to tell you."

"I changed my mind." For one thing, after that night, she figured he'd never speak to her again. It would be a memory, just for her.

Now they were… here.

"A lot of things, I guess," Jack said, looking at her. "Life. For the longest time, I felt like I was just here, stagnant. I wanted to be a photographer and at some point, I became that person on the opposite side of the lens, waiting for a flash that never came. I'm closer to thirty than twenty-five and suddenly—I don't know what I wished for. I wished for anything. I wished for what I needed, I guess."

Just like he dreamed that day at Artist's Quarter.

He nudged her. "Stop it."

"What?"

"I can hear the gears turning," he said. "What did you wish for?"

Katherine opened her mouth before she stopped, glancing at him.

"What? I showed you mine, now you show me yours."

She rolled her eyes, but Katherine thought back to when she wished. Long after the stars fell from their highest point, the sun was already mostly up, but she figured that it wasn't much worse than wishing on a ceiling as she leaned over the edge of the bridge overlooking Ash river the next day.

Turning her gaze back to the townhouse, she thought of Avril and Jack and the night she had with them, and for the first time in her whole existence, it was the first time, for just a second, Katherine didn't feel alone.

So, she wished the most ridiculous of wishes that she was certain would never come true. Not for her.

She almost said it now. What did she wish for?

You.

A yell cut her off.

It was something between a shout and a screech as the sound of leaves and branches crunched underneath what was inexplicably a person, feet in front of them.

"What the hell happened?" Jack screamed right back into the darkness. He stomped toward the silhouette from where Katherine froze in her tracks.

"Jack?"

"Jace?" Jack reached out a hand that was slapped away.

"Jace?" another voice called out ahead of them. More branches crunched until a larger figure stepped in front of them. Katherine's eyes began to adjust, seeing the similarity in height with the man with a tight haircut around his ears where Jack's had begun to grow out, or else Katherine might've guessed they were twins.

Instead, they were just brothers.

The three of them.

"Jack?"

"Jed." Jack looked up from Jace until all three of them were looking at the eldest brother, eyes flicking back and forth.

Both of them seemed to ignore the brother still on the ground, grunting through his teeth as he reached down toward his lower leg. Katherine moved toward him, and even in the dark, there was no mistaking the slick shadows smearing his pants.

Jed, on the other hand, stepped over the two of them, throwing his arm around Jack.

"Welcome home, little brother."

Jack gave a stiff laugh. "You didn't think I was coming."

"Leann told me, but no." Jed clapped him on the back. "Good to see you anyway."

Jack reached a hand around to the back of his head.

Katherine kneeled down in front of Jace, his eyes, when he looked up at her, were the same molten honey as Jack's. She swallowed at how they glowed. "Are you all right?"

"No, I am not fucking all right," Jace snapped. His one hand gripped and stretched around air with pain. "Fuck!"

"Looks like a rock caught you." Jed crouched down beside Katherine and inspected the gash. Blood gushed down Jace's leg. It looked like someone had sliced a chunk out of his calf.

Jace swatted Jed's hand away.

"Well, don't touch it! Shit!" Closing his eyes, he attempted to take a deep cleansing breath but only came out with expletives.

"You're fine. What a welcome home, hey Jack?" Jed said, waving him over.

Without a question, the two men each threw one of their younger brother's arms around their shoulders, hauling him back off the ground. As they did, another stream of blood dripped onto the leaf-covered ground.

"We aren't far from camp," Jed explained. Both of them were doing a better job of ignoring the protests coming from Jace than Katherine was. Slowly she followed behind, catching Jack glance back to her to make sure she was still there. "You two came looking for us?"

"We stopped at the house first."

"Figures," Jed replied. He hauled Jace farther up on his shoulder.

It granted him a hiss.

Jack looked straight ahead. In the near distance, the light from a fire began to light up the trees, and a cleared path. "Is he in a good mood?"

"Considering that his one son is piss drunk after coming home late from a party down the way and another one is coming back to camp with more complaints than he already openly announced on the way out here," Jed recounted with a shrug. "Could be worse."

Again, Jack glanced back at Katherine. His eyes widened slightly.

She bit her lip so as not to smile. So far, she liked Jed. She liked him a lot.

"So, what happened out there?" The question came from the burlier man across the flames of the campsite. Turning around, whatever else he was about to say died on his lips.

The two brothers, with the youngest slung over their shoulders, paused on the edge of the site.

Jack visibly swallowed as Brian stared at them. "Hi, Dad."

For a long moment, there was only silence and the crackle of fire.

"Jack."

Without another word between the group, Jed spoke up, guiding Jack to help set Jace down at the edge of the fire. The flames and lanterns were bright. In this light, Jace's leg looked angry behind ripped jeans.

Brian walked with them as he settled against one of the over-turned logs. "What happened now?"

"Jace apparently had a little accident," explained Jed. "I sadly was not there to see it."

"Accident?" Jace seethed. "These two came out of nowhere. I thought they were a bear or something."

"He fell," Jed finished simply. "On a rock."

Kneeling down beside his youngest son, Brian whistled as he started to roll up Jace's pant leg. For a minute, Katherine was sure he was going to get a boot to the face. "Must've been one heck of a fall."

"Clumsy again, Jace?" The final brother, Katherine knew to be Jeremy, sat up from the darkness somewhere across the fire. Long, dark strands of hair fell across his brow. "This is why I told you all before that I would have been the better choice to help and get more dry firewood. And Jack is way too short to be a bear. Or did you think it was Pat wandering the trees after you?"

"Shut up. You're drunk."

"Still," Jeremey said, voice slow and even.

Katherine pressed her lips together not to laugh. It was relatively easy when she glanced back to Jace, who was still seething. Her mouth went dry at the wound. A perfect slice trailed up his calf before he sounded off another round of expletives into the trees.

"Jesus!" Jace screeched.

Brian pressed his weight into the open space with what looked like a shirt.

Beside her, the sudden pressure of Jack leaned up against her. She noted his unease.

Katherine nudged her hand against his, without waiting for permission to slip hers into his like they did that day out in Ashton on their adventure together, she gave it a squeeze.

Brian's face contorted as the blood flowing from the long gash down Jace's leg slowed, but did not stop. "This is going to need stitches, Jace."

"Are you going to have to take him to the hospital?" Katherine suddenly spoke up.

The three faces in front of her all turned as if just noticing she was there.

Brian looked around to his other sons, a dry laugh escaping his lips. "Anyone here have a needle?"

Jed huffed a similar laugh.

So did Jack, somewhere in his chest that rocked against her.

Only did Katherine raise her hand, trying to mimic the sound in jest, not noticing until Brian turned back to his middle son at her side how serious he indeed was.

CHAPTER TWENTY-FIVE

"Not so happy about that magic bag of yours now, are you?"

"Shut up," Katherine breathed after she pulled out her sewing kit from the very bottom of her tote, now sitting in damp dirt beside her and a log. Mud cushioned her knees as she kneeled down.

Jace was still going on about something. At this point, she managed to tune him out, mostly anyway.

At the very least, she knew he was still conscious despite the slightly oozing wound.

"Are you sure you can do this, Kitten?" Jack asked, more serious this time. His voice sounded as if he stood a few feet away rather than leaning over her shoulder. "It's a distance from the house, but we could still pack him up and carry him there."

And then what?

At her stunned expression, Brian tactfully informed her that the nearest hospital was a good hour away, not to mention the walk back with Jace. Out of the five men, Jace was by far the tallest. The hospital would just piece him back together with a needle and string anyway—just like she could. In theory.

Closing her eyes, she focused on her hand not shaking as she held the needle. After letting it heat over the open fire, Jack's father threaded it for her. She wasn't sure she could have kept her hand steady enough to do it herself anyway.

"Shouldn't we, I don't know, numb him or something?"

"With what?" Jed asked.

Promptly, Brian handed over a wide flat bottle from a bag labeled Supplies. The bottle was also clearly labeled. Bourbon. Without further ado, he doused a healthy amount over the open wound.

Jace's low howl echoed through the space until silence settled back around them.

Katherine's lips parted from the shock alone.

Next to her, she was pleased to see that Jack looked the same, his skin turning a strange pallor in the glow of the fire.

Brian only took a deep breath and nodded. Taking a sip of the liquor, he passed it down to his son, who was still breathing heavily. "That'll work. Drink up, Jacey."

Who were these people?

She had met people who liked to be beaten for a living, as well as the rest of Ashton's underworld. She met drag queens, bikers, catcallers, and art students who thought two highly of their coffee orders. Yet, her hand was still shaking.

"Close your eyes for me, Kitten," vibrated behind her ear.

Still holding the sterilized needle between her thumb and forefinger, Katherine shut her eyes without protest. She could still see the flicker of the flames behind her eyelids.

But all she could feel was the long, deep breath that coursed through Jack's chest against her back. In and out. She followed the movement. Once, twice...

Her hand stopped shaking.

"Looks like we are both going to be doing scary shit tonight, huh?"

She nodded, opening up her eyes. Here she went. Deep breath.

"Okay."

The moment her needle punctured Jace's skin, his mouth went to the top of the bourbon bottle to conceal his grunt of agony.

Katherine felt her chest heave to the side.

"Oh my god," someone coughed a few feet away, likely the eldest of Jack's brothers. He covered his mouth with his hand, no doubt to hide a smile.

Katherine shut her eyes again.

Deep breaths. Deep breaths.

"You gonna be sick there, Kitten?"

Swallowing down the involuntary gag, Katherine glared behind herself, whispering. "Shut the fuck up, Jack."

"Since when did you get such a mouth on you?" he murmured into her neck so low she almost shivered.

Since about the moment she decided that she could become a plastic surgeon and stitch Jack's brother up, apparently that was when she found her voice, a quiet plea.

"Back up."

"I'm just here in case you pass out or do something else wildly crazy like what my father just made you agree to."

"I will stab you," she warned.

"Aw, but then you will have to stitch me back up, sweetheart," Jack said, leaning forward once more. "And we are obviously not ready for those kinds of games yet."

"My god, are you going to take forever?" Jace snapped, looking away from where the needle punctured his skin.

Oh, right.

"Just take another sip of the whiskey and let Jack's girl do her work, will you?" Brian said. His eyes quickly adjusted and he looked in Katherine and Jack's direction. "I don't think you want to be taunting the lady with the needle about to go into your leg."

"You really don't have to do this, Kit."

It was just like fabric. Very thick, moving fabric.

"Everyone needs to shut up right now and get back," she snapped. Her voice even sounded stern to her. But they were too close. Everyone was too close, watching her. "If I'm doing this, I need space."

After a short moment of silence, Brian took lead once more. "Well, you heard the lady. Give her some room before Jace bleeds out on our favorite campsite, yeah?"

Well, there was no turning back now.

Staring back down at the wound again, trying to imagine it like a blank canvas, precut fabric.

Gritting his teeth, Jace swore a few more times as she got to work, not warning him this time.

His jaw locked. He looked at her from her knees to the top of her head, where she was sure there was a rat's nest after a long day of work and passing out in Jack's Jeep. "You're my brother's girlfriend?"

"Um." Katherine swallowed, focusing on what she was doing. It wasn't so bad once she got started. "Not exactly."

"Where did you meet him?"

"I met him at work."

"Work?"

Katherine nodded. "I'm an apprentice for my aunt. I met him and some friends at one of my stops. Jack helped me out."

Jace's smile was as focused as his gaze. "Bet he did."

Glancing up at him, Katherine gave the thread an extra little tug.

He grunted with pain. "What the hell?"

Katherine didn't answer. She only shrugged.

"So, who are you then?"

"What do you mean?"

Jace's jaw was tight, eyes looking to the point of tears as he held them back. "You know what I mean."

"I am just a friend."

"Is that what we are calling it now?" Jace asked with a snort. "Or are we blind?"

Katherine looked up and glared at him. Need she remind him she had his bloody leg and a needle at her disposal right now? Her hand could easily just—slip.

"Obviously not. In case you haven't noticed, I am sewing your leg back together."

He made a low muttering sound.

"What's your problem?"

"Besides the fact that some chick is sewing up my leg in the middle of the woods?"

That was what she was going for. She sure didn't want to talk about how his blood was staining her fingernails. "Jack said that you were close once out of the rest of them. It doesn't seem like it."

"He said that?"

Again, she nodded.

"Jack's a liar." Jace let out a hiss of breath as Katherine paused.

Turning to look back down, she squinted and shoved the needle back through again. He only needed one more, just to be sure.

"My god—could you at least try to be a little nicer about that?"

"Sorry," Katherine apologized. Still, she might even say that her stitches were looking rather nice. If only Emilie could see her now.

"How old are you anyway?"

"I'm twenty."

"Twenty," Jace repeated. His eyes stayed on hers before she made them turn back down to her work there. She needed to focus. "I'm eighteen."

"You graduate this year then?"

"Nope. Graduated last spring."

So had Katherine.

Sucking on the inside of her cheek, Katherine cupped his leg, trying to get a better light as she made her way up the cut.

"He was nervous to come back."

"He should've been nervous," Jace choked back. "He doesn't even care."

"He cares."

"Man, give that guy an award." Jace gave a single clap.

Lifting Jace's pant leg up a little farther to ensure she didn't miss anything, Katherine noticed the stark lines and dark swirls of a tattoo coating his thigh.

He jerked his leg away, wincing. "It's just marker."

"It's really good."

Jace said nothing. He only looked at her, less angry, more unsure.

"Is your hand okay?" Katherine asked. "I saw you looking at it before. I know how careful you probably are about your hands as an artist—"

"I'm not an artist," Jace snapped. Only this time, his voice was less angry, more unsure.

Katherine leaned back to her kit on the edge of her bag. She found the small embroidery scissors she bought herself the other week. She hadn't thought the first time she'd be using them would be for this. Birth by blood. She clipped the extra thread.

"All done."

Jace only looked at her, not even glancing at his leg.

"Can we come back now?"

Katherine turned toward Jed's voice. On the other side of the site, she also noticed Jeremy again. His head was propped up on a cushion of leaves, sleeping.

"Finished," she confirmed as they drew closer.

"Here," Jack said, getting to her first, helping her up. He tilted a bottle of water, so it ran over her hands. She scrubbed them together until she saw the darkness begin to fade, like shadows running back into the night surrounding them.

"Thanks."

"Hello there," a voice cut between them. Turning, Katherine met a pair of round, honey-shaded eyes. A family trait, then. "I'm Brian."

Katherine blinked twice. "Kit."

"Kit," he repeated with a nod. He glanced back at Jack with a twitch of his lips before turning away again, focusing on her.

"You stitch my youngest up good?" Brian gave a crooked smile at her work. There was no doubt looking at it now that it was a little haphazard, sure to produce a decent scar.

Still, Katherine tried to imitate the well-meaning smirk. "Good as he's going to get."

Brian's mouth pressed back together, a laugh at the corner of his lips before he settled with a simple nod. "Nice to meet you, sweetheart. Sorry this had to happen so soon after your arrival, but hell, sure tells me a lot about you."

Shutting her eyes, Katherine shook her head.

Jace, finally, was silent behind them, looking at the fire and up at the stars.

"You okay, Kitten?" a deep voice interrupted. The tone was so low she was sure only she could hear.

Jack's one hand came around the back of her neck, pressing lightly.

It felt good. Almost like a massage, but not at all the massage she needed as tension only began to dissipate down her spine. It felt like something had fallen off of her shoulders in only the last few minutes.

"You good?" he asked, close as if only for her to hear.

"Perfect. I'm basically ready for med school now."

"Impressive."

"Well, now that we got this mess sorted and Jeremy is already half in his grave, we all best get some sleep or else your mother will have my head," Brian said, looking over to Jed.

Jack cleared his throat. "We'll head back to the house, then."

"It's too dark to walk back now," Jed said.

Katherine didn't really see how the darkness now was different from a half hour ago, but she looked around nonetheless.

"We'll be fine," Jack argued.

"No, your brother is right," Brian said as he poked at the fire with another stick. He didn't look back up toward Jack. "You two will stay here for the night. We don't want another incident."

"We can walk—"

"Two to a tent," Brian directed. "Jed, stay with Jer to make sure he doesn't get sick on himself. Jace?"

The youngest finally looked back up. "What?"

"You'll bunk with me and give Kit and your brother the tent you set up. I'll keep an eye on that leg."

Jace shrugged. It looked like he, too, was now focused on not looking in Jack's direction.

He tensed beside her. Still, he didn't argue. Helping Jed again to haul Jeremy into a tent, murmuring to themselves. Brian, doing the same with Jace. Katherine walked over to the green canvas tent on the end.

Unzipping the front flap, inside was a single sleeping bag and blanket.

"You sure you're okay, Kit?" Jack appeared behind her.

She nodded, kicking off her shoes that were speckled in a healthy coating of mud and blood. Katherine crawled inside. Sitting down, she watched as Jack did the same.

He zipped the flap up behind him. "This okay? We can still head back to the house if you want."

"It's fine," she assured him. It was no different than sleeping on the same couch, really.

"Scooch over then, let's figure this out." In a simple motion, Jack unzipped the sleeping bag, opening it up, so it spread over the canvas floor. Grabbing the quilt next, he shook it out until it fell over the top. Glancing up at Katherine as he worked, a strange smile crossed his face. "You look like you've come from war."

Looking down at her legs, smeared in earth, she couldn't imagine the rest of her looked much better. She crossed her arms over one another. "I think you should be thanking me."

"Oh, I know." He gave a reassuring smile.

With a wave, he motioned for her to get under the blanket. The cold, now that she had finished her task tonight and stopped walking, started to seep into her bones.

"I'm going to get them all dirty."

"They'll wash. Me, on the other hand." He wagged his eyebrows.

Katherine swatted him as she crawled under the blanket. It was still cold, but less so as she wrapped the soft flannel around her. "You know, I've never been camping."

"What a great way to start."

She only shrugged. Brian was right, after all. It sure told everyone a lot about her. Told her something too. "How are you?"

"What do you mean?"

Katherine only stared at him. They both knew what she meant.

He motioned for her to move over as he got situated. Reaching for the battery-powered lantern, he flicked the button, cascading them back into darkness. On her back, she looked up toward the tent ceiling, listening as he shuffled to get comfortable.

With a huff, he turned toward her.

Still, Katherine didn't move. If she did, she was pretty sure she'd startle him.

"I didn't expect much coming back," Jack said. "I mean, I know it could've all gone so much worse already."

"What did you picture? Your dad screaming at you? Telling you not to come back?"

Jack didn't answer.

That must've been exactly what he pictured. "Jack, from what I see, your family missed you. Maybe they are a little mad, like Jace."

"Jace?"

She nodded before she realized that he couldn't see her. "Jace seems to have you at the top of some sort of list. Out of everyone, it's him I'd watch for."

Jack chuckled.

"Your mom looks like she would've run to Ashton to find you sooner if she knew that you wanted her to," Katherine went on. "And your dad... your dad wants to forgive you."

"You think?"

"I think it's the forgetting he is having problems with," Katherine added. "And Jeremy, well, who knows if he even realizes you're here yet."

Another laugh escaped. A small smile curved her own lips at the sound. "What did happen, though?"

"I thought I told you how I left."

"You did, I just mean—Jace. He seems more than a little angry."

"Right." Jack took a deep breath. "Jace thinks that I left him behind, and I did in a way. I left them all, but to him, I left him."

"What do you mean?"

"I told you before that out of all the brothers, I was closest with Jace."

Again, Katherine nodded to herself.

"When I was in high school and the idea of running off to the city formed in my head, I told him about it. We'd make these grand plans together about what we would do and what Ashton would be like."

"Like you make plans about traveling with your photography."

Jack paused. "Right. Anyway, eventually, after a few years of fighting with my dad about what I thought I was doing with my life, I did leave. I left early one morning to catch the bus, and I stopped by his bedroom before I left to tell him where I was going. He nearly started yelling loud enough to out me before I reached the front door. I told him I wouldn't be gone forever. I'd come back."

Something in Katherine's chest stopped beating at the admission. "But you didn't."

"I didn't."

He left him. He left them all, just like that, and he didn't look back. At least, to them, it didn't look it.

Katherine thought about her mother on the day she left, birthday candles melting on the pink frosting flowers. She thought about her father, who barely exchanged much of a conversation near the end. She wasn't sure she would let them back in.

But then again, they were never really hers.

Jack let loose a heavy sigh. "It feels crazy being back here."

"In a tent?"

"Yeah, Kit, in a tent." He nudged her with his foot.

She nudged his back. "It'll be okay."

"How do you know?"

"Because they love you."

The tent went quiet again at the simple truth without the threat of a single dare. They didn't need it now. They just were, and it was getting easier.

Katherine curled herself, bringing the blanket with her when she closed her eyes. Her lids were so heavy, she couldn't keep them open even after her nap in Jack's Jeep.

"Stars, you're shaking the tent."

"Sorry."

"Come here." Jack's arms reached out and before Katherine could realize what he was doing, Jack pulled her tighter against him. Twisting around, she could still smell the remnants of his soap. "Better?"

Her heart hammered in her chest. "Better."

After another moment, Katherine let some of the tension of being so close to him, held by him, leach out of her. She relaxed against him. Her head in the crook of his arm, it was oddly comfortable, how they fit.

"Hey, Jack?" Katherine whispered.

"Yeah?"

"Why did you invite me to come home with you?"

"You offered."

She did.

"And, I wanted you here," Jack whispered as if only talking to himself. "I always want you here."

Slowly, as if only grazing her skin, Jack's hand swept up the side of her leg. Starting at her knee, his fingertips traced up over her exposed thigh.

Keeping her breath steady, Katherine's hand, that remained flat against his chest, gently moved. Sliding it upward, she felt the way his muscles tensed, just enough, as she positioned her palm on his shoulder. Her thumb traced a small circle on his neck.

His fingers trailed over her hip, making the same circular motion as they said nothing in the silence. The back of his nails brushed against her ribs. The feeling, even through her shirt, sent shivers throughout her body.

The reaction only made him bring her closer.

She never imagined Jack to be soft, careful. From the first time she saw him, all she saw was a man that wanted something and went for it, only now, here she was.

Jack had her.

They fell asleep like that, carefully taking turns in the darkness. Eyes closed, they touched and grazed hands against skin, like no one was watching, not even them. They touched as if one wrong move would cause the tether between awake and sleep to snap. There, they drifted off asleep without noticing where their simple touches, tangled in each other, ended.

CHAPTER TWENTY-SIX

*F*or sleeping on the ground, Katherine was surprisingly comfortable when she woke up. Stretching, she felt another leg between hers, and her head curled against a chest.

Jack's chest, that she could now very clearly see herself literally drooling over in the morning sunlight.

Shifting, Jack blinked a few times as if he, too, was shocked at the position they were in. Recovering just as quickly, his arm rounded her shoulders with a squeeze. "Morning."

What was happening?

Not willing to risk asking, Katherine slowly peeled herself away, the cool air a stark contrast to Jack's skin. His hair stuck up in different directions on either side. She smoothed down one side before her eyes widened.

What was she doing?

He didn't seem to notice before her hand snapped back into its own personal space. Sitting up alongside her, she heard shuffling. Jack reached forward to unzip the front of the tent. The dreary sunlight poured in on them.

"Finally." Jed was on the other side. "Come on, we are packing up to get Jace back and help set up for the party later."

Slipping out from the tent, Katherine adjusted her clothes while Jack stretched his arms up toward the sky. The hem of his shirt raised, exposing a slice of his stomach.

"Hey, Jack."

"Hey, Jer." Jack smiled. "How are you doing?"

"Besides the fact I feel like I just got ran over by a truck?" Jeremy asked. His eyes skittered toward Katherine. "Who's this?"

"Man, you really remember nothing from last night, do you?" Jed said, shoving things into bags. Most of the camp was already cleaned up, looking very different than it did in the darkness.

Jeremy only shrugged, a hand still at his forehead.

"This is Kit," Jack introduced.

"We ready to make our way home?" Brian asked from the other side of the fire pit. Jace was there too, propping himself up against a tree.

One at a time, they nodded. Jack went back to his position that he was in last night, under Jace's one arm while Jed took the other. They were right, the walk back felt a lot longer than it did when they went searching for them last night.

Katherine kept her eyes on Jack most of the way there, otherwise looking over the large expanse of property. Trees and fields extended out from their footsteps as they trudged their way back to the large farmhouse.

The back screen door opened, Jack and Jed stepped through with Jace first.

A woman inside that wasn't Jack's mother stood up immediately at the sight of them. Her eyes immediately found Jed's, her husband's.

He was somehow still gleeful in delight toward his brother's whining since they got in eyeshot of the house.

"Oh my god, what happened?" Leann exclaimed. Her eyes caught on Jace's leg.

Jack grunted as he set his brother down on the uneven kitchen chair.

Jed let go and moved to Leann. He gave her a quick kiss, careful not to squish the baby clinging to her chest. "What are you doing here so early?"

"I'm helping Emily get the food and things together for the party later."

"The kids?" Jed asked.

Katherine twisted her neck around to see if Jack said anything, but his mouth remained closed as a loud wall of screaming children ran into the hall.

Jack swooped the one toddler up into his arms without question.

With a wide smile, the little boy buried his face into Jack's neck as he gestured to be picked up. Jack looked like he had won the lottery.

Leann's eyes widened too as they landed on Jack. She nearly sprung forward to wrap a hand around his wide shoulders. "Now, do my eyes deceive me? Is it really Jack Carver back from the dead?"

"You know that I never died, nor rose," Jack replied blandly. He gave her a warm squeeze. At the gesture, the small boy squirmed to be let back down to the ground. The moment his tiny feet touched the scratched hardwood, he was back to running toward the front of the house.

No one looked concerned about where he might end up.

"Might as well have," Leann proclaimed. "You said you were coming, and I still wasn't sure you'd be here."

"Well, here I am."

Leann's dark caramel eyes flicked toward Katherine. "And this is..."

"That's Kit, baby," Jed filled in. "She's Jack's girl."

Jack's mouth parted, but he only blinked, unsure what to say.

So did Katherine.

His sister-in-law only widened her eyes in delight. "You're the one he told me about. It is so great to meet you. After Jack practically left his sweetheart at the altar way back when, we worried that he was never going to find someone steady," Leann chattered.

Jack's voice finally found itself, tense. "Leann."

"Oh." Katherine's face turned away so not to look back at Jack. "Me and—we're not exactly—"

Leann was having none of it, adjusting her baby a little higher into the crook of her elbow. She gave an easy nod. *Right.*

Katherine felt her shoulders try to melt into the rest of her body.

"Kit here sewed up Jace last night when the two of them found him on their way to the campsite."

Leann turned back to her with another renewed look of intrigue.

A gasp sounded from the other doorway.

Brian put up a hand to Jack's mom as she stared at her youngest son, covered in blood and dirt from the knee down. "Emily, it is not as bad as it looks."

"It totally is," Jace countered.

"What happened?"

"The boy fell is all," Brian explained, lifting a hand toward the back of his head.

"On what? An ax?"

"A rock actually," Jed said.

"Much less cinematic," added Jeremy.

"Well, you couldn't have taken him to Roberts?" Emily conceded, kneeling down to look at the wound.

"He's not getting back in town till tonight."

Roberts? Katherine mouthed.

Leann noticed first, mouthing back the answer. *Town doctor.*

Katherine didn't even know such things existed anymore.

"It all worked out since Kit was there."

Emily's eyes flew to hers. "You did this?"

With a shrug, Katherine crossed her arms. It felt like a dream now.

Surprisingly, Emily began to laugh. Katherine couldn't help but smile at the reaction. Loud chortles of laughter came out of her until she reached up to wipe away a tear. "Well, now you'll definitely have a story to tell Emilie when you get home."

That she sure would.

"Go get a shower and clean yourself up, Jace, and put some disinfectant on that."

With a huff, Jace pushed himself back up off the chair and limped away, grabbing on to the wall for support.

Emily continued to watch his ascent with a shake of her head before turning back to her other boys. They averted their eyes. "I assume after your late night, the rest of you are still prepared to set up for the party later?"

One by one, they nodded heavy heads, heading back toward the door they just came in.

"Kit can stay here with us and help," Leann added, putting a hand on her shoulder the moment Jack's eyes searched for her across the room.

They stuck to Katherine for a long moment, as if trying to see if she was okay with the arrangement.

Emily nodded with a smile. "Brian, will you show Jack where everything is, please?"

For a long moment, Brian stared at his wife as if they were sharing a silent language. He nodded. "Let's go."

Jack peeked over his shoulder, sharing a few words of his own with Katherine. Less assessing, this time it looked something like, *save me.*

Biting her lip not to laugh at the dramatics, Emily had already put an arm around Katherine's shoulders, leading her to the stairs. "Let's get you cleaned up before you help us with the food too, shall we?"

Brought to Emily and Brian's bathroom off their room, the farmhouse looked like it must've been renovated at some point, keeping most of the floors and fixtures, but the rest like the bathroom was designed fresh and new with a large soaking tub in the corner and a walk-in shower. Emily showed her how to adjust the faucet as the water rained down.

"I'll leave out some clothes for you to wear when you get out. Holler if you need anything."

Katherine nodded. Listening for when the steps retreated behind the closed door, Katherine slowly stripped off each layer of her clothes, seeing all the specks of dirt and muck she accumulated over the past twenty-four hours. She almost wanted to laugh as she looked in the mirror. She did look like she came home from war, however odd.

The water was warm as it fell against her, and though the soap, though it didn't smell like the kind she had been using from the farmer's market, it gently scrubbed away the grime. She let the water smooth down her hair as well, coming back out feeling much fresher and cleaner than when she went in.

The clothes Jack's mom left out for her fit decently, nothing falling off her entirely, even if she wasn't used to wearing jeans, hadn't in a long time. The tight fabric hugged her thighs as she made her way back down the stairs to the kitchen.

The radio played gently to the sounds of knives hitting cutting boards.

Emily waved her knife in a surprisingly unthreatening way when she caught Katherine lingering at the entrance. "Come on in. You can help me and Leann prep a few things for the party till Jack gets back."

Katherine gave a small smile toward Leann, moving forward. "You think they'll be okay?"

"Brian and Jack?" She rolled her eyes. "They'll be fine. They aren't a lot alike, the two of them, but one thing they are is stubborn."

Katherine walked toward the counter filled with vegetables. "You're making the food for your own anniversary party?"

"Eh, a little here and there. Everyone brings something. So, prepare to eat all you can and dance it back off." Emily laughed like a songbird and shrugged, glancing at Leann next to her. "I hope everyone has fun. The farms haven't gotten together in a long while. Once all the kids grow up, it's harder to make things happen. But now our babies are having babies and it is like the magic starts all over again."

Not knowing what to say, Katherine continued to stand, swaying side to side.

Emily shook her head. "Come, help us."

At the command, Katherine pushed up the thick sleeves of her sweater as she was handed a silver bowl. She stared down at its empty contents.

"Take the corn and shuck the husk away from the cob. Ears in that bowl, husks in the other to dry out." Leann demonstrated as she spoke, peeling the outer part of the corn away in one swift motion. She handed the next to Katherine.

"We donate the intact husks when we can to the church, after. They make the palms from husks when they run out around Easter time," Emily explained, still focused on her tiny chopped peppers.

Katherine imagined Jack and his family, dressed in their Sunday best for church service. She had never been to church before, but nodded to Emily like she knew what it meant. The closest thing Katherine knew to religion was whatever pagan following her aunt Emilie used to run off to one night a month, dressed in drapery cross-stitched with every color.

Emilie asked her if she would like to come with her a few times when she first got to Ashton, to meet people. She never took her up on the offer.

"The town, from what Jack told me, seems really close," Katherine commented softly. She fought to get the end of the husk off and into the metal bowl. It clanged when her elbow connected.

Heat coated her cheeks.

"It's a great group of people." Emily thankfully did not comment or look at her struggle as they both set to their tasks. "Did your mom ever teach you how to cook?"

"I'm very good at making tea."

Emily laughed.

The only reason Katherine even knew how to do that was because of Emilie, as well as when she was still in high school. The home economics teacher didn't have a home to attend of her own, so she ran clubs on cooking and what Katherine was there for each week, sewing.

Katherine was the only one who showed up for a whole semester. Each day in the overly sterile classroom with baby dolls stacked in the corner, the home studies teacher would make tea on one of the three kitchen stations before showing Katherine how to turn on the sewing machine. They made silly things like pillows or hemmed the many skirts she picked up from the thrift shop she worked at.

The hot water would boil and sing usually right when they finished instruction, then her teacher would get distracted and prattle about how lovely it was for a student to finally show interest in simple things. She was ultimately determined to make Katherine a good little housewife.

"My mother left when I was young," Katherine explained.

"Ah, that's right. I'm sorry. I remember Emilie saying something like that when I last talked with her. Feels like a while ago."

"Don't be sorry," Katherine said. She gave the poor woman a smile. "It's alright."

"I just can't imagine it. Especially as a little girl, growing up without a mother. I mean my boys, they're heathens. They could and would fend for themselves, but it's different, I guess, in my mind." Emily shrugged. "Once you are done there, would you mind emptying the strainer for me? I swear I make more messes than I clean."

Finishing off the rest of the corn, Katherine rinsed her hands before beginning to stack plates. Gently, Katherine stacked them in the cabinet above her head. The ceramic clanged against one another. Coming off her toes, Emily was watching her. So was Leann.

Both smiled.

A little while later, caught as the three of them chatted, the back door slid open again. Jack stepped inside, followed by Brian.

He came up beside her and touched her elbow. "Ready to go get ready for the party?"

Katherine glanced at the other two women.

"We are all set to go," Emily confirmed. "See you two in a bit."

"Bye, Kit," Leann called.

Katherine gave a small wave as Jack led her back outside. After a minute of walking through the thick grass, noticing all the tables and chairs set up that weren't there earlier, she looked at Jack.

"How did it go?"

"Good."

"Yeah?" Katherine gave a hesitant smile.

"I think anyway."

Katherine remained silent, watching Jack's jaw work as he tried to form a better answer.

"He forgave me."

"Well, that's good, isn't it?"

"Just like that." Jack shook his head. "He didn't say it like that, of course, but I expected him to be a lot madder, you know. Maybe that is just how I remember him back then. But there we were walking. I let him walk me halfway around the property in the opposite direction for a good second, thinking that he was going to take me out back somewhere and shoot me. But no. He just kept talking about what kind of man I was and who I wanted to be, and then just said..."

"What?"

"That he understood what I did. Why I did it, though he didn't like my reasons most of the time. Family is family," Jack said. He blinked once, like he was still trying to decipher this strange code of forgiveness his father laid out for him. "No matter what."

Katherine gave a tight nod, looking around the farm. It definitely was, here. One big family. For a while, Katherine barely even knew what that looked like.

"We talked about other things too."

"Yeah?" Katherine nudged him. "You talked about me, didn't you?"

He turned, eyes completely focused on her. "You made quite the impression."

"You totally talked about me." She beamed, though she didn't believe it herself. "Where are we going, anyway? I thought we would be staying in the house."

"We'll be under a roof tonight, don't worry. We are staying in the barn."

"Barn?" She looked up at the looming building in front of her. She assumed it would be larger than it was. Still, she glanced at Jack.

Jack smirked at her hesitancy. "Where did your sense of adventure go, Kit?"

"Probably into your brother's leg."

He laughed.

Unlatching a small door of the building encapsulated in darkness, Katherine stayed back a few steps. The overgrown tendrils of grass tickled her ankles. Jack leaned around the doorframe, and all was light. Jack held the door open until Katherine made her way past them, sealing them in with a large pane of wood, inside what Katherine was not sure she would ever simply describe as a barn.

Fairy lights of all lengths hung from the rafters of the tall ceiling, swooping around the corners and around the door they entered. The entire barn had been converted into one of the largest studio apartments she had ever seen. A couch curved around the right corner. A wooden counter led back as the kitchen, breaking apart the rooms, including the bed that was piled with puffed comforters tucked neatly into the frame.

"Wow."

Her and Jack's bags were already sitting on the bed in front of them. The latch gave a hard click as it shut behind them.

"My older brothers' humble abode. They decided that the house was too small once they got to high school. This was their summer project."

It was amazing. Katherine froze only a few steps into the barn —home. Touching her hand against the edge of the counter, she could imagine herself sitting on the couch, looking out the window as snow fell. It was due any day now. She would make hot chocolate on the hot plate in the small kitchenette. She could imagine herself in that bed right over there, curled up in quilted hexagons.

Katherine looked back over her shoulder. Jack was leaning against the door, watching her.

"What is it?"

Katherine shrugged. She put her hands out to get a bit of space. She was being stupid, really. "It's stunning."

"The barn?" Jack smiled like it was a sort of crazy notion. "It is nothing really."

But it was. A summer project and this place was more of a home to Jack and his brothers, she could feel it, than any home she had lived in before.

Two days ago, she was sipping tea and listening to college kids curse the world after she tore up a dancer very unprofessionally, and now she had stumbled into another branch of wonderland. Only it was warmer than the sort of wonderland she felt DuCain was when she met Jack with all the colors swirling in his gaze.

One big wonderland. That was what he was.

She ran her teeth along her bottom lip before sucking on them.

"I'm glad you're here," Jack said softly, as if reminding her.

"Me too."

"And though you look very cute in my mother's clothes, not to mention the jeans. Shall we get ready for what a Saturday night at the Carver Farm has in store?"

CHAPTER TWENTY-SEVEN

*I*t would be a lie to say that Jack had never watched a woman get dressed before. He watched them get dressed, undressed, and put on a show while doing it. Watching Kit as she got dressed, however, trumped them all. She put herself together, steady preparedness one layer at a time.

Each movement was easy to Kit. At some point, she'd gotten rather good at transforming herself into the person Jack always saw her as. She stood tall and simply at ease with herself when she shook her hair in the mirror. A simple black dress slipped over her frame. The sleeves started below her shoulders and framed her collarbones with a frill of lace, and the hem landed just past her knees, easily hiding her garters that Jack eyed from across the room. He remembered the set from their photo shoot the other day.

Kit carefully attached each brooch Avril entrusted her with to the fabric wrapped around her pelvis.

And there she was, puckering her lips with the rosy red hue she applied with the pad of her finger.

Coming up behind her, Jack touched the center of the ribbon

she tied around her neck. He adjusted the shape, turning it just so.

"You look stunning." His thumb slipped beneath her ribbon, a gentle caress. He couldn't help himself after the night before in the tent, the way it felt so right for him to be so close, her against him.

He had to control himself, whether or not the rest of the town thought the two of them were anything more than—well, whatever they were.

Stepping back, he released her and cleared his throat.

She stared at him; mouth lightly parted as if sorting her words. Not finding them, Kit reached for her tennis shoes left by the door. They didn't scream anniversary elegance but did a backyard celebration. She gripped the doorframe as she slipped one on.

With a twirl, she grinned at him the way she did when she tried to copy his. He began to understand what she meant. That smile—it made him crumble.

"That. Do it again."

"What?" Kit asked again, laughing.

"That, right there. That smile!" He put a hand to his heart. "All of it is perfection, and you still worry about winning them over, don't you?"

"You're crazy." She shook her head as he approached her in his own sort of party bests when it came to the farm. Jeans and a nice shirt tucked in. His one hand pressed against the door above her until she was in a shadowy cave of Jack.

"Aren't we all?" he asked.

Kit inhaled but didn't let it out for another moment. The sharp, nervous feeling was back in his ribs, but it was all Kit and honey as she breathed again.

They really needed to get out the door and to the party that was probably already starting without them.

She must've been thinking the same thing as her hand slid toward the door handle. "Well, you hold a special place in crazy."

"Do I? Where?"

"Right between the c and r, if I am not mistaken."

"And here I thought I was near the z."

"Oh, you're there too. You're all over crazy," Kit confirmed, taking the extra scarf layer she left by the door to wrap around her shoulders. Though thin, it brought out the rich mahogany of her eyes.

The night was cold, but in the short distance, as they made their way to the houses, Jack could already hear the voices.

Kit studied him. "You're in a good mood."

"It's been a good day so far. Oddly good."

"I'm glad." Though her voice seemed stilted.

The rib-breaking emotions were making their medieval torture methods known again. "I can feel you're nervous."

Her face squished. "What?"

"I can feel it all in my ribs," Jack admitted, gesturing in the region. "I wasn't sure what it was at first, but don't like it, stop."

"I can't help that I'm anxious."

"Stop." Jack grabbed her hand before they made it to the outskirts of the party. "Look at me. Don't be anxious."

"Wow, so helpful," Kit teased.

He shook his head. Reaching out to bring her chin back to face him. Her eyes came with it. "I'm not done. Look at me. Everyone already seems taken with you. I'm serious. If they could trade me in for you, I don't think they'd mind at this rate if I ever came back. Even my dad said he liked you."

"He did?"

"He did."

"Truth?"

He rolled his eyes. "Truth, and everyone else, if you want to meet anyone else tonight, will love you too. What's not to love?"

Her eyebrows raised as if she was compiling a comprehensive list.

He flicked her nose.

"Hey!"

He caught her hand before it could land anywhere important. "You'll be perfect." Everything felt perfect right now.

"I think you're lying."

"I gave no promises," Jack insisted, but began to lead them farther into the small crowd of neighbors. "We eat, drink, dance, and be merry."

"There is dancing?"

Jack nodded.

"Like line dancing?"

"Depends on how late we stay, Kitten." The pain in his ribs eased, but was still there. "I'll be by your side all night. Okay?"

"Okay."

THE FARMHOUSE LOOKED like a concert was about to begin. Lights flickered on as the sun began to set earlier than the day before and the thrum of voices calling for more green beer bottles to be passed, their own music.

Jack led Katherine farther into the crowd, already picking apart plates of tart-smelling apple pies and burgers layered with more toppings than Katherine could ever imagine attempting to eat at once. People turned to take glances at the two of them as they passed, wandering through the groups who asked where Jack had been and why Jace was hiding. By the time they got to the house, Katherine felt that she had met the entire town.

"Sangria, beer, liquor?" Jack offered. He scooped a beer out of the ice bucket before turning back to her.

"Sangria?"

"Daring." In a cherry red Solo cup, he lifted the pitcher set to the side with a cloth draped over it and filled it to the top line.

The dark liquid had pieces of fruit floating in it. Katherine took a hesitant sip.

Her eyes widened at the dry sweetness.

Jack smiled. "Good?"

He topped her off at the assent just as Brian, head down, meandered to the middle of the dance floor.

"Hello, everyone!" Brian called out to his audience. "Before we get started—"

A few hollers and whistles rang out.

"I would just like to say a few words about my lovely bride over there. Emily, you have been nothing but the world. You are someone who held up my world, even. Over the past many years, that woman, mine right there, has been my best friend from the first time we danced here in her parents' backyard after saying our I dos. I'd say 'em again." Brian cleared his throat. "I don't think I can say much more besides throwing up some thanks to God for us and our wonderful community here. And of course, the fact that I have all my sons here tonight. Cheers, everyone."

Bottles and cups clanged together in their striking symphony.

Jack tilted his bottle against her cup with a hollow sound as he stared into her eyes. Each of them took a sip and Katherine tasted the sweetness of sangria slide over her tongue. She had to be careful drinking these. Though the air was cold, each sip made her feel warm, all the way down to her toes.

"I'll be right back," Jack spoke into her ear. His hand grazed her ribbon again, giving it a little tug before walking off toward where Brian and Emily kissed, surrounded by others.

"I know, they're disgusting. Ruins everyone's night, don't they?" a voice next to her joked.

Katherine turned to see a golden-eyed boy with shoulder-length wavy hair. The color of his eyes nearly matched a few strands, a complement to olive skin.

He extended a hand to the side. "Jeremy."

"Kit."

"Oh, I know." Jeremy nodded. "I was sober enough to remember you this morning."

Katherine took another sip of her drink, holding it with two hands.

"You brought our lost brother home," Jeremy said. "An impressive feat, to say the least. Why are you looking at me like that?"

"Sorry. You kind of look like Fabio."

"What?" Jeremy laughed. It washed over her, rich and warm like maple syrup.

"I'm sorry. I had a whole cup of this red wine juice with fruit in it already. I should know better than to speak," Katherine rambled. Where was Jack?

"It's the hair, isn't it?" Jeremy said, not commenting on her verbal drunkenness. "I honestly only grew it out because it bothered my mother to no end, but now..."

He shrugged.

Katherine gave a small smile. She sure knew how to make a first impression. "I like your hair."

"Thanks. How are you enjoying the party?" he asked.

After a moment, Katherine looked around the area. It was gorgeous. She could imagine this place over forty years ago, Emily in a white dress walking under the swooping white fairy lights. It was gorgeous. Picturesque. Still, Katherine shrugged as she swayed to the music. Side to side.

"It's a fishbowl."

She narrowed her eyes at Jack's brother.

"See that man that was talking with my mom a while ago? He's been staring at us ever since Jack walked over to make peace with my dad's friends." Jeremy leaned back farther into the tree, hiding behind a branch with her. "He'll continue to stare, especially with me whispering like this to you right now. He'll also likely pass the information on to his wife that everyone thinks is the real chatty one. Probably already thinking you're switching one brother for another."

Katherine's eyes widened, jaw parting in shock as she looked out the corner of her eye toward the man. He looked down toward his plate of homemade salt and vinegar chips.

Jeremey's long waves blew to one side.

"You know all the dirt," Katherine said slyly.

Jeremy only nodded in slight satisfaction at the compliment. "Have to around this town. There are two kinds of people. Those who know the gossip—"

"And those who are being gossiped about," Katherine filled in.

"Exactly. That girl over there?" With a tip of his pointed chin, Jeremy referenced across the crowd toward a girl holding up her plastic cup for lemonade. She had big eyes and light brown hair that curled on the edges around her shoulders. She was pretty. Very soft pretty actually. "That's Claudia. She and Jack used to date throughout the last two years of high school, on and off. Until she met some guy in a secretarial class last year, she was still bitter that our very own Jack left her virginal at the altar."

Jack. At the altar. Eyes wide, she tossed her gaze back to the girl again, a demure sort of beauty, Katherine could imagine the two of them walking along the farm together. Her in her cowboy boots and him with his arm fitting perfectly around her waist.

"You're kidding."

He laughed. "Kinda. By the eleventh grade, that girl was practically boasting to half the town that Jack and she were screwing and getting married after graduation. Of course, my brother had other plans that didn't include a ring."

The plans of hopping out his window in the middle of the night and running away from his family and wannabe-wife, becoming an ex-photography student and professional beater of kinky individuals. Yeah, she knew of those plans.

The thought made her smile just as Jack looped a warm arm back around her shoulders.

"Trying to steal my girl, Jer?"

Jeremy only shrugged with a playful expression on his face. He put his hands in his pockets. "Wouldn't dream of it."

"Especially not with Olivia around here somewhere. Where is she anyway?"

Olivia? Katherine looked up at Jeremy. If Olivia was anything like Jeremy, maybe she would have someone to latch onto for a few hours whenever Jack was pulled away in another decade-fixing conversation.

Jeremy looked around, but didn't appear to be searching. "We actually broke it off a while ago after I came back from training, Jack."

"Oh."

"Yep." Another shrug. "Things happen."

For some reason, Katherine could tell it wasn't just a few things. A tinge of sorrow laced his words.

"I'm going to go and get some food," Jeremy diverted. "Have fun, guys. See ya, Kit."

Katherine gave a small wave while Jack steered her back toward the front of the house where a few groups had gathered. "That's sad."

"Yeah," Jack agreed. "I can't believe he didn't say anything before now. My mom wants to see you, though. Apparently, you guys got along earlier."

Jack dropped her off in front of his mother. Katherine turned around to say something, her mouth tingling with Jeremy's next witty joke of farmer Jack being escorted down the aisle with a shotgun on him, but Jack was already gone. He wandered toward another group of men his father called out for him to join.

"Sorry, isn't every day you have to reintroduce your lost son to society," Emily teased. "How are you doing? Enjoying the sangria?" She lifted a cup of her own. "Be careful. Our delightful neighbor makes it. She always puts in a few more shots of brandy than anyone should put into sangria."

No wonder Katherine felt a strange mixture of warm joy

instead of cold November fear at the prospect of so many people staring at her right then. She could feel eyes from all angles.

Another pair seemed to get even closer to them.

"Oh! Hello Claudie, how are you, sweetheart?" Jack's mom enveloped the girl in a tight hug before letting go.

Claudia turned with laughter. "Hi, Mrs. Carver. How are you?"

"Just fine. Having a wonderful anniversary so far with the help of everyone." Still holding on to Claudia's tiny hand, Emily turned to Katherine. "You should meet Kit."

Katherine gave a hesitant smile. "Hello."

"Hi," Claudia said, cheerful as ever. "You must be Jack's new girl."

"That she is," Emily answered for her before Katherine even had the chance to flounder. Maybe Emily was sticking up for her. Right as Katherine thought this, however, Emily continued. "I'll leave you girls alone. Don't need an old woman like me interfering with good conversation. I need a refill anyway."

"Well, it was good to see you." Claudia smiled.

"You too, Claudia."

As Emily walked away, Katherine felt all of that sangria-fueled joy die.

Claudia pulled Katherine forward with as much force as if she was a rag doll. Though Claudia was small, she had one impressive grip as she placed the two of them in a small group of girls that all looked the same. Like little plaid-covered clones.

"Ladies, this is Kit. She is Jack's new girl," Claudia said.

A few of the girls smiled. Nearly all of them assessed her, up and down, before meeting her eyes.

Katherine took a sip of her drink. She was almost out. Avril would have been proud. "Hello."

"I heard Jack came home and brought a girl with him," a girl with deep-set eyes said. "I figured the first part was true, but seeing is believing."

"I hear you're from the city," another girl added in before Katherine could say anything. Not that she knew what to say. Did she defend herself? Say thank you? All seemed like the right and wrong response. She tucked a piece of pin-straight hair behind her ear. "That must be exciting."

Katherine let the last sip of her sangria burn with brandy all the way down her throat before answering. "It is. Have you been?"

"Oh no. I'd love to visit maybe one day and see the sights. Honestly though, I don't even know what I would do there."

"What do you do, Kit?" Claudia asked, cocking her head kindly. "Do you go to school?"

"I work for my aunt actually." Suddenly, she was having flashbacks to that day at the square.

"That must be nice."

"It is," Katherine said with a smile. Emilie was probably bustling to clean up the place before shutting down for the night right now, if she ended up feeling better today, enough to open. Katherine should've called her earlier. "I love the work I do. I sew, mainly."

"Oh my gosh, Leah loves to sew too, don't you, Leah?" Claudia turned toward the smallest of the ladies with long hair pinned up in braids on either side.

Leah carefully nursed her own Solo cup, peeking up from the rim. "I have been making quilts and skirts and things for the farmer's market."

Katherine saw a few large quilts stitched in swirls inside of Emily's living room as well as on the bed in the barn. She wondered if maybe a few of them were Leah's. They were gorgeous, not to mention exceedingly warm. Katherine thought of the one she had wrapped around her shoulders last night after they crawled into the tent.

"So, what do you do exactly?"

"Oh." Katherine smiled. "My aunt runs a lingerie store."

Leah went pink.

"Scandalous," one of the other girls said.

They all leaned farther into the circle, intrigued.

"Not really," Katherine said softly, looking toward her feet. She couldn't imagine what they would think if they knew where Jack worked, let alone the things that she saw on her daily errands. "We run the shop together right now. There is a lot we do from designing new things, to delivering pieces and other supplies to people who order them around the city."

"I'm surprised that Jack lets you do such things."

"What do you mean?" Katherine asked.

"Wasn't he jealous, Claudie?"

Jealous? Except for that one time in DuCain when Devil approached her, Katherine couldn't see Jack as jealous, at least not to that degree.

Claudia only rolled her eyes, tossing a look over her shoulder. Jack's laugh boomed across the yard.

Katherine narrowed hers. "He appreciates my work and what I do. Both of which he has seen plenty of actually."

Puckering their lips, a few of the girls apparently caught Katherine's second meaning. She wanted to say even more about it. Katherine had the intense desire to tell them all about how Jack laced her up in corsets and had taken photos of her he joked about plastering the walls with. Tell them how he spoke to her without a smirk on his face when he was serious, how he slept next to her at night and that somehow, she figured it was more intimate than any of the times he must've fucked half of them under the bleachers in high school. All of a sudden, she wasn't afraid to tell the whole town about her and Jack.

"My, my."

"Don't scare her," Claudia said, biting on her bottom lip. "It is just, well, you know."

"When Jack says that he is going to stick around for a while. He means stick around until it feels like a while to him."

"Of course, he did bring you home." Another chimed back in. Katherine was pretty sure it was Leah, though she did not turn her head to make sure. "He must love you. Maybe the city has changed more than just his hair."

He must love her.

"His hair is what drew everyone in around here."

"He did have great hair, though it's shorter now."

"His eyes," Katherine cut in, the other words still tossing themselves against her skull.

He must love her.

"What was that?"

"His eyes and his smile—" That was what she noticed first.

They never saw him.

Katherine looked over her shoulder in the direction Claudia did moments ago, but Jack was no longer there. He must have gone inside or around the back of the house without her.

He must love her.

Why did she even let those words get to her? She knew they weren't right, this was all a charade she played inside of her head.

A few of the girls looked down into their hands while the others continued to appraise Katherine like the new prize mare. She couldn't help but think they knew she wouldn't win any prizes, her pedigree not up to their standards.

"Are you alright?"

Katherine nodded, continuing to take a few steps away. The girls looked amused when she nearly tripped over her feet.

"I am just going to—" Katherine grit her teeth together, unable to say anything more. She shook her cup. It hung limply by her side.

Claudia, pretty little Claudia with a voice like ice, smiled the cheeriest smile. "Alright, well, I'll see you hopefully."

Of course. She couldn't help herself, giving an almost respectful half-hearted wave to the rest to the girls who quickly lessened the space between one another now that Katherine slid away. Stomping through the high patches of grass, she noticed how dark it had become. The fairy lights they hung early in the day illuminated the space of laughing faces filling their plates and starting to dance in small movements on the makeshift dance floor under the big swooping tree.

Katherine bit the inside of her cheek, looking at them all.

"Are you all right there, Kit?" Brian asked. His hand reached out in a comforting way, but Katherine had already taken a few steps past him before she paused.

"Yes. I am. Thank you. I just needed a moment for some fresh air."

"How about you dance with me instead?"

"Oh, I'm not much of a dancer."

"For some reason, I don't think that's true." He extended a large hand once more. "Come on. For an old guy on his anniversary."

Huffing with a light smile, Katherine nodded. Her hand felt small inside of his, callused yet somehow soft as he already began to lead her back to the center of the dance floor. "All right."

"So, tell me, sweetheart, what's wrong?"

"Nothing is wrong. It's a lovely party."

He raised an inquisitive eyebrow.

Katherine only shook her head, trying not to look down at her feet she was sure were a step away from stomping on his. "Just thinking is all."

"No good can come of that most of the time."

That she knew.

"Want to talk about it instead of thinking?"

"Not really." If she was being honest. "It's... a lot."

"Hm. I think I know the feeling. For the longest time, you know, I didn't think my son would come back. The rest, they were independent enough, but they always came home when I whistled out the back door. Jack, on the other hand, was always someone I knew would press curfew until the last second. He got a watch one time just to prove it to me when he sauntered on in late one night with his shirt inside out."

Katherine chuckled.

"If you like that one, I have plenty more," said Brian. "But like I said, he was always his own person. He reminded me a lot of his mother compared to me. For the longest time, she always wanted to run away to that city your aunt did, after she went away, closer to Ashton for school and I had to drive back and forth every few days just to see her. She used to talk about that city all the time, and I saw how Jack's eyes lit up. She came back, though. Jack—"

"Jack made the city his home."

"I suppose he did."

"He did," Katherine repeated. "Honestly, Mr. Carver—"

"Brian."

"You say that Jack isn't a family guy, but he is someone who smiles at everyone, whether it be in a good or bad way. He grins so often that when he smiles at you, it is hard to tell whether or not it's actually real or for you. He never ceases to make me feel special when he does smile at me, though, whatever that means. He and his friends gave me a family I never had before, since I came to the city. And though, it isn't always perfect, and sometimes we don't make the best decisions, or we forget to call each other once in a while, what family is perfect, really? Speaking from my perspective, I know it doesn't mean much."

"It does."

"Your son has been one of the best people I have ever met." Katherine sniffed, not realizing the clouds in her eyes, she quickly blinked to clear them.

"I love that boy, whether he wants me to or not," Brian told her.

"He knows."

"You so sure?"

Thinking for a minute, Katherine scrunched her nose with a smile. "No."

Brian let out a loud, howling laugh. Now she knew where Jack got it from as it echoed around them.

"I like you, Kit. If you ever need anyone too, you let me know. I know what it is like not to have a family. My parents weren't around a lot. Not like I made sure that this family would try to be. If you stick around, know that I'll be here." He gave the nod, and the statement was sealed.

LIPS PARTING, Katherine stared at him. A family. Him and Emily and Jack—they were offering up family like it was free to go around and Katherine didn't know what to say. Pressure pulsed against the back of her eyes.

"Thank you." She took a step back, escaping his gentle hands as the song came to a close. She pointed behind her. "I just... like I said, I need a second. Thank you."

Turning on her heel, Katherine moved across the field, away from everyone and not caring exactly where she was going. She just needed a minute to think or—

Katherine had to sniff back a breath of air that had caught in her throat.

It was stupid that she was even thinking of her and Jack. Together. For some reason though, every time someone said it; Jack's girl, boyfriend, girlfriend, love, family—Katherine couldn't help the feelings that were stirred at the possibility that was never going to happen.

Katherine never had a family. She never expected to.

Just like she couldn't expect for it to happen now.

To do otherwise would just be another fantasy. Another infatuation she could not let herself linger in.

Because she and Jack weren't together, whether or not everyone else here thought so, and she wasn't strong enough to reject it.

She knew who she was, and she also knew in extraordinary

detail how Jack could have any girl in the country. Maybe even Avril, if he got up the courage to do more than just grin at her and watch her walk away.

Her hands lifted into her hair and squeezed the curls tight.

Maybe the girls here were just willing to say the things that Katherine wasn't. That he didn't love her. He never said anything —did anything. Katherine didn't even know if he liked her for anything other than the fact that Avril wasn't here right now to fill her space ever since she left and she forced herself back into his life that night.

A distraction. That's what she was.

Maybe she could take that and face it without this complete upheaval. She could understand it even on some human level.

And yet, her heart clenched, so did the bones holding it up. She couldn't help herself.

Oh god, she was more than just infatuated with Jack.

Infatuated with the world she could not have, yet was now surrounding her, all hers if she would only open her hands and take it like the girl who knew who she was and where she was meant to be and didn't fear anyone taking those things away from her.

She was in love with Jack.

It was only then, as she turned in her agony, she noticed the glowing eyes staring at her in the darkness.

CHAPTER TWENTY-EIGHT

"*A*h!" Leaping backward, Katherine attempted to fall on her feet. Like most times in the dark, however, she effectively fell on her butt.

"Hey, hey." A voice came up behind her, holding her under her arms and lifting her back up to her feet. Laughter ensued from the deep bellowing of her savior's chest. It rang so loud through his chest that the stars above Katherine shook. "You're all right."

"Eyes. There. Animal."

"That's just Pat."

"Pat? What?" Leaning into Jack's chest while her eyes adjusted, Katherine did not see a rabid mountain lion in front of her, but a very large, brown, "Cow."

"Just Pat."

"The cow has a name."

He chortled. Actually chortled.

Oh god, it was worse. Katherine wasn't falling in love with Jack. She stared at him with wide, pained eyes, afraid to blink.

She was in love with him.

He rubbed his hands up and down her arms before stepping

closer to the cow. The creature looked like it was smiling at them. "Not only does Pat have a name, but Pat here..."

The cow fell into Jack the moment he approached. Maybe that is what people meant when they went cow tipping. Or was it dipping? Either way, this cow let out a tiny moo as it nuzzled the man who was holding up at least a ton.

"Pat here is basically part dog and now free roams the property. Pat was born on this farm when all of us brothers were old enough to watch. He's basically been the fifth brother from when we realized he was a boy."

"Lot of male energy around this place, huh?"

Jack extended a hand. "Come here."

She shook her head at the offer. No matter how much Pat might have been a brother to him, Pat was still a large animal that moments ago Katherine believed was ready to attack as much as any mountain lion.

Gently, Jack took her hand and extended it toward Pat, who had not moved another inch until her hand met with the side of his surprisingly soft head. If anything, he leaned farther into it, much unlike a lion and more like a very large dog.

Katherine sadly pursed her lips, continuing to pet Pat even when Jack took his hand away. He was sort of cute.

"You okay?" Jack asked her softly, as if afraid to spook her.

"Yeah," Katherine said, her voice still shaky. "I'm fine."

"You don't seem fine."

She let her hand fall away from Pat. He didn't seem to mind standing there, watching the two of them in the darkness through the sound of crickets and faded eighties hits. Jack appeared a tad more concerned.

"My dad told me where you went. He looked a little worried."

Weren't they all a little worried at this rate? What had her life turned into?

Putting a hand to her head, her glasses jostled onto the one side of her face. Maybe it was her arms that were cold again or the sky was bright with stars, or the fact that Jack was just standing there, waiting.

Katherine had to say it, something, as she stood there because she couldn't think of another wish right now to make it all go away.

"I really like you, okay?"

Jack's grin reappeared. "I would sure hope so."

"No." Katherine heard the way that sounded. "No, you don't get it."

Her voice was stiff, and he noticed. Instead of moving, he only offered a hand.

She couldn't take it.

"I kissed you," she whispered, words collapsing in on one another. "I kissed you that night and you said nothing. But no, that's not it. Since then, everything has been so amazing. You've been my friend and I—"

She wanted him.

Did she have to spell it out for him? "If you are going to go back to Penelope, or Claudia, or—"

"You make it sound as if I have a harem."

"Or Avril."

"Avril?"

"I know you say that is old news or whatever, but I still see how you look at her." Katherine clenched her teeth together so she wouldn't scream. It cracked out of the back of her throat anyway. "You look at her how I've always imagined you would look at me. For so long, I've come up with these stupid thoughts of you in my head, and I wanted you to look at me like that."

It might always be someone like Avril. Confident and wild. The vixen who Katherine loved even when it felt like she took a dagger and stabbed a hole through both their chests.

"Avril?" Jack repeated, reaching that hand up to run through his hair.

He certainly didn't sound outraged about it.

"Yes."

"From the moment I first walked into DuCain and saw you two sitting on the edge of the stage, the first thing I thought was, how perfect you two looked together. Laughing and looking up as the lights shined down on you like some sign from heaven. How perfect you were."

"You said you were jealous."

"I am! Obviously." Katherine swallowed the thickness in her throat. Still, the burn of tears made its way to her eyes. "I've been jealous of everyone my entire life and I don't know how to stop. I am the big green monster! So yes, I was jealous of your friendship and your lives that looked so worth living, and how you love her when I've somehow loved you from the minute I first laid eyes on you like some infatuated little girl.

"And me," Katherine forced out. "I'm just—"

"You are not *just* anything." Jack reached out for her hand.

She pulled it away, slipping back another step, unable to look at him as she retreated. Unlike Avril, she wasn't a queen. She was never good at fighting wars. She always lost.

"Look at me."

"Stop it." She took another step away. She needed a minute to clear her head, to pretend this all never happened, and then they could go back to doing what they were before. It must've been the sangria or something causing her big mouth to open and start like this.

"Kitten."

No one wanted her. How could she even entertain the possibility? Her breath cracked with a low, despicable laugh.

"I love you and you can't even look at me."

Katherine's head snapped back up. "What?"

Jack's lip curled. "How I look at you—I look at you and I feel like I can't breathe. I look at you and for all the good reasons in the world, I can't find one good enough to stop."

Lips pressed together; Katherine stared at him to make sure she was breathing.

"You said you loved me," Jack reminded.

"So?" she asked. So what if she loved him? "I love you and I don't know why; I just do. But we can be friends. We are so good at being friends and you've been so nice to me and helping me—"

"Friends?"

"Not only am I jealous, it turns out that my heart is greedy, but it's okay. You and Avril are my family and I don't have anyone else. We can just be friends."

She just didn't want to be alone.

For so long, she thought she was good at being alone, but it looked like she was wrong. Wishes on stars didn't come true just because you begged and pleaded for years on one.

"Did you not just hear me, Kit?"

"What?"

"I asked if you just heard what I said a minute ago while you were all up in your head convincing yourself anything but."

Katherine bit her lip, letting him gently put his hands on her arms.

"I said, Kit, I love you," Jack said. "Do I need to say it again?"

A few times would probably be best.

"I love you, so I'm going to need you to keep being able to look at me when I do this."

Before Katherine could get words out from her numb lips, whatever they were meant to be, Jack's hand gripped her hair.

Then his lips crashed on top of hers.

CHAPTER TWENTY-NINE

*T*he first time Jack realized he kissed Kit was about two-and-a-half seconds after he did it. She opened her mouth and breathed into him with a gasp that sounded more like a laugh meant to be bottled inside of him. Maybe it was the sangria he had that was stronger than he remembered, or the night, cold when not close to the someone else, but none of that mattered.

He didn't care what she was about to say next, challenging him for another truth. All he knew was that he had to kiss her. His mouth covered hers, drawing her close with the hand he shoved to her hair so she couldn't run away. Damn anyone who watched—who stared wantonly as he devoured one of many spots on her he'd clearly been starving for.

Pulling back, he looked down at her and what was there wasn't shiny eyes or regret or unsureness. No, after a second, her eyes met with his and he saw her teeth pop out of the corners of her mouth before she grinned, beaming up at him.

No, it was the first time Jack realized he kissed Kit.

No, he didn't just like Kit.

No, hell no. It was the first time in Jack's life his heart sank in his chest as if someone had just sucker punched him in the gut. It was the first time he realized, just like after he said it; he was in love with Kit.

He had been since the moment they looked up at the ceiling and both must've wished on nothingness for everything.

He felt the force of her desire radiating from her, and he loved the way that she responded to him, opening her mouth and kissing him with such a force he was sure she was going to devour him. If so, he'd die happy. Arms surrounding her waist, he touched her however he could, grazed her through the thin layer she had on as they crumbled against each other to the ground, no string holding them up and apart for so long.

Too long.

He needed to kiss, touch, and taste every inch of her. Rolling on top of her, for now, this would have to do as he ran his tongue up the column of her throat.

She shook at the sensation, and he could feel the sharp pounding echo of her heartbeat on his taste buds.

She was so delicious.

Jack gave a laugh before sighing against her throat. The sound only caused Katherine's hand to tremble more as she clumsily fought to get past his shirt. She tugged each of his shirt buttons. There was a quiet pop.

"My new sidekick, Kitten the Button Popper."

"Shh…" She could barely breathe, trying to regain herself through steadying breaths.

She must've almost wanted this as much as he did.

He wanted her more than anything.

A hand squeezed her thigh. "I need you to answer me. Do you want me to stop?"

With the question, he knew he would stop if she said the word. Stop. Periwinkle. Anything out of the ordinary and he would stop. He would stop whispering, kissing, touching—

He strained against his zipper as he nipped the skin of her collarbones.

Katherine immediately shook her head, letting her body relax limply into him. "No. Don't stop."

"Thank god," he rumbled, shoving her back against him. Grabbing her one leg, he looped it around his hip.

She groaned as he leaned against her.

"You think I don't want you now?"

"I'm almost convinced," she said, breathless.

"Then we will have to do something about that."

Bending his neck back down for another kiss, there was nothing like kissing Kit, her lips were warm and full. His teeth scraped her bottom lip, and a sound shook out of her mouth and shot straight down through his stomach.

"How could you ever think I could want anyone but you, Kit? All this time from the first night you sat next to me in that kitchen, I knew there was something about you."

"I thought you said that I was just one of Avril's lost things."

"No." Jack shook his head, forehead pressed against hers. "I changed my mind. You're mine."

With new fervor, he kissed her, needing to be closer to her in any way possible, her hips arching up into his. He groaned against her lips and at the sound, she whimpered. His hands eased over her front again, feeling the way her body curved under him by the time he pushed the fabric of her panties to the side.

She was so wet for him, slipping a finger inside, teasing the delicate flesh until her head fell back with a gasp of pleasure. Reaching down, he released himself from his jeans, the air cold but the space between the two of them hot, and he was burning as he brushed up against the inside of her thigh.

Reaching down, she took him into her hand, gently teasing before stroking him once.

He growled, muscles taut with restraint.

Blinking, she looked down at him with wide eyes, those swollen lips parted.

"What is it, Kitten? Do you want me inside of you?" Jack asked, his voice surprisingly breathless.

With a single tip of her chin, she met his eyes. "Please."

She asked so nicely.

"Put your arms around my neck," Jack directed, his mouth colliding with hers again as he swiftly thrust into her.

The suddenness of him filling her, the certainness of how he fit so perfectly inside, startled her enough that a gasp escaped loud enough that she brought her hand up from his shoulder to cover her mouth. Someone would hear her, not that he cared.

They really weren't that far away from the main party, but he was a bit preoccupied with their party of two.

Her eyes were wide as she looked at him, mouth parted as he seated himself inside of her, so tight and warm around him. Taking a deep breath, she shut her eyes again, and he waited a moment until she squirmed, only then did Jack adjust, pulling out before pushing right back into her. A low gasp was met with his movements.

Kit's hands gripped his shoulders as he pressed hard into her, wanting to feel every piece of her. They said nothing, only stared at each other in awe, so close they shared breath between them as they gazed on.

Glancing down between them at the sight of them joined, Kit tightened around him as she moaned.

Jack loved that sound, sliding his tongue into her mouth to taste it as he thrust into her, propelling them farther into the ground as he cupped the back of her head. He groaned with her, and the sound undid Kit as she broke. She clamped her legs around his back, gasping before going stiff in his arms, tightening around him as he sank deeper.

Her fingers slipped under his shirt, cutting into his shoulder blades. And Jack, too, felt himself fall over the edge. Never had anything felt like this before, he arched into her and held her tight against his body.

They could hear the rough pants echoing between them as Jack held her up in his arms. He didn't want to let go, not yet, as they slowly came back down. Looking at her, she stared back with the sweetness of honey.

Love. Desire. Longing.

Those were the emotions, weren't they? What he'd sensed from her, tingeing the rest for so long.

Carefully, Jack pulled out of her, settling with an arm still around her waist. A small shadow of red came away with him.

"No." He must've whispered before looking back up at Kit, still held in his arms. He clutched her tight, as if he needed her to pound breath back into his lungs. "You didn't say anything?"

Why the hell didn't she say anything?

The look of horror on his face must've been worth it to her nonetheless.

All Kit did was let her lips spread wide, and laugh.

CHAPTER THIRTY

"You look scandalized," said Katherine. Jack remained openmouthed at the discovery he made. Katherine couldn't help the laugh that exploded out of her at his shock.

His lips were swollen and cheeks a flushed red. Katherine reached up and brushed a few strands of hair away from his forehead. Her fingers twitched when they weren't on him, desperately trying to find their way back right where they should be.

"I told you I wasn't very popular."

"Why didn't you say anything?"

Katherine took a deep breath, steadying herself with her legs still spread open, him perched between them. "I thought maybe you knew."

Of course, she was wrong about that.

"And, I worried you'd stop."

He looked at me as if he couldn't believe what he was hearing. "Hell yes, I would've stopped."

"Then that's why."

"I sure would've stopped for a good five minutes until we

made it back to the barn so you wouldn't have lost your virginity outside on the ground."

He ran a hand through his hair, eyes wide. "I would've—I could've hurt you."

"It didn't hurt."

"No?"

"Well..." She paused, thinking about how her heart raced, knowing exactly what was coming as his fingers skirted between her legs and he pressed against her. The moment he pushed himself into her, it burned, but it wasn't long before she'd needed to move, arching her hips against him. She felt the blush rise to her cheeks. "Not a lot."

"Dear Lord."

"I thought you weren't religious."

"I think I might start," Jack said, exasperated. Looking back up to her face, something shifted. Moving forward, he cupped the back of her head and drew her close. "It looks like I have a lot of making up to do."

Jack carried her across the field through his own tiny bursts of laughter when she clung to him. In the distance, she could still see the party going on, voices drifting out toward them by the time they made it back to the barn.

When the door closed behind him, they were back in silence. Katherine was set on her feet as she toed out of her shoes. Twisting around, she stared at Jack as she moved backward.

He cocked his head at her with a sly smirk. "What are you doing?"

Not panicking, for the first time, Katherine felt oddly at ease. One shoulder swayed in front of her, then the other. Through the barn walls, she could still hear the music playing from the house. She extended her hand.

He took it, pulling her back into him.

"You want to dance?" he murmured into her hair. With another step, he put one leg between hers, dipping her back. He was her own Patrick Swayze, teaching her to dance and bend to the soft beat still playing. They moved as if they were meant to be dancing together, moving together.

With a twirl, Katherine let go of his hand and finally felt okay to dance alone, to let him see her as she smoothed her hands down her body and reached for the bottom of her dress, pulling the hip-hugging fabric up overhead. A pin still in her hair tumbled to the floor as she still attempted to look coy. She swayed her hips and tossed her dress to the side.

Jack chuckled louder. Even his cheeks burned. "You got the start down. Now all you have to get is the dancing. I'm sure Rosin has some openings."

Katherine snickered with him.

"Don't laugh—you are abso-fucking-lutely going to get on that stage one day. You hear me? I'm serious. For now, though," Jack nudged her deviously with his nose as he gripped the edge of her garter belt. Slowly unlatching each glimmering brooch, he set them up on the table. One after another.

Amethyst. Diamond. Ruby. Emerald. They seemed to shiver just as Katherine did at the touch.

"Let me help you with that. I believe I have some making up to do."

When Jack touched her body, she was surprised that she didn't melt.

Jack guided her back onto the bed.

At her height, she leaned forward and didn't stop herself before she pressed a kiss against the side of his neck. His mouth fell open at the touch, and she continued to caress down to his chest before looking back up at him.

"Kiss me."

Taking her hands in either of his, he happily obliged. His mouth found hers, and it was like breathing. Hands above her head, she breathed in, feeling Jack wrapping her stockings around the headboard until they were attached to her wrists in a knot.

Her heart pounded in her chest, hard and steady. Still, Jack kissed her, long slow kisses on her mouth before moving lower against the side of her neck. Katherine writhed against him, trying to touch—but not being able to.

Jack laughed at the game he created. He nipped and pressed soft, soothing kisses and languid licks down her throat. He paused when he reached her breasts, taking one of her nipples into his mouth, and sucked.

She gasped.

Jack hummed against her skin, continuing his onslaught of pinching and teasing her nipples with his teeth and hot mouth that slid down her stomach.

"So responsive." He swirled a single finger back and forth along her slick folds. "If I had known you were all mine, Kitten, you know what I would've done the first time?"

Katherine swallowed, looking down at him and that finger he dragged up and down the inside of her thigh. "What?"

"I would've brought you back here, spread you out in front of me, and took my time with you. I would have kissed and teased and made you come before I put myself inside of you. We would've started slow. So slow, you'd be begging me to pick up the pace. Pleading with me for more."

She was pretty sure she was about to do that right now.

"And what are you going to do now?"

Jack gave a heady smile from where he was positioned between her legs. Dipping down, he pressed a kiss against the apex of her thighs.

Katherine arched and murmured another few words that caused Jack to stop, hot breath laughing against needy skin.

"Jack," she gasped, the sound trailing into new octaves. She squirmed, unsure whether she wanted to pull him away or press him deeper. She quivered at the vibration of him as she decided.

What a gorgeous laugh.

And luckily, she didn't want to decide. No, Jack took all her decisions for himself. He devoured her until she was panting, tongue languishing her with long strokes. His eyes glowed as he peeked up at her and she stared down through her lashes. He tested each movement and what made her gasp. He dug his hands deep into her hips until she groaned.

The sounds only encouraged him, each movement between them rough and goading as he sucked and licked places she didn't know could cause her to make the sounds that escaped her lips. She bucked against him, hands stretching open in a pitiful attempt to free herself from the bindings he created, keeping her right where he wanted her.

With another sweep of his tongue, a finger slipped inside of her. The intrusion was sweeter than any of her own in the past. Her mouth opened as if ready to close over a breath that was not already held in her lungs and Jack stopped.

Her entire body paused, withering in frustration while he chuckled low and deep. He kissed each peak of her pelvis, moving his finger in and out so *so* slowly.

She tilted her hips farther up to him as if in offering.

"So eager."

Something like that. Two fingers moved in and out of her faster, now teasing a space inside of her she had never found. He placed a breath of a kiss over her parted lips. "Come for me, Kitten."

As if all she needed was permission, her hips lifted off the mattress. Pressure wound in her stomach as she came into his mouth.

"Beautiful." Jack lifted his head up, giving her a kiss there where she shivered and then on her lips. She could taste herself while his hands reached back up and undid the taut bindings around her wrists.

Hands free, all she could do was lift her chin for another kiss.

He gave one, looking at her differently than he normally did, almost fondly, when he pulled away. "Little freak. Now roll over."

Katherine rolled over before she questioned why.

Looking over her shoulder up toward Jack as he kneeled—he looked good kneeling. All of him looked good.

"What was that?"

"I said," Katherine panted, "You look pretty good kneeling."

That grin of his spread farther than she had ever seen before. His eyes glittered more than any of the champagne-colored crystals downstairs.

"Well, you look pretty good with your ass in the air, Kitten." He slapped it once to a rewarding yelp.

From behind, he slipped a finger inside of her, and then another once more until her wetness coated her thighs. "No pain?"

She was pretty sure her moan into the sheet was enough of an answer.

"Ready?"

Certainly, much more than she was the first time, but she didn't care. It was wonderful. Everything was perfect as she hummed the word.

She was going to die if he didn't get inside her already.

"That would just be a shame since I have already started a long list of things me and you need to do together, Kitten," Jack said, her words must've been spoken aloud. "We may not be playing games right now, but darling, I think you would be very put out if you missed any of it, especially when we do."

Katherine felt a light burning sort of pain once more as he began to enter her again, replacing his fingers. Only this time she breathed instead of gasped in shock. A low sound escaped her throat. Her body arched, leaning back to take even more of him.

"Good girl." Jack bit the outer corner of his lip. "Who knew, I should have brought lube."

Katherine gave a nervous chuckle.

He pushed into her, filling her inch by inch. There was a tightness, but after another moment, Jack was moving almost completely out before pushing back in. As Jack moved in her, his hands slid down either side of her body. They gripped her hips hard enough that she groaned and pinched her nipples until she gasped. One of his hands continued the journey, reaching low to find the space where they connected.

His other hand gripped the sheet to steady himself. Katherine reached out and felt down the veins of his hand. She wrapped her fingers around his thumb, imagining a red thread there, a string connecting the two of them.

She swore he gasped at the act. Felt his eyes stare at her chipped nails bitten short.

"Kit," Jack breathed, leaning farther over top of her body as he continued to thrust into her. Tightness in his voice. Tightness everywhere.

All Katherine wanted was more, lifting herself to meet him, breathing his breaths until she could no longer keep up the pace and became limp as he drove himself into her, using her, hand on her hip digging so far in Katherine groaned at the pain until she came from the combination of pleasure and the sweetest pain inflicted on her body.

A low groan seemed to sneak up on Jack, catching in the back of his throat. He thrust into her a few more times, his body relaxing into hers as if they could melt together in silence.

Pulling out of her with a slight grunt, Jack rolled off the bed and wandered over to the trash across the room, where he easily slipped off the condom. Katherine collapsed, ear against the mattress. All she could hear was the wanton rhythm of her heart.

Wow.

What was Avril going to say?

The thought made her cringe internally.

And grin. Laugh even once more.

"That might be one of the best sounds I have heard all night."

A hand ran up her leg as Jack sat back down. He looked over her with a long sweeping look. "Ever. Not that the other ones were not uniquely encouraging. Open up. Please, with that mouth, there is no need for conservative knees."

He flicked them once.

Her legs fell open. She was too tired to contest.

"Like magic." With the cloth in his hand, he gently wiped Katherine off.

She shuddered at the sensitive friction, not realizing how sore she was already if the bit of blood on the towel was any indication. "Ouch."

"You didn't seem to think so. What was that about wanting to just be friends again, Kitten?"

"Mm," Katherine hummed as he put the towel aside. She said a lot of things that didn't seem to matter anymore.

The only thing that did, through her hooded eyes, was this moment, right now. It was after all, just like magic. Him. Her. A single wish, and she closed her eyes with it all right in front of her.

CHAPTER THIRTY-ONE

"*W*here are you going?" Jack peeked an eye open from where they at last landed at the foot of the bed.

"Tea."

"It's almost past midnight."

"It is never too late for tea," Katherine softly protested, crawling out from the hot sheets that curled around her like they were planning a suffocation attempt. "And right now, my brain feels like it might explode, and I doubt you would be pleased about having to help your family redecorate. So, when I don't know what to do, Emilie has informed me, you make tea."

He mumbled something that couldn't have been complimentary.

"I'll be right back."

His hand loosened as she stepped out of his grasp.

As she walked, there was a soreness between her legs, not in a bad way, but odd. Biting her lip so as not to smile that it was caused by Jack, she grabbed one of the quilts, likely made by one of Jack's ex-girlfriend's minions, to wrap around herself.

It was a really nice blanket.

"You have no more tea," she said, turning back from the small kitchenette to inform Jack, but he rolled over, already asleep.

With a huff, Katherine paced the kitchen back and forth a few times before she slipped on Jack's pajama pants, a red plaid, and cinched them as tight as she could to her hips. Pulling Jack's oversized sweatshirt over the top, Katherine kept the lanterns by the barn door on to light a path toward the main house. The party dissolved into only a few low voices.

One of them was unmistakable, the loud guffaw of Brian Craver.

Katherine smiled to herself as she stepped into the kitchen and slid the door shut behind her. Her steps must have seemed as nervous as she was as they came to a halt. She wasn't the only one in the kitchen.

Emily's eyes lifted from where she shut off the tap of the sink, washed dishes in the strainer.

She raised her thin eyebrows as she took in Katherine's getup.

"I'm sorry," Katherine said immediately, without thinking about the words. "I didn't think anyone would still be up and was just… looking for tea."

Emily waved a hand. "Come in. I know we have some somewhere."

"It's all right, really. I couldn't sleep yet."

She smiled. "I know the feeling. Parties have always gotten me a little too overstimulated. I'll be tired and cleaning up for days, but it was a good one, wasn't it?"

Katherine bit her lip as she looked down at herself again. Yeah, it was a good one.

Avril was right, after all. She wanted to tell Emily, though she doubted Jack's mother knew who the vixen was. What a difference a single Saturday night party could make.

Emily giggled toward Katherine's giddy expression and shrugged. "I am not going to ask. Don't worry. After four boys, I've learned better."

"Thank you."

"As I said, I just hope everyone had fun, besides my youngest, of course, who has been complaining upstairs for most of the day. I never did thank you for stitching him back up, did I?"

"It's going to scar horribly."

She only shrugged. "Men like those kinds of things. They make good stories for women to fawn over."

Katherine never thought of it like that.

"The neighbors haven't gotten together in a long while. Once all the kids grow up, it's harder to make things happen. But now our babies are having babies and it is like the magic starts all back over again. So, thank you."

"For what?"

"I didn't need Brian to tell me that you are the reason my son decided to come home, so just thank you. I missed him. We all did, I think. He brings a certain personality to us all."

Not knowing what to say, Katherine continued to stand, swaying side to side.

"Don't just keep standing in the doorway, Kit. Come in."

The house was quiet, save for the two of them. She yanked the door shut behind her. It was only then that Katherine could really take in the home, warn and warm. Photos lined the walls where the kitchen met the living room.

"Your home," Katherine began. "It's wonderful."

Emily smiled. "Thank you. When it comes down to it, it's always been nice staying where I grew up."

"Even after your time in the city?"

Emily paused before she nodded. "The city is where I learned all about myself. I was never a gentlewoman. It was why me and your aunt got along so well, I think. We evened each other out. But in the end, I knew where I belonged in my life, and I haven't regretted choosing Brian or my family for a moment, even if it did take me away from the glamour. I'm glad I had the chance to see a different life, whether or not I chose it." Emily dried off a large bowl.

Katherine gave the woman a smile back. She was sure it was brimming with everything she had felt in the past few hours. Joy. Fear. Excitement and utmost happiness as she leaned over the counter. Katherine shook her head as she approached. The tile was cool against her fingertips.

Emily shrugged. "Don't mind me if I'm rambling."

"I do it all the time."

"It's nice to have another girl in the house," Emily said. "It's just, as a mother, I can't help but pry. I've held it in long enough and now that you are standing in front of me—Jack never told me that you two were together. Or told Leann, that is, until he called to say that he was coming."

"He talked about me?" Katherine asked, before quickly correcting herself. "I mean, we weren't together. Not exactly."

She wasn't sure what they were now.

The baggy clothing couldn't have looked very convincing if she spouted the past line of just friends, so she didn't.

She didn't want to.

"You seem good for him, Kit."

Katherine shrugged. "He's good on his own. Most of the time anyway."

Emily chuckled. "I have to ask something."

Katherine twisted back around with wide eyes. She fidgeted with the edge of the sweatshirt. "Of course."

"Is he still taking photos?"

Katherine's chest visually deflated as she heard the emotion in Emily's voice.

Slowly, she nodded. "Yes. Not so much until recently, from what I gather. But, yes. Weddings and… other things. Jack is very talented."

After another moment, Emily nodded along with her.

"I always thought so too. Good night, Kit."

"'Night."

KATHERINE REMOVED the baggy pants and hoodie before she crawled underneath the blankets.

"Your feet are cold," Jack commented, but didn't recoil.

Rolling over, she blew into his ear.

Jack swatted her away like a fly. "Sleep."

Of course, even with all the energy flowing through her, she was afraid to go to sleep as if, when she woke, it would all disappear, but she would. But first, Katherine had to ask. "Why did you leave?"

"Leave where?"

"Here. Your little farm town. Why did you leave?"

With a huff, Jack turned over to face her. He blinked a few times, noticing her face and carefully removing her glasses to put on the nightstand beside them.

She smiled at the casual act.

"Honestly?"

"Truth," Katherine said.

He sighed. "I never felt like I was meant to be here. For years. Everyone in this kind of town has their place. I never did."

"What do you mean?"

"I mean… Jed has the farm to take over. Jer works part time on the farm and part time at the local airport, now, after he was injured after joining the air force."

"There's an airport around here?"

"A small one. They fly old warplanes off a short track along with jumpers. It's more of a pastime for him than anything. Jace spends his time with him there, too," Jack explained.

"Jace flies?" For some reason, she couldn't see it.

"Nah, Jace helps work on the planes when they need him. He paints the old ones to look how they once did. Jer's been flying since he was about thirteen. Or wanted to fly since then. I don't remember."

"My friends from high school too, they only ever saw themselves here in some way, shape, or form, getting married after graduation or following in someone else's footsteps. But me?" Jack shook his head.

"It's funny, I think," Katherine mused. "How we end up certain places. Do you think you'll ever actually go?"

"Hm?"

"You said, before, with your photography, that one day you wanted to run away. You wanted to travel and see the world that way. Do you think you'll ever do it? Once and for all?"

"I don't know," Jack confessed, eyes half open with effort, but he didn't take them off of her. "I buy a ticket almost every year."

"What?"

"At random times," he explained. "When I see that the prices on flights are low—to Nevada or California or anywhere overseas—I book the flight. I print out the ticket and stick it on the fridge. When I had roommates, they thought I was nuts."

"What happened that you never went?" Katherine asked.

"I don't know. Didn't feel right. I always ended up canceling the ticket and getting at least a partial refund. I had a job at DuCain. I was friends with Avril. I was having a hell of a good time."

"You got scared."

"Maybe." He confessed the word carefully, as if it was glass. Jack peeked at her from his hooded eyes. "For now, I'll settle with taking over Ashton. Become king and rule over the city with an iron rod held by a very suggestive fist. Print all your naughty lingerie pictures after we put them up online and plaster the streets."

"You better not."

He only smiled and pulled her closer into his chest. "We'll

have to see, won't we? Maybe I'll pick up my camera some more. Make decisions. Right now, I want to sleep."

He cuddled her farther into him. She never pictured Jack as a cuddler, but now it felt right.

Katherine pressed her nose into his shoulder, giving it a featherlight kiss. She wanted to remember this moment before they had to return to reality, even though that was what right now was.

Soon enough, the world would see her creations, once they returned to the city and she had enough guts to hit publish. She and Jack—would they take places in the court of Ash together? The thought of it didn't seem so scary anymore. Even less, the thought of returning to the shop.

This was all real.

Her heart sped up a single beat as she thought it. In a few days, Jack had become one of the most important people in her life. Not that there were many, but right now, there was one.

"Did you ever get your tea?" Jack mumbled sleepily.

Katherine thought for a second before curling herself into him. Her arms wrapped around his stomach, unwilling to let go. Not just yet. "No."

CHAPTER THIRTY-TWO

*T*he phone rang four times.

She rolled back over under the dark covers of the bed, the adamant noise never lasted long. A wrong number, perhaps. On the fourth and final ring, Katherine felt the bed shift. A light kiss pressed against her temple and then again down her spine. With a short groan, she rolled toward the tyrant kisser himself. She blinked slowly up at him.

His hair went in two different directions. "Go back to sleep."

"I'm awake." She closed her eyes though as she said it. "Why are you up?"

"Go back to sleep for a little while longer."

"Don't want to... waste the day."

"You won't waste the day," Jack promised. She could hear the amusement in his voice. "I'll be back in a few minutes. I'll bring tea. I will even leave the bag in so you can over-steep it."

Katherine hummed in appreciation. She tugged the heavy blankets tighter around herself as he left. Nose in Jack's pillow, she smelled the fresh air and wood fire from the previous night.

She might've drifted for a minute too, but it couldn't have been long.

The trill of her missing phone echoed through the barn. With a groan, Katherine peeled herself out from under the covers. It sounded like it was coming from the floor on the other side of the bed. Reaching between the cracks, she pulled it back out and pressed it to her ear.

"Hello?"

"Is this Katherine Passin?"

She sat up a little straighter, rubbing the corners of her squinting eyes, trying to see the number on the screen she didn't recognize. "This is she."

Though, to be honest, she still wasn't quite awake enough to be sure. Sangria was still running through her veins instead of blood.

"This is St. Augustine's hospital calling on behalf of Emilie Passin Walker…"

Katherine barely heard the conversation. When she caught up, she stumbled out from the warm blankets and across the cold floor, tugging the skirt that she wore the day she arrived, still covered in dirt, over her bitten and caressed hips as only one thought rang through her mind.

Emilie was sick. Emilie was in the hospital in Ashton.

She had to go. She had to get there right now.

She would be there soon, she promised the nurse on the phone.

St. Augustine's hospital. She had to remember that too. Looking at her missed calls, though, she wasn't sure they would let her forget.

That was who all the calls were, every single one of them.

She barely noticed how damp the ground was. From tipped-over cups no one had bothered to clean up from the yard of the cold weather turning air to rain, she did not know. She made her way across the field and backyard, grass snagging on her ankles with every step as she walked until she finally yanked open the back door into the main house.

She scanned the room, lit only slightly in the still-dark morning haze. She only caught one dark blond head. "Do you know where Jack is?"

"Do I know where Jack is?" Jace repeated the question. With the tip of his pointer finger, he pushed his heavy coffee mug toward the middle of the table he sat at.

She didn't have time for this.

"This is serious, Jace."

"Since when have they been calling you? Let me guess, yesterday?" Jace asked blandly. He held his head in one hand, elbow digging into the table. "Didn't you conveniently not have your phone on you by then?"

None of that mattered. Eyebrows creasing in frustration, Jace looked at her with as much consideration as an eye roll.

"Seriously, you aren't getting this yet? I thought he said you were smart. Smartest girl he ever met."

"Getting what?"

"Jack," Jace repeated, bored. "Jack had your phone. Your dying aunt has been calling since he had your phone. He shows up while you are working for your aunt. God, put two and two together."

Katherine didn't know what to say. She had to find Jack. She needed to get dressed. She needed to get out of here and back to the city to see Emilie, because she was not dying. She couldn't be and would've told Jace as much, but no sound managed past her half-parted lips.

"How do you know this?"

Jace only sighed. "What do you think he is doing here so early in the morning talking to my mother about?"

Katherine looked up toward the ceiling, there were no stars, only footsteps.

"I have been stuck here for the past how many years of my life and you don't think I get him better than you do? Honestly. What do you take Jack for, an angel? He's been helping Emilie. Yes, your Emilie. From what I heard, he's been helping her out and getting some extra cash on the side by taking care of the child she had shoved on her only to find out, gasp, he loves her? Sounds like fake drama to me but happily ever after to you."

Katherine didn't understand. She only stared at Jace. She thought she had talked to him already. That Jace was like her in a different way, just a boy sad about his brother, sad about being constantly left behind by those who told them they wouldn't. And then... now—

"He'll leave, you know. He makes you care and then leaves, just like he does everyone. Have you not noticed that no one else volunteered to be his BFF to greet his family after a decade?"

Gritting her teeth, Katherine couldn't think. She couldn't understand what he was saying because he was lying.

He was the liar, not Jack.

"Jace, the only person you have to thank for whatever shitty life you are living is yourself." She could feel the pressure building, held back behind her eyes. "If you want to leave this place, leave! What's stopping you? You're an artist who paints planes and his legs because he's too much of a coward to show the world what he has to offer? Or you're an asshole who lives in this small town doing what you hate for the rest of your life? Up to you. For now, stop fucking up everyone else's lives and fix your own."

Jace only stared at her.

So did Jack. He stood in the hall. He held no tea. Only his own hands, looking at her with wide eyes.

Katherine swallowed that look, and for once, she was not the person who didn't look away first.

"I have to go."

MAYBE SHE WAS WRONG.

"Please, say something. Let me talk to you. I can explain," Jack begged before the car turned silent for the longest car ride Katherine had ever been on.

Longer than even the bus trip she took to Ashton, wondering if she should jump off at one of the rest stops before she hit ground zero.

She was wrong, wrong, *wrong* now, and she could do nothing about it. There was no place to jump, no place to turn back and see where she made her mistake from the second she stepped into DuCain and saw the most beautiful people in the world who so suddenly let her enter their gorgeous lives.

It wasn't like her to not notice these things. She was not gullible, and yet here she was. She kept her eyes shut in an attempt for Jack to think she was asleep until she finally stood in a hospital asking for a room number. She hadn't been in a hospital since she was ten and had to have her tonsils taken out. It smelled the same. Like disinfectant and stale air, keeping away the outside monsters of disease while keeping everyone else in.

Keeping Emilie in.

"Stop looking at me like that." Emilie turned her head from the pillow and rolled her eyes as Katherine approached. "You look like someone ran over your dog."

"Emilie."

"What? Now I'm not allowed to make jokes?"

Standing beside the hospital bed, Katherine ran her hand over the edge of a pale blue hospital blanket. Definitely not the best fabric to comfort someone. Make them itch half their skin off, maybe. She let it fall back onto the edge of the mattress covered in wires.

"Kit."

"Why didn't you say anything?"

"I had a spell." Emilie threw a dismissive wave toward the other side of the tiny room.

"You have cancer, Emilie."

Not blinking, Emilie shrugged, letting out a long breath. She'd had cancer for a long time.

"Why didn't you tell me?"

"Katherine."

She never used her real name.

"Why didn't you tell me? You could have told me. I could have helped you and not been running around like some—some—"

"Twenty-year-old?"

"That is not the point. I'm not a child." She hated that she even had to say such a thing.

"I know, I know. But that's the point, sweetie, and I didn't want to tell you."

She couldn't trust her. Was that it? Looking off to the other side of the room where the beige wallpaper began to peel away from the corner, just like in the living room back in the house, Katherine inhaled, but no air came back out. The only thing that formed was a burning sensation behind her eyes.

"No, Kit. Look at me," Emilie said. She reached up until just the tips of her too long fake nails grazed the edge of her cheek. "I didn't want to tell you because I was selfish, okay? I knew what was happening for a long time now. That is why I have been having my friend stop in so often to help and take me to appointments—"

"I could have helped you."

"You did, Kit. You did more for that shop and the people I know in the city than I have been able to do in years. The shop is thriving, you know, being up with my ledgers every night."

Katherine looked back down at her hands to let out a light laugh.

"I love this city. I knew you would too if you gave it a chance. I knew I was sick long before you even showed up on my doorstep. You have lost so many people already, I wasn't ready to tell you that you were going to lose another."

"Em."

A tear slipped, not from Katherine, but Emilie.

"Woo." She brushed it away. Gone as if it was never there. It occurred to Katherine that she had rarely seen her aunt without makeup on. Pinks and purples and even green lipstick never ceased to surprise her. Now, Emilie looked very plain, very pale. "No crying. No need for it except to clear some pimples. There is so much left I should have... so many things I need to tell you."

"It is alright, Emilie. Don't worry about anything. I will figure out everything else. I'll find somewhere to go."

Emilie began to shake her head.

Katherine shook her own head as she thought about the options she had. She thought about Avril, who she hadn't seen in weeks, and she thought about Jack left waiting outside the door. "Us Passins always somehow find somewhere to run off to."

"No, Kit, that is not what I meant. I'm leaving you the shop."

What? She must have heard her wrong.

"I am leaving you everything," Emilie said.

"Em."

"No. Now you be quiet and listen to me. You used to be so silent all the time. It almost scared me, and now look at you." She gestured meekly toward Katherine, standing, one garter tack broken and her hair completely skewed to the right. "You are so alive."

Katherine might have been crying now. She might have been crying for some time.

"Emilie, I can't."

"What are you talking about?"

"You can't give this to me. It isn't mine. Don't you have someone else or..."

"You?" Emilie smiled weakly, clasping her hand on top of Katherine's. Now, when she looked down, she still had to look at her.

"I can't take over the shop. I can't take over everything."

"Of course you can. It's time. It is your turn."

Another tear collapsed with Kit's body hunched over their hands.

"You've been practically running the shop since you got here. Why do you think I have been giving you so much to do? Why do you think I made you stay up until three a.m. until you got those pieces sewn together so perfectly you couldn't tell which were mine and which were yours? You have talent, Kit. If you can't trust your aunt, trust your mentor, trust me."

Trust her. Trust. Emilie must have seen the wavering in Katherine's eyes, but wearily guided her to lie in bed beside her.

"Kit, don't you worry. The world isn't done with me yet. It has you."

hen Katherine stepped out of Emilie's room, she found Jack sitting against the wall in an uneven waiting room chair. It rocked to one side when he sprung to his feet. He was still wearing his work boots from the barn. They stomped with each step until he met her across the laminate tile.

"How is she?"

How was she? Katherine closed her eyes and took a deep breath. She released it out of her mouth just like she knew to. To let the pain fade. Only this time, it grew.

"Why didn't you tell me?"

"I wanted to." Jack's voice filled with something that almost sounded like regret surrounding the rest of his sincerity. But Katherine could hear none of it. "I wanted to tell you about Emilie, I really did, but I made a promise, Kit. I'm a horrible liar, but I made a promise."

"Why didn't you tell me?" She was owed an explanation. She was owed something. Anything really, other than the nothing that was coming out of Jack's mouth.

"I couldn't. She begged me not to and ever since I came to the city, Emilie has been there for me when I was fucked up or needed cash, so when she asked for a favor—You know that I couldn't." He said it all like it was so simple.

"You wouldn't. All of this was a lie."

"An oversight."

"Was watching me crumble some sort of goal for you? Because here I am! Take it in." Tears streaked down Katherine's face as quickly as she shoved them away. How pitiful she looked. How perfect for the exact same person Avril, who she also thought was the only friend she'd ever made, warned her not to trust.

The people in Ashton were sleek and dangerous.

For a minute there, Katherine thought she was a little dangerous too. But she wasn't. She was soft and naïve.

"No." Jack's face looked crushed. He reached out only for her to take a step back, nearly falling into the cream-colored wall. "That's not what I meant. You know what I meant."

"Then why the hell don't you say it now?"

To that, he had no answer. He only stared at her, cracks in both their facades.

"Say it." She gave him another chance but knew that he wouldn't take it before he even did, mouth opening and closing like a gaping fish. "Right, you can't. Because didn't you know?"

"Didn't I know what?"

"Did you not know that the only reason you are even talking to me right now is because Emilie paid you to watch over her immature little niece like a work whoring spy? That first day when we met. It was all a lie whether or not Avril was roped into it." Katherine pounded on her hand, smacking it against her leg with every word. "I am pretty positive that you did know. Actually, I am one-hundred-percent positive."

Jack's anger began to dissipate, but she could see it there, still right in the corner of his twitching lips.

"You don't actually want me."

"I want you. How many times do you want me to say it? Because like I told you before, Kit, I'll say it a million more if I have to. I want you. You're mine."

"You didn't even want to be my friend."

His teeth gritted as he looked down toward his feet. "I do now. I have for a long time. When Emilie asked me—At the beginning—You aren't even the same person who you were in my head then, Kit. You weren't just some stupid twenty-year-old like I was, trying to find themselves in life. You are life."

Katherine could barely hear him anymore over the roar of it all. Emilie was leaving her. He was going to leave her.

He was never hers to begin with.

"You need to go."

"Don't do this, Kit," Jack pleaded, his voice struggling to remain steady. "Not now."

"I am alone out here with my aunt and I leave for a few days and it is all gone. And you did this to me. I have no one anymore. No one. Not even Avril talks to me anymore."

"You know she isn't talking to anyone right now."

He never wanted Katherine; she knew it. He was going to leave her the moment his chivalry to a dead woman was up and crawl back into anyone else's sequin-filled lap that never needed any help to be more than whatever Katherine was. Less.

"You need to go. Now."

"Katherine." Jack reached out to gently grip her wrist, but she yanked it behind her before he could. He looked after that hand as if it had slapped him instead.

"No. Listen to me. You need to go now so I can go back in there and watch the only measure of family I have left die hooked up to tubes in an empty hospital room."

"I am your family; don't you see that? You said it! Me and Avril and everyone. We are your family. Let me be here."

They were nothing.

"What a fucked-up family we'd be."

"That's what I have been trying to tell you."

Was he joking? Tears streamed down her cheeks. "Leave."

"God, Kit. I want to be here for you. I want to be here—with you. I'm trying to make up for my mistakes. I'm trying to keep my promises."

By betraying her—taunting her with her stupid dreams and wishes on stars that made no difference in the end. She shook her head over and over again.

"Look at me," Jack pleaded, reaching out for her arm.

She shoved him away. "Go."

"Just let me explain."

"I don't want you to explain," Katherine screamed. "Leave, like you do everyone else!"

The nurse's station behind them hushed at her rising voice. Katherine didn't know if she'd ever been so loud, and she didn't even care.

Neither, it seemed, did Jack.

"You say that you don't want people to leave you? Whenever there is one question of someone's loyalty or how they goddamn feel about you, you are the one who runs away. Do you not see that? You are the problem here right now!"

"W-what?"

Face red with held-in anger or fear or whatever it was that coursed the bright red blood throughout his body, he gestured to the space between them, a whole other being in the tiny hallway filled with bustling bodies and the beeping of blood pressure machines going up and up and up.

"You! You push everyone away."

Katherine was frozen as the words floated in the air between them. She pushed them all away. She knew it wasn't true. That all of this, that Emilie's death even was not her fault, that her parents leaving on their own accord without her was not her fault, but deep down somewhere it all seemed to click.

Yes, her. Her fault all along.

Slowly, she nodded. "Have a n-nice rest of your night, Jack."

His hands hung on either side, almost stunned by the single gesture of the words. "Kit. I—"

Turning around, Katherine barely even noticed the resident doctor holding the clipboard in his hands tightly. His wide glasses tilted to the side. "Miss Passin?"

Peeking back over her shoulder, Jack still stood there, his eyes wide toward the doctor. Once, Katherine would've told him to come with her. To hold her hand while she held Emilie's and watched her leave the world in a bed lonely without the quilts made of all the states she visited and scattered with ribbons and strawberry pincushions. Now, Katherine dipped her head and followed the doctor back down the hallway, feeling Jack's eyes follow her even as he did not.

OUTSIDE THE HOSPITAL, the wind whipped with the beginnings of the first snowstorm as Katherine wandered along the sidewalk back and forth, back and forth, until she was walking straight again. She walked like she used to back home when she needed to get out of the one-story home miles away that smelled like dust bunnies and dried bottles of her mother's favorite perfume her father couldn't convince himself to get rid of. Alone again.

She couldn't help herself when she arrived at the tall apartment building.

She didn't remember how she got there or knew where it was, only that she snuck rather easily into the elevator before it closed, going up nine floors. She had never been inside this building before, yet somehow, as if Emilie's intuition was already rubbing off on her, Katherine knew exactly where she was going.

It was the only place she had left to go.

Knocking once, twice, five times, the door finally whipped open, but only an inch.

"Avril."

A whisper of red hair fell partially in front of her face.

"Kit. What are you doing here?"

"I didn't know where else to go. Emilie was really sick and Jack—"

"Go away."

Shocked, Katherine almost took a step back, farther into the hallway. Instead, something came over her as she shoved the big toe of her shoe in the doorway. It burned when the door tried to crush it. "What?"

"Move."

"No. Avril, please. Is something wrong?"

"Nothing is wrong."

"Then what is going on?"

"Get out of here, Kit," Avril snarled, kicking Katherine's foot away before she peeked behind. "Go."

"No." She had done everything that Avril had asked of her, and now it was her turn. It was her fucking turn. "Avril, please, I need you."

"And I need you to leave. If I wanted to talk to a skittish mouse with no idea how desperate she sounds, I would call you or go and talk to some random chick scraping up pennies in the subway."

The words felt like a bullet wedging itself farther and farther into her chest until she almost couldn't breathe.

"Avril."

"Leave me alone. Leave."

"But."

"I don't want you here!"

I don't want you.

"Okay," Katherine murmured the word until she almost couldn't hear the sounds choking out of her. "Alright."

Gritting her teeth together, the redness around Avril's eyes seemed suddenly a lot more prominent than it did when she was yelling at her. "Please, Kit. Leave me. Go and run your dead Emilie's shop and leave me here. Leave me alone."

The door slammed in her face, leaving her in the fancy carpeted hallway with no other noise to be heard. The only sound Katherine could hear was the ragged breathing as her chest heaved, trying to catch the next breath that was already supposed to be filling her lungs but wasn't. She stumbled back into the wall behind her.

Her heart felt as heavy as the breaths she took. Her hands as light as air, she ripped one of the three bejeweled pins off her garter and pitched it at the door before her. "Fuck you, Avril!"

Katherine cried as she fell toward the swirling carpet. The next brooch found itself in her hand, glittering with red rubies. She could have sworn she threw it just as hard, but it only rolled off her palm and onto the floor. The third brooch caught and pulled under her skirt. The clip broke before it finally came loose, until it shone up at Katherine, the stark purple amethyst. It winked.

Winked.

Stupid brooch. She was supposed to keep them safe. She was supposed to be safe, but Katherine only fell to the floor along with them. "Fuck you."

After what felt like an hour but could have been only minutes, Katherine gathered up the still intact gold and jewels in her arms. She stumbled into the elevator and out the door to a taxi, not even caring that she barely had enough cash to pay once she arrived back at the shop. Keys shaking, she struggled to turn the lock.

Avril knew.

She knew that Emilie had died. She had probably known that

Jack didn't actually love her at all. They were playing her this entire time and she had believed them.

Leave her alone.

For once, it seemed fate had brought her right back around to the place and things she found herself very good at.

CHAPTER THIRTY-FOUR

The funeral was quiet. Katherine had no one to call, and Emilie had told most of her friends she didn't want an affair. Katherine wore the shoes Avril gave her, slightly scuffed now around the heel. She tied her curls back into a low bun with one of Emilie's scarves. She wore the simple black dress with sleeves that ended just below her elbows, shoulders covered with Emilie's fringed piano shawl.

It was the same dress she wore for Jack's parents' anniversary party.

The urn felt too light in her hands.

An old friend of Emilie's lifted Katherine's glasses for her, only for her hankie to come away dry. She didn't seem to notice.

"I just can't believe he didn't show up."

Her father was not a cruel man. He was not mean or uncaring. He was simply indifferent. Katherine didn't realize how much so until now.

Handing the urn to Emilie's chosen confidant to get to place her in her final resting place in the ground, Katherine's hands now felt even lighter. Felt the way they did when she never blew out her pretty pink birthday cake with yellow frosting flowers the day her mother left. Felt the way she did when the note her father left her slid off the table and she never bothered to pick it back up or throw it away. She felt nearly the same way as she did when she accidentally gave the cab driver a nickel instead of a quarter the other night after she left Avril's apartment in the city, and he said nothing.

She was hollow.

Go home, get some sleep, those who came to the cemetery advised to her empty blinking eyes.

Right. Sure. She would do that. Right away.

But Katherine was not in the mood to be taking any orders, well-meaning or otherwise.

She let the cabs pass her by on the walk home through a prophetic mist that turned into thin drops of rain beating down on her, slipping down around her temples. Katherine's shoulders slumped and let the rest of her body melt with it with every step across the gritty pavement. Eyes down, she even slipped off her shoes halfway home, watching for glass hidden against the cracks.

Turning the block, her eyes met a pair of very scuffed black dress shoes sitting on the shop's stoop. Katherine followed the legs attached to them all the way up to their familiar face. He looked good in a suit. His tie wasn't clipped down, just hanging there, swaying away from his crisp gray button-down.

Jack's expression looked about as pained as she felt.

The skin on her forehead creased together, causing a new line of rain to trail down the side of her face. "Were you…"

Was he at the funeral? Katherine couldn't remember seeing him there, though it seemed like a stupid question in her mind now, seeing him there in front of her. In a suit. Staring at her.

He gave a small, almost unnoticeable nod.

"Kit, I—"

"Don't. Please." Katherine clenched a hand over her chest. She felt a snag in the beats.

"I need to talk to you," Jack forced on anyway. "What I said—"

It didn't matter. None of it. Not him or her or the shop that she signed the papers for this morning to say that it now legally belonged to her mattered anymore. At least not right now.

Katherine tried to look away, but it was as if she knew that his hand would flinch. He would try to reach out and bring her eyes in line with him only a few inches higher than her own. "You don't have to say anything."

"You're right. I need a whole damn soliloquy."

How poetic. Katherine blinked slowly before taking another step closer to Jack. Around him. She dug for her keys.

"Please."

Finding the cold silver edge of her keys, she let the grooves dig into her palm. "You lied. This whole time, you lied to me. Why would I want to talk to a liar?"

Jack looked pained. "That's fair."

She hated that expression. Of course, it was fair. It was the truth.

"Let's go inside. Or hell, let's get out of here and go to Keys. Get some tea," Jack began to ramble on about not knowing what to do and warm drinks. "You look like you're freezing. Just, let's talk."

"I have to go," Katherine said, though she had nowhere to go at all. Two steps up. A flight to the apartment. A few more to the bed. Go home. Alone.

Rest, they told her.

Jack's eyes flicked toward the upstairs window. The rain began to beat on his shoulders. He only nodded. "Yeah, I do too. Good night, Kit."

Good night, Jack.

Katherine opened the door and used all her strength to shut and lock it behind her.

By the time she got up the stairs and locked the second door leading to the shop behind her, Katherine's hands shook. She snatched her phone up from where it was sitting beside the bed. Left there, after she couldn't handle hitting decline every time Jack attempted to call. Now, Katherine pressed the hot plastic frame of the phone harder against her ear. The same ringing voice of her father's voice mail answered that she had reached the current owner of the number. Hitting the end call, she was too irritated to listen.

She hit redial again and again.

"Don't you care?" she screamed into the voice mail on her eighth—no, ninth try. "Don't you care that your sister is dead, you ass?"

THE SHOP WAS CLOSED, and the days passed by slowly.

They were running out of tea. Katherine's blood was filled with sugar and her eyes caked in purple smudges as she continued to work.

She wasn't sure how many rounds of hot water fermented tea leaves sat nearly untouched in Emilie's faded mugs over the past week after she made them, taken a sip, and left them to rot.

Katherine nudged the mug to check for dust, though found it only rested on top of thin waxy sugar cake wrappers before she answered the door.

"I don't usually do house calls anymore," said the man who entered wearing a loose suit.

Slightly graying around the sides, his hands gently gripped a laptop and binder in his hands. Katherine focused on them, unable to look anyone in the eye, but especially him. The lawyer. He would know she was a hack—that she did this.

"But Emilie was a friend to me once."

So it seemed that's what a lot of people said. The shop phone had been going off for days with condolences, and Katherine had given up on answering. The city was Emilie's home, Emilie's family.

Katherine left them that way.

"Thank you for coming," Katherine replied, guiding him inside to the table. The living space was still a mess of her things. She didn't feel right sleeping in Emilie's bed just yet. "How does this work?"

"Well, I go over her will that she left. We'll sign some paperwork and then I will get out of your hair."

Katherine nodded. She could do that.

"All right then. Let's get started. According to the will of Emilie Passin Walker..."

All the words blended together. Everything went to Kit just as she said. Sign on the dotted line and she owned a house. A store. Even Emilie's name, currently attached to it, was hers somehow.

"Is that it?"

"And there is one more person in her will."

Katherine looked up at the man, adjusting his narrow glasses. "Who?"

"A Jack Carver."

CHAPTER THIRTY-FIVE

*J*ack realized he didn't want to live without Kit when he kneeled at the grave. It felt too formal though, he could just imagine Emilie whacking him on the back and laughing at him, so he adjusted until he sat in front of the fresh stone, legs crossed.

She wanted to be cremated so no one would touch her body, but still be buried in the earth where no one could take her.

She liked to cause a fuss.

"Hey, Emilie." He looked around, feeling a little silly, but he went on. "I was at your funeral, though I stood in the back. I was too much of a coward even then to face your niece—not that she noticed I was there."

The entire time at the funeral, it was a small affair, but still, many who knew her came. Nik from DuCain, the girls from Rosin, others around town who knew her by name or reputation. And Kit, her family, was there, clutching the ashes and nodding as people came to pay their respects.

She did not smile.

She did not cry.

She did not waver.

Jack wavered. Jack bit his cheek as he waited in the short line and bowed out before anyone even moved. He couldn't stand looking at her like that. He couldn't bear that he had caused her pain.

They should've told her sooner. They should've told her the moment he realized that she had feelings—that he couldn't see a day without her somewhere in it, even for a second. It wasn't supposed to be like this. He was just supposed to make sure she was taken care of and wasn't hurt.

And what did he do?

"Do you think she'll ever forgive me?" Jack asked, feeling silly as he looked around. "I know you'd say yes if you were here, but you aren't, and we really fucked up, Em. I really fucked up."

All the things he yelled at her as she screamed in grief.

He tugged at the roots of his hair as his jaw clenched.

"I don't know what I'm going to do."

CHAPTER THIRTY-SIX

*W*hen she made it back inside the chilled first floor of the shop, instead of turning to her left where the workroom was, where the tea hid for special necessary occasions, Katherine wandered toward the other wall. Standing before the phone, she let the plastic shake one more time before reaching out, snatching it and its high-pitched noise away.

She pressed the phone tight to her ear and murmured a hello instead of asking who the hell kept calling. Her voice sounded hazy, unused to speaking to anyone but the kettle who screeched back too loudly.

The phone was starting to mock her too.

"Thank goodness, I have been trying to get a hold of someone for days."

"I'm sorry." Katherine held the phone with two hands. How silly a landline was. So much harder not to pick up. "The shop has been closed for the past few weeks due to…"

A death.

The owner's death.

"A change in management." How stupid that phrase sounded. Katherine shook her head, though the woman on the other side of the line clearly could not see it, nor how Katherine let her head fall back toward the ceiling. Maybe she shouldn't have answered.

A few witch's globes made of hand-blown glass to capture bad energy hung from the supporting beam. How had she never noticed them before? Greens and pinks twinkled in the swaths of light, cutting through the windowpanes.

"Is that why the website looks all shiny and new?" the woman asked. "I was just curious about when the order I placed would be shipped. It didn't really say anything, and it's a holiday gift."

"Right." Katherine hesitated, feeling her forehead wrinkle before she understood what the woman was asking. "Of course."

Website?

"Where did you order, again?"

"On your shop's website," the woman repeated. This time, slowly.

"Would you just hold for a moment?" Looking around, Katherine found the laptop beneath the register she left there. Hitting the power button, time passed in years, centuries once the internet loaded and she found the link sitting in her email.

EMS Lingerie, in stark swirling script, lit up the screen. A single star was positioned right above, between the M and S.

Em's.

All the photos were there. Her photos. A face soft and unaware that her stretch marks and curves were also everywhere on the internet in Chantilly lace and night-sky satin stared back at her with something she could only classify as unabashed vibrance.

Katherine's eyes stretched wide.

She looked beautiful.

He had done it. Hadn't he? Jack had done this.

Switching back to the other tab, she saw the email there. Jack's email was the one that sent her the link. And under it was a single line.

I warned you. You can change the name if you like, but I think it has a nice ring to it.

"No effing way," Katherine murmured under her breath.

"I'm sorry." A small chuckle came from inside her ear. "What was that?"

"Right. I am sorry again." Katherine came up with some sort of excuse for swearing at a customer. She blinked, feeling one of her first tears in days slide down her cheek. She flicked the sudden emotion away quickly, clearing her voice. "Like you said, new website and all."

"It seems it is working out for you. I saw a few postings online and thought the pieces were absolutely gorgeous. I figured I had to jump on and get my order in quickly before it was too late."

Quite a few of the listings said only two words beneath the items. Sold Out.

Katherine's eyes widened at the words. "Thank you for bringing the orders to my attention. I will get your order out to you as soon as the mailman comes around. Gift wrapped and everything."

"Thank you so much." She could hear the woman smiling through the phone. "I am sure my niece will love it."

"Thank you," Katherine replied. She hit the end call button and hung the phone back up without looking. Her eyes couldn't be torn away from the computer screen as she scrolled.

She couldn't believe it. Everything she had imagined, drawn up, and set to work with her limited coding knowledge, was in front of her. Better than she had ever imagined.

Bringing the laptop filled with a spreadsheet of unfilled orders with her to where the tea was hidden, she flicked the light on in the workroom.

Grabbing supplies from each cabinet in the silence, her eyes caught on the old record player. Passing by the light switch, she ran her hand over the edge of the mint green plastic. Gently, as if touching an old artifact that had never been seen before, she dropped the pin on the record and the room filled with the fulfilling hum of The Beatles in strawberry fields.

Letting her hips sway side to side, Katherine let her body dance to the slow strange beat until she was rolling up ribbon and lace into their respective drawers across the drafting table. Sweeping through the shop, she set to cleaning the entire place as the rest of the record played. When it stopped, she flipped through the box for another and set the needle back down to play again.

She had a lot of orders to catch up on.

———

Leaning over her worktable, Katherine ran scissors through the length of sky-blue fabric, ignoring the incessant pounding at the door. Facing the other direction, Katherine didn't know if they could see her, but turned around anyway to look at the dull unlit shop before her. It was bustling with color again with all the orders she'd stayed up over the last week making, they were spread out to be tagged and packaged before being sent out in the morning. Everything was exactly how Emilie had left it. Only no one was there.

A knock came again.

A dirty-blond boy stood at the sparkling front door.

Katherine paused, frozen in the middle of the shop. She almost expected another one of Emilie's old friends to be at the door, checking in on her, or even her own father, finally showing up to do some good in his life, but it wasn't.

She clutched her warm, fluff-lined robe she hadn't taken off for the past few days closer to her chest.

For a long second, Katherine only stared at Jack's younger brother.

Jace's golden eyes widened in a wince for whatever was about to come. It was obvious, if not by her appearance, by her lack of greeting that Katherine had no well wishes to speak of. But maybe it was the fact that he showed up. Here. In Ashton. At her shop, that made her pause in stagnant shock.

Or maybe for the fact he at least had the decency to be ready to beg from where he was, kneeling before the entrance on his knees.

Katherine raised her eyebrows at the sight.

Jace's mouth twisted to the side. A withering smile bloomed and something harsh caught in Katherine's chest at it.

That smile.

With her bare foot, Katherine shoved his shoulder back. He had to catch himself before he went toppling down the wide steps. He caught himself just in time, hand covered in hard pebbles. He turned back to look at her again, as if he wasn't quite sure anymore that he arrived at the correct address.

All he could see at this one was cold rage—easily sparked whenever she dared to think about him or Jack or what her life was weeks ago, before it was all taken away from her.

"Kit—"

"What do you think you're doing here?"

Jace's mouth hung open. He hoped the right explanation would buzz into his mouth. When it didn't come, he stood and brushed off his knees. "I didn't—I don't know, okay?"

Katherine closed her eyes. Shook her head. Behind his form, she noticed a stuffed backpack lying on the step.

Her eyes flicked back to his guilty grin.

Please say he didn't do what she thought he did.

"I just got here, and I realized I had no clue what to do next. I don't even know my goddamn brother's address to go begging on his doorstep first." As Jace spoke, one word at a time, Jace picked at the ridges around his fingers. Some of his cuticles were already raw with color.

Katherine put a hand to her head. Oh, why yes, he did do exactly what she thought he did.

"I didn't know where to go," he stammered. "So, yeah, here I am, I guess, begging on his girlfriend's front... is this considered a stoop or storefront? I didn't know you owned the place. Pretty impressive."

"It's recently acquired," Katherine replied without emotion. "I am not his girlfriend."

She was never his anything. Not really.

Jace, for once, hesitated, raising one eyebrow. "You're kidding me, right?"

Katherine reached for the door. Maybe if she shut and opened it again, he would be gone. Maybe this was all a terrible stress-induced anxiety dream.

"Please!" Jace stretched out a hand. If Katherine was an ounce crueler, she could have let the creaky wood door slam on his fingers. Instead, she caught it just as he gasped. "Wait."

"Please," he repeated. "I don't have anywhere else to go."

Looking Jace up and down again, his body looked as leached as his coat did, dripping from the rain. He must've walked through the storm that morning to get there. He almost looked as rough as Katherine did.

He had nowhere else to go.

She felt her own shoulders slide down her back with a sigh. "Fine."

"Yeah?" A glimmer of hope startled his expression.

"Yeah." Before Katherine could question herself, she slammed the door closed and turned back into the shop before heading upstairs. Carver boys, always getting in the way of her work. "Wait there."

CLOTHES FELT strange on Katherine's skin. After spending the past weeks in varying states of dress and cleanliness, perhaps that was a good thing. Change. Even the air felt different outside than it did flowing through the cracked windows inside the house.

She tucked the hem of her sweater into her long skirt.

"Where are we going?" Jace asked, hiking his backpack up a little farther on his back. With how full it was, fabric pulled away from his body until it looked like a shell. "So you live, like, in the shop? Nice skirt, by the way, you headed to the prairie anytime soon?"

She pretended she didn't hear any of the questions, especially the last one.

"It's loud here, huh?"

Did Katherine ever sound like that? She honestly didn't think she did. She sure hoped that she didn't. Jace went on and on, filling up the silence until his voice turned to a long hum in Katherine's ears. She held the door open for him once they reached their destination, swinging her arm until he finally went into Keys before her. Inside the café was decorated in green and red lights.

The only reason she knew it was Christmas was the fact of how many orders came in with various gift requests and in shades of green or red. Katherine preferred the less ostentatious silver and gold herself.

"Miss Kit."

Marley. At his gruff, joyful voice, it was as if the fog around Katherine began to separate. "You remember me."

With a single nod, he grabbed two wide-rimmed mugs off the top of the espresso machine. "Never forget a face. I'm sorry to hear about Emilie, she was a good woman," he said.

Katherine nodded, holding back the rush of emotion that pulsed behind her eyes at the sentiment. "Thank you."

His gaze landed on Jace. "And if I'm not mistaken, you are a new one."

Jace, for once silent in the past twenty minutes, dipped his chin down until half his mouth was concealed by his rust-colored, hand-knit scarf.

Staring at the pulls and tight knits and pearls, Katherine could imagine Emily sitting in their living room before the fire, making it for a gift. The only thing Emilie could not do was knit. Maybe Emily tried to teach her once.

Katherine shook the thought away, stretching her hands inside her oversized coat pockets.

"What can I get you two?" Marley cut through her thoughts.

"Tea please, Marley."

"What kind?"

"Surprise me."

"And you, Carver boy?"

Jace looked shocked at the correct assumption. "Uh, coffee."

"Comin' right up."

"How does he know me?"

"Jack." Even the name made her sigh. She didn't want to talk about Jack. Yet there she was, drifting back to the table in the corner where she and Jack sat when he first brought her to Keys. Jace followed like a lost dog.

There was no missing, however, the interested looks Jace gave the many art students with more piercings and impressive streaks of color etched through their hair than he must have thought possible.

"He brought me here once."

Jace sat. The plush chair seemed to encapsulate him.

"So, what brings you to Ashton?" Katherine finally dared to ask.

"Oh, right. That." He lifted a hand, running it through his hair. It was growing out from the cropped buzz she had seen on the farm. "Would you believe me if I said that I don't know? I just grabbed my backpack. It was that easy. Of course, my heart was about to explode out of my chest the whole bus ride here."

"You took the bus in?" Katherine narrowed her eyes.

"Yeah, I called up a few people and they agreed to take me to the town over. I mean, they probably didn't know where I was going once I got there, but—"

"Wait." She was getting even more confused. "Does anyone know where you are?"

"I thought I made this clear by the whole showing up on your doorstep thing."

"Jace."

"Kit," he mocked in a deep voice.

"You have to call your mom. You have to go home. You have to—" Though to be honest, Katherine had no idea what Jace should do. He was sitting right in front of her now. In Ashton. That all was clear. And she wasn't exactly in the place to be giving advice.

Katherine cradled her head in the palm of her hand.

"Tea for the lady. And coffee." Marley set down the enormous mugs that got a smile from Jace. Taking in the difference of expression between the two of them, he didn't linger.

Plain English breakfast tea wafted up Katherine's nose.

Jace attempted to fill the space, clear up the mess he made that only seemed to get messier. "Look, I wanted to do this, okay? And after what you said—"

"What I said?" She certainly did not remember telling him to pull a Jack and run away from home.

"I don't know. I mean, you said something. Something like how I should get off my ass, basically. To do something about my life. Stop my complaining. Something like that."

She did say that.

"And when I got here, look at me, Kit. You have to get what I'm saying. When I stepped off that bus at the port authority, freaking out wondering if I had enough cash to get a bus back home before anyone noticed I was gone, relief." Jace spread his arms as if his newfound zen was a jacket he also did not have on any longer as he made himself at home.

Katherine picked up her cup and looked down into the deep, dark contents. She didn't ask for honey or milk.

"You know, you don't look all that great."

"Wow. Thanks," Katherine said. "In case you forgot, my aunt died."

Jace stopped to think before he spoke this time. His manic grin turned somber. "Right. My condolences."

Katherine looked around the space again, away from Jace. Every time she looked at him, her stomach ached.

"Thanks, too, for not calling my brother right away before. I appreciate it."

"We aren't exactly talking right now," explained Katherine. "Why would you even think—"

"It just seemed like you guys loved each other or whatever, don't mind me trying to be a considerate human being and ask about your life."

"He was only being nice to me because of Emilie."

"You don't really believe that, do you?"

Maybe. Sort of. The whole devious plot of it was starting to wear on her, if she was being honest. But it was the only thing that made some sort of sense.

Even if it wasn't much.

"No thanks to you," she said simply.

He rolled his eyes.

"Jack fucking thinks you are the best thing in the world. He's been calling my mother for the past few weeks and couldn't stop talking about you, which, yeah, we both know, isn't that rare, but it was all you," Jace said.

"He didn't."

"Oh, he did. My mother was practically planning the wedding by the time they got off the phone, whether you guys are together anymore or not. I'd call her if I were you in case you aren't interested in amber yellow, whatever that is, for your bridesmaid dresses."

Katherine remained silent, brushing away a piece of hair from her eyes.

"My brother misses you. If you guys fought..."

He didn't know the half of it. Didn't he know after all that it wasn't Jack that ran? It was her. Katherine was the one who pushed everyone away.

The truth of it picked open another hole she had been trying to ignore the past week.

"I don't want to talk about Jack."

"Fine." He lifted his cup to his lips and took a tentative sip. Whatever he tasted seemed to be a pleasant surprise.

"Do you even have a plan?" she dared to ask.

"Sort of. I mean, of course I do. I want to do art."

The image of the marker drawing on Jace's thigh flashed to mind.

"Tattoos specifically," Jace clarified. "Did you know back in town there is literally not a single tattoo shop in a hundred miles?"

It wouldn't take much for Katherine to believe it.

"Ashton just feels right. Like I am supposed to be here. From the moment I got off the bus, I knew. This is it. I'm finally doing something right. I know it."

Katherine couldn't say anything against that. "So, this is what you want to do? Stay in the city and find yourself."

"Basically."

Well, then there was only one thing to do. Katherine dug through her bag and extended her phone across the table. "Call your brother."

"I can't."

"It's your only option right now. Call him."

Jace took the phone.

To say that Jack was shocked to hear his brother's voice come out of a number that was most certainly not his own was an understatement if it was to be judged by Jace's deflated expression. One word at a time, Jace managed to get out a semblance of the story he told Katherine before pausing. "Yeah, I'm here. I'm at Keys with Kit."

At the mention of Katherine's name over the phone Jace spoke into before hanging up, she stood from the table, slowly getting ready. She could only imagine Jack halfway across town by now. "I should go."

"You aren't going to wait with me?"

"No," Katherine said. She wrapped her scarf tighter around her neck. "I can't."

"I know that I said things."

He said a whole lot of things. More things than Katherine did if she remembered correctly, and her things made Jace jump on a bus this morning without a plan once he got to his destination.

"Just don't torture my brother."

"He made his decisions," Katherine countered. She wasn't the one to clean those decisions up.

"But you have to talk to him."

"I know." At the very least, through her anger, she did know that. She knew that eventually she had to talk to him. She wanted to talk to him. To see him. But deep inside all that, the idea of it all hurt. "Just not now."

After a breath, Jace blinked a few times. He nodded.

"Thanks."

Jace shook his head now. "I think that is what I am supposed to say."

"No." Katherine was pretty sure this time. "Just take it."

"You're welcome then."

"You too," she said, enveloping him in a hug before she thought better of it.

He didn't let go until she did.

She must have looked like she needed it.

CHAPTER THIRTY-SEVEN

*T*he first time Jack ever pictured his future, it was him on the farm just like his parents. Kids ran around. He was seven. The next time, Jack pictured himself on the cover of a magazine, or rather, his photos would be. It was around the time his grandmother used to praise him whenever they went to go get them developed at the pharmacy. He held on to that image for a long time, before adding Avril to the mix, his life a constant stream of laughter and parties.

The most recent vision Jack had of his life was Kit.

She haunted his dreams and mind as if she died rather than Emilie. Bits and pieces of all those lives he thought he might lead blended into one, but Kit was always there.

Now, he might as well have thrown it all away, and he didn't know what to do in order to fix it.

"I want to come with you."

"You are not coming with," Jack said to his brother with a hand on the steering wheel. They drove alongside the dreary river, though Jace didn't seem very interested in taking in the scenery. "I am dropping you off so I can get to work, I'm already late. You are going to go in for your final portfolio interview and then hopefully finish moving into student housing. Put on a smile and pretend to be charming."

Jack couldn't believe all that somehow happened in the past few weeks after his brother showed up with only a grin. The first words out of his mouth when he picked him up at Keys were slow, through exposed teeth.

"Please don't kill me."

Marley, who overheard behind the counter, really liked Jace's sense of humor.

They both had gone home for Christmas after Jack called his family to tell them where their youngest ran off to. Only his mother noticed Jace was gone, and no one seemed all that concerned compared to when Jack did basically the same thing, though he had more of a plan going in. His brother was gripping onto his coattails and hoping for the best ever since Jack let him stay on Avril's couch.

He was lucky The Ashton Institute of Art and Design even had second-semester openings for people like him. He was lucky that Jack knew enough about them to sign him up for an open interview slot. As they walked into the auditorium, already half the seats in the front section were filled with potential academics that looked a lot cleaner and more pressed compared to his brother.

"Do my eyes deceive me?"

Jack didn't answer as a figure walked toward him. He nudged his brother to go and sit down with the rest of the non-punctual art academics. Hands shoved in his pockets, he had to pull one out in surprise at the hand extended.

"Nice to see you, Jack."

He chuckled. "Why do I think that's not true?"

"Ah, you weren't all that bad," his old professor said. He hadn't changed much over the past few years. Gray speckled the once young and spry photography buff who made them study too much Ansel Adams, but still the same.

Still made Jack shuffle his feet as he looked around the auditorium to see if any others noticed their exchange. "No?"

"I've had worse."

Jack chuckled.

"What are you doing here?"

"My brother." Jack gestured over to the shaggy-haired kid. He
didn't look so out of place among them all, holding his large
folder of his work. "He decided to follow in my footsteps."

"Photography?" Oddly enough, the professor's eyebrows went
up as if in interest.

"Art."

"Too bad. You know, I always thought you showed promise."

Jack's eyes narrowed.

"It's true."

"Before or after you helped throw me out?" Jack asked.

"We both know that's not how it went down."

"No?"

He shook his head. "I would've helped you stay, Jack. All you
had to do was ask."

But Jack didn't ask back then. He left about a day after being
put on probation with the academic board.

"Your work was rough, ill-planned, of course, but in the end,
whatever you turned in always struck me as different. You never
tried to imitate. I can only hope your brother will be the same in
whatever he decides to pursue."

For some reason, Jack had no doubt Jace would somehow
surprise them all. He already did.

"Do you still work in the field?"

"The field?"

"Photography."

"Oh." Jack paused, taken off guard by the question. He tilted
his chin. "I do. Not how I always wanted to, but I've kept up
with it."

"I'm glad to hear that," his old professor said with a smile. "It did kill me that we let you slip away. I would love to see more of your portfolio sometime. A good friend of mine has actually been looking for photographers, but everyone else I've sent to him hasn't been up to the task. Maybe?"

He gave a long look at Jack.

Without realizing what he was doing, Jack reached into his back pocket and pulled out his wallet. Inside was one of the few old cards he still had and occasionally gave out at the weddings he worked at. Otherwise, the one he handed over now was slightly faded and bent.

His old professor tapped it knowingly. "Good to know the city still hasn't broken a dream, huh? I have to get going since the board is going to start soon. Watch your phone if you get a call."

The city built by dreamers hasn't broken dreams.

Just the dreamer.

An odd, sensitive patch struck the base of his spine as his old professor turned around and walked back down the aisle. Rolling his shoulders to get rid of the twitch, with another nod at his brother, Jack walked out into the atrium. He lifted his phone to his ear.

It rang twice before turning to voice mail. The beep sounded and for once, Jack didn't hit the end call button.

"Yo, Queen. Where the hell are you? Answer your phone."

Sliding the screen back to black, Jack paused before putting it back into his pocket.

He'd called her at least seven times in the past month since Emilie died, encouraging her to show up to the funeral. She never answered.

Something stirred in his stomach that something was wrong. So much so, his vision swam with a sudden wave of nausea, though that could've also been from the shot he had after setting up the final DuCain run through for New Year's earlier and needed to get back to. Tonight was the big night.

Every day leading up to it, whenever the doors opened, he waited for Kit to walk through with her big notebook and plans.

She never did.

With another hit of a button on the way back to his car, he heard the ringing, and someone picked up.

"Hello?"

"Reed, it's Jack."

Reed remained silent on the other line as Jack told him everything he needed and didn't need to know. He told him about Kit and Emilie, and finally Avril.

"I know this is what she always does, but..."

The pause said enough for both of them.

"I'll find her," Reed said simply. "Thanks for letting me know."

HE ALMOST THOUGHT Avril had shown back up under all their noses when he made a pit stop at Rosin. Everything Kit had already managed to plan down to the minor details began to go off at Rosin without a hitch. It looked the same at DuCain.

Decorations were set, strung, tasteful and sparkling as the clock above the door ticked closer to the new year. Glasses were clinking and the crowd was full of people wearing their best. Peeking around the curtain where one of the girls from Rosin, transitioned from there to DuCain, danced, there was only one thing wrong—besides the obvious.

Jack rounded the corner back toward the dungeons, looking around through the thick stream of faces.

"Have you seen Evie?"

The girl in the spaghetti straps looked at him with wide eyes.

He rolled his. Looping around, he came face-to-face with Devil.

"Expecting someone else? Nice eyeliner."

Jack's lip curled in disgust. "Have you seen Evie?"

"Who?"

"Of course not," he said, walking away. "Bother me again, how about when you can actually be useful!"

Coming up from the main crowd, Jack spotted Nik. Shimmering gold combed through their hair. Nik's eyes also streaked similarly, caught on Jack the moment he stomped toward them.

"Where's Evie?"

They shook their head. "Don't worry about it, Jack. She's probably just running late. We'll find her."

"Then go and find her."

He had enough to worry about without adding Evie to the list. Half the reason she chose her was because the girl was punctual. She'd show up an hour early to her appointments according to the logbook, whether it was because she was bored or truly wanted to get here on time without the subway breaking down on her.

The other half was that, at least with Evie, he didn't have to worry about getting unnecessary pestering anymore. Not after he yelled at her when he got back from home about where Kit was.

Not his finest moment.

Walking over to the other side of the stage, the clock at the back of the house ticked. Clapping erupted from the space as they waited for the next thing to come on.

Nik squeezed through a group of people.

"Evie here?" Jack asked.

"They're here. Just get on stage."

Nearly shoved out onto the stage, Jack was met with the sound he loved. Drunken joy and excitement. There was another reason he didn't mind being the main event before the midnight ball dropped. Half the people here wouldn't care what happened on stage as long as they remembered they were here for it.

All of it.

Taking a deep breath, he looked down at his black shoes. He

took a step, and then another. Each movement was deliberate, as the indifferent mask he schooled himself in over the years slipped into place.

And he breathed, running through the scene they practiced a few dozen times through his head.

He thought of reminding Kit the same words he thought to himself, remembering the way her chest rose so close to his.

In and out.

He looked up to where the person likely did the same as they took a step to meet him.

Kit stood on the other end of the stage.

CHAPTER THIRTY-EIGHT

*T*hey'd never played this kind of game before.

Katherine's breath shook between her ribs from the moment she stepped out on stage. Jack's eyes widening just enough that she knew he definitely wasn't expecting her. Neither was she really when she showed up at DuCain, knowing he would be here. The only person she couldn't find was Evie as Nik searched the back rooms, stumbling across her instead.

"Have you seen Evie?" Nik asked, eyes wide as the rumble of clapping hands died down above.

She shook her head. "I haven't seen her."

Swearing, Nik continued to search. She hadn't called in. She should've been at the club hours ago.

Truth or dare? Katherine asked herself, freezing in the middle of the dungeon hallway, clenching and unclenching her hands into fists.

"I'll do it. I'll go."

But still, nothing could prepare her for what those words entailed as she looked across the stage in front of her, lit with the lights that always shined down on Jack the first time she ever saw him, and now she was under them too.

The crowd cried in a roar for fresh blood.

Frozen in her confidence, her steps, Katherine could barely see the crowd in the darkness surrounding them. All eyes were on her.

She could only listen and focus on him as he stalked toward her.

She expected him to whisper, What are you doing here? What do you think you are doing?

But instead, Jack growled a single word. "Kneel."

As she had been taught by Evie, she carefully slid down, like candle wax down a stem. Before Jack, her eyes positioned downward.

Until his finger lifted her chin back up.

"Well, isn't this a surprise," Jack murmured so low Katherine knew only she could hear. "I thought you said you didn't like surprises."

"I live to please."

"Is that so?" Jack grinned. "Eyes on me, Kitten."

Where else would they go?

Up, down, stand, kneel. Jack traced his fingers across her skin but went no further, and somehow the crowd seemed just as pleased by the change of pace as he did. They watched her. All eyes were on her, unlike all the other times when she walked into DuCain. There were questions in their eyes then.

What was she doing here?

Now there was the answer, and when Katherine caught a gaze among the stage lights flickering in and out with her gasp of breath when Jack ordered her to crawl and she did so without question, there was no confusion on anyone's faces.

There were different games, other than impact, which Jack insisted he didn't play live anymore without practicing the set first, Katherine remembered. This was pure obedience. Humiliation. Submission.

But to Katherine, as she tilted her chin down and let her gaze glow back up at him, in their own little world together for just this moment, she needed to say nothing. Explain nothing. Be nothing.

And it felt like devotion.

An order to stand.

Katherine stood.

An order to look at him.

Her eyes were already there.

Then, just like she imagined after seeing another girl on stage once.

Jack sauntered across the stage as if there was one more game he wanted to play and slammed his mouth onto hers.

DuCain went wild.

Her heart hammered in her chest as they stumbled off into the wings together. She couldn't tell who was tugging the other more, trying to get backstage before she was twisted up against the dungeon door and there was nowhere else to go.

There was nowhere else Katherine wanted to go. She wanted this right now, Jack on her and to never leave, never to say a word and they could keep pretending, at least for a little while, that everything was okay. They were both performers at DuCain and made such perfect partners—fit so perfectly against each other.

His lips captured hers and she pulled him close against her, feeling the rough fabric of his pants skid between her knees. She shut off her brain, trying not to think of anything or anyone else. She needed this, his mouth on her.

Jack's hands gripped into her sides before he broke to pull back. His breath was heavy and erratic. "I thought…"

"I don't know yet."

She barely knew what she just did. All she wanted to do was say yes, forgive and let it all go, but the moment she stepped off stage, the moment he looked at her, every lie from him and Emilie crashed back into her and she couldn't help but wonder— was the act over?

Was that smile for her?

She kissed him anyway, relishing the hot compulsion he had over her, around her, as he slid a hand to the back of her neck so she couldn't escape. She put her arms back around his shoulders, hugging him close as she tugged at the collar of his shirt as the tension between them melted.

It was perfectly right here as he nipped at her bottom lip with a gentle tug. Katherine's chest heaved with want. She missed him. How could she have not?

"Jack."

"What?" he snapped at the interruption.

Nik stood there in the darkness a few steps away. Their phone hung by their side as they looked between the two of them.

"It's Avril."

And Katherine and Jack were both suddenly free of any words they may or may not have had left held between bodies so close.

CHAPTER THIRTY-NINE

"*I* never even knew Avril had a brother," Katherine said softly. She tried to ignore the pain she felt all over whenever she looked at him in the Jeep.

They drove down the highway toward their unknown destination and the engine roared underneath and filled the space.

Jack adjusted himself in his seat, running his hand through his dirty hair, clearing his throat. "Yeah... neither did I. I always thought she was joking. But Reed just told me."

She nodded.

"Kit."

"Stop," Katherine choked. She could still feel him on her lips, forcing herself not to reach up and touch them. "Just because I—"

"Came to DuCain? Got on stage with me?" Jack supplied.

"Just because I didn't want to see all the work we did crash and burn—we don't have to do this right now. We can't do this right now."

Jack huffed. His hands gripped the steering wheel tighter. "I just..."

Just.

"Please, Jack. Don't. We have to... we have to focus on Avril right now. We have to find her brother, whatever his name is."

"Kellen."

"Kellen. We will find him and get back to the city. That is all we have to do. Focus on her," Katherine said, the final part delicately.

"That's going to be hard."

"Don't."

"Because the only person I have been able to think about for the past weeks has been you."

Katherine said nothing. If she did, she would've had to say the same thing.

"Truth or dare, Kit?"

"I don't want to play."

"I see it differently," Jack countered. "Truth or dare?"

Still, she didn't answer. Not until she shut her eyes. "Truth. I missed you. Is that what you want to hear? Is that what you want me to say? I missed you and your stupid smile and everything about you, and that I feel like you stole my entire life that took me twenty years to build up in my head before it was finally right in front of me. Then, it was all suddenly gone, and it was your fault because you lied, and I took your truth when you told me that you hated secrets. Is that what you want me to say to you, right now?"

Tears brimmed out of her eyes.

Jack said nothing.

She forced her eyes to stay open for the entire ride on the highway that became darker as they left the city in near silence. The car lights were the only thing pulsing over the white lines, leading them closer to their destination. Pulling up outside of the hotel bar, there was one thing that Katherine had only seen before in the movies. There was a sign hanging off the edge of the building, underneath, rocky dirt parking spaces for a long line of motorcycles.

Jack came around to the passenger door before Katherine had a chance to unlock her seat belt.

"Avril's brother is a biker?"

He turned, noticing the extreme number of Harleys at the same moment. "Damn. I thought she was kidding."

"Avril. Kidding?"

Were they talking about the same person?

Jack's lips dropped from his sad smile. "You have a point."

Walking through the side door, a few glances were immediately tossed in their direction. The bar was packed with bodies, leather, and pints of watery beer scattered on the tops of tables.

Jack looped his arm around Katherine, leading her farther into the crowd cheering at the football game on television, no doubt a replay from earlier in the week. The men and few women yelled and swore with every pass anyway.

"How are we going to find him?" Katherine asked, looking around. From what she gathered, it wasn't like they had a wanted poster or even a photograph from Avril to go off of.

Leaning down over her shoulder, Jack was about to reply when his and the rest of the voices in the bar were cut off.

"Get the fuck away from me." A statement that once Avril would have screamed came out low and empty through the bar. It was not loud but penetrating. It ended in a sour laugh.

Katherine paused at the sound of that resonating tone. That accent.

"Well, I think we found him."

The man had a head of fire slouched over his elbows, positioned on the wood bar top. He was tall and broad. At least that's how he appeared from where Katherine and Jack approached him from, squished between other large men in jackets. He and Avril looked similar. Soft face and dull green eyes blinking down into his beer.

After a moment, Kellen huffed and looked up into their stares. He looked faintly bored, resting his freckled face against one fist.

"And what are you two fancy faces doing hangin' out in these parts? Did you get lost?"

Katherine shook her head. "We—We've been looking for someone actually."

"Oh yeah?" Kellen looked her up and down. His eyes were a lot more vibrant than they were a moment ago. Almost alien. She felt Jack's hand stiffen on her lower back. "Poor bugger."

"No," Katherine stuttered. "I mean, we are here looking for you—Kellen McClair?"

At the sound of his full name, even the man on the other side of Kellen seemed a little more interested in Katherine. Without looking, Kellen whipped his hand back to wave his friends off.

"Is that so?" He tapped the corners of his pint glass.

"It is. It's Avril actually, your sister."

"I know who my sister is."

"I didn't—she needs you," Katherine insisted. This was Avril's brother—her family, and yet he could not look less interested.

"And if you knew who my sister was, you would also know that she doesn't need anyone. Especially me."

"She needs you now. Please."

Kellen still did not look convinced. Actually, he took a sip of his drink and rolled his eyes at Katherine's attempt at sincerity. "Really? The last time I saw my sister was on a cover of some sex magazine at a truck stop in Oklahoma a year or two ago. Looked like it was sellin' pretty damn well. Looks like she is also doing pretty damn well. The time before that, I left her on some steps somewhere in some sucky suburbs." Kellen gestured around him with a shrug. "I left for my brothers and my family. She got her own, and I got my own. We have an understanding."

Jack cleared his throat, finally coming alive. "We are Avril's family."

"Good." Kellen tipped his imaginary hat to him. "Then you go help her."

Both of them stood in stunned silence. Katherine leaned into

Jack, hoping that it would give some semblance of her needing backup. This was clearly not going as smoothly as either of them planned.

"Look," Jack began. He breathed deeply before he continued. It looked like the signature McClair attitude was wearing on both of their patience and insomnia. "We love Avril. Get it? We wouldn't be here if we didn't have to be. Your sister is in trouble and asked for you—I don't know. All I do know is that Reed, who is probably a better brother to her than you, knows that for some reason you are the only one who can help her right now."

"What's wrong with her? She lost another fight? Run away?"

"She hasn't left her boyfriend's apartment in almost three months," Katherine whispered.

"What?" Kellen's head whipped toward them. The rest of him swayed.

"I saw her a few weeks ago."

"You did?" Jack leaned to see Katherine's face.

Her gaze remained firmly on Kellen. "I didn't think anything of it. I mean, she left dancing. She said she needed a break. The other day, though, when I went to her, she yelled. Not that that is out of the ordinary, but she wouldn't open the door all the way."

Kellen still stared at her, unsure.

It dawned on her then. "She gave me these."

Without hesitation, Katherine reached toward her knees and drew her skirt up as high as it could go on the one side. She didn't feel the stares. They didn't matter anymore. What did was the three sparkling brooches that had belonged to Avril and Avril's mother, hanging from her garter belt of ribbons.

His sea-green eyes attached to the precious stones. "Let me finish my drink."

SHOVING the seat back until it clicked into position, Kellen stretched out in the back seat after screaming at his friends to take his bike back to the house. He had business to attend to. And no, it wasn't any of their fucking business.

Jack held out a hand to help Katherine climb in before rounding to the driver's seat.

"Do you want me to drive for a bit?" Katherine asked. "You drove all the way here and must be tired."

Jack looked at her as if she was joking. "Kit, I don't mean to be rude, but you look like you haven't slept in days."

"I haven't."

"What?" Jack's amused expression suddenly turned stern.

Katherine only shrugged. She didn't need to be chastised. She was fine. She was still awake and moving, wasn't she?

"I've had a lot of orders to catch up on," Katherine said hesitantly. "It seems someone published the shop's website without me."

He visibly swallowed as the Jeep groaned back to life. "Do you like it?"

"The pictures—they're beautiful, Jack."

A groan came from behind them. "My god, are you two going to screw in the front seat or are we going?"

Shaking his head, Jack put the Jeep in reverse and made sure that Katherine and big brother McClair both had their seat belts on before they reached the highway. They were all back in darkness even as the radio dial burned a dull blue but didn't play a single song, even though Katherine questioned it from Kellen's constant humming.

Leaning back, Katherine almost found whatever he was singing in the back of his throat soothing.

Katherine opened her eyes again to a big red sign shining into her line of vision after what she thought was only a few miles later. "What are you doing?"

Jack peeked over his shoulder before rolling down his window. He ordered into the tiny black fast-food box. French fries. A milkshake.

"Get me a burger, man," Kellen mumbled loudly from the back seat. His eyes were closed as he kicked up his feet on the edge of the center console. "God, you just had to need me when I was a pint of fuckin' whisky in, dinna ya?"

Katherine looked to Jack. He shrugged his shoulders. Neither of them could be sure if he was talking to them or the swirling sky. He stretched his tattoo-covered arms upward. Katherine swore that he must have thought the smog-covered stars were going to reach down and pick him straight up out of the Jeep at that moment.

Instead, the worker reached out and handed Jack a grease-filled paper bag and a large cup, striped straw included.

"If you haven't slept in days, I don't even want to ask about what you've been eating." He handed everything to Katherine, who handed the bag with a cheeseburger back to Kellen. Kellen immediately fished it out of the bag before they were even on the road. He moaned in drunken delight.

Jack pressed his lips together in an attempt not to smile.

Katherine couldn't hold herself together that well as the deep sounds continued in the back seat. She let loose a choked giggle. "What are you doing back there?"

"I am enjoying this fantastic piece of American culture, my non-friends," Kellen said. "Oh, so good."

"I'm glad that you are enjoying yourself," Jack said, teeth bright against the low car lights.

"You should hear me in bed."

Definitely Avril's brother. Katherine looked at Jack, extending a floppy fry toward his face. She had to lean over the milkshake in the cup holder to get close enough to him. She almost second-guessed herself. Why did she do that? She could imagine herself teasing Jack, doing something fun like this a few weeks ago, but now they weren't together. If they were ever truly together.

Before she could lean back into her own seat, he opened his

mouth to snatch the fry. His face flinched from the salt. "Where did they come from again?"

"Space. Another planet. For sure."

Katherine slumped back in her seat. Jack lifted up the Styrofoam cup in his hand and fed the straw to her lips until she tasted the sweet cookies and cream ice cream. She took a second sip before he put it back in the holder. She could see why Kellen was moaning now. It felt like she hadn't had real food in days.

Perhaps she hadn't.

Jack kept his eyes steady on the road. He didn't even notice when she stared at him. How badly she wanted to say thank you but couldn't.

When Kellen finished his burger and some of Katherine's fries, she'd handed them back one by one, his head fell back, snoring softly.

Leaning her own head against the window, she glanced at Jack.

He seemed to notice her staring, but made an effort not to look.

"Truth or dare, Jack?"

"I thought you said you didn't want to play?" he murmured.

She waited.

"Truth. I wanted to tell you. At first, when I was helping Emilie get set up for you to come, she just kept talking about you. She told me everything about her sweet little niece who sewed just like her and was going to learn the business. She asked me to meet you, be friends and show you around the city so you'd have someone if something did happen earlier than expected. She made me promise, though, on some metaphorical deathbed of hers, that I wouldn't tell you that she was sick. Sicker than you knew anyway.

"Of course, I didn't see you all summer, and I didn't seek you out. I sort of figured, better off for the both of us. But then you did show up, and Avril knew exactly who you were. I met you.

You weren't just some little niece in the city for somewhere to sleep and a good time. You were you," Jack drifted. "I did try to stay away. I tried to keep distance between us, but—"

He glanced at her, unable to help himself anymore. "It literally hurt me every time I thought about it. I told my mom, but she didn't know what to do either. I even called Emilie trying to get her to tell you around the time she kept getting sicker after coming off her medication, wanting to make sure the shop was set and as ready as she knew how to make it for you. I know I should've told you."

Katherine didn't say anything. She didn't know what to say.

"I'm terrible at secrets, you're right. But I'm very good at making promises."

"I just feel so stupid," whispered Katherine when she was sure he was finished. "I've been left over and over again, and this time I could've had a warning. There were signs everywhere, and I overlooked them all."

The amount of foundation over yellowing skin that Emilie kept stocked. Her random trips to visit friends. The spring convention she kept mentioning to Katherine was one she was pretty sure she wouldn't have come back from.

"All of it was right in front of me. I was just too hung up on doing my work and making her proud. Too hung up on you. To think she wanted me to be."

"What is so wrong with that?"

"What?" Katherine didn't understand.

"That Emilie wanted you to be happy," Jack said. "Didn't I make you happy?"

He did. "Too much."

They drove for a few minutes before Katherine swallowed the rock lodged in her throat. "Why does it hurt so much?"

Jack only had one answer. "Because it matters."

"Too much."

CHAPTER FORTY

*K*atherine stood only a step farther than Jack in the doorway of the ornate riverside townhouse. The castle. Tiny puddles collected at her feet, fed by droplets dripping from the tips of her hair all the way down her back. Her gaze followed Kellen while he carried Avril up the carpeted staircase.

It was Jack and him that managed to get her out of the ninth-floor apartment at all. She yelled at them the moment they walked in, curled up in the one corner, she screeched for them to leave her alone.

"Please, just don't fucking touch me." Avril's voice sounded small, yet still held as much bite as it ever did.

Kellen still reached for her. Trying to lift her off the floor, the moment he tugged, she screamed. Kellen's eyes widened as much as the rest of us as he looked toward the door.

"Where the hell is he? Huh, Aves? Where the fuck is this asshole? I will raise hell, meet Satan himself, and beat this moth-erfucker!" Kellen's voice burst through the walls.

Someone was bound to call the police.

Katherine looked from the door back to Reed again. Maybe they should.

Without a word, Jack brushed up behind the two of them and made his way inside. He said something to Kellen or Avril or the two of them. All Katherine could see next was Avril being lifted into his arms.

It was hard not to notice the tears streaming down Kellen's face. He didn't move to wipe them away. They weren't ashamed. He wasn't. Neither was Avril, as she kept her gaze straight ahead, one step at a time. She waited for the car door to be opened before entering the Jeep as rain pounded down on them. Reed climbed in on one side of her, Kellen the other, where she tipped over into him.

Settling her in his lap, Kellen brushed her long, knotted hair away from her temples. Pieces turned into thick dreads from being so long unbrushed or washed from anything but the drops of rain it caught. The strands looked dull, like the fire had gone out.

"Why, Avie? How did you let this happen, love?"

Somehow, she looked even smaller than Katherine had ever seen her before, cradled in her brother's arms when they got back to the house. It was as if she could fade into him.

Without questioning it, Katherine followed. She took her time up each step, feeling Jack's eyes on her as she went. By the time she got to the top of the stairs, she could already hear Avril's voice, sharp and direct.

"No. No!" Avril batted away Reed's hands, sending the little white pill across the room. "Get the hell away from me."

"Aves, please. Just take it. It will help you sleep."

"Get away from me," she repeated, but she was crying now. Avril shook her head at her best friend, if only so the tears would disappear toward her hairline.

Reed placed the water glass aside and leaned closer. With a sigh, his forehead nearly pressed against hers. They looked at each other, eye to eye, where tears seemed to jump between the two. They spoke in whimpers.

"You know I won't take it," Avril sputtered. "I don't want to take them."

"I promise you you'll be fine. They're yours from last time when you hurt your back, remember? I will be right here. I would never let anything bad happen."

Avril only stared at him, eyes half shut.

"I can't. Not now."

"Please? Just one." Reed poured another pill out of a nearly full prescription bottle. He extended it toward her. "For me? There you go—thank you. Take a big sip of water."

Reed smoothed down the big puff of curls on Avril's unkempt head. The bright red looked dark and dull, as if it hadn't been washed in days, weeks. Once she drank the full cup, the glass clattered over on its side.

She didn't or did not care to notice. "Where's Kellen?"

"In the other room, getting cleaned up. Just like you, darling."

"I'm tired."

"You should rest."

Avril's deep breath shook when she let it back out. It sounded like glass rattling in her lungs. "I haven't seen him in so long."

"I know." Reed gave her a peck on the forehead. The act was almost brotherly, but not quite. "Katherine?"

Reed turned toward where she stood respectfully, still in the doorway. She was far enough away from them still, so that Avril wouldn't even have to know that she was there. She was far enough away from the action for Katherine to believe she could still walk away from these people and Jack and everything else if she needed to. But like the rest of them, Reed wanted to break that.

He gave her the type of understanding look that said he knew more about her than nearly anyone else ever did before them. "Can you help me?"

Katherine could not bring herself to answer. She only closed Avril's bedroom door behind her. The last time she had been inside, they were playing dress-up. Cleaning out a closet to start a new life that turned out to nearly end them both. By the time she got to the bed where Avril gave her hotness ratings for each article of clothing she had tried on months ago, Reed was already attempting to peel away Avril's sweater. Underneath, another fitted shirt rode up, stuck to what looked like paint.

Katherine narrowed her eyes on it. Reed did not seem to notice.

"Oh, Kit," Avril murmured her name a few more times. It sounded slurred. "One hell of a shit show tonight, huh?"

Was she drinking? Katherine mouthed.

Reed's eyes widened. The thought hadn't occurred to him. Either way, whatever sleeping meds he gave Avril were taking effect.

Katherine gave Avril a pained smile. She kneeled down in front of her and Reed, finally, since they left the apartment building, took a step back.

"I am going to help take off your pants. Is that okay?" Katherine asked.

Even Avril's laugh, low and cracked, sounded wrong. "Well, since you asked so nicely."

Without any other discourse, Katherine got to work. She slipped her fingers carefully into the waistband of the sweats Kellen must have put her in before they left. At the light tug over her hips, Avril flinched. Waiting for any complaint that never came, Katherine slipped the soft gray cotton over Avril's calves. She handed the limp fabric to Reed.

"Gentle, gentle, so gentle," Avril continued to muse. "You wouldn't have made it anywhere in Ash till we found ya."

Trying to ignore the string of her words, Katherine could not help herself. She looked back at Reed. He shook his head at her. Don't listen to her right now, the motion seemed to say.

Lifting her knees from the plush rug, Katherine returned to stand before Avril. "Arms up."

With a huff, Avril did as she was told, lifting her elbows partway. Better than nothing. Each arm removed from its respective sleeve, Katherine took the bottom and lifted. At the sudden yank, Avril made a sharp gasp.

The shirt free, Katherine could fully see the paint that trailed up Avril's lower back. Splotches of dark purples and yellow expanded the longer she stared.

"Did he do this?" Katherine's voice asked the dreaded question before she could decide not to. She tried to bring back Avril's attention, slowly slipping. "Avril. Did he do this to your back?"

Reed just stood, gaping at the damage.

"An accident is all. Stop. I'm fine. Always fine." Avril's eyelashes fluttered.

Katherine took the fresh cotton shirt from Reed. She managed to pull it over Avril's head before she sloped to the side. Reed and Avril took the ends of a blanket, layering them over her prone body. She was so small beneath them.

It was only then Katherine realized her hands were shaking. She did not know why, the mixture of fear and sadness and anger brewing black in her bloodstream.

Careful not to jolt the bed, Reed led Katherine back out into the hallway. The house was eerily quiet.

"Thank you," he nearly whispered.

Katherine couldn't accept the words. "I should have known. I was there the other week and I saw her—I should have known."

"No. Don't you think that, darling." Reed reached out to place a hand on her arm. "Avril is very good at making the world see what she wants them to see. And if she doesn't even fully know what is in front of her. No one would've questioned her. Not even me."

He didn't see her that night, though. Half naked when she answered the door. She was screaming at Katherine when she told her to go. Pleading. And yet Katherine was far too caught up in herself. Her own grief and the lies she had been fed.

"I am just glad we got her into bed and convinced her to take something to get some rest."

"Right," Katherine said. "She is still afraid, isn't she? She didn't want to take the pills."

"I wanted to take her to the hospital," Reed said, confirming she was not wrong to wonder. "Kellen thought it would only make her worse. I agree. You know about her mom, right?"

Of course. Katherine couldn't help but remember what Avril told her about her mother, trying to piece it together like a strange puzzle that didn't quite fit. The bathroom floors. Mental illness. The beautiful brooches are still sitting in Katherine's coat pocket. The pills.

"She won't admit it, but Avril is terrified of being like her mother. And now—"

"She walked right into mommy dearest's footsteps," Kellen finished.

CHAPTER FORTY-ONE

*W*hen Jack stared through the door, he knew why he'd thought he loved Avril for so long. She was strong and fierce and didn't take anyone's shit. Maybe, like Kit, he too wanted to be like her. More like the both of them, from the moment he arrived in Ashton.

Everyone wanted something that never existed.

He stared at Reed as Avril's number one braced himself against the kitchen island. It took long enough for them to get her settled, and then again when she tried to get back out of bed, but now the house was quiet. It might've been the quietest it ever had been with so many inside its walls at once.

"Reed," Jack started.

He put up a hand, eyes closed. "Don't."

"I'm so sorry."

"What did I just say?" Reed grit. He shook his head as his hand dropped. His dark eyes were rimmed in red when they opened to look at him again. They looked painful.

"It's not your fault, man," Jack tried again.

"I should've known. I wasn't paying attention."

Jack knew what he meant. All this time in the past few

months when she was in and out of the city—was she ever really gone? Or were there just moments she came back outside, grasping at something she thought was slipping through her fingers?

She let it all go.

For that fucker.

"She didn't want you to," Jack said, coming up next to him, though they both kept their voices low. He ran a hand through his hair, catching himself in the hallway. "It was all me. I fucked up. I fucked up big time when I told you that I would take care of her."

Bitterness and salt stuffed the back of Jack's throat as he felt Reed's sorrow. He swallowed his own to make room.

"I told you I would make sure that she didn't get into anything bad. I should've known that something was off, that she didn't feel the same way anymore," Jack said, remembering the conversation they had years ago when Reed started to pull back from the scene, wanting to do something different.

He wanted to make his own sort of passion that wasn't attached to hers.

"Just say it."

The space between Reed's eyes creased. "Say what?"

"I told you so," Jack offered. "That I'm exactly the kind of person you said I was in the beginning. Someone who attaches and disappoints."

"You remember that?"

"I remember a hell of a lot more than I wish I did, Reed."

Reed huffed through his lips. "You are a lot of things, Jack. But, one thing you are not is someone who disappoints. You made her happy, Jack. From that night you led our escape from that party, I saw that look in her eyes. You were like this shiny new idea she wouldn't be able to leave behind."

Jack licked his lips as Reed took a deep breath.

"Even if you've been a pain in my ass, you took my place when

I needed to get away and see the world and mess up my own life a little. You were the only one who called me when they realized she was gone for too long and something wasn't right. I even had to contact her agent and PR person who then asked me why she wasn't posting online as often as she used to be anymore."

Jack watched him take a deep breath as he stood back up, heading down the hall back to the stairs.

"You're a lot of things, Jack," Reed said, shoulders slumped. "But you're not a disappointment. Whether or not you think so."

Opening his mouth, Jack shut it again, not sure what else to say for once.

How Reed seemed to know exactly what he was thinking, he also didn't know.

"We'll figure this out. None of this is what was supposed to happen. It's not right, but Queen will be alright. I will make sure of it. She's been through worse." His jaw clenched, tense as Reed began a sort of imaginary list in his head. Jack couldn't imagine a time where it must not have been full. "Maybe I'll send her to another city with her friends for a while, or see what she wants to do after I contact her old therapist and somehow convince her to go to the doctor for her back which should be an adventure in and of itself."

"How is it?"

"Her back?"

Jack nodded. He heard the screech Avril made from upstairs as Reed and Kit got her down to rest. He felt the tenderness of skin flooding his senses as he lifted her off the ground and into his arms with Kellen back at that fucker's apartment. If that guy did something. If she couldn't dance again—Jack didn't know what Avril would do.

He had quite a few ideas about what he'd do.

Reed paused and looked at him, again seeming to know his exact line of thought. "From what I could see and get out of her— my bet is that it's a lot worse than she's trying to put it off as. If I had to try and walk her out of there myself, I'm not sure what would have happened. But now, we'll figure it out. She'll get to the doctor that fixed her back up the last time she tweaked it a few years ago. I'll call him in the morning. You, though?"

"What?"

Reed paused as he stepped up the first step upstairs. His stare turned into the living room. He gave Jack that expression he knew well now from Reed. Just like old times. Was he really that stupid?

"I'm not interested enough to give advice or anything. Just don't screw that up."

Jack glanced out into the living room at Kit's form curled up on the couch in the morning darkness. Across from her in the corner lounge, Kellen was already asleep, making tiny noises from the back of his throat. Other than the hair, the resemblance wasn't like him and his brothers, but—he shook his head at everything.

None of this was right.

"Why do you care?" Jack gripped the railing.

"Because out of everyone Avril has brought home, I think I mind her the least. Good night, Jack."

"'Night." Jack watched Reed's retreating form go back upstairs and make the right turn into Queen's room. Pausing on the stairs, he looked back into the living room again toward Kit.

Kit, who laughed at his jokes.

Kit, who held his hand without question.

Kit, who kneeled at his feet and scrunched her nose up at him.

Kit, who let him dream.

Yeah, he was pretty sure he already screwed up, big time.

CHAPTER FORTY-TWO

*S*he was beginning to see how so many people could call the riverside townhouse home. Lying on the couch, if she closed her eyes, it was almost like she was back to fall, as the air chilled her lungs until she came inside and laid down after finishing her work alongside Jack. The blanket cocooned her as she curled her knees.

But then she blinked.

The house was quiet and dark, with no old film playing on mute in front of her.

Avril's brother slammed the fridge door shut in the other room.

Groaning as she sat up, she wasn't sure if she even fell asleep since she laid down for just a second. She didn't remember dreaming or sleeping, only thinking everything and anything, and her mind wouldn't stop.

It was the new year. She rang the year in on stage with Jack, kissing while people out in the crowd celebrated the clock hitting midnight without them even realizing. And now she was back on the couch.

Only he wasn't across from her. A deep pain resounded in her chest.

Slipping off the couch, Katherine stood, and like a homing beacon, she began to make her way up the stairs she had walked up and down so many times now. The first time, she thought, was when Avril brought her back here after going to her boyfriend's apartment. She dressed her up for a party they didn't go to, and she met Jack. Sober this time.

Katherine let the blanket around her shoulders trail behind her. The thick cover billowed until she came to a stop in front of the door. She had, surprisingly, never passed. Shutting her eyes, Katherine bit her lip, unsure if she should knock.

Should she do anything?

The door opened in front of her.

Her lips parted, looking back and forth from the floor to him. Those melting eyes dripped down. She clenched the blanket tighter around her. "How did you—"

"The shadows," Jack answered, glancing down to where her feet reflected under the doorway.

She shook her head. Right, of course.

"Do you…" Jack hesitated before he stepped to the side. "Do you want to come in?"

Suddenly awkward, Katherine could only nod as she crossed the threshold. Looking around, like all things with Jack, it was surprisingly clean in a *know where everything is in the mess* sort of way.

His bed was only slightly undone. Shoes kicked at the one side along with his phone plugged in on the nightstand.

Katherine pointed at it, suddenly remembering. Guilt settled over her. "Did you give them a proper goodbye that day? When we left for Emilie."

"I called them later, and I ended up taking a trip back over Christmas because of my brother and everything. Thank you for taking care of him that day. But, don't worry. They understood."

"They knew," Katherine said. It wasn't a question. Of course, they knew.

Everyone knew.

He gave another short nod.

"I—"

"You don't need to say anything," Jack said suddenly. "I know I was pushy probably earlier and I know that I would be pissed."

"I was so angry," she whispered. No, she needed to talk. She needed to do something. She couldn't sleep or focus. She needed to do this, however it ended. Jack seemed to see the thoughts cross her face. "I am still so angry with you and Emilie and everyone."

"You should be. You can be."

"That whole time, it was like I was a souvenir you picked up in Ashton along the way from scheming with Em. You could have just bought a T-shirt."

"That isn't fair."

She knew that he was right, though, no matter if it was fair or not. Sort of anyway. "I had to deal with her dying all on my own."

"You didn't have to be alone," Jack said, fighting to keep his voice easy. "If it makes you feel any better, Emilie and I did not intend for this to happen. I actually got a very stern talking to when I did call my parents' house."

It did make her feel better. Sort of. It also made her think of Emilie. She most likely was trying not to laugh or ask Jack for details on how their relationship came to be after making it very clear that Jack was to simply be her coercive spy throughout the entire lecture.

"And you know that's not how I feel about you."

She did. And she didn't. Or at least she didn't want to. Her head, like the days and weeks before, still felt foggy. "I still don't —I can't trust you. Or maybe it isn't that. I don't know."

"What can I do?"

She shook her head. "Honestly, I don't know."

She didn't feel safe anymore, she wanted to say.

But that wasn't true. As he stepped forward, arms extended at either side, Jack pulled her into his arms. She hadn't realized that she'd been shaking underneath her blanket. The pressure to not cry snuck up on her.

"How about this?"

Katherine bit her lip.

"You didn't have to go through it all alone, Kit," Jack murmured into her hair, squeezing her tighter. Her glasses dug into the side of her nose. "That's what I've been trying to tell you all this time. I didn't want you to deal with it alone. I wanted to be there for you. I wanted to be with you."

An unsteady breath escaped from her lungs as she looped her arms back around him.

"You are so strong, Kit. You are so amazing. I don't get how anyone hasn't seen it. But you can cry now. I got you, even if it is only right now, okay? You can cry. You don't have to be alone."

Katherine had been holding it in all this time. Every pain and tear and anger when she wanted to pick up that old sewing machine only Emilie used in the corner of the workspace because it barely worked anymore and throw it across the room. So now, she did cry. She buried her face into Jack's chest and wept.

Her body racked with the sobs she'd been holding in. She cried and cried all the way to the bed, where Jack tucked her in and pulled her back against him. She cried until she almost wanted to laugh, eyes so heavy and lulled by the gentle strokes Jack's hand made up and down her back.

She laid her head against his form, and he did not reject the weight. She didn't feel safe, she said, but that perhaps was the biggest lie she was telling herself. For her whole life, she didn't feel safe or right. Safe, right now, was the only thing that could lull her to sleep, being back in his arms.

She just…

"Never just."

She brought her eyes right back up to his, filled with warm melting honey that could easily sweep her under. She wanted them too. It would all be so much easier if she could go back to months ago, when it was all just a dream in her head. So, she went back there.

SHE WOKE UP TO SCREAMS.

The space in the bed beside her was vacant.

"Don't you dare save me again! You hear me, you fucker?" Avril's cry was unmistakable as it traveled down the stairs and toward the front door, partly opened.

Katherine stood there, along with Jack, who was already helping her up off the ground. The siblings continued their screaming match from the steps all the way to the front door. It was obvious that they'd missed something. Reed held his head in the palm of his hand as he watched, unsure whether to intervene.

"I was proud of you," Kellen snarled. "I fuckin' was, A. I saw your picture on the guys' magazines with that friend of yours in there—" Kellen threw a hand toward Jack.

Katherine looked up at him.

"The last time you called was my fifteenth birthday," Avril said.

With a nod, Kellen shook his head like he didn't want to hear about such things. "The guys, they tried to hide the print from me, I could tell. One night when they had it out, though, I snatched it from their hands. I hadn't seen you in about five years, A, but I knew it was you before I searched for the names. Corset and boobs and whatever the hell that thing was in your hand..."

"A riding crop," Avril whispered so softly.

"They waited for my reaction. I think they thought I'd be angry. When I held that magazine, I looked at them, and I smiled. Queen. So proud." He shook his head now, as if in a ridiculous sort of memory. "My sister was another woman in the sex indus-try, whatever that meant, but I was proud, because I could see it. That spark in your eye. It reminded me of you back then. But... it's gone now."

If Avril didn't feel the punch in her chest from those words that carried in the air of the Riverside house, Katherine did.

"You don't need me, you know it. You never did."

"I know."

In other words, Kellen seemed to take that as a resolution. He opened the door the rest of the way, heading into the gray morn-ing. Only Avril went after him, hobbling.

Avril's fingers gripped the doorframe. "Show up and leave. That's the little boy you were and turned into? This is what you decided to keep doing?"

He didn't say anything. He just stood there. Staring at Avril from the bottom step of the stoop.

"Fine. I don't need you. I don't fucking need you!" Avril shrieked, cried. It was all one and the same. Emotion she must have been keeping in a box and stored far away. "Go!"

Given permission by the Queen, Kellen gave a single nod and walked toward the dark beat-up car that was situated on the side of the street. Traffic honked their horns behind the vehicle until finally going around.

At the sight of Kellen's first foot hitting the concrete, however, Avril tried to take another step outside, bare legged and unsteady.

"Don't you leave." Avril's fist slammed down against the side of the townhouse so hard Katherine thought she heard a crack. Through the sounds Avril made in the back of her throat between words she could not say.

Kellen opened the car door and slid in. The car quickly kicked into gear, turning right at the end of the block.

"You goddamn bastard!" Avril yelled. "Bastard!"

Katherine took a step forward, but Jack held her back with a single hand. Reed was already there. Pulling her back into the townhouse, he held her against his chest, carrying her until it seemed neither of them could take her weight anymore, sliding to the floor of the foyer.

"We are going to get you back, okay?" Reed cradled Avril in his arms.

Lying on the floor, Avril sniffed, but no longer looked like she cried with a clenched jaw. Her fingers traced patterns of the tiles and faded stains, barely holding on to him. It was like she wasn't even there anymore.

"Hear me, Queen? We are going to piece you back together."

"My name is Avril."

CHAPTER FORTY-THREE

"Is there anything I can do?" Katherine asked not long after they all woke up. Whatever it was that triggered Avril took it out of her just as quickly, Reed and Jack helping her back upstairs before she started to crawl. "I could stay and watch Avril or make some tea."

"She does make a hell of a cup of tea," Jack murmured.

Katherine glanced toward him as he shoved his hands in his pockets.

"No, it's all good. Thank you, Kit."

Jack cleared his throat. "You want me to give you a ride home?"

Looking him up and down, Katherine felt different, off again, as if whatever it was that they shared the night before really was a dream. She nodded, nonetheless. "Okay."

When they got back outside, the rain had already begun to die down. Scattered shards of mist made Katherine feel as if she was forming a second layer of skin under the lamp glow before they reached the Jeep. Jack turned on the radio but didn't try to say anything until they were in front of Emilie's—her shop.

Jack pushed the car into park. "I would like some tea."

Turning toward him, she stared at Jack, who looked right back at her, regret in his eyes, almost like a small boy prepared to beg.

Katherine closed her eyes, rubbed under her glasses before she reached for the handle. "You don't even like tea."

He shrugged.

"I would still love a cup."

Taking a deep breath, Katherine awarded him a single nod. One cup couldn't hurt things. "Come on, then."

Though she had been getting the shop on track the past few weeks, it would be a lie if Katherine said that she was following through for the rest of her life. The apartment showed as much. What the customers saw downstairs was what mattered for right now, she told herself. Not the fact that she had been living off of old tea leaves and Little Debbie snack cakes for the past few weeks.

"Sorry, this is all we have left," Katherine said. After making a pot out of habit, even though she knew he wouldn't drink it, she handed Jack an Archie comic mug filled with the last type of tea she had in the house, a deep red color and swirling with the scent of vanilla and berries.

"Birthday tea," Jack recalled.

She hadn't realized her hands were shaking until he wrapped his hands around hers.

She sighed. Letting them rest there, his over hers for a moment longer. Maybe letting him in wasn't such a good idea. The place was a mess. Emilie's things everywhere were a mess. She was a mess.

She pulled away from him, sitting down in the only other place she could. On the pull-out couch, she still couldn't help herself from using it. It creaked under her weight.

"So, what did you want to talk about?" Katherine asked.

Jack stared at her for a long moment. He even took a second to bring the tea to his lips and take a sip, forcing himself not to cringe by the tic in his jaw before setting the cup aside and Katherine could see that it wasn't a tic, it was a smile. A smug smirk of a smile as Jack forced himself not to laugh.

Katherine raised her eyebrows anyway, pressing her lips together.

She hadn't seen that smile in a long time. At least, it felt that way.

"Kitten, you crack me up," Jack said softly. "We do have things to talk about, don't we? No? Then, I'll stay simple. I love you, Kit."

"Jack."

"Or was that too vague?"

"You don't—you don't have to say it." She didn't want him to say it. Her mind pulsed from all the information that was slowly collecting in the corners of everything she previously knew to begin with.

Everything still hurt inside of her and she couldn't be sure what was from him, what was from Emilie, and what was just from her anymore. She didn't need him to say the words that would scatter the feelings wrapped up in a knot of unforgiving string, somehow attaching the two of them together any further.

"Kit."

"I just—" She tried to stop him.

"No—"

"But—"

"Stop talking." Jack smiled a sad smile. A tear slipped down and around his nose. She hadn't even seen it collecting there. "What can I do? What can I say to make this better? Do I need to tell you what happened? About how I gave Emilie a deathbed promise before she was dead, and I've regretted it since the moment I met you?"

"You already said that."

"But I'll say it again. I will tell you anything you need to fix this, Kit."

"But you don't have to."

"That's true."

Katherine's heart stopped in her chest for a solid second. "That's right—"

"So now, can I declare my love without you having an existential crisis now?"

What did he think all of this was? Mouth parted open; Katherine pressed her lips together. She thought about what he said earlier.

Was happiness with someone, what Emilie wanted for her, such a bad thing?

Joy. It was what meant most to her. Always. Looking around the various brightly shaded wallpapers and hundred-dollar Hermes scarves hanging from doorknobs only illustrated the thought.

"Good," Jack breathed. "Because I fucking love you, Kit—and yes. God, yes. I mean it."

"You don't mean that."

He looked at her like she had to be kidding. That small smile he forced to stay there only continued to break over and over again. "I do."

Yet Katherine still shook her head. All of this, it wasn't right. She was supposed to be getting back to life, all right and perfectly. Alone.

"I don't want to leave you. I am yours. Don't you get that yet? I thought you were mine. Yours," Jack stammered. "I thought we were going to come back here—take over DuCain together. Take over this whole goddamn city."

Katherine felt the tears slipping out from the corners of her eyes, still fighting with herself. She needed to stop. She needed to take him before he changed his mind or— "That was Avril, though, Jack. You wanted that for you and Avril, and you shouldn't settle. You've always wanted to be a king standing alongside the queen, taking over the world with traveling and your photography and parties. You deserve that."

"I am no king."

Then they must not have been talking about the same person. Tapping her foot, Katherine stood.

"Don't walk away," Jack said.

Throwing her arms out to either side, water dripped from her coat. She must've forgotten to take it off.

She looked at him, ripping an arm out of either sleeve before dropping it back to the floor. "Don't you get it yet, Jack? I have nowhere to go."

The realization settled into Katherine's bones all over again. This shop. The apartment above it with buckling hardwood stained and battered from the moment it was installed in the nineteenth century. All of it was hers, from the thousand dollars' worth of silk she always admired to the tiny pieces of costume jewelry her aunt collected.

She had a life here. Emilie did. She lived and raged and danced through the streets of Ash since the moment she stepped across the river. What she had brought back in physical objects and she hoarded were memories.

Now it was all Katherine's, and she had nowhere to go.

She was here.

"Well then." Jack nodded slowly. "It is a good thing that I will always be right next to you."

Katherine could have sobbed. Instead, she let him move toward her when she faltered on her feet, cupping the side of her face with his hand as she made out another question. "Why would you want this?"

"Want what? You? Who wouldn't want you, Kitten?" The thought seemed as if it was completely incredulous to him. "It's stupid, really. I've been asking myself the same question since the minute I met you that night on the kitchen floor. I asked you, 'What did you think of me?'"

"Magnificent," Katherine quoted herself.

Jack nodded, a tear in the corner of his eye. "I love you. Can you ever forgive me?"

The words settled themselves into the very marrow of her bones. The taut string of fate settled between the two of them, wound and tugged tight until both bodies were held against each other, gasping for the warm air passed between them, around the sorrow and pain they had been both given and had caused.

Katherine had caused just as much as she had given, she was sure. Maybe more.

Her hand reached up to run through Jack's hair, beginning to get shaggy around the sides. Near the back, she gripped tight. "I forgive you."

His shoulders slumped in relief.

"I love you too."

"You don't have to just say it," Jack teased her with a sniff.

She closed her eyes and laughed into his skin. "Do you want me to take it back?"

He laughed with her, hugging her tight to his chest. She felt his warm skin, his heart beating strong and fast. "Never. I won't let you."

She could feel his head shake at the top of her slick, sweat-caked hair. Neither of them seemed to care. She only cared how relieved his eyes looked when he lifted her chin to look at him in the eyes. "But you can say it again, if you'd like."

He was pushing his luck. She'd let him. She was too tired to notice anything but the way his lips were moving ever so slowly over each word.

"I've loved you since I first walked into DuCain on a delivery and saw you up on that stage. Eyeliner and everything," Katherine tried to joke. "I always thought you looked kind of hot in that eyeliner."

"Kind of?"

"Undeniably."

"That sounds more correct."

Their words murmured between chapped lips and the pull of their mouths before they finally ended the torture and crashed in on one another.

Neither of them was quite sure who had kissed the other first. Such things didn't matter. Not in the slightest. There was no fighting. They were done fighting for the night. There was only the immediate and luscious movement of kisses as they mixed with the drying saltwater still coating their cheeks. Katherine's glasses were pushed up toward her forehead before Jack carefully took them off her face, setting them on the table next to the antique sewing machine.

Katherine reached back up around his neck and pulled his mouth back to hers. They met again, and Katherine felt the thrill of energy coursing from Jack's lips all the way down to the bottom of her stomach. The softest, most intimate kiss she ever experienced, though few.

She opened her mouth, and his expert tongue pressed gently against hers. Fingers dug into the back of her neck as they guided one another back down the hallway toward the bedroom. One step at a time, they tumbled toward the bed.

Hitting the edge of the mattress, unlike the first time they had ever been together, Katherine was not nervous. She shook from the thrill and brewing joy alone. Jack bent his head as he leaned over her and kissed her long and deep. He slid his hands under her skirt. The new pressure caused her to moan softly in the back of her throat.

She was on fire, and the first thing to go was anything separating her skin from his.

Katherine let Jack hold her up as she reached out, tugging his shirt over his head. She ran her hands over his chest and stomach, remembering the small scars and the way he felt while he undressed her.

When they both were equally bare, he pulled her close and bit and kissed the sensitive skin of her neck and shoulders.

She squirmed backward, Jack gripping her waist and pulling her back toward him. She stretched out beneath him and his mouth was on hers, a gleeful laugh breaking between each kiss, an onslaught of his attack. Nothing was really funny. It was as if they couldn't stop the sensation passing between them, not that they wanted to.

Each kiss and languid movement were warm and wet and more intense than Katherine had ever experienced with him or anyone. Her heart pounded wildly against his chest.

They kissed and touched, too sore and exhausted to tease.

No, she needed him right now, and the feeling appeared to be mutual. Words were done, they'd spoken too many already, so now their hands told the other what they needed to know.

I love you. This matters. You matter.

Jack's lip scraped along Katherine's jaw as he pressed himself against her, and her hips rose to meet him even as his hand slipped between the two. He made a sound, a quiet hiss when he felt how slick she was.

Pressing her lips together, Katherine held back a pained whimper when he pulled back to look down at her. "I can't wait any longer."

Shaking her head, neither could she, squirming beneath him for more. She let him spread her legs and positioned himself at her entrance before gently pushing the head of him inside of her. Both of them made a sort of noise, mingling between their mouths which widened as if trying to catch it. With each plunge, Jack seated himself farther and farther. Moving the final inch inside of her, Jack looked down at her in wonder.

She placed her hand over his heart and looked up to stare at him as he began to move, not long after he began, however, Jack peered down and grinned.

Katherine's eyes widened as he tucked his arm around her back and pulled her on top of him. Knees on either side of his hips, Katherine braced her hands where only one remained.

"How much did you miss me, again?"

So much.

At the question, Katherine shifted her hips in answer. She lifted herself before rolling her hips back into his pelvis on the way down.

He choked on whatever else he was going to say, his hands finding a new position on her hips as he lifted his chest to take the tip of her breast into his mouth. She shuddered, trying to keep moving, feeling their muscles flex against each other as she rode him.

Glancing over his shoulder, Katherine caught their reflection in the vanity mirror. She made a high-pitched sound as she watched the people, that couldn't be her. At her slowing pace, Jack wrapped his arms around her back, meeting her halfway as they moved in and out, slow and steady, until both of them were misted with a fine sheen of sweat, eyes shimmering.

She caught Jack staring back in the mirror. "You like the way we look, Kitten?"

Katherine leaned down, pulling up a sheet to fist in her hand.

"Hold on to me," Jack directed. "I got you."

Immediately, her other hand looped around his neck while her breasts rubbed against the stubble of his chest. With his thumb, Jack circled the apex of where they met as he began to thrust inside of her faster now, moving with each of her breaths as she begged and pleaded into his hair. They made no effort anymore to silence their cries and pleas.

The sensations were too much as they coursed through her body, twisting her against him until she came with a gasp, legs squeezing around him.

Jack still held on to her, pushing into her with ease twice before he made a low sound and shuddered as he pulsed inside of her. Still, he did not let her go.

There was silence echoing in Katherine's ears that sounded like him breathing, and she didn't want to let him go either, letting the aching seconds go on, letting the heat surface back up to her cheeks as she felt them joined so completely.

Seeming to sense her thought, Jack placed gentle kisses down the side of her neck until they lifted their heads to look at each other. He was flushed, hair pressed down on the one side where she'd gripped it. So utterly beautiful.

He let his lips skim over hers, shivering, before lifting her off of him with a heavy sigh. They simply lay there, side by side on the mattress, staring and listening to each other's breathing calm, comforted by cushioned pillows.

Katherine curled into the crook of his neck. "I'm so tired."

"Me too," Jack said, laughter coating his words. Both of them held each other close, though melted farther into the mattress.

"We have a lot to do, huh?"

Jack nodded so their foreheads touched. "I think we should start with sleep."

"Then showers."

"Definitely showers." He nestled right below her ear and jaw, giving her a sniff.

"I wouldn't be talking." Katherine pulled back to see him better, pulling the thin comforter that smelled like homemade rosewater perfume over the two of them. Jack tangled his leg around both of hers. He shut his eyes for a second before opening them again. There was contentment there she had not seen since they were on the farm together. Tangled in different sheets.

A whole other time and a knot in their string.

She traced his cheekbones. "You still have glitter and a healthy amount of eyeliner coating your face."

"You just said you liked it." He wagged his eyebrows.

Leaning in, she wiped a line off his cheekbones and smoothed it onto her own. They both laid in the impending darkness of the messy room, staring at each other as sirens rumbled outside, half asleep and covered in glitter. That, Katherine figured at this point, was exactly what Ashton was made of.

Eyeliner, glitter, and sweat.

"I do."

"Then," Jack whispered, nuzzling into her. "I'll have to tell you something else. Yesterday was my last night working at DuCain."

Katherine's lips parted, not expecting that.

"So, I have a few more things I hope you'll say yes to. First of all, once more, being with me."

CHAPTER FORTY-FOUR

They only left the apartment for food. He filled her in on his plans while she finished up the orders. Katherine still had plenty to do. They cleaned up the apartment. They laughed, finding another quilt in the oven when they went to turn it on. They smiled while eating macaroni and cheese, curled up on the couch that was, for the first time, for Katherine, a couch—however lumpy.

Otherwise, they spent most of their time in bed, pretending for at least a few hours when they needed to that the world didn't exist. It was just them, one of them who found their ankle tied to the bottom bedpost after waking up from a nap.

When they finally came up for air, the city felt like a dream coursing around them. The river held steady, its dark waters gently flowing beneath them as they made their way across it in the Jeep. The door to the townhouse was unlocked, but clicked when they shut it behind them.

Jack's hands smoothly caught the neck of her coat and Katherine easily slid out. The heavy wool no longer stuck to her skin after showering again this morning, only her hair as she swept it over her shoulder. The oriental rugs, even the walls, lacked the saturated energy that had assaulted Katherine the first time she had come into the riverside house. It hummed as if abandoned.

In the kitchen archway, Reed leaned against the dark gray wall. He tilted his mop of hair to their left toward the living room. The television above the fireplace was on, but the volume buzzed so low it was unlikely that anyone could hear what the characters drinking cappuccinos on a lime green couch were saying.

Not that Avril was watching. A book sat splayed in her lap, her planner, but she stared only at the stone mantelpiece. Her eyes flickered when Katherine walked in, Jack close behind. His hand was positioned gently on her lower back.

"'Morning," Katherine said softly, letting her lips turn up.

She looked better.

A lot better than she did before.

Avril's purple-rimmed eyes had positioned themselves on Jack's hand, locking on the two of them. A smug, unfeeling smile broke through her chapped lips.

"Oh, I see." Avril cleared her throat as she lifted a hand toward the two of them. "You two are in love now. Fabulous. Didn't see that one coming."

Though sarcastic, her voice held very little care.

"How are you doin', Queen?" Jack asked. Leaving Katherine, he perched on the arm of the couch.

Avril didn't even glance at him.

"Well?" Avril simply asked, eyeing Kit. "Any other news besides you suddenly being fun?"

"Avril."

"What?" she asked. "What are you going to say to me?"

Katherine stood in front of her. Nothing. She honestly could not find the right words to say anything. Still, she was there. That was what mattered right now, she was certain.

"That's right. I'm fine, sweet little Kit. Go. I don't need your pity." For the first time, there was no hostility in Avril's voice. Only emptiness.

Katherine was pretty sure she preferred it the other way around.

"I don't pity you." Katherine formed each word as they sounded. There was a long pause that now Katherine couldn't help but fill. Moving over to her other side, Katherine kneeled down on the carpet, stretching her legs to the side. "I opened the shop back up finally, you know. I'm going to fix it up. Paint the walls that are peeling from the hideous wallpaper underneath. Rainbow stripes just don't go with ivory lace, you know?"

Avril didn't answer.

"You should come by sometime," Katherine went on. "Try on and model a few of my new pieces that have been selling online. You would look gorgeous in them. I finished the corset, by the way. It's all yours."

"I don't need it."

"A deal is a deal," Katherine said with a nod. "And the green I picked will make your eyes—"

"I don't give a fuck about your shop or your corset, Kit."

Jack stood and took a step around the glass coffee table toward Katherine. She lifted her hand up out of her lap, trusting him to catch her meaning. She was fine.

This was not fine, but she was fine.

Glancing back at Jack, however, she wasn't so sure that he was. It appeared he couldn't stand what they were looking at. Couldn't stand how the room felt like it was slowly dancing inward, like in a strange game of torture. He looked like he might very well be sick.

Avril sat there as if she was taken ill, legs tucked under a thick puff of blankets. A cup of water sat next to her on the coffee table, untouched and unmarred by lipstick she no longer had even slightly staining her grimace.

"Go." Avril waved a limp, unmanicured hand toward the door without emotion. "Have your happily fucking ever after."

Jack turned away. The palm of his hand that was on the back of her neck gently tugged her shoulder before he went alone toward the front door. He'd wait for her.

With a nod of understanding, Katherine pushed herself up to standing. Reaching down, she began to lift her thick, itchy skirt away from her tights.

"What? Do I get a show now?" Avril chided. It looked like she was about to go on, but her chapped lips paused mid-purse once she saw what Katherine unclipped and held in her hand.

Without pausing, Katherine walked closer to Avril, who sat frozen. She dropped the three brooches that had been given to her months ago in their rightful Queen's lap. Katherine promised that she would keep them safe. And she did.

Avril picked up the one pin decorated with what looked like tiny rubies, glittering in the shape of a rose. She turned it until it winked, a personality captured in the jewels.

Katherine left Avril with the brooch still glinting up at her.

She shook her head, breaking out of the thought the moment Jack came up behind her. He looped his arm over her shoulders, directing her back into the Jeep.

They'd try again, he said. She was going to be fine.

Katherine nodded and let him go on as she looked down into her hand at the single item she decided to keep, just for now. Someone would have to come for it eventually after all, even if it took months or years. She'd have to.

"Ready to go?"

Katherine hummed as she tilted the deep purple amethyst brooch between her thumb and forefinger. Just like the ruby one did toward Avril, it winked.

EPILOGUE

*J*ack crushed her closer to him, and she could feel his heat even better than the four layers she wore each day, plus an extra sweatshirt he got her before they boarded the plane for their extended work and relaxation trip. They made their way through the Netherlands, Germany, and now for the relaxation pit stop portion since Jack sold off most of his photos to the company contract he was hired for not long after the new year, France. Paris, specifically.

She'd been giddy when they got off the plane. Though the weather was gray since they landed, looking out the window of their cab, she could still see the streets. Right before her eyes was the Seine she'd only seen in a book before. She felt even better when she finally had enough coverage at the hotel to make a phone call to check in with the shop when she woke up.

Peeling her eyes open, she dragged the sheet with her as she reached for her phone on the nightstand and dialed the shop's landline it seemed Emilie did have a reason to keep.

She left the keys with the intern she hired to ship out premade orders each week, and so far, she hadn't heard anything bad had happened.

No one picked up.

They'd be back in Ashton soon enough now.

"Everything is fine," Jack murmured into her hair when she set the phone back down.

Katherine wrapped her arms around herself. "I know."

"Then why are you worrying?"

"Why are you pulling your weird emotional ESP on me?"

Jack laughed, pulling her tighter against him. A low sound vibrated in his chest. "I wouldn't need to even if I was trying, Kitten."

Letting herself fall against him, she closed her eyes. He was so warm. The entire room was so cozy and comfortable. "Why do you always have to bring me somewhere so cold?"

"So that I can hold you like this, of course," Jack breathed against her neck, tangling them farther in the stiff sheets. "And it's not that cold."

"Says you."

"I have you to warm me."

He had a point. Relaxing, she was suddenly jolted awake as his hands skimmed playfully down her sides.

"Are you ready for your day out in Paris?" Jack murmured into her skin.

Katherine hummed at the sensation it sent through her ribs. "Where are we going?"

"I have everything planned."

"You do?" She giggled as he began to plant kisses up her spine. At this rate, she was beginning to think his plans didn't include leaving this room, and with how tired she was, Katherine wasn't sure she minded.

They could order room service, sleep off whatever kind of jet lag she was experiencing before calling the shop again—

"I do," Jack agreed. "Unfortunately, though, they do include getting out of this bed."

"And putting on clothes?"

"Though it may be the city of love and light, the Parisians do appreciate clothing."

Jack swatted her on the butt. "Go. Get dressed before I change my mind."

She gave him a little shimmy as she headed toward her suitcase.

He only flopped over on his back and admired her. "What did I do to get so lucky?"

"Make a deal with my aunt, who kept your kinky secrets for years?"

"Ah, that's right."

She was happy to remind him. The more she talked about Emilie, the less sting there was left about any of it. It was more like a running joke now, and she loved to hear Jack's laugh. She turned back around with a scrunch of her nose and watched him smile.

"I'm changing my mind," he warned.

"Don't you dare."

Jack began to roll himself out of the large bed. "Better hurry."

Grinning, Katherine gathered her clothes against her chest before running toward the bathroom. Within the next half hour, she managed to shower without getting too distracted by Jack, who climbed in with her and got dressed in one of her simple black circle skirts and blouse. She didn't want to attract too much attention from any locals.

Jack whistled when she came out of the bathroom.

She felt her face flush as he extended his hand.

"Ready to go?"

Katherine nodded, slapping her hand down in his like how they always did when they explored a new city. It was funny how many it had already been in the past two months. "Let's go."

They started at the Louvre. Wandering through the different corners of the museum, Katherine dragged him through each exhibit, staring up at the statue of Nike and squinting through her glasses before Jack propped her up to see over the crowd taking photos in front of the *Mona Lisa*. He gave her a twirl in front of the *Bath of Venus* and pulled her back into him with an easy movement before the exhibit guard noticed.

It was like they were back in Ashton for a moment, posing in front of the different original artworks she'd never seen before. Stepping back, she gave a little curtsy, causing a few stares. She only kept hers on his as he pulled her back through the Tuileries gardens, popping a raspberry macaron past her lips as they went.

They wandered through the short stretch of the catacombs. Jack hugged her close as they passed a tight patch of skulls surrounding the tunnels.

Looking up at him, he shrugged. "What?"

She pointed at him and laughed as he shoved her finger down.

Along with several others, the tour guide seemed to frown upon her reaction.

The man behind the counter of the patisserie didn't, however, when Katherine bit into her crepe folded between pieces of wax. Licking her lips, she let the chocolate drop down from the corners of her mouth. Jack leaned in and licked it away.

The only looks they accumulated then were gentle looks of admiration between the two of them before they started to walk alongside the river again, stopping at tea shops and modistes where Katherine keened over the stunning fabrics, and finally Shakespeare & Co.

Standing outside, Jack lifted his phone to take a photo of her as she smiled beneath the green and yellow sign.

"Beautiful." He nodded before they went in, hiding between the shelves before the sun started to set. They crossed the short bridge between it and the island, where tourists began to disperse around Notre Dame.

Katherine tilted her head up, exhausted but happy, as she took in the large structure and gargoyles leaning over the edges.

"Kit," Jack observed. "Look down."

Stepping back before she did, Katherine realized where she stood. Her feet rested on the top of a metallic eight-point gold star. Point Zero. The very center of Paris.

"Did you know," Jack said, directing her back to stand on the very center. "It's said if you stand on the star of Notre Dame, you will return to Paris one day. You also get a wish."

Katherine's eyes widened as she twirled around to face him. She was pretty sure that all her wishes on stars were used up by now. She was about to tell him so before he turned her back toward the cathedral, leaning in with his hands on her shoulders.

"Make a wish," Jack whispered softly.

Closing her eyes, Katherine couldn't think of anything specific. She only let a feeling wash over her as she stood there in the center of the city, but she wished. Wished and wished and wished.

When she opened her eyes back up, Jack was in front of her.

"Your turn."

Switching places, Jack stood on the golden star and shut his eyes the same as she did. He squeezed them tight before he opened them again.

"Good one?" Katherine asked him.

"I can't tell you all my wishes, can I?"

She hummed but didn't press before he took her hand back into his, walking her over to the side pillar of the cathedral. "Where are we going? Inside? To that show you were talking about in Montmartre?"

"First, to the top. You've never been one to be afraid of heights, have you?"

Rolling her eyes, they climbed each step round and around, him slightly behind her until they reached the top of the Notre Dame. Coming out of the staircase, they breathed in the light all around them. They could even see some real stars just starting to appear far in the distance.

Jack listened to her intake of breath as he walked up behind.

"You like it?"

"Jack," Katherine breathed, unable to tear her eyes away from the view.

She could see lights from the Eiffel Tower and hear all the sounds around her. If she closed her eyes, she could almost imagine she was home in Ashton, only she wasn't. She was here in Paris, with Jack. And that perhaps was as close to home as she ever wanted to be, all her life.

"This is amazing. I can't believe you did this, and what else did you say you have planned?" Katherine asked, still basking.

"I have plenty planned. You're just going to have to be surprised. But right now…" Jack cleared his throat. "I need to ask you a question."

"What?"

"Truth or dare?"

Heart stopping in her chest, Katherine knew exactly the right answer for once, without a doubt or worry.

She turned around to face him on one knee.

"Dare."

ACKNOWLEDGMENTS

I always thought I knew what I was going to write when I got this point. The dream of writing a book, these books with these characters, has been sitting in my head for a long time. But now that I am here, thinking of all the people I have to thank, I'm both intimidated as well as immensely grateful.

Firstly, this book would not have been started and finished without a special group of people who agreed during an independent creative writing workshop to let me turn in chapters each week instead of short stories. Thank you so much to Carling Ramsdell, who believed in and worked her magic on this story until the very end (and likely read the most versions of it), Amanda Gillette, and Alyssa Clauhs. Along with them, the person who made the group of misfit writers of all genres come together, Elise Burke Parcha. You truly have my greatest thanks and admiration.

To Taylor Whelan, I genuinely am having a hard time finding words to thank you for coming back into my life when I needed a friend as well as someone to obsess over fantastic books with on the daily. You have shared your excitement and wisdom for my stories just as much as any bestseller, and I am forever thankful for you.

To my family, I feel like I need to give the largest shout-out of all. I love you and I am so grateful to have been able to start this journey, this dream of mine, with support and plenty of hope when luck just doesn't seem cut it.

To everyone throughout the years who let me borrow a pen I never returned, thank you.

And finally, to my eighth-grade English teacher, Mrs. Thompson, who encouraged my writing and at the end of the year jotted down a quote in my yearbook with the message *"Your quote is not yet written, but it will be!"*

Is it written yet?

ABOUT THE AUTHOR

Kendra Mase is a voracious reader who always dreamed of having her own stories on the shelves. She holds a BA in English Publishing and Editing and is a graduate of The Columbia Publishing Course in New York City. *The Strings That Hold Us Together* is her first novel.

Made in the USA
Middletown, DE
22 September 2021